eden burning

Deirdre Quiery

urbanepublications.com

First published in Great Britain in 2015
by Urbane Publications Ltd
Suite 3, Brown Europe House, 33/34 Gleamingwood Drive,
Chatham, Kent ME5 8RZ
Copyright © Deirdre Quiery, 2015

ISBN 978-1-909273-90-0
EPUB 978-1-909273-91-7
KINDLE 978-1-909273-92-4

Design and Typeset by Julie Martin

Cover by Julie Martin

Printed and bound by CPI (Group) Ltd, Croydon, CR0 4YY

urbanepublications.com

The publisher supports the Forest Stewardship Council® (FSC®), the leading international forest-certification organisation.
This book is made from acid-free paper from an FSC®-certified provider. FSC is the only forest-certification scheme
supported by the leading environmental organisations, including Greenpeace.

Door to Silence – John Main

"The purification that leads to purity of heart ... is a consuming fire. We must not be afraid of the purifying fire.

*We must have confidence in the fire because it is the fire of love ... It is the fire **who** is love". ***

*reproduced with the kind permission of the World Community for Christian Meditation

For Martin – my Guardian Angel – always by my side dancing along the slippery path of life.

Acknowledgements

Gosh – where to begin? Maybe I start with my parents George and Doreen from whom I learnt so much about love. They asked so little from me – well nothing from me and gave so much without any expectation or demands. You will see their essences in my second novel "Gurtha". I also want to thank Martin's parents Elsie and Hooksie for welcoming me into the family and giving me a haven of peace only a few years after the setting of "Eden Burning" in 1972. What a joy it was to see the waves pounding Portstewart Strand compared to watching the petrol bombs explode on the Crumlin Road. That beauty inspired me to write the scene about Cedric and Jenny towards the end of "Eden Burning."

Then it has to be Martin. How I loved those morning walks in the mountains when we would talk about what might happen to Tom and Lily. Martin would always come up with great ideas and twists for the story. So together the characters were born – Eden Burning is our baby!

Rachel Connor has been a source of inspiration and motivation with the quality of her feedback and encouragement. She knows that writers need to write badly if they are to improve and so enormous thanks to Rachel for persevering with all of the early drafts and helping to carve a way forward towards the final full stop.

A special thanks to Matthew Smith from Urbane Publications whose Monday evening email changed my life! Since that email,

I've grown to respect and to be fascinated by Matthew's true collaboration with the writer. He never fails to amaze me.

To allow you time to read the book – let me briefly mention others whose contributions were so significant either in providing me with the motivation to keep going or in practically providing editing and feedback. There has to be a special thanks to Alan and Agnes McLaughlin and Peter and Liz Richardson who provided financial support during the economic crisis in 2009 which allowed me to start writing "Eden Burning".

Thanks also to Cornerstone Literary Consultancy, David Walker, Mary McMenamin, Mark and Heather Quiery, John and Linda Burridge, Natascha Czech, Ivo and Rose Van Der Werff, Marie-Claire Primel, Bill Hoagland, Elspeth Bannister, Mary and David Smith, Lilo Heine, Janice and John Brooke, Diamantina Messaris, Deirdre Shannon and Michael Boyce, Penny and David Lee, Caroline and Ben Warner, Pep and Maria Vicens, Catalina and Paco, Ingrid and Kike, Natalia, Ricardo, Marga (1) and Bernardo, Doris, Walter, Miguel, Kike, Bettina, Joachim, David and Nuria, Marga (2), Monica, Lucia, Nadal, Rebecca, Loli, Rosa, Jose, Shinzen Young, Geraldine Glover, Dolores and Paul McCloskey; and of course the cats – Paloma, Ulysses, Jemima and Bumper.

* If I Loved You lyrics reproduced with the kind permission of Reprise Records.
**Song for Ireland lyrics copyright Phil and June Colclough

Wednesday 12th January 1972

A velvet purple curtain glimmered golden at the edges of the Confessional box like a total eclipse of the sun. Tom sat on the bench, feet perched on the kneeler with hands joined in prayer. He listened to the hum of voices inside. It was surely Mrs McLaughlin with Father Anthony. He couldn't hear the content of what she was saying, but her voice rose and fell with a fingerprint rhythm. He raised his eyes towards the main altar where a familiar red light flickered beside the tabernacle, indicating the presence of God. He closed his eyes and prayed.

"Don't let them murder Rose."

Thunder rumbled, then crackled in the distance over Black Mountain and the lights of the Church momentarily flashed on and off. Tom felt the sweat on his hands as the brass knob turned sharply and the Confessional door squeaked open. He rubbed them on his brown corduroy trousers.

Tom listened to Mrs McLaughlin's brogues briskly clump across the marble floor towards the exit at the rear of the Church. When the wooden door thumped closed, he looked around to make sure that he was alone, then heaved himself to his feet, opened the Confessional door, blessed himself, and in the darkness whispered to Father Anthony, "Father, get me a gun."

Father Anthony pushed open the confessional grill, stuck his curly black head through the small window and looked Tom in the eyes.

"What on earth are you talking about Tom? What do you mean a gun?"

"They're going to kill Rose."

"Who in God's name?"

"Cedric and William."

"Who are they for Christ's sake?"

"Paddy's killers."

Father Anthony pulled his head quickly back through the window. He leaned forward and clasped his hands together, bit his right knuckles before sitting up and resting his head against the back of his chair.

"Christ Almighty," he whispered. "Christ on a bicycle. Not Paddy's killers. Not Rose."

Tom leaned forward, peering into the Confessional through the wooden lattice window. Father Anthony pulled at the white collar around his neck, sat forward and looked directly into Tom's eyes.

"We can't stop them with a gun, Tom."

Tom slowly shook his head. "This is not murder."

"Tom, you know it is."

Tom squeezed his hand into a fist and hammered on the lattice. He pushed his face against the wood. His lips pressed slightly through the lattice like soft putty. His teeth touched the pinewood as he rasped.

"Have you not heard a thing I've said? They're going to kill Rose. How many times do I need to say it before you hear it?"

"What has happened to you Tom?" Father Anthony asked in a soft voice.

Tom stayed on his knees and slowly took a white cotton handkerchief from his trouser pocket. He opened it carefully, removed his glasses and wiped them. Holding the glasses in his hands he raised his eyes to plead with Father Anthony.

"Have you forgotten what they did to Paddy and Michael?"

Father Anthony was the right person to find him a gun. He approached Father Anthony because he knew that one of the other priests – Father Martin – had a gun which he used when he went hunting rabbits up Cave Hill in the summer. Tom thought that Father Anthony could be persuaded to get hold of Father Martin's gun. He didn't expect Father Anthony to pull the trigger or to aim the gun at Cedric. Tom was prepared to do that. If Tom had to kill Cedric to save Rose's life that was the way it would be.

Anyone who had known Tom before the evening of Wednesday 12th January would never have believed that he was capable of contemplating murder. It was no wonder that Father Anthony felt totally confused. Tom was the most saintly man he had ever met; in or out of Confession. Saintly in Father Anthony's mind did not mean "perfect" but someone who imperfectly struggled to put God's will first in their lives.

Tom understood that the natural world worked within preordained rules and within a primordial order, annihilating and creating simultaneously. The sun rose and set at its prescribed times with each passing allowing light to flood the earth or darkness to cloak it. Seasons came and went in a disciplined manner. There was beauty in this order. Tom heard conkers thump onto the sodden ground or patiently watched a sycamore leaf flutter in an autumn breeze and settle into the moist earth, before disintegrating to nourish the tree from which it came. Tom felt familiar in the rhythm of this natural world where a fuzzy cloud appeared from nowhere and held form on a still day before morphing, dissolving, reforming, moving and disappearing. He knew the importance of touching cherry blossom on the tree as it burst into life. Nature, apart from man, was at home in its rhythm, in harmony with God – the "prime mover" setting the world in motion.

For Tom, man was different – thirsting for water like a fish in the sea, trapped in time and space, restless to escape his sentence of movement on the earth, looking for stillness within an incessant burning, twisting desire for life and a fear of death. It was Tom who knew how to find stillness in silence. It was Tom who could feel his thoughts settle like waves swishing onto sand after a storm or slowly rolling like a billiard ball to a halt on a velvet table. It was Tom who had shown Father Anthony what it meant to be a man of peace, patience and forgiveness. It was Tom who had helped Father Anthony to recover a sense of hope and faith in the living.

Yet this same Tom was asking the impossible. "Will you help me? Get me a gun."

Father Anthony rubbed his eyes with the palms of his hands and lowered his head, grasping the crucifix around his neck.

"What's going on Tom? Tell me everything you know."

Tom sighed with relief.

"On Tuesday Paddy's killers spotted Rose walking home from school. They were in a black taxi driving along the Crumlin Road, looking for a target. She caught their attention. They had seen her before coming out from Mass."

Tom removed his glasses and gulped at the air like a fish on a hook. He placed the glasses on the floor beside the kneeler. He laid his head on crossed arms and sniffed tears to the back of his throat.

"She was in the wrong place at the wrong time. They only had to see her to add her to their list."

"What list?"

"The list of people they plan to murder. That's what happened to Paddy and Michael. They were on the list." He raised his head, took a deep in breath and sighed. "I'd rather die than have what happened to Paddy happen to Rose."

"Tom, Rose isn't going to be murdered."

"How do you know? How can you be so sure?"

Tom raised his head and stared into Father Anthony's eyes. He wiped his nose with the back of his hand. He wiped it again with the sleeve of his jacket.

"There were three of them in the taxi – Cedric, his brother Peter and his father William. When they saw Rose, Cedric and William joked about her being their next victim. Peter was in the back seat of the taxi. Peter then heard what they were saying – about their plans to kill her."

"How do you know this?"

"Tonight Peter came to see Rose after Mass, to warn her."

"I'm confused. Why did he do that? Is he not one of the murderers?"

"I don't know why." Tom shook his head. "It seems that he is terrified of his father and brother. Rose said that he didn't want to be involved in the killings. He wants the murders to stop. He wants out."

"Are you sure Peter is to be trusted?"

"Rose thinks so. I don't know what to think."

Father Anthony pushed open the half door of the Confessional which led onto the side aisle. He turned the knob on the heavy wooden door on the Confessor's side, gently opening it. Tom slid onto the floor and curled up like a snail, holding his head in his hands.

Father Anthony knelt in the darkness and pulled Tom towards him, holding him in his arms. "Tom, let's go to the Sacristy. It's easier to talk there."

He placed his arm around Tom's shoulders. They leant against each other as they edged up the side aisle towards the Sacristy door. Once seated and with a cup of tea in his hands, Tom explained.

"This evening Peter gave Rose Molly's engagement ring. I recognised it immediately. Paddy had it with him the night he was murdered. I saw it with my own eyes. It's proof that they killed Paddy. They took Molly's ring. He had it in his trouser pocket that night when he left me." Tom slurped mouthfuls of hot sweet tea. "What do we do now? I've told Rose and Lily to stay indoors and not to open the door to anyone."

"Shouldn't we call the Police?" asked Father Anthony.

"How do we know that Cedric and William haven't got connections with the Police? Can we risk that?"

Tom's voice was a little stronger. He placed the china teacup firmly on the saucer and rubbed his hand on his sleeve.

"Once we know that Rose is safe we'll make sure that the Police know who killed Paddy and Michael. Let's make sure that Rose is safe first. Do you remember the prison guard in the Crumlin Road jail who poisoned Roger Cochrane? You have to be careful who you trust. Wouldn't you have thought that Roger would be safe enough behind bars? Can you believe that it was a guard who put the arsenic in Roger's custard?"

Father Anthony got to his feet. He brought his hands to his face and mumbled through his fingers. "I'll speak with Father Martin."

"Don't be long. I have to get back to Lily and Rose." Tom sat with his hands joined on his lap. His breathing had returned to normal, the clamminess on his hands had gone. He felt momentarily calm now that he had taken some action, no matter how small. He took a deep breath and tried to allow the fledging peace within him to grow.

•••

Father Anthony couldn't believe the difference that twelve hours had made to his sense of well-being. Only that morning he had been meditating in his cell, experiencing the deepest peace and tranquillity of his life, naively believing that he would never again give in to temptation. He truly believed this morning that he had an epiphany during his meditation that returned him to a state of innocence, wiping clean his fifteen year old sin. This same state of grace would now enable him to be eternally faithful to his vocation. Yet here he was, standing in front of Father Martin making plans to be party to a murder.

Father Anthony watched Father Martin scratch his head and then rest his joined hands on top of his stomach, sticking the thumbs through the cord twisted around his waist.

"Shouldn't we inform the Rector?"

Father Anthony vigorously shook his head.

"He's not here. Remember he's giving a retreat at Mount Argus."

"I still think that we need to talk to him. He needs to know."

Father Anthony's right eye twitched slightly.

"We haven't time to waste tracking down the Rector. What do you think Christ would do? Slouch in a chair and think about the best protocol to follow?"

"I don't think he would look for a gun – do you?" Father Martin's face was slightly twisted as though he didn't know whether to laugh or cry. "What about your sermon on Christmas Day about the meaning of the "powerlessness" of Christ and how we were meant to imitate it? How come you've changed your mind?" Father Martin crossed his legs at the ankles and moved his toes up and down in his sandals. He removed his hands from his waist and tapped the leather arms of the chair as though to hurry a response from Father Anthony.

Father Anthony jumped to his feet, rubbed both hands through his curly dark hair and responded in a strained but powerful whisper.

"Rose's death isn't going to bring peace to Northern Ireland. If it was as simple as the powerless dying creating a change of heart in the killers, we would have had peace years ago. We don't need another murder on our doorstep. Christ had a mission to fulfil. What's Rose's mission in life? Do you know? I would like her to live and find that out."

Father Martin shook his head. "I still see an inconsistency in what you are saying, but I can see that there's no stopping you. Let me show you how the gun works." Father Martin pulled himself heavily from the armchair. "It's only ever been used for rabbits."

Father Anthony took the rifle out of Father Martin's hands.

"Here are the bullets." Father Martin handed him six bullets about an inch and a half long.

"How do I use it?"

Father Martin shook his head and took the gun from Father Anthony, clicking a cartridge into place and then emptying it again.

"I'll aim for the legs."

"Let's hope he's not too skinny. A rabbit is an easier target than skinny legs."

"Pray that we don't need to use it at all."

"Of course."

"I'll explain to Tom what we'll do. Will you do the evening Mass tomorrow for me? I'll take guard outside."

"That goes without saying."

Father Anthony kept his eyes on the sandaled feet of Father Martin and walked behind him towards the oak door. Before Father Martin could turn the doorknob, the door shuddered under the pressure of two strong blows. Father Martin glanced nervously at Father Anthony. He turned the doorknob and pulled the door towards him, revealing the smiling face of the Rector.

"You're the very two I am looking for."

The Rector strode purposefully into the room and standing with his back to the crackling fire warmed his hands.

"I've had an interesting chat with Tom…"

"What happened to the Retreat at Mount Argus?" Father Anthony interrupted, hiding the gun behind his back.

"Let's just say I heard a voice whisper to me in the darkness that I needed to be here. Curious don't you think? Now, what do we do about Cedric?"

Father Anthony and Father Martin exchanged nervous glances. The Rector smiled.

"Father Anthony, take that ridiculous gun from behind your back and put it on the chair where we can all see it. Father Martin, I want to talk to you alone, this minute. Father Anthony you can keep an eye on the gun until we return. Although I don't think it's going anywhere do you?"

Father Anthony flushed red and dropped the gun on the floor, then retrieved it carefully and placed it on the leather chair.

chapter 1

Friday 31st December 1971

Cedric looked at his reflection in the darkened window of the Black Beetle pub. He combed his fringe off his forehead, pulled a few strands forward, slipped the comb into his back pocket and looked at his watch.

"Five, four, three, two and we have … one."

A bomb exploded in the distance.

"Yes … that's what we want … on time."

Cedric smiled at William and reached over to clink his glass.

"Come on Peter, cheer up, it may never happen! Happy New Year!"

Everyone else in the Black Beetle was standing on their feet, arms around one another singing and swaying in the smoke. "Should auld acquaintance be forgot …"

William smoothed a single long strand of dark hair over his bald head and leant forward to clink Cedric's glass a second time. "I hope the fuckers roast in Hell. On second thoughts, Hell is too good for them. Cheers. Happy New Year son."

A second bomb rumbled in the distance.

"Crumlin Road; Ardoyne if Sammy P is on time."

Peter wiped beads of sweat from his forehead with the palm of his hand before reaching for the salt and vinegar crisps in the middle of the table. The crisps rasped against the roof of his mouth. He choked and coughed. His stomach was doing circles like a twin tub washing machine on a fast spin.

"Looks like Sammy P has done a good job. I like a man who knows the importance of being on time." Cedric gave a thumbs up to William, and pulled out the comb from his back pocket and slowly combed the fringe once more off his forehead. He took a deep breath, closed his eyes and listened. A woman screeched at the front door – like a turkey getting its neck wrung, or someone descending at speed on a fairground big dipper. He couldn't work out whether she was enjoying herself or whether she was in pain. Without opening his eyes he decided that she was enjoying herself. He tapped his feet on the carpeted floor. It was soothing. For a moment the contact of his foot against the soft carpet was rhythmic and gentle like a heartbeat. He inhaled the cigarette and cigar smoke like incense in a church and began to count.

"Five, four, three, two, one ...We have blast off!"

There was a third thump. This one was sharper, longer, lasting more than a second. WHOOOOMP.

"Well done Sammy P!"

Peter stood up, rubbing his salty hands on his jeans. He looked towards the door.

"Shouldn't we go home? Mum's alone."

William reached for his jacket hanging on the back of a chair. "Cedric?"

"It's not often that we're first out of here." Cedric waved at Jenny behind the bar. She blew a kiss at him. She was wearing a red polo neck jumper and jeans, with her hair curling onto her shoulders. There was a crown of artificial white daisies on top.

"I'll be with you in a minute." Cedric pushed his way through the crowd towards Jenny.

•••

On the Crumlin Road, Rose surfaced from deep sleep, opening her eyes in the darkness of the bedroom. It took a few seconds for her to realise that the noise was coming from downstairs. She tried to work out what was happening. There was an insistent banging on the front door. Her heart started to race. She instinctively tried to slow it down by breathing deeply but her body felt paralysed under the blankets. It was as much as she could do to turn her head slowly to the right and squint at the alarm clock beside her. Light from the full moon fell onto a rectangle on the worn green carpet and the objects in the room emerged as recognisable shapes. The white faced clock showed five minutes to midnight. Her heart beat even more quickly although she wouldn't have thought that possible, her breathing quickened and she moved, jumping out of bed and searching the bedroom for something warm to throw on top of her pyjamas. She spotted her favourite purple coat with its fluffy lamb's wool sleeves hanging on the back of bedroom door and ran towards it, pulling it over the pink brushed cotton pyjamas.

She recognised the voice now which was attached to the pounding of the door. It had to be Matt.

"Get out of bed. It's the British Army."

Rose fumbled with the buttons on her coat, threw open the bedroom door and ran down the first flight of stairs in bare feet, jumping two steps at a time.

"Tom, Lily, waken up." She thumped on the bedroom door to her left. She heard the light tread of Lily's slippers behind the closed door. "I'll find out what's happening," Rose shouted as she ran along the landing towards the last flight of stairs. She gripped the top of the bannister, took a deep breath, then let the bannister go and forced herself to jump two and even three steps at a time, before reaching the bottom and sprinting towards the front door. A soldier hammered urgently on the glass window.

"Wake up! There's not much time."

Rose lifted the metal bar from its catches and placed it against the wall on her left, turning the lock and swinging the door open.

"Matt, what are you doing here?" Rose whispered, looking over her shoulder to see if Tom and Lily were about.

Matt sighed in relief, tightening the strap of his helmet and pulling on his gloves.

"Rose, it's a car bomb. Get Tom and Lily. It's about to go off. The bomb disposal guys say it is a big one." Matt pointed at a white Ford Cortina parked two doors away, on the pavement at the corner of Brompton Park.

"Is there anyone next door? I can't get a response."

"The Maloney family. But they're not there tonight. They've gone to visit Nuala's sister."

Matt sighed. "They're not going to have much of a house to come back to if this goes off."

Rose looked past Matt to see two soldiers peering through the back windows of the Ford Cortina. They shouted at Matt.

"It's about to go! Run! Get out of here!"

Matt grabbed Rose's hand and pulled her towards the gate.

"No Matt. I can't leave Tom and Lily. You go. Go!"

Rose's hand slipped from Matt's gloved fingers. She took two steps towards the front door. Matt sprinted with the two soldiers through the wrought iron gates, into the Church grounds. Rose was rooted, bolted to the floor. Matt was inside the gates of Holy Cross Church when the bomb exploded. It started with a small rumble and built to a massive roar as Rose saw the car disintegrate. She instinctively moved her hands to cover her ears as the full force of the bomb swept towards her. It thundered to a recognisable BOOOOOM. The glass from the parlour windows to her right, the upstairs bedroom, and even further up in the attic exploded, dropping in a glittering fountain of glass. Her body swayed and she felt herself losing balance as the plaster ceilings collapsed above her. The roar continued as the plaster crumbled and the wallpaper lay in strips on the floor. After the initial explosion Rose could still hear a high pitched continuous ringing in her ears. She felt the stinging of small splinters of glass pierce both the soles of her feet and toes as she ran up the flight of stairs. She didn't care. There was only one thought in her head.

"Tom, Lily where are you?"

She tripped on a mound of fallen plaster on the landing, struggling to her feet as the hall lights flickered on and off. As she pulled herself off the floor, she looked up and could see stars twinkling above. It was as though she had fallen through a crevice and could see the sky from the jagged edge of the hole through which she had slipped.

Tom emerged flustered in his striped crumpled pyjamas and bare feet.

"Rose – are you alright?"

"Yes." Rose ran towards him, forgetting the pain from the glass sticking into her feet.

Lily appeared breathless behind Tom. She threw her arms around them both.

"Oh my God, have a look at the bed."

Lily held her hands to her face. The bed was covered with glass and plaster. A triangular piece of glass pierced the pillow. From the bedroom door, it looked like a sail on a small yacht.

"Tom's head was right there." Lily pointed at the pillow.

"Come on everyone. There could be a second bomb. We need to find out what's happening."

Lily tightened the belt on her dressing gown.

"Quick. Downstairs."

Mr Langley the next door neighbour stood at his front door smoking his pipe.

"Mr Langley. Are you OK?" Lily patted him on the arm.

"Well, I'm not bad at all – considering." He tapped his tobacco on the wall and refilled the pipe. "I could be worse." He gave Lily one of his slow smiles, holding the pipe in his hand, and then with a wink, he placed it back in his mouth and took a deep puff.

"Here's Father Anthony." Lily shivered, crossing her arms.

Father Anthony stumbled onto the Crumlin Road. His long black woollen habit swirled around him in the freezing breeze. His dark curly hair glistened like oil in the light of the moon. As he neared them, Lily pointed at his sandaled feet,

"You'll catch your death of cold Father."

Father Anthony rubbed his hands. "Forget about me. What about you all here? Has anyone been hurt?"

Rose stood beside Lily. Father Anthony looked at her feet which were covered in blood.

"You OK?"

Rose smiled at him. "I'm fine. It looks worse than it is. It's only a few scratches. Lily aren't you going to offer Father Anthony a cup of tea?"

Father Anthony followed Rose's gaze across the road.

"Are you looking for someone?"

Rose shook her head. "No."

Father Anthony followed Lily down the hallway as Tom brushed a path ahead of them.

Rose stood in the doorway and looked across the road

again for Matt. Her heart sank as she watched him jump into the armoured jeep. What would happen to him? As soon as he disappeared from sight she felt her stomach starting to churn once again. The driver swung out across the Crumlin Road to block oncoming traffic. She couldn't tell if Matt could see her. She wanted to wave at him but she couldn't as Mr Langley would see. She turned towards Mr Langley and looked into his eyes.

"Did you have any damage to the house Mr Langley?"

"Only the windows – you and the Maloney's have taken the brunt of it. I've got folk inside who will be boarding up the windows for me within the next hour."

"Well, that's not so bad." Rose patted Mr Langley on the shoulder. "You know where we are if you need any help. Goodnight Mr Langley."

Rose closed the front door gently and joined everyone in the sitting room.

The reality of how close they had all come to dying hadn't hit home. That would happen the next day when they realised the extent of the damage and there was time to reflect. For now, it was Lily as always who made an attempt to lighten the mood before going to bed,

"You're not going to believe this Rose." Lily held a banana in her hand. "The bomb perfectly skinned a banana."

"You're pulling my leg."

"I swear. It jumped out of the fruit bowl, skinned itself and lay there on the kitchen floor asking for someone to eat it."

"So now we have not only a walking but a talking banana." Father Anthony winked at Rose over a rim of his cup of tea. "What's your Aunt Lily like?"

chapter 2

Saturday 1st January 1972

Eileen cut a slice of white lard and placed it on the hot frying pan. She fried six slices of bacon, the edges shrivelling and kissing each other. She prised them apart, pressing them flat against the spitting fat. They bubbled up and the edges gradually browned. She turned to the six thick Cookstown pork sausages, stabbing each of them twice with a fork. Fat squirted into the pan as the sides burst open. She turned them round, watching the stripes of crusty brown spread over pink flesh. Bacon and sausages were placed into a Pyrex dish in the oven while she fried soda and potato bread, eggs, tomatoes and black pudding.

She rustled among the ironed shirts to find a white cotton tablecloth with which she covered the table. She found a small red candle, lit it and placed it in the centre of the table with a few sprigs of holly. A cuckoo jerked out from the clock hanging on the wall beside the door, calling its punctuated song for nine o'clock.

Upstairs, Cedric washed and shaved, splashed himself with Old Spice before carefully putting on a striped blue and pink cotton shirt with a white collar. He fingered the perfect crease Eileen had ironed into the sleeves and then fiddled with the gold dolphin cufflinks.

"Why do they always make the bloody button holes too small?" He muttered under his breath, before opening the drawer filled with neatly rolled ties and finding a smaller set of blue crystal cufflinks. He sat on the bed to pull on a pair of navy corduroy trousers and a matching soft navy blue cashmere jumper. His dark hair curled onto the white collar of his shirt. He chose a pink silk tie spotted with blue hearts. He reached into the drawer for Eileen's present.

Cedric ambled into the kitchen, one hand behind his back.

"Morning Mum. Happy New Year. How did you sleep?" He kissed her on the cheek.

"Not bad. What about you? What time did you get in?"

Eileen plucked a stray black hair from his shoulder.

"Not much after midnight. I thought you would still be up."

"I was in bed for 11. Did you have a good New Year's Eve?"

"Not a lot changes in the Black Beetle for New Year's Eve."

"I take that for a no then? Made any New Year's Resolutions?"

"I've nothing to improve. You know that." He gave Eileen a second kiss.

"You smell nice. What's that you've got?"

"A New Year's present for you."

Cedric handed Eileen the long narrow box covered in silver wrapping paper with a red satin bow.

"Thank you." Eileen removed the wrapping paper meticulously, folding it in four and setting it on the table. Inside the box lay a string of pearls like a row of small moons on red velvet.

"You shouldn't have. You've already given me a Christmas present. They're beautiful, though."

Cedric took the pearls from his mother's hands and placed them carefully around her neck. The clasp snapped closed.

"They look great."

Eileen laughed, rolling the pearls in her fingers. "Sit down you big softy. Breakfast is nearly ready. Tell me about Jenny. Have you got around to asking her out?"

"No."

"You should do. She's a lovely girl from what you've told me."

The kitchen door squeaked open as William limped into the room.

"Morning all."

"Happy New Year. Ready for breakfast?"

"Fed the cats?" William looked around the kitchen.

"Of course. Here's Bouncer looking for you."

A mop of a striped tiger cat jumped onto William's knee, turned around twice and settled comfortably on top of his brown corduroy trousers. William stroked his head, feeling the long soft silky fur beneath his fingers. Bouncer looked at him through half closed eyes, digging his claws into William's thighs, gently swishing his tail.

"Honourable creatures aren't they?" William smiled at Eileen.

"Why do you say that?" Eileen buttered the toasted wheaten bread.

"They don't lie. Not like human beings." Eileen blushed slightly red but William didn't notice.

Five minutes later Peter was last to appear for breakfast. Wrapped in a green cotton dressing gown and brown leather slippers he sat down facing Cedric and held his head for a few seconds in his hands.

"What's the matter?" Eileen placed a mug of tea beside him.

"I hate this time of year."

"Oh dear, will a fried egg make any difference?"

Eileen tweaked his hair. Peter held out his plate.

"You've too much time on your hands, that's what's wrong with you," Cedric mumbled through a half-eaten pork sausage. "Remember that you've work to do tomorrow. That will stop you feeling sorry for yourself."

"Don't be mean Cedric." Eileen topped up Cedric's tea.

"What's happening tomorrow?"

"Nothing special." Cedric tapped a dollop of tomato ketchup onto his plate.

"We have a visit to do."

Eileen helped Cedric to a second piece of potato bread.

"What kind of visit?"

"Showing Peter the ropes in case he wants to stay in the family business rather than waste his time at University next year."

"Cedric – if you can't say something nice, say nothing." Eileen spoke in a gentle voice, resting a hand on Cedric's shoulder and smiling at Peter. "Peter's not going to waste his time. He's going to be a doctor and help people. You help people too in your own way don't you?"

Cedric returned alone to the Black Beetle at two o'clock. He sat with a pint of Guinness watching Jenny. She was laughing with Sammy P who was propped up on a stool at the bar. From a distance he couldn't hear what she was saying, he only saw the playful way she threw a bottle of Guinness in the air as though it was a cocktail shaker catching it behind her back. She opened it and the Guinness went everywhere. Sammy P wiped foam from his face. Jenny helped him dry off with a paper tissue. She was wearing a long pink wraparound skirt with cream crocheted top. Her brown hair waved down to her waist. Over her fringe she wore a braid of artificial daisies. She had pink tights, yellow leg warmers and yellow platform shoes.

Cedric carried the empty glass to the counter.

"Hi Cedric. What will you be having?" Jenny smiled.

"Nothing thanks. I've had enough."

"Is this a change for the New Year?" Jenny leant on the counter. Cedric noticed her gently glossed lips; the blue eye shadow, eye-liner and rose blusher across the top of her cheeks.

"Could be." He coughed. His face reddened. "Jenny." There was silence.

Jenny looked at Cedric. His eyes were deep blue with a circle of black around the iris. His face was lean – not a trace of fat or loose flesh, smooth wrinkle free skin.

"Would you like to go out for dinner?"

Silence.

"Is this an official date?"

"You could say so." Cedric wiped at his forehead with a cotton handkerchief.

"When have you got in mind?"

"What about Tuesday ... around eight?"

"What about tonight? I'm free at six? I've got a few days off now after the holidays." Jenny held her head in her hands, elbow on the counter. "See – I'm keen."

"Tonight is not so good. I've got to talk to Dad ... You know William."

"Of course I know William. He's almost a resident here." Jenny laughed. "Like yourself. I'll see you Tuesday then. Where are we going?"

"Not here. The Queen's Head. I'll drive."

chapter 3

Sunday 2nd January 1972

William was born in 1910 in Belfast around the time that Lord Carson was made leader of the Ulster Unionist Party. His father served in the Ulster Volunteers under Carson and James Craig. In the womb he heard 'No surrender' and angry arguments around the dinner table between his father who did not support Home Rule and his mother who did. Even in the womb, his tiny foetus was flooded with 'flight or fight' chemicals and the patterns were laid for William's so called 'unknown thoughts' – called 'unknown' because they are formed before language. Baby William, traumatised even before being born, feeling threatened and insecure, created a protection system which became his cage, his prison. "I exist but only under the threat of not existing." Baby William in the womb and in the early years of life wanted an answer to the "big" question – "Will you always be there for me unconditionally?" William's parents didn't answer "yes" because no-one had ever been there unconditionally for them. So, the answer was "no", even if it was never stated explicitly. William learnt that the love he received was conditional – he never felt himself loved.

He needed to find someone to blame for the constant sense of dissatisfaction which gnawed away at his innards. He needed to do something to escape the unbearable loneliness of his existence. He learnt survival strategies – to repress what felt uncomfortable, to deny that anything was wrong, and to project onto others all the hate, anger, resentment and disgust which fermented inside. He also learnt to project onto Eileen the qualities of gentleness, kindness and sensitivity which he denied in himself.

William remembered the Easter Rising in Dublin in 1916 although he was only six at the time. His father lifted every dinner plate from the cupboard and smashed them against the wall of the kitchen, shouting "No surrender!"

His mother, brush and shovel in her hand, swept up every single fragment without saying a word. She served him his dinner that evening on a small piece plate. He made no comment, poured himself a large whiskey, lit a cigar and muttered again "No surrender."

When William was twelve the British soldiers left Ireland and a bloody Civil War broke out in the South between the Free State Soldiers and the Irregulars. There were stories in the papers every day in the North about dreadful happenings within families, where a father would betray a son or an uncle a nephew. There was treachery and even jealously when someone would be murdered because they were too popular, or had more money or were a rival in love. Eight years after William married Eileen the Republic of Ireland was granted full independence from Britain – it was one of the darkest days of William's life. William felt that he had lost something. Something had been stolen from him which was a warning of worse to come.

When William was forty-six, he attended a meeting of

Loyalists with Cedric in the Ulster Unionist Party Offices in Glengall Street, committed to defend Protestant areas from the threat of the IRA. He was part of the vigilante patrols, setting up street barricades and drawing up lists of IRA suspects. In the same year with Peter only a baby, William and Cedric were rioting on the Shankill Road and burning Catholics out of their homes. They joined the Ulster Protestant Volunteers in 1966 and were involved in bombing campaigns on behalf of 'God and Ulster'. In 1969 William and Cedric marched in illegal counter demonstrations against the Northern Ireland Civil Rights movement. Peter had never been involved in any of these activities. He played rugby, strummed the guitar and studied with dreams of going to Queen's University.

Eileen knew nothing about the rioting, the bombings or the marching. It was of course a curious marriage – very similar in many ways to that of William's father and mother – with the exception that William seldom raised his voice at home and Eileen never did. It was a family of 'not knowing'. Eileen didn't know much about what William and Cedric did when they left 18 Elmwood Terrace every day. Peter didn't know that behind the screen of running a taxi business, William and Cedric were murderers. Although William had murdered on his own before Cedric joined him, with Cedric at his side the experience of murder created a bond between them which deepened their relationship. Secrecy gave security and meaning within a world which threatened to tear them apart. They were more like 'blood brothers' than father and son. Peter, living on the periphery of their lives, was increasingly a threat to this security. If he found out what was happening, he could squeal to the police. They had no concerns about Eileen interfering with what they did – she was too much taken up with life within the walls of 18 Elmwood Terrace, her art and the daily routine of taking care of Peter, Cedric and William. Peter was different; he had a dangerous curiosity about life.

In December 1971 Cedric encouraged William to get Peter involved in the planned murders. It had become difficult to ignore the fact that not only had Peter curiosity about life, but had a heart. In listening to the Ten o'clock News or reading the headlines in the daily paper, Peter commented on the horror behind the killings. He talked with Eileen about the impact of murder on the family left behind. He commented on the pain, the confusion, the desperation, the fear that rippled through the extended family. William and Cedric stared at each other in silence across the table with a sense of irritation, discomfort and increasing annoyance at each word falling from Peter's mouth. Without knowing it Peter held up a mirror to William and Cedric. Although they looked away, they still registered what they saw in the mirror. A person with a heart like Peter on the other hand was free. A sensitive heart within a free person was dangerous. It made the person difficult to control.

William and Cedric entrapped Peter by using the oldest trick in the world. They told him a lie. They asked Peter to come for a drive with them on Sunday 2nd January to look at a new house for Eileen. It was on the Woodvale Road with beautiful gardens to the front and back. If Peter thought that the house was something Eileen could be interested in, they would put their house on Elmwood Terrace on the market and they could be moved in before the end of the summer. They had no intention of showing Peter any house. Peter thought that it was odd that they wanted him to look at it on a Sunday when the estate agents were closed.

"If we speak to the owners directly they can skip out the estate agent and save ourselves a fortune." Cedric rubbed his hands together and nodded knowingly to William.

Peter shifted in his seat and tugged his left ear lobe.

"But the estate agent has already probably put a lot of effort into the sale. He's been out the cost of advertising and you wouldn't even know that the house was for sale if there wasn't a board outside."

"You have a lot to learn about life," Cedric replied.

"Isn't the Woodvale Road unsafe?"

Peter knew that there was no sign of The Troubles coming to an end. How would Eileen be able to do her weeding and seeding plants with the daily riots in North Belfast?

"You can't have everything for the prices we can afford. The houses are cheaper where there is a little bit of 'Trouble'. You can't deny that the Woodvale Road could almost be called residential?"

Cedric leaned forward and patted Peter on the shoulder.

Peter shrugged Cedric's hand free.

"Won't Eileen miss the cherry tree?"

Cedric and William laughed at one another, slapped each other on the shoulder and then slapped Peter on the back saying,

"It's a dream house. She will love it. She can plant another cherry tree and a bloody apple tree and there's a weeping willow in the front garden. Didn't Eileen always say that she would love to have a weeping willow? We're only asking you to have a look. If you don't like it, we'll stay in Elmwood Terrace. This is all about Eileen."

"At seven thirty? It will be dark. We won't see the garden properly." Peter wrinkled his nose.

"We can see the garden another day. We're not going to be living in the fucking garden. It's the inside of the house that we need to see. It's fucking dark here for most of the year and so we might as well see what it looks like in the dark."

They drove up the Shankill Road, and along the Woodvale

Road. Peter saw the spires of Holy Cross Church.

"Which one is it?"

William and Cedric laughed at one another.

"What did we tell you? You've a lot to learn about life."

They swung the car from the Woodvale Road onto the Crumlin Road. They drove past the sentry look out, past Ardoyne Hall and accelerated past Holy Cross Church on the right.

At ten minutes to eight they saw Paddy on the left hand side of the road walking to work.

"I told you he would be here." Cedric glanced sideways at William before looking over his shoulder at Peter who was sitting upright in the back seat, looking through the front window.

"You're just about to learn about life brother."

The car screeched to a halt.

"Let's introduce you to Paddy."

Paddy was thirty-five, living on his own in lodgings in a terraced house in Butler Street, off the Crumlin Road. His landlady, Anne, cooked his breakfast during the week and he made his own arrangements for the weekend. Sometimes that meant a Chinese take-away or fish and chips from 'The Last Supper' on the Crumlin Road. His bed-sit was on the first floor, with a bed, a wash basin, television and a stove where he boiled a kettle for tea or warmed Heinz tomato soup to take the chill out of his winter bones. He polished the window which looked onto Butler Street with a newspaper. From the window he would watch crowds of mourners hanging around the corner outside Blackwood's shop with its display of brassieres and men's socks waiting for a funeral to pass by.

He would count the steps leading up to Holy Cross Church, through the hedges and shrubs into the Grove as a meditation, letting his gaze move to the metal gate at the top of the steps where soldiers from the Welsh Guards stood looking at him, rifles cradled in arms, bulletproof jackets fastened tightly, hard helmets hanging from belts. He loved the symmetry of Holy Cross Church – with its twin towers reaching into a cloudy sky – a cross on top of each spire, three stained glass windows above the tall arched wooden front door, the jutting side altars. For Paddy the church was like Noah's Ark – capable of providing safety and shelter in the tumultuous seas surrounding it. Paddy stood at the back of a crowded church for the annual 'mission'. He listened with gratitude to the practical guidance given by the missionary priests on how to respond to the chaos outside. Each sentence was like a brick from the solid towers stacked one on top of the other in his head to bring the strength and security of Holy Cross Church into the confusion within his mind.

On the bedside table there was a black and white framed photograph of his parents, arm in arm on their wedding day. His mother wore a garland of artificial roses around her head and held a bouquet of fresh lilies. She had a lost look in her eyes, as though she had moved away from the present moment and would return after the photo was taken. Beside her, stood his father with Brylcreemed shiny flat black hair, parted on the left, and a dull, brittle, surprisingly orange moustache suspended over his upper lip like a yard brush. He had a proud look in his eye as if he had returned from safari with a Bengali tiger which he alone was responsible for shooting. Unlike his mother, Paddy's father's look knew the historic nature of this opening and closing of a shutter, this explosion of light snatching and preserving a moment in time.

There was a second colour photograph in a shell frame. Paddy stood side by side with a smiling girl, with long brown hair, a psychedelic swirling print T-shirt and bell bottom Levi jeans. Paddy had short dark hair, a broad square face, almond shaped eyes with long dark eyelashes, a relaxed hypnotic smile – one of those smiles which when you met him face to face, seemed to take a long time to ebb into place. You found yourself falling into a deep state of peace as the smile spread across his face. Paddy held a cigarette in his right hand and squeezed the fourth finger on Molly's hand with his left. He planned to marry Molly.

The night before Molly's thirtieth birthday on Friday 25th November 1971, they danced together in Ardoyne Hall to The Wandering Cowboys singing Frank Sinatra's 'And then I go and spoil it all by saying something stupid, like I love you'. Paddy stumbled over the Fox Trot and the Quick Step but when he held Molly for a Viennese Waltz, he moved with her like two waves in love on the sea.

Paddy took Molly's right hand as they sat together, the smoke settling into a comforting blanket around them, the lights dim against a gentle hum of voices.

"Molly, your hand is empty. We'll have to sort that out."

Molly smiled at him with her hazel green eyes. "What have you got in mind Mr Paddy? Are you going to get me a pair of woolly gloves for my birthday then? They're freezing".

She held his right hand. Paddy felt the silky softness of her finger tips send shivers of joy right down to his toes. Paddy leant forward, to kiss her softly on the lips. With his eyes closed, Paddy felt the boundary of his lips meeting the boundary of Molly. A fizzy champagne sweetness spreads through him, leaving him not knowing where he ends and Molly begins. For a few seconds Paddy and Molly disappeared into the kiss, into the emptiness, into the place where there is no Paddy and no Molly. He opened his eyes as the Wandering Cowboys took a break and Frank Sinatra sang on tape.

"*If I loved you, time and again, I would try to say, all I'd want you to know. If I loved you, words wouldn't come in an easy way, round in circles, I'd go. Longing to tell you but afraid and shy. I'd let my golden chances pass me by. Soon you'd leave me. Off you would go in a mist of days never, never to know, how I love you, if I loved you."*

Paddy whispered, "Tomorrow it's your birthday. I've booked a table at The Crawfordsburn Inn."

"Paddy, you can't afford it."

"I'm not taking no for an answer. I've booked a taxi to take us there and back. I'll be there to collect you at seven." It was Friday.

Paddy helped Molly on with her coat in the porch of the Hall. They shouted goodbyes over their shoulders as Molly struggled to open Paddy's umbrella, stepping from Ardoyne Hall into the lashing rain with its meteorite of solid crystal drops showering in front of the approaching car headlights. A black taxi approached from further up the Crumlin Road, Paddy pulled Molly back into the porch. His breathing quickening, his heart thumping as the rounded contour of the shiny black taxi rolled slowly past.

"You know to be careful of the black taxis Molly? Always order one in advance and make sure you know the driver."

"Sure, how many times are you going to tell me that Paddy? I don't plan to take a taxi – the bus does the job for me. It's only the odd time when Mother has a hospital appointment; Brendan is as good as gold and he gives me a lift. Don't worry yourself about me."

She caught his hand as they dashed across the Crumlin Road into Brompton Park, bumping against each other, laughing now as Paddy, holding the umbrella, fought with the wind to keep it from turning inside out.

A six man foot patrol from the newly arrived Welsh Guards

walked down Brompton Park ahead of them. Black silhouettes walking slowly in silence, like Zen monks one behind the other, hugging fences, skimming small brick walls, occasionally bending on one knee, pointing a rifle with its infrared light down the street, signalling to one another, occasionally running a few yards, stopping still, turning backwards, pointing the rifle up Brompton Park towards Ardoyne Hall.

Next day at two in the afternoon, with the rain still thumping on her pink umbrella, Molly took a right turn off Royal Avenue into Cornmarket. No-one knew why. She had told Paddy that she was going to Sinclair's to buy a dress. Why did she not keep walking down Royal Avenue? Sinclair's was on the right, far away from Cornmarket. Instead, she splashed through a few puddles of rainwater, her shoes now soaked through, her hands mottled blue, purple and white by the cold northerly wind, making it hard to grip the handle of the umbrella. She stopped to fasten the bottom button on her raincoat which flapped open, allowing the rain to seep into the hem of her grey woollen dress as if it were blotting paper. Her left high heel caught in a drain as she stepped onto the pavement, heading towards Brands and Normans on the corner. She bent over, her left foot bare, wrestling with the stiletto. She had just managed to free the heel when the IRA bomb exploded.

Molly didn't see the car bomb. Her head was down; her right hand clutched the patent leather stiletto, the fourth finger wrapped around the heel, as she tugged it the last inch from the drain. She heard the roar and rush of the explosion, the push and pull of the air around her. Everything moved except Molly, who stayed still. She lifted her head. Everything was in slow motion. Glass splintered from the shop windows in front of her, cascading onto the ground, showering around her like an exploding supernova. There were no voices, no screams. Did

Molly scream? She didn't know. It's was as though all sounds were sucked into the roar around her. Everything trembled, slowly shuddered, crumbled, breaking apart, disintegrating, as Molly loosened her grip, falling into stillness.

Paddy was alone in his bedsit when the telephone rang downstairs. Anne wiped the flour from her hands onto her white apron. She was making scones for afternoon tea. She lifted the phone.

"Please God no! How can I tell him? Is there any way it can be a mistake? Are you sure it's Molly?"

There was silence. Anne replaced the receiver slowly, like a priest laying the Host to be consecrated on the gold paten. She stepped back, her eyes still on the telephone as she blessed herself, removed her apron, and hung it on a hook in the kitchen, taking time to catch her breath, wiping the trailing beads of sweat with a cotton handkerchief as she climbed the stairs to knock on Paddy's door.

Paddy never cried when his parents died. Like Tom's mother he had never shed a single tear in his life. When Anne told him the news about Molly, the tears burst onto his cheeks like a geyser opening in a newly discovered oil field. He sobbed uncontrollably, throwing himself on top of the bed, crying until the white pillow case was sopping wet. He turned the pillow over, felt the coolness of the dry cotton bring a fleeting sense of comfort, before waves of tears gushed and overwhelmed him once again.

Anne sat with him for fifteen minutes, hands on her lap, on the armchair beside the television, watching him lying on the bed, face down, hands covering his ears as though someone who he didn't want to hear was talking to him. It was Anne's voice that he heard, saying "Molly's dead. Molly's dead." Anne sat silently but her voice repeated in his head. "Molly's dead."

"Please leave me alone Anne," he whispered in a muffled voice, "leave me alone, if you don't mind."

Anne prised herself awkwardly from the armchair and made her way to the door, patting Tom firmly on the back the way you would pat a horse. The patting made his feet flap. Hanging over the end of the bed were two long, shiny size eleven shoes which flapped helplessly up and down like a fish treading water with its tail. She opened the door gently, turned the knob reluctantly, hesitating as she turned to look at his heaving shoulders, his feet now unmoving, suspended in silence over the edge of his warm winter quilt.

"I'll make you a pot of tea and a fresh scone. It'll do you good."

Paddy didn't reply. He was unmoving. The tray of tea and cherry scones arrived and sat on the table in front of the armchair by the television until Anne took them away the following morning as Paddy showered.

After showering, Paddy prepared to put on the clothes he had planned to wear to take Molly to the Crawfordsburn Inn for her birthday. He softly touched the wool of the navy blue pinstripe suit, opened the new white shirt from its cellophane wrapping, spread it on the bed, and then searched for the silver cufflinks – a present from Molly – and found the light blue silk tie with its pink scattering of hearts and gold stars. He knelt naked on the floor beside the bed, spreading his arms over the clothes resting his head on the shirt and tie.

"Molly. Can you hear me Molly? Are you there?"

He remembered his father saying, "I don't believe in a life after death. No-one has come back and told me about it. It's a load of nonsense."

His mother stayed silent. She believed in a God who loved her, who had counted the hairs on her head, who loved her into being, who named and chose her in the womb. She believed in a Holy Spirit who moved through her, bringing her peace, giving her patience, making her gentle and opening her to love.

Paddy pressed his head into the shirt, sinking into the quilt, believing in a God and not believing in a God. The love he knew from his mother and from Molly was from God. He believed that love needed his mother and Molly to be held – the way you need a cup to hold tea or clouds to cover sky or the sky to hold the emptiness of space – to hold the universe. He was able to drink the love of God from the cup of his mother and from Molly. Now that the cup was gone, where was the love of God? Paddy knew that the love of God was in him. For a fleeting second, he knew that it was also imprisoned in the hearts of whoever killed Molly. Paddy imagined that love, intangible, gently trying to escape from the impenetrable hardened hearts of Molly's killers. Couldn't they feel its movement? Didn't they recognise it? Couldn't they feel it at night when they lay in bed, struggling to be free?

As he lay with his head on the bed in silence, these thoughts were his prayers. He wondered whether now that the cup of Molly was broken maybe her love was free, pouring around him, flowing over his body.

Paddy let his thoughts ramble like this because that is the way he prayed to God. Molly was a beautiful china cup that had been smashed. All of the plans he had for their future were now shattered, scattered into space.

He asked God why He didn't allow Molly to appear in the room. He made her once, He could make her again. He could perform miracles. He thought that He heard God telling him (or was it only his own thoughts?) that Molly could never die. God whispered to him in the beating of his heart, that the love he drank from the cup he thought was Molly could never die.

He pulled himself heavily to his feet, and slowly put on the clothes draped over the bed. He opened the drawer beside his bed, removing a small jewellery box. He slowly flicked open the golden clip revealing Molly's engagement ring, a heart shaped solitaire diamond, half a carat, size J.

He had prepared a speech for Molly which he planned to say beside the open burning fire in the Crawfordsburn Inn. As he wrote it, he imagined a cold November wind howling outside, the logs crackling and spitting inside, sending the most wonderful woody perfumed incense, cleansing his soul, as he asked Molly to marry him.

He took the solitaire from its box, clutching the ring tightly in his hand, closing his eyes, squeezing them tight. He licked the last salty drops rolling onto his lips, placing the heart solitaire into his trouser pocket, sitting on the edge of the bed in silence.

•••

It was only a few months since Father Anthony had buried Molly. Paddy continued to work as a security guard at Flax Mill, working one week on nights, the next on days. He dreaded nights. He told Father Anthony in confession, "Once the rioting starts, I am caught in the middle. I stay in the security hut. I need the money. What can I do? I need to pay the bills. I bring a book and brew a pot of tea or listen to the radio. I'm frightened, Father. I'm terrified."

Father Anthony replied, "It's only human to be afraid. Christ is within you. You're not on your own Paddy"

"I feel alone."

Father Anthony patted Paddy's head. "Even Christ felt alone. There is a difference between being alone and being on your own."

Kneeling in the confessional on the 12th January, Tom

reminded Father Anthony. "Do you remember what happened then?" Tom's glasses steamed up. He removed them again, took the cotton handkerchief from his pocket, and wiped the glasses slowly in a clockwise direction, remembering the night before Paddy was murdered.

"Tom, will you have the other half?" Paddy had asked. Tom shook his head, laughing. "Sure it was a full pint Paddy, it wasn't a half. Lily will be expecting me home. But go on then. I can't be late though."

Tom scratched an itch on his left leg waiting for Paddy to return with the pints. They sat on the plastic black sofa and Paddy took Molly's ring from his pocket. He touched the ring the way he caressed his rosary crucifix.

"Tom, there isn't five minutes of a day goes by when I don't think of her. I carry this ring with me everywhere."

Tom took the ring from Paddy and looked at it.

"Yes, I can see this on Molly's hand. She would have loved it."

"How do I keep going Tom?"

"It will get easier Paddy. I know it doesn't feel that way now, but it will get easier. You will enjoy life again. It will be possible."

At seven-thirty Paddy rubbed his mouth with the back of his hand, the creamy top of the Guinness still frothy on his moustache. Tom thought that he saw him wipe away a tear. He wasn't sure because Paddy quickly took his hand and shook it. It was a strong handshake, as if he was off to America or Australia and he wouldn't be seeing him for a long time.

"Tom, Happy New Year and be sure to tell Lily and Rose I was asking for them. Tell Rose, I want to hear her New Year's Resolutions. I need some inspiration. It's been one hell of a year." His long black lashes blinked twice as his famous slow smile spread across his face. "Sure you die if you worry and you die if you don't, so why worry?" He gave him another half-smile, holding him in a long, steady gaze.

It was ten to eight on the evening of Sunday 2nd January 1972. A bitterly cold northerly wind battered through the Grove, whipping leaves across the Crumlin Road. Black ice shone like the oily back of an enormous cockroach as Paddy wiped a drip from the end of his nose with the sleeve of his woollen jacket. He searched in his pocket for a handkerchief, retrieving a tissue, coughing and spitting out phlegm as he walked past Herbert Street, his metal-capped security boots clicking on the pavement. He sighed as he looked down the Crumlin Road. "Not far to go now." He whispered. The silence enveloped him in a thick blanket. There were no lookouts on the street corners, no-one scouting for soldiers or police; no-one trying to start a riot by throwing bricks at the sentry post above the chapel. He glanced at his watch, five to eight. He was on time. A car screeched to a halt behind him.

Paddy hadn't time to run into Flax Street or to knock on a door on the Crumlin Road. Before he knew it the back door of a black taxi swung open. The front door followed. Cedric jumped out from the passenger seat wearing a black leather jacket, black gloves and blue jeans. He stood in front of Paddy, his arms by his sides – deep blue eyes, shoulder length black hair. He looked calmly at Paddy, smiling. "Where do you think you're going?"

"Work," whispered Paddy, hands in pockets, fingering the rosary beads in the right pocket and Molly's solitaire in the left.

"Not till after we've had a little chat. I don't think you told us everything we needed to know. Get in the back."

Paddy's stomach heaved as he stumbled into the back seat beside Peter, sturdy, pale faced with balding strawberry blonde hair – some might call red – light blue eyes and almost no eyelashes or eyebrows giving his face a babyish look. Peter wasn't there the week before when Paddy was picked up and interrogated by Cedric and William. Now a voice in his head screamed, 'Let me out of here.'

He tried unsuccessfully to swallow, struggling for air. It wasn't fear in his body, but terror. His body tingled all over, confusing terror with bliss, or awe – every nerve in his body vibrated with anticipation. Currents of electricity shot up and down from his toes to the top of his head. He sensed Peter beside him looking at him then quickly looking away. William, the driver pressed the accelerator to the floor. The car sped past the Mill where Paddy was due to clock in, down the Crumlin Road, past the Mater Hospital, slowing to the speed limit as it approached the Crumlin Road jail. William swung the taxi sharply right, almost lifting it onto two wheels at Carlisle Circus and headed for the Shankill. Peter was thrown against Paddy. He pulled himself away, shrivelling as though Paddy was acid. Paddy wondered for a moment whether it was worth opening the door and risk throwing himself from the taxi at forty miles an hour. If he tried to escape, would it make matters worse? After all, didn't they let him go last week? Maybe he could make a run for it when they stopped – that's if they didn't kill him first.

He couldn't block the memory of Brendan McKee's nineteen stab wounds. Nineteen. Why did he not die from the first one? They said that Brendan didn't die in the taxi. Worse was to follow.

"I'll run for it when they stop," Paddy whispered to himself. "I've nothing to lose." He gripped the rosary in his right pocket. He searched in his left pocket for the heart solitaire. Without moving his left hand from his trouser pocket, he managed to squeeze the ring over his small finger. He got it all the way up to his knuckle but no further. He touched the diamond with his thumb.

Paddy knew what happened to people taken by the drivers of black taxis. Few escaped. He tried not to remember the Ardoyne gossip about how they died. "This is what it feels like," he thought. "It's not real," he told himself, "someone is going to stop the film. There's going to be a commercial break. I'm going to get out of this car and I'm going to be told it's a bad joke or a nightmare."

After Molly died, Paddy had nightmares almost every night. He dreamt that he was trying to lock up and go home from the Mill, but he couldn't get the front door to close. He didn't want anyone to think that he had left it carelessly open. That would cost him his job. He rushed to find Andrew, his boss, to explain that the door wouldn't close. Andrew walked with him in the darkness to the front door of the Mill, tried to close it and saw for himself that what Paddy was saying was true. It was simply impossible. They nodded at each other, shrugged their shoulders, left the door open and walked away.

The dream morphed. Paddy was alone on his way to work, walking towards the front door. The glass door swung slowly open outwards. He stopped. Something was inside waiting for him – he saw a deliberateness in the way the door opened, as though whatever was in there knew that he was only few steps away. What did it want of him? His body filled with fear, terror, energy rippling, zapping, vibrating bubbles shooting from head to toe as his feet were rooted to the ground. The fear wakened him. His heart beat wildly as he opened his eyes in relief. "It's only a nightmare". His pulse returned to normal as he comfortingly took in the familiar view of his small bedsit – the table set for breakfast next morning, teacup upside down on the saucer. Chivers marmalade with a small teaspoon on top of it, a bottle of HP brown sauce and one of Heinz tomato sauce. A white teapot covered with the red tea cosy Molly had knitted for him. Anne knew that he liked to be alone in the morning so she brought his cooked breakfast to his room while the other lodgers ate downstairs in the dining room. As he surveyed the comfort of his breakfast table, he wondered why the fear in his nightmare was worse than any fear experienced when awake. Is it God opening the door for me or the Devil? He wondered was he shaking with awe and terror at the mystery of an unknown God waiting for him, or was it the terror of the unfathomable evil of the Devil? He wasn't sure.

Now in the taxi he traced the rough outline of Christ's body on the crucifix of his rosary with his fingers. He prayed, "Jesus, Son of God, have mercy on me, a sinner." The same prayer said during nights in his security hut. The Jesus Prayer of the third century Desert Fathers fleeing into the solitude of the Egyptian Desert to find God within. Paddy repeated the Jesus Prayer until he didn't hear the sound of the taxi changing gears, until all he heard were the words in his head. Then the words were a pulse beating in his heart and there was silence. He kept repeating, "Jesus, Son of God, have mercy on me, a sinner." The taxi stopped, Cedric jumped out from the passenger seat, opened the back door where Paddy was sitting, pulled him onto the pavement outside the Black Beetle pub.

"Take him to the lock up." Cedric said to Peter.

Paddy fell to his knees, his legs buckling under him. This was his last chance to escape, where he was meant to run, not kneel. William opened the driver's door, walked slowly around the front of the car where the headlights still shone. He handed Cedric a long rectangular box. Cedric caught the wooden box like a rugby ball, its bronze clip closed, and he swung the box at Paddy, hitting him on the neck. Paddy groaned, folding to the ground, both feet caught by Peter who dragged him, head bumping on the rough pavement past the Black Beetle.

•••

"Kill me! Please kill me!" Screamed Paddy, his words faintly heard in the semi-darkness of a neighbour's bedroom. The room smelt strongly of polish. A white net curtain filtered the light from the streetlamp outside, casting moving shadows onto the wall to the left. The neighbour opened her eyes with a start, lying perfectly still, sweeping the room with a glance from left to right to see if anyone was there. The next day The Irish News reported that an unnamed neighbour heard Paddy O'Connor's plea to be killed at four in the morning. Hearing his cries, the neighbour didn't call the police, or run out of the house and knock on the door of the lockup garage next door. She sat up in bed, listened carefully to make sure she hadn't imagined it. "Kill me. Kill me," Paddy repeated in a lower voice, weeping. His voice floated into the room, this time as a ghostly shimmer of a sound, which wouldn't have wakened her if she had been asleep. Reaching over to the bedside table she switched the radio on. Then lay back in bed, breathing deeply. She concentrated on Frank Sinatra singing 'My Way'. She needn't have bothered because Paddy never spoke again. Those were his last words.

Paddy was in a place beyond fear, beyond courage – a place of surrender. Inside the garage, Cedric smiled to himself. He hadn't finished with Paddy yet. Paddy was hanging naked, upside down from a rafter. Cedric's rough hands twisted the rope ever tighter around his neck, reducing his panting and intermittent screams to a harsh rasping choking. Cedric tightened and loosened the rope as he lounged back in a rickety chair, lighting a cigarette, resting it hands free on his lips for a few seconds, inhaling; before leaning forward, slowly puffing out hoops of smoke, drifting them towards Paddy. When he was about to die, Cedric loosened the noose again. Paddy gasped. He didn't want to breathe. His body wanted to survive, Paddy wanted to die.

When a cat chases a mouse, the mouse tries to escape at first. Even if it finds itself in a corner with no obvious way out, it will run around the skirting board, searching. The cat will follow, jumping into the air then falling with its full weight in a pounce. It draws the mouse into the air with its two paws, throwing it even higher towards the ceiling. It watches it fall onto the ground then rolls it with its paw from left to right, from right to left. The mouse still thinks it can escape, it makes a dart north-east but the cat has north-east, north-west, south-east, south-west covered. With a swipe of the paw the mouse is brought back to the centre. There is a moment before the kill, when the cat looks at the mouse, alone on the ground, eyes wide open, brown, bright, sparkling. The look they now exchange is different. It is intense, magnetic, absorbing, hypnotic. It might almost be mistaken as a look of love. In that moment before the kill, the mouse knows how to die. When the mouse lies dead on the cold tiles of a kitchen floor, the cat is no longer interested. It walks away, head in the air, without looking back at the still warm but lifeless body of its prey.

An hour and a half later Cedric decided that Paddy would be allowed to die. What went through Cedric's head as he looked at Paddy hanging naked upside down from the ceiling? As Cedric cut the rope and Paddy thumped heavily onto the concrete floor, Cedric muttered to Paddy, "Why did you make me do it? You gave me no choice." He shook his head. "I had no choice."

Cedric stroked Paddy's hair as he loosened the noose for the last time.

Dawn broke over Belfast Lough, a thread of gold tracing along the horizon, a misty orange veiling the fading stars.

Blackbirds sang energetically, hopping along the top of the yard wall then swooping gracefully onto the pavement. The grass growing through the pavement cracks frozen white. Even the hairs on the inside of Cedric's nose bristled and froze as he breathed in, dragging Paddy's dead body from the garage, dumping it in the entry, leaning against a neighbour's back yard door. Paddy was doubled over like an unwanted scarecrow left for the bin men.

Cedric pulled on black leather gloves, exhaled deeply, blowing white puffs of vapour in front of his face. He rubbed his arms to warm them as he approached the black taxi. He lifted a small heart shaped solitaire diamond ring out of his pocket. He looked at it under the street light – sparkling, a star fallen to earth, bound in gold. He slipped it into his trouser pocket.

chapter 4

Monday 3rd January 1972

"Mum – where are you?" Cedric opened the door into the kitchen. There was no sign of Eileen. He raised his voice and there was a slight sound of anxiety in the second call. "Where are you Mum?" He looked behind the door, remembering how she had hidden behind the door when he was three and how he had cried thinking she had disappeared and that he was alone in the world. He remembered how she laughed at him to see him in such a panic, with his mouth wide open screaming, tears running down his face.

"You're OK Cedric. Don't be silly. I'm here."

She knelt down on the floor and hugged him and he felt the fear subside and he looked into her face and mimicked her smile.

She smiled even more broadly. He felt the warm peace return to his belly, melting the ball of fear. He knew that warmth as Eileen, his Mum.

Eileen opened the back door with the empty can of cat food in her hand.

"Cedric – what are you doing up so early?"

"I have a present for you."

"Don't be mad. You've given me too many presents for Christmas and then the lovely pearls. You must stop. You're spoiling me. What's all this about?" Eileen looked a little puzzled as she peeled the sellotape carefully from the pink and white hearts wrapping paper.

She then slowly opened a small white box in which lay a heart shaped diamond solitaire ring, glittering in the light from the chandelier dangling over the table. Eileen tried the ring on her right hand, fourth finger. It was a perfect fit. She moved the ring towards the chandelier watching the diamond sparkle even more brightly – a kaleidoscope of dazzling blue, green, pink and yellow. The light shimmered and sparkled like flames in a roaring white fire.

"It's beautiful Cedric. But it must have cost you a fortune."

"I won it in a game of poker last night." Cedric opened the top button on his shirt and loosened his tie. "It didn't cost me a penny."

"You can't take that from someone because you've won it at cards. You must give it back. Someone will be missing this. It belongs to someone else. It meant something to them. I can't take it." Eileen handed it back to Cedric. "Give it back to the person you won it from. Who was it?"

"It was no-one you know Mum. He was a stranger passing through who knew the rules. He played the game and lost." He closed his hand around hers. "It's yours."

Eileen clipped a strand of hair which had fallen across her face into her French plait. She raised her head to look into Cedric's eyes. His lips were smiling but his eyes were disconnected from the smile which gave the impression of his face being divided into two parts. It was hard to know which half to believe – the red, spider-webbed and anguished eyes or the broad smile with its ivory white teeth. Eileen settled on the lower half of his face, mesmerised by the evenness and whiteness of his teeth – her eyes scanning right and left as though to discover a flaw.

"How did he take it?" Eileen kept her eyes on Cedric's teeth.

"Take what?" Cedric smiled even more broadly, tapping Eileen on the nose with his index finger.

"Losing the ring of course." Eileen instinctively twitched her nose twice like a rabbit.

"How would I know?" Cedric reached for a chair at the kitchen table.

"You could tell from his expression couldn't you whether he was upset or not?" Eileen filled the kettle for tea.

"That's what I would expect a woman to say. A man plays by the rules. It was only a game of poker remember? You're meant to keep your face straight."

"Men have hearts too you know." Eileen topped the teapot up with boiling water and didn't look at Cedric as she whispered. "It isn't only about your friend playing poker, what about her?"

"Who?" Cedric drummed his fingers on the kitchen table.

"The person the ring was meant for ... who it belonged to."

She poured his tea into a china cup. Cedric twisted a small band of gold on his left pinky finger. "That's the kind of thinking that would do your head in if you let it."

•••

Cedric, William and Peter returned to the Black Beetle the afternoon after Paddy had been murdered. The pub looked neglected from the outside with black paint curling on wooden window frames. There was a worn, muddy Guinness mat at the front door to wipe your feet and the door itself was riddled with woodworm. The windows were dusty and finger stained.

Cedric swaggered through the open front door, followed by William and Peter. A faint shaft of sunlight fell through the open door onto the wooden boards by the bar. Cedric strutted into the rectangle, as though into a spotlight on stage, as the cigarette smoke swirled in clouds around him. Frank, the bar owner, immediately jumped to his feet and rushed behind the bar, pushing through the groups of men huddled in the darkness around tables, playing cards, dominoes or talking in whispers.

"Get them whatever they want. It's on the house." Frank shouted at Richard the barman.

There was a steady background hum of talking. To the right of the bar there was a television showing the Chester horse races. At the table closest to the television, two men compared betting tickets.

"Another beaten docket Sammy P?" shouted Cedric across the bar. Sammy P smiled back, waving his ticket in the air, rolling his eyes to the ceiling. Richard scurried to Cedric seated beside the billiard table in an enclosed booth. "What are you having? Frank says it's on the house."

"Let's have three pints of the black stuff and three whiskey chasers."

Richard wiped the table with a damp cloth and hurried back to the bar. He piled the drinks onto a small circular tray and breathing heavily moved quickly towards the booth. As he approached Cedric's table Richard's feet seemed to tie themselves in knots and he lurched forward – the tray leaving his hand and causing a wall of black liquid to cascade on top of Cedric and William.

The bar filled with silence. All eyes were on the small booth, waiting for someone to break the silence.

Richard took a deep breath. "I'm really sorry."

Cedric mopped his face with a handkerchief. Cedric looked at Richard who trembled in front of him, shoulders bent over, wringing his hands.

"I'm really sorry."

Frank had dropped to his hunkers behind the bar, looking over the top, with his hands over his ears.

Cedric coughed, looked at William and then Peter. William nodded. "We'll have the same round again. This time throw a towel in if you don't mind."

Richard sighed. "I'll get you that right away." Minutes later he carefully balanced the three pints and whiskey on the small circular tin tray.

"How long did it take you to finish the job last night?'" asked William knocking back a whiskey.

"I took my time. No need to rush these things if you want to do a quality job," Cedric smirked.

"What are you talking about?" Peter asked. "He didn't look as though he was long for this world when you took him to the lock up."

"Well, there you go. Out of the goodness of my heart, you might say that I let him live a little longer. Oh by the way – well done Peter. I forgot to offer you my congratulations. You're no longer a Mammy's boy. You're in it now with us. I didn't think you had it in you." Cedric slapped Peter across the head.

"Put a notch in your guitar to remember your first one. You'll never forget it. You can be proud of yourself," William quipped.

Peter wiped away the beads of sweat, rolling through his strawberry blonde sideburns.

"I didn't do anything."

He breathed heavily. His legs splayed open, the neck of his rugby shirt showed thick curly red hair. He rubbed his right hand over the matted curls, pushing to one side the pint of Guinness in front of him. He scratched a scab on his left hand. Cedric leaned forward and stared into Peter's eyes.

"Try telling that to the Police. I don't think it will hold up in the Crumlin Road Courthouse, do you? You're the intelligent one in the family after all."

Peter felt his stomach and throat constricting, his breathing getting shallower, his eyes narrowing. He struggled to get the words out. "You might be in there yourself soon watching the paint flake off the walls."

"Boys, boys, let's not start fighting. Let's stay focused." William signalled to the barman. "Same again."

"Not for me." Peter pushed his almost full pint across the table.

•••

On the afternoon of the Tuesday 3rd January while Michael McGuckin played bowls in Ardoyne Hall. Tom, Rose and Lily were at home. Lily was painting, Rose was in her bedroom studying and Tom was fixing a leak in the bathroom toilet. He had screwed in a metal tray to catch drips from the cistern and a tube from the tray ran into the back of the basin beside the bath. It was a temporary measure until how he could find out how to fix it properly.

While he adjusted the tubing into the basin, Lily went into the kitchen and poured an inch of turpentine into four clean jam jars. She carried them into the sitting room, placed a fifth empty jar for the paintbrushes on a small table. She touched the brushes with her fingers to see if they were soft. She lifted a wooden palette and pressed a line of Prussian blue, Titan Rose, Cadmium Yellow and Platinum White, Black, Violet Blue. She mixed cadmium yellow with blue to make her favourite turquoise green, adding white to make it shimmer. She placed a postcard of Belfast Harbour at sunset on one side of the table. With the canvas on the easel, she mixed more blue with violet, thinning it with the turpentine. The Lough glistened with the lights from nearby Whitehouse. It was difficult to distinguish the dark blue water from an almost black sky. Streetlights and house lights twinkled like golden stars, studded into the hills. After Lily had finished mixing the colours, she traced the first line between the hill and the sky and the second line between the disappearing land and the beginning of the Lough. On canvas the land and sky merged. Lily placed her brush back into the turpentine and make circles in the Prussian blue on canvas with her fingers. She was not aware of time passing. There was only now, only the mixing, the movement of her hand without thought, the creation of shadows and light. Without thinking her fingers scooped up and mixed on canvas blue with yellow, red with violet, her breathing relaxed, her gaze intently disappearing into the painting.

"British bastards! Go home!" A clatter of stones hit metal.

Tom shouted down to Lily, "They're at it again."

Tom ran downstairs into the hallway and placed the metal bar on its hooks. A handful of rioters gathered at the top of Brompton Park hurling broken pavement at the army lookout post.

"British bastards! Go home!" Within minutes there were more than a hundred rioters outside. Tom walked down the hallway towards the sitting room.

"What's happening?" Lily looked up from her painting and wiped her fingers on an old towel.

"They're warming up to riot. We should be in full flow in about fifteen minutes. How are you getting on with the painting?" Tom stood beside Lily as she dabbed yellow into the dark mountains.

"It will have to dry before I can do more. But I have time."

"When is the exhibition opening?"

"Saturday. I'm quitting now. What do you think?"

"I like it. You don't need touch it. It's done. All you need to do is sign it."

A bus rumbled along the road, stopping outside the front door. Tom shook his head at Lily, "It's odd that they are still running the buses."

"Get out!" A voice screamed outside.

"I'll check." Tom touched Lily on the shoulder, walked quickly into the hallway and into the parlour. He looked out from behind the white lace curtain. A driver still sitting in the seat fumbled with the catch of the door. Two rioters with guns stood facing him. "Hurry up."

"It's stuck." The driver kept his head down pulling wildly at the catch. It opened.

He raised both arms into the air. In a high pitched voiced squeaked, "Don't hurt me. Take the money." He pushed a leather bag into the hands of one of the rioters before jumping from the bus and running down the Crumlin Road. Two rioters jumped from the bus. One lit a cloth and pushed it into the neck of a bottle filled with petrol.

"Stand back." He threw the petrol bomb through the open door.

"Get back." He yelled at the approaching wave of rioters. "The petrol tank is going to explode."

The rioters scattered into Brompton Park like a flock of sheep chased by a mad dog. Tom took a deep breath and ran towards the parlour door, shouting upstairs to Rose. "Rose, get downstairs. There's a bus outside. The tank is going to go at any minute."

Rose hadn't even time to open the bedroom door before the petrol tank exploded, shaking the windows in the parlour but not breaking them. Outside flames danced into a black night sky, sparks shooting into the fading light. The rioters cheered as reinforcements in the form of six Saracen tanks trundled along the Crumlin Road, the window flaps opened and rubber bullets bounced into the crowd.

A familiar cheer was heard. The soldiers inside the Saracen lowered the metal eyelids, leaving enough room to fire rubber bullets into the crowd. "Poom ... poom ... poom."

The rioters cheered, "More. More. More."

Tom said, "It will have quietened down for Mass. It always does."

That was the Tom that Lily knew – the Tom who was patient, kind and tender. It was the Tom with big shoulders. The Tom you could always depend upon to take you through the worst of whatever life would throw at you. Tom was born in 1920, nine years before The Great Depression swept across the ocean from America to hit Belfast with the fury of a hurricane. His father was of a stocky build, with bushy red hair, sideburns and a curious sprinkling of small brown freckles, dotted down the bridge of his nose and forming a heavy nucleus around his left eye, giving the impression that he was wearing an eye patch.

Tom father's feet and legs appeared rooted in the earth, making him walk slowly, as though extracting them one at a time from beneath the earth's boggy surface. His nickname was Elfie. Tom inherited his red curly hair and freckly face from his father and his height and slim build from his mother. She had long black wavy hair which fell onto her shoulders like a silk scarf, deep brown eyes bulged as her wide mouth opened, screaming at Elfie when he came home drunk on a Friday night. She towered over him, flicking the dishcloth at his bowed head, biting her lower lip, shouting, "You pig. You pig. The children are starving." On the rare occasion when his father ventured to respond, his mother shouted, "There you go. What do you expect from a pig but a grunt?" Flicking the dishcloth with increasing fury, catching him this time on the nose or eyelid.

Tom's mother's genes may have bobbed on a Spanish Armada galleon blessed by Pope Sixtus V. Setting sail from Lisbon in 1588, the galleons were forced to sail around the north of Scotland towards the craggy coast of Donegal, then south past the towering cliffs of Clare, fighting to continue even further south while repeatedly being driven relentlessly north and east by the Gulf Stream. The ships had lost anchors in an earlier battle so were at the mercy of seventy foot waves. Cavalry horses were dragged from below decks, slithered and struggled on the salty wooden floor before being thrown into the tumultuous seas to lighten the load on board. Ships lurched into the air, balancing for a moment on the crests of gigantic waves before following the horses headlong into the depths of the Atlantic. Some of the ships couldn't escape the pull and lure of the granite rocks off shore. The bellies of ships pierced by shards of rock. Tom's DNA maybe struggled lacerated from the rocks, slipping the last few inches into shallow water, from where it was possible to stagger, fall and eventually collapse into the embrace of lugworms nesting in the sodden sand. Breathing air from the space between the worms, spitting and coughing blood and sea water, his lungs vigorously filtering the sweet sense of air, snivelling, almost lifeless, head pressed more deeply into the sand, as though wanting to return to a warm centre that was unmoving and solid. The wind whipping onto his back, forcing him to twist and burrow into the sand – yet making him almost smile at the sweet pain of being alive. He raised his eyes to see in the distance two misty shapes approaching through the driving rain struggling to carry a long plank of wood between them; their cloaks swirling into the air like flapping dragon's wings. He soon felt the soft touch of a hand against his shoulder, rolling him onto his back. He looked into the Irishman's eyes, as though into his father's, as he was gently hoisted onto a rough wooden stretcher and carried to safety, hidden from the English.

The defeat of the Spanish Armada was one of those decisive moments of destiny, forever changing the course of Irish history. The Protestants believed that God was on their side because it was the winds sent from God that destroyed the Armada and not the English. Even Philip II of Spain, when he heard of the result of the expedition, declared, "I sent the Armada against men, not God's winds and waves."

During the days of the Great Depression, Tom's mother would say, "Tom, go and see if you can find any money someone might have dropped on the pavement. If you find any buy three quarters a pound of cod for dinner. Ask Mr Fishy to skin and bone it." Tom walked slowly down the Horseshoe bend towards Ardoyne, scouring the pavement for a miracle. As he reached the shops, there lying glittering in the gutter at the side of the road was a sparkling silvery half crown. He picked it up, felt the coldness of it in his hand, ran straight over to Mr Fishy to ask for his cod to be boned and skinned.

Elfie's father used to sell horses and do a bit of painting and decorating for a living. For a while he also sold coal, driving it around in a cart pulled by one of his horses. The other horses galloped around the field beside the house, cutting up the turf with their sharpened hooves until a buyer could be found for them. Elfie planted potatoes in the turned up soil. He made a carousel of wooden horses, painted with outdoor gloss, mostly cream coloured with ochre manes and titan rose harnesses. He drove around North Belfast charging a halfpenny for a ride, allowing the children to go around only once, playing tinned music as the horses moved up and down. The children laughed, clung on for dear life, crying when it stopped. "Will you not give them another go?" the mothers asked. Tom's father sometimes said "Yes", eyeing the mother up and down to see if she was good looking.

Tom never understood why Elfie spent less time at home after his third child John died in childbirth.

After dinner on Friday evenings when Elfie was home, he asked for "*the chocolate*" to be brought to the table. Pushing the dinner plate to one side, he threw himself back in the chair, his legs splayed to the right and left and slowly peeled back the silvery foil. All six eyes watched him as he popped one, two, three squares into his mouth at once. He closed his eyes as he sucked, letting the chocolate slowly melt without looking even once at the children. Then Elfie found another way of finding pleasure in life. He found himself another woman.

Tom would escape into the field at the back of house after his evening meal and lay in the long grass with cowslips tickling his cheeks. He breathed in the smell of the damp clover, buttercups and dandelions and prayed for his father. He prayed his father would not die and go to hell but that God would change him, make a saint out of him and that when he died, he would go to heaven. Tom thought 'that's what we were put on earth for – to become saints – to be Divine instruments – holy flutes allowing God to whistle tunes through us'. It was hard for Tom to imagine his father becoming a saint but his mother gently reminded him, "For God nothing is impossible."

One evening when Tom came back from daydreaming and praying in the garden, Elfie told him that he was putting his mother into Purdysburn mental hospital.

"She needs help."

"What do you mean she needs help?"

"She's not well. There's nothing that we can do for her on our own."

Tom worried that maybe his prayers weren't good enough. Couldn't God hear him? His mother tried to explain to him that he could pray to God by listening to Him rather than talking to Him. She told him that God knew every thought in his head.

"He knows your thoughts before you know them yourself – even the thoughts you don't want to know."

His mother accepted the fact that she had to go to Purdysburn, saying, "God's ways are not our ways". Tom didn't know what that meant. Did it mean that Elfie was right and that his mother needed to go into Purdysburn or did it mean that she was going into Purdysburn like a martyr, helpless to resist Elfie and surrendering to the will of God?

Only the week before, Dickie who worked with Tom asked, "Do you want to see a picture of your father?" A photograph was thrust into Tom's face, of his father with his arms around another woman with short straight hair cut in a bob, unlike his mother's long wavy hair. He was dancing with her in the Plaza Ballroom. They were both smiling for the camera. The woman's left hand caught in his father's right hand was held close to his shoulder. His father's cheek pressed against her cheek. They were intimately squashed together like pieces of putty settling into one another. Tom studied the photo as Dickie smirked. Tom handed it back. "You can keep the photo Dickie. Thanks."

"I have another if you want of him lying face down in the cabbages?"

"No thanks Dickie. Keep it."

Tom's mother didn't last long in Purdysburn. Within a month she was dead. The day before she died Tom visited her in hospital and she told him, "Tom, I have something for you." She reached into the bedside cabinet and took out a small silver medal. On one side there was an image of Our Lady of Mount Carmel with the words 'Virgo Carmel'. On the back there was an image of the Sacred Heart with Jesus pointing to his heart. It was the size of a large thumbnail. Tom placed it in his pocket. Later with a small safety pin he pinned it to the inside of his shirt. She also gave him a small book with curled up corners, smelling of mothballs. It had a picture on the front of a medieval man bent over a walking stick. He had a long beard and a tight fitting skull cap and rested his hand on the shoulder of a kneeling friend. The book was called 'The Book of the Lover and the Beloved' by Ramon Llull. Ramon's name in gold leaf was sunk deep into the frayed edges of the purple hard cover.

The day before his mother died, Tom held her hand. He knew that she couldn't have long to live. It was unbearable to think of her not existing. Her death, her 'goneness' was much more unbearable than the thought of dying himself. He looked away for a moment to the left, fixing his gaze on the white wall. It was as though in that simple head movement she had disappeared. She had gone. She was dead. The movement of his head was an echo of death. He should get used to it.

He turned back to her, feeling the immense poignancy of her presence, all of her being here and yet soon to be gone. The deep love for her settled in his stomach, churning with the knowledge of what would come.

"Let me show you." She took the book from him and carefully turned a few pages. "There is a short meditation for each day." She opened the book at Verse 9.

"So the Beloved asked: "If I double your trials, will you still be patient?" The Lover answered: "Yes, so you may double also my love."

His mother asked, "Why do trials double love?"

"They allow you to find patience – to know God's heart beat," Tom replied without hesitation.

His mother nodded. "Yes. That's true. Patience, like love is tested and purified in the fires of suffering. Suffering becomes love if you know how to suffer."

"How did you learn?"

"Life taught me. It will teach you too if you let it."

He took the small book from his mother and put it into his jacket pocket with the medal to Our Lady of Mount Carmel. He threw his arms around his mother as she lay propped up on the pillows. Tears rolled down his face as he whispered, "I don't want you to die." Even as he said it, he knew it was a crazy thing to say. She had to die. Whatever is born has to die. His mother looked at him with a tangible gentleness, her head tilted to one side, smiling softly, with the kind of smile that wanted to tell Tom something more than could be told with words. She didn't move her arms to hold him. Her arms stayed crossed on her lap. She then looked at him again quizzically as Tom pulled back, rubbing the tears from his cheeks with the back of his hand. She whispered, "You're lucky. You can cry. I've never been able to cry."

Tom threw his arms around her once more. Tom's mother caressed his hair with soft even strokes.

"It's my time Tom. You have to let me go."

As Tom worked carving grooves in the leg of an oak chair, his thoughts were constantly of his mother and her approaching death. He didn't know what he could do to help her. He could only think of her. By keeping images of her in his mind, he felt her presence filling him, wiping out any other reality. As he turned the back of the chair in his hands, the smoothness of the warm oak reminded him of her skin, the curve of the wood, her nose, the warmth of the sun shining on his back, her caress. His body flooded with a sweet sadness, a melancholy, a piercing poignancy. The image of his mother now seemed to sink from his head to his heart. He couldn't clearly see her at all but felt her essence beating within his heart. At ten minutes past four he experienced a stabbing sensation above the groin on his right side. He sat still on the chair on which he had been carving.

Was it the beginning of appendicitis? He pressed his hand into his side and felt his body flood with a mingling of peace and joy. In the peace was the sinking sensation of silence. He felt as though he was dropping through clouds of feathers, breathing slowly and deeply. The accompanying feeling of joy was as though he was simultaneously being lifted back up again to the surface. The feeling was so extraordinary that he wanted to laugh out loud. He felt light, buoyant, bubbling with a sense of anticipation and pleasure as though he was waiting at a railway station for a long lost friend arriving on the approaching train. He found himself observing these unusual sensations in his body with confusion. His body was being playful – like a kitten bouncing up a tree in the garden, patting with its paw at a flower or like a lamb jumping high into the air. Why, he wondered, did he feel so sublimely happy with his mother dying? Later that evening, when he returned to the hospital to visit his mother, Nurse Anne rested her hand on his shoulder. "I'm so sorry. Your mother passed away at ten past four. Would you like to see her?"

When Tom saw his mother, she was lying on her side. The bedspread with its tiny roses covered her shoulders. He approached her, slowly, cautiously, seeing first her open mouth, spidery red veins around her nose, closed eyes. Her long black hair spread over the pillow like an oil slick. Her body gurgled and he could have sworn it moved. For a moment Tom thought that she hadn't died, that they had made a mistake and that she was only asleep. He touched her forehead. It was cold and hard. He looked at her closed eyes. They were solid, slightly open but he couldn't see the eyes themselves which before had looked at him, sparkling like the twinkling surface of a summer sea, or on occasion pierced him like the thrust of a sword in fencing. No, her lashes were sealed as though with glue. He stroked her silky fine hair against the pillow case. He fingered her arm through the long cotton sleeve of her nightdress. It was still warm. He held her hand for the last time, her chipped nails, long fingers that wanted to play the piano but never did or would. He squeezed her hand tight, wanting to see her fingers flutter like a butterfly and settle once more onto the sheets.

When Tom left his mother, the world had changed. Everyone he now looked at, it seemed as though he was seeing through them – seeing into them. Their bodies were moving but the people themselves didn't know what moved them or even that they were being moved. Tom knew. Tom didn't see the world through his eyes anymore. It seemed as though he was looking at the world from no fixed point at all, although if he was asked, he would have tried to say that it now seemed as though he was seeing from his heart – not a fixed point in his physical heart but from his heart which was now everywhere. Tom had the sense that he was a part of everything that existed and that like an air plant, he was taking all the nourishment he needed from the air. Everything that he needed was in his breathing. When he breathed in, he breathed in the whole Universe and when he breathed out he breathed out the Universe. He didn't really know whether he was breathing in and out the Universe or whether it was breathing in and out Tom. It didn't matter which way it was. He was intimately connected with everything around him.

Sitting on the number 57 bus rolling along the Crumlin Road, it now seemed to Tom as though everyone was made up from part of someone else – Ena Martin had his mother's lips, Roísin McKeever his mother's hair, and Angela McFadden his mother's feet. It went on like that until he felt that his mother hadn't died but had only been redistributed around Belfast in the smiles, the laughter, the joy, the sorrow, the sadness of everyone he met. God the artist had painted everyone from the same palate of paint. Colours were dotted onto bodies like canvases. When he found himself filled with a sense of peace, he didn't know whether he was at peace himself or whether it was his mother who was at peace within him.

He could feel her breathing inside of him. She was there in his nose, in the sensation of air moving along his nostrils into the back of his throat as he breathed in. She was there in the warm air he breathed out through his mouth. She was there in the beating of his heart, in the touch of his chisel against the cherry wood. He no longer felt that he was one person. Neither did he feel that he was two people but rather that he was one and two people at the same time.

When Tom went to daily Mass and received Communion he used to feel that the host dissolving on his tongue symbolised everything on earth that he needed to survive. To make the bread, someone needed to sow the wheat, it needed sun and water, it needed someone to harvest, someone to grind the wheat, someone to mix the wheat with water and to add salt. It needed another fire like the sun in miniature to cook the bread. It needed someone to cut the bread, a van to transport it, a priest to be present as mediator between God and man. When the bread dissolved on his tongue he felt he was receiving the whole Universe that had created it for him.

In those days after his mother died, Tom felt when he went to Mass that his body was the host on the tongue of God. That God was receiving him and giving thanks for Tom's being – that he was dissolving, dying on the tongue of God. His death and his mother's life and death were this – small appearings and disappearings on the tongue of God who received them into himself. It was God who was transformed by eating them. These thoughts and feelings didn't last very long at all – maybe at most for three days, until he had a dream.

In the dream Tom saw his mother eagerly scrambling over smooth red rocks, jumping like a goat from rock to rock, and climbing the mountain at great speed and with great dexterity. He slowly followed behind, looking for foot holds, grasping at the rocks with his hands to pull himself forward. He was amazed at the progress his mother was making. As he looked up, he could see that she had reached the top of the mountain. He wanted to shout at her to be careful, not to go so fast and to remember that she had a weak heart. He didn't shout. Instead he watched her sitting peacefully at the summit on smooth red rocks. Her hands were again on her lap. She stared straight ahead, into the distance, towards the horizon. She didn't look at Tom at all. Her expression was serene, joyful with a mysterious ineffable quality – a look beyond emotion. Tom kept watching his mother. It seemed as though she was telling him something that he couldn't really understand. It had something to do with her serenity – something to do with going beyond emotions. There was something important about the fact that she wasn't looking at him but was looking straight ahead. She could have turned and smiled at him. Why didn't she? She knew he was there right below her, looking up.

•••

Elfie remarried within two months of Tom's mother's death and moved into a terraced house in Ardoyne. With his new wife, the woman in Dickie's photograph, he started a second family.

It was only then that Elfie confided to Tom that he used to hide from his own father when he came home from work. His father would search the house, looking for him. Elfie hid in the glory hole under the stairs. He listened as his father drew closer. He heard him turn the knob on the glory hole door. He saw a hairy arm reach down towards him in the darkness and seconds later, Elfie's father dragged him screaming into the sitting room. Elfie curled up on the floor, pulling his arms in around his head, withdrawing into himself like a snail into its shell. Elfie's father removed his leather belt with its metal buckle and thrashed Elfie making sure the metal buckle cracked repeatedly onto his spine until he was too tired to hit him anymore. Elfie's mother sat in the rocking chair crocheting a table cloth with white linen thread. Tom wondered if it was then that his father's heart had turned to stone. He prayed that his father would be given a new heart of flesh like the one promised in Ezekiel. He wanted his father to receive a heart that knew how to suffer, a heart that could throb with a conscience and learn how to love.

Years later, on a cold wintery February in 1939, Elfie lifted a pint of Guinness in the Crown Bar in Belfast. He held the glass perfectly vertical before taking the first sip, the creamy top sticking to his upper lip. "What will you be having?" he called to Danny, Eddie and Sam. The frothy cream settled slowly at the bottom of the glass as he struggled to his feet, squeezed out of the cubicle, to walk with heavy slow feet to the bar. He placed four pints of Guinness on a wooden tray, walked back towards the cubicle, placed the tray precariously on the edge of the rectangular oak table. Then he held his hands in the air as if he had remembered something important to say, or wanted to ask permission to speak. He coughed gently, patting the air, as if acknowledging an invisible wall. A hush fell over the bar. The silence spread to the enclosed cubicles, bounced off the opaque etched glass windows, the dusty arched mirrors, the fleur-de-lis, the marble pillars. Elfie smiled and with a small nod of his head to the right and left, acknowledging the silence or surrendering, he took another step forward, towards the table, where the tray, now holding one pint of Guinness, was stable. His lips moved but no words could be heard. His arms and shoulders circled while his legs remained steady on the tiled floor. The circle widened. His lips moved again, this time two words were heard by everyone.

"Thank you."

He dropped backwards, falling in a perfect 90 degrees arc to the floor, his head crashing onto the polished black and white mosaic tiling, breaking open like a dropped Easter egg. A thin snail trail of blood oozed from his nose, the sunlight danced on his curly red ringlets, forming a halo around his head. It was the first time in his life that Elfie had said thank you for anything.

Tom on the other hand was a man who was a grateful for life. Shortly after his father's death, his gratitude turned to Lily who appeared in his world.

Lily met Tom in the Plaza Ballroom at a tea dance where the men sat on the right hand side of the room and the women sat on the left. It was 1939 just before the start of the Second World War. The women waited patiently to be asked to dance. Sometimes it could happen that you were left alone. You were known then as a 'wall flower'. It was one of the worst things that could happen to you. You would be forced to sit and look at your lacy gloves and pray for the dance to end with an excruciating burning pain in your belly. That night Lily arrived with two girlfriends. She didn't know Tom. She waited for the music to start. Those five minutes after the music started were magic. In the five minutes as she looked across the room, time seemed to move into eternity where nothing happened and yet everything happened. She felt as though in her head danced all of the stars in the Universe and in her heart swished all of the waves from every ocean.

Everything stopped when she spotted Dominic Green talking to Paddy Moran. Dominic had curly blonde hair and blue eyes. He was neither too tall nor too small. He had more of a kind of chunky stocky rugby player build which gave you a sense of confidence in his ability to defend you if necessary. His face was fiery red as though he was embarrassed or had been drinking. The latter wasn't true as he was a Pioneer which meant that he had taken a vow not to take any alcoholic drink at all. He had kept to that vow. Lily thought that was a good sign in an Irishman – staying true to your vows. He was a great dancer and a little bit shy. All of the girls were dying for him to ask them to dance. Lily rolled up a piece of paper into a ball and threw it across the room. It bounced off Dominic's head. He stopped his conversation with Paddy Moran and looked across the room at Lily, who waved at him and stuck her tongue out. The music started and Dominic squashed his cigarette butt under his shiny black shoe and headed straight across the room to ask Lily to dance.

"You're a cheeky one."

"There's no point being shy. We're only here once. Tell the Truth and shame the Devil. Sure you know you're a gorgeous man and all the girls are falling at your feet."

Lily swirled around into Dominic's arms. Dominic whirled her across the floor into the quick step, the fox trot and tango. Then they had two cups of tea and a slice of madeira cake.

What should have happened next was that Dominic should have asked permission to walk Lily home. He didn't. Lily waited as the music ended, tapping her feet on the floor, humming the words of the last song as coats were being put on and the hall began to slowly empty.

"Lily, I'm sorry but tonight I'm working the night shift at the ship yard. Would you mind Tom walking you home? He's a good man. Not as good as I am mind you. I would like you to remember that."

Tom mysteriously appeared at Dominic's side. Lily felt her stomach sink. On the left stood Dominic with his curly blonde hair, his to-die-for blue eyes, his tailored black suit, white shirt, blue silk tie and the shiniest shoes that had ever been seen in Ireland. Beside him Tom with his long narrow face, straight nose, bushy eyebrows and an insignificant mouth. Although only nineteen his hair was already quite thin on top with a wide parting that you could drive a tram through. It is true that he had rather beautiful blue eyes – even more beautiful than Dominic's – but they were hidden behind a pair of thick round black glasses which gave him a sense of being beautiful but at a distance. That night he wore a white crumpled shirt, black tie and a mottled green v-neck jumper, woollen trousers and brown boots ragged at the edges with one of the bootlaces trailing the floor.

Tom held out his hand to shake Lily's.

"You've drawn the short straw tonight Tom."

"Now, Lily I think that it is you who has drawn the short straw. Sure, I must be the luckiest man in Belfast."

As Tom walked Lily home, he listened to her talk about her Grandmother Martha who played the harp and piano and who used to live in a small castle perched on a cliff edge in Donegal. "That's when there was money in the family. It all disappeared and no-one knows where or how".

"They don't have an idea?"

"Well everyone says that it was Grandfather Dennis who played Poker and drank himself silly. He lost the castle in a poker game but won it back again by the end of the week. Martha locked him in his bedroom one night he came home drunk and she said that he tied the sheets together and climbed down onto the cliff face and they found him in a bar three hours later in his pyjamas and slippers."

"I like his style." Tom dropped his head and saw Lily's dainty ankles wobbling on the cobbled street.

"Can I help?" He reached an arm towards her.

Lily stopped and looked at Tom.

"You're a gentleman. Thank you." She slipped her arm through his and nestled against his shoulder. "You're a good listener Tom."

"You're a good talker. Together we're a good pair don't you think?" Tom squeezed Lily's hand through the woollen glove. As Tom held Lily's to say goodbye, he took a deep breath and asked, "Lily, will you come with me next Saturday to the Plaza?"

Lily looked straight into his eyes.

"What will Dominic say?"

"I hope he will say that he will be honoured to be Best Man."

They were married on Saturday 2nd November 1940 at Holy Cross Church Ardoyne. The sun shone brightly through the stained glass windows as they exchanged vows. Dominic Green stood on Tom's left as Best Man. A pregnant Catherine, Tom's sister, stood on Lily's right as Maid of Honour and Catherine's husband Leo was an usher.

On Tom's wedding day, Catherine was only newly married herself to Leo Wilson, a Protestant who worked in the shipyard in Belfast. Leo was five foot five, with auburn hair and hazel eyes. He looked everyone directly in the eye when he met them, shook hands and then he would hug them. Tom towered over him. Leo held out his hand. Tom caught it and they shook hands, their hands rising and falling between them like passionate waves in a turbulent sea. Leo smiled, his face wide open, hazel eyes twinkling into Tom's. Then he dropped Tom's hand and hugged Tom. His arms around Tom's shoulders, his feet on tip toes, head pressed against Tom's woollen jacket.

"Good to meet you Tom. Catherine told me all about you."

Tom patted his back, smiling at Catherine, over Leo's shoulders.

On Friday 1st November 1940, Leo was having lunch in the shipyard when he heard the low drone of the Junker 107 as it disappeared into a thundery grey cloud, the swastika swallowed up by a billowing dragon-like breath. The nose emerged seconds later, two propellers, wings dipping to circle over the dockyard. He slowly chewed his sandwich without taking his eyes off the plane which hung in the air like a sleepy queen wasp searching for her nest.

A four month pregnant Catherine had made his lunch that morning. Leo watched, sipping his tea as Catherine cut the bread into triangles and placed two cheese and tomato sandwiches with a slice of apple pie into his lunch box. Her blonde hair curled in a Veronica Lake-like style to her shoulders. She placed the lunch box beside his jacket, lifted the stainless steel teapot, topping his cup up with hot tea.

"What will we call the twins?"

"You decide".

"Maybe we should wait until they're born. Everyone says it's easier."

"If we have a boy, I would like to call him Jonas." Catherine ruffled Leo's hair with her hand.

"Jonas?"

"Yes."

Leo caught Catherine's hand and kissed it.

"If we have a girl, let's call her Maria."

"Maria, it will be then."

"What if we have two boys or two girls?" Leo sprawled back on the chair.

"We won't." Catherine shook her head. "I know we will have a boy and a girl."

Later that morning, Leo found himself a quiet place in the shipyard, away from the clanging metal, the cursing and swearing. He watched the route of the mysterious lone aircraft tracing a circle in and out of the puffy cumulous clouds, placed the apple pie on the ground to his left, rough puff pastry with a sprinkling of caramelised sugar. The German plane turned towards him dropping even lower into Belfast harbour. The November sunlight twinkled on the rippling waves. Seconds later a huge block of concrete smashed onto the ground beside him. It whistled past his shoulder, plucking a strand of wool from his Aran jumper, before it buried itself in the cement ground, splintering at the edges, throwing up a small cloud of dust. He looked around. There was no-one to be seen. There was no-one to be heard – only silence. How did he not hear someone carrying a block of that size? There was no laughing, no-one sniggering and not even the sound of scurrying footsteps. The apple pie with its juicy cooking apples was squelched, and plastered against the red brick wall. A hollow clunking of metal thumped in the distance.

Leo gathered his coat from the ground, struggling to push his left arm into the woollen sleeve. It was cold away from the shelter of the wall where a weak November sun warmed him. The humid air with icy tentacles now touched his ankles, penetrating his thin woollen socks. He shivered, walking slowly, aligning his breathing with his footsteps to calm his racing heart. Outside the shipyard, Dan O' Sullivan was leaning against the red brick wall with his famous pet lion on a lead. He let the lead out a foot or two and the lion snarled at Leo, raising its left paw into the air. Dan laughed a low cackling kind of laugh. He lengthened the lead by a few inches as he took a puff on his cigarette. Leo kept his eyes on the ground, didn't quicken his pace but kept walking. The lion growled after him – tugging on the lead and scratching at the ground.

A week later as Leo hammered and shaped a metal panel the roar from over one hundred Henkel planes drowned the hiss of his blow torch. An air raid siren wailed. He flicked the blow torch off, turning to Sammy. "Come on Sammy. This is for real. Let's head for the shelter." Sammy McAfee dropped his hammer on the ground, his face white. He had already started to run before Leo finished his sentence. They joined twenty other men who were stumbling, running, sprinting. The Henkel's were now flying low, directly overhead. Sammy panted, gasping as beads of sweat gathered around his balding head then rolling onto his cheeks. Leo saw a pilot staring straight ahead through a glass greenhouse nose. Anti-aircraft guns fired rhythmically into the sky. The first bomb dropped like a rugby ball, hitting the building in which Leo and Sammy had been working. Everything appeared to be in slow motion, including Leo's breathing. It didn't feel that he was running. More that he was a passenger in a body which was running. His feet pounded the concrete path, his arms moved rhythmically up and down and his legs continued to run when he heard machine gunfire stippling the concrete pavement in front of him. The second bomb dropped onto the ground six feet in front of Leo. The Henkel put its nose into the air and climbed noisily into the blue sky. The pilot looked down at Sammy and Leo, scattered bodies twisting and settling onto the ground.

Five months later on Easter Tuesday 15th April 1941 a lone reconnaissance Junker 107 circled over Belfast while in Windsor Park spectators watched Distillery beat Linfield 3-1. Everyone's eyes were on the match. No-one knew that two hundred bombers had left Northern France for Belfast.

In the Royal Victoria Hospital, Catherine removed her wedding ring and diamond engagement ring and placed them in a small jewellery box which she hid in the bedside cabinet. An air raid siren wailed into life outside the hospital. Catherine lay back on the pillow. She placed the palms of both hands on her stomach and felt the babies pushing and stretching inside, pressing against her womb. She gasped. "What will happen to them?"

"They will be loved." Sister Susan smiled, squeezing Catherine's hand.

"If only Leo were still alive." Catherine closed her eyes and took a deep breath as her body rippled in the aftermath of contraction. "I can no longer see his face when I close my eyes or hear his voice. He's gone." Catherine felt her throat tightening. She struggled to breathe as her body contracted again.

Sister Susan stroked Catherine's hair. "You'll see him in the babies."

"It won't be the same." Catherine's face twisted and tears rolled onto her lips which she licked as though she was in the desert and they were the only water available.

As Catherine writhed and pushed in the last stages of labour to give birth to twins, she didn't see the night sky lit up with flares or the black outlines of Junker 88s, Dornier's and Henkel's flying in formation over Belfast. Bombs began to fall on the Waterworks. Had they made a mistake? Why were they bombing the Waterworks? 95,000 incendiaries later, with Belfast in flames and no water anywhere, everyone knew that it was no mistake. Mines parachuted silently onto the Antrim Road before exploding. In the confusion, in the Royal Victoria Hospital, Catherine gave birth to a boy and a girl. A fire alarm shrilled into life as Robert Magee delivered Jonas the second baby and cut the umbilical cord. Maria lay wrapped in a warm cotton blanket nestling quietly in Catherine's arms. Catherine leaned forward on the pillow and whispered, "Sister Susan, would you hold the babies. Mr Magee, please would you be kind enough to pass me a glass of water?"

Susan sat on the bed beside Catherine holding the twins. Catherine took the tumbler of water from Mr Magee, poured a few drops over the head of Jonas, "Jonas, I baptise you in the name of the Father, the Son and the Holy Spirit, Amen." She pressed a cross with her thumb onto his forehead. The water trickled over his dark black hair onto the sheets. She leant over kissing him on the forehead, before turning to Maria. "Maria, I baptise you in the name of the Father, the Son and the Holy Spirit, Amen." Maria's fine blonde hair held the drops of water for a few seconds before they rolled onto the sheets. Sister Susan returned the babies to Catherine's arms as the room shuddered. Catherine didn't hear the bombs exploding as she looked into the eyes of Jonas and disappeared into a world without words or sounds.

Susan sighed, glancing at Mr Magee.

"Do what you have to do." Catherine whispered without lifting her gaze from the twins.

Outside the Theatre, Mr Magee and Sister Susan ran along the narrow corridor, skidding on broken glass on their way to Ward 1.

Mr Magee took a deep intake of breath and shouted, "I'll take Ward 1. Check Ward 2."

Susan nodded, stopping for a minute outside Ward 1 as Mr Magee pulled open the wooden doors and disappeared inside.

"What happened to the emergency generator?" Susan heard moans and whimpers drifting along the corridor. She looked back to see if Mr Magee was in Ward 1. Yes. He must be. He was nowhere to be seen. She then walked slowly, touching the walls as though guided by Braille. She approached a T-junction.

"Now right", she muttered to herself. She could run. The sounds of crying were stronger now. She looked through the windows on her right as incendiaries continued to float into the courtyard below. A fighter plane swooped low. Susan dived for the floor as machine gunfire shattered the windows. Shards of glass tinkled onto the marble floors; two triangular fragments exploded from the wooden window frames, piercing Susan's back with arrow precision.

From Ward 2, a shadowy shape of a woman wearing a long white nightdress and blue slippers glided towards Susan. The woman stopped, touched the wall on her right, balancing before moving forward hesitantly. First bending over Susan's crumpled body she knelt and took Susan's pulse. There was no movement. She pulled herself up, holding the wall and stepping over Susan continued along the corridor.

Back in Theatre, Catherine breathed deeply as a bomb exploded nearby, rattling the metal bed. The lights went out. The blackness of the room fell like a blanket over the bed. The twins didn't move. Catherine listened. She couldn't see any shapes at all; only feel the warmth of Jonas and Maria in her arms. She leant over to assure herself of their breathing and then slowly rested her head against the pillow. She closed her eyes. Her body was gently throbbing. Her heart beat like a drum softened with a wool covering being rhythmically stroked. For the first time since Leo died, she felt a smile forming on her face, her lips opening and stretching towards her ears. Her body rippled with pleasure. She squeezed her arms tight to her body.

In the space behind her closed eyes appeared a dark violet blue circle. It became luminous, expanding to extinguish the blackness around it. It came closer. Then it spontaneously broke apart, splintering into white light which settled like snow crystals on a floor. On top of the glimmering crystals stood Leo. She gasped. It was the first time that she had been able to see Leo in her imagination since he had died. He smiled at her now with his arms wide open – the way he had held them open on their wedding day, when he turned around on the altar, took two steps towards her and kissed her after the priest said, "I now pronounce you man and wife."

On her wedding day, Lily sang 'Panis Angelicus'. Catherine listened again to violins playing in the background as Lily's voice harmonised with Tom's. Now, with her eyes closed, Leo took two steps towards her. Her thighs and lower legs tingled with excitement. Leo's face was inches away. His eyes were smiling yet full of tears and as he closed his eyes, Catherine whispered, "Open them. Open them." He had to keep looking at her, or he might disappear again.

She didn't hear the door of the theatre open or the click of heels across the concrete floor. She didn't see the long knife in the man's right hand or see him twist it and touch the blade with his fingers. She felt the first cold touch of its edge against her neck, sliding deeply from left to right. She heard Jonas cry and the sound of scuffling feet stopping as the theatre door slammed shut.

Catherine held Maria tight. With her eyes closed, the blue light gone, the white crystal snow melted, Leo was still there smiling. Catherine felt the soft touch of his lips press against hers. She smelt him warm and spiced with Wrights cold tar soap. She heard him breathing close against her or was it her own breathing? She rubbed her nose against his and tasted for the last time the saltiness of his kiss.

Outside in the corridor the woman walked towards the theatre. The flickering flames from multiple fires outside now made it easier for her to see. The emergency generator spluttered into life. The light for the theatre flashed on and off for a few seconds and then steadied on. The woman cautiously opened the theatre door. The broken glass from the corridor floor crunched and squeaked under the weight of wood. The room was in darkness. At first she couldn't see very well, and then gradually the light from the corridor illuminated Catherine lying in bed, head to one side on the pillow with Maria and Jonas crying gently in her arms. The stranger stopped at the side of the bed. The twins fell silent.

The woman first saw Catherine's blue theatre gown covered in blood. Then her eyes moved from the blood-stained chest, to the gaping wound in Catherine's throat. The woman screamed. The scream curdled into a vacuum. There was a faint movement in Catherine's chest – a slight rising and falling. Then as the stranger moved closer, Catherine took a deep shuddering breath, quickly exhaled, her body convulsing for the last time. The twins cried, waving arms into the air, kicking vigorously underneath the white cotton blankets. The woman removed Jonas from Catherine's embrace.

"Don't cry, baby. Don't cry. You're safe now. I'll take care of you. Come to Mummy." She cradled Jonas against her chest, ignoring the shrill cries from Maria as she turned and walked quickly towards the open theatre door. She pulled it firmly closed behind her, whispering "You're safe now. Mummy will take care of you." The Exit sign flickered as the woman opened a side door to the car park. She disappeared for a moment, lost in dozens of people huddling together for protection from the bitterly cold northerly wind. She emerged as a man covering her shoulders with a blanket guided her towards a dark shadowy figure pushing his way through the crowd towards her. Under the silvery light of an Easter moon, he embraced the woman and then the child. They kissed. He then kissed Jonas as the bombs continued to fall and the terraced houses on the Grosvenor Road, trembled and crumbled.

Catherine had been dead only ten minutes when Mr Magee stumbled through debris on his way back to theatre. He slipped on water gushing from a broken pipe, crashing arms outstretched onto the floor, slithering forward a few yards before resting his head for a few seconds on his arms, whimpering uncontrollably and then pulling himself onto his knees. The generator rumbled into full power and low level lighting brightened the previously darkened rooms. His hands were slippery with blood. He slowly removed two large fragments of glass from his left hand, leaning against the wall, holding his breath. Pulling a handkerchief from his pocket he twisted it around his hand before walking briskly along the corridor and pushing open the door into theatre.

His breathing quickened, a metallic taste of fear coated his tongue. He swallowed. Each breath descended into his gut like a ball of fire as he took Catherine's pulse. Maria slept in Catherine's arms. She occasionally made small snuffling hedgehog noises. Mr Magee gently opened Catherine's arms and removed Maria who opened her eyes but didn't resist as he held her with one arm, and with the other pulled the blood stained sheet over Catherine's head. Through the broken windows the sky flickered, as though in a thunderstorm. The Henkel and Junker bombers flashed in and out of view from behind the hospital's east wing, cumulous clouds and the slated roofs of the Grosvenor and Falls.

•••

Early on Wednesday 16th April 1941, Eamon de Valera, Taoiseach in the Republic of Ireland, wakened to the shrill alarm of the telephone in his room. Minutes later thirteen fire engines were dispatched to the North. Bodies were laid out in an open air market near Smithfield as Lord Haw Haw on the radio from Hamburg said that he would give the people of Belfast time to bury their dead before the next attack. He hoped that the people of Belfast liked their "Easter Eggs".

Mr Magee the surgeon explained to Tom, "We don't know what happened. We have no idea who killed Catherine, or why they killed her or who took Jonas. It may have been the same person but maybe not. He handed Maria to Tom.

"A beauty." Maria lay in Tom's arms staring at him the way a Siamese cat would look at you, unblinking, in silence, with big open blue eyes. Her long fingers gripped his thumb.

"Oh. There's something else you should know." Mr Magee slapped his head with his hand and then walked slowly to the back of the room where on a long wooden table, rubbing his chin; he picked up a file with notes.

"For what it is worth, I can tell you that Jonas had an unusual birthmark to the left of his navel – three small hearts rising in a vertical line towards his heart. Catherine baptised Jonas and Maria. This was found in the drawer beside her bed." He handed over Catherine's small ring box. "One of the staff found it."

Tom opened the box. He fingered the diamond engagement ring.

"Catherine's wedding ring isn't here."

"It was chaos last night." Mr Magee rubbed his eyes with his knuckles. "It was absolute madness. The wedding ring could be anywhere."

For many years Tom tried unsuccessfully to find out who killed Catherine and who had taken Jonas. He visited every primary school in Belfast, showing photos of Maria, asking if there were any boys who resembled her. He drew the birthmark time after time on pieces of paper. They shook their heads. "No."

Tom and Lily lived with baby Maria on a small farm on the Horseshoe Bend until they had saved enough money to put a deposit on a small end of terrace house in Glenbryn Park, on the outskirts of Ardoyne, North Belfast. Lily found a job as an assistant in Saville's jewellery shop on Royal Avenue. Mr Saville educated her on the world of diamonds on returning from his numerous buying trips to Antwerp. Maria grew into a beautiful woman with blonde wavy hair all the way to her waist, piercing blue eyes, delicate eyebrows, and a ballet dancer's gait. For Tom and Lily she was a perfect child. They couldn't have asked for better.

One Sunday afternoon the week before Maria's fifteenth birthday, Lily gathered her paintbrushes and placed them in empty jam jars as Tom read the Sunday papers.

"Tom, can we give Maria Catherine's engagement ring on her birthday next week?"

"I was thinking of keeping it for her twenty-first." Tom scanned the obituary columns. "Harry Dunlop died on Friday."

"What age was he?" Lily squeezed acrylics onto the palette.

"Seventeen."

"There you go. Nobody knows when they will die. Maria mightn't make it to twenty one."

"Lily don't say that."

"It's the truth. Life is uncertain. Didn't your mother always say 'the truth hurts'? Let Maria enjoy the ring now. Ask Father Anthony to bless it."

Lily mixed blue with yellow and then dotted in platinum white.

Tom put the paper to one side. He looked through the

window where buds were opening on the cherry trees in the garden.

"So you think it's a good idea to give Maria Catherine's ring?"

"I do. Remember Marilyn – 'Diamonds are a girl's best friend.'"

"You don't think it might bring…?" He hesitated and rubbed his leg.

"Nonsense. It won't bring bad luck. A diamond is a wonderful symbol of mystery and magic." Lily straightened the canvas on the easel.

"Did you know …?" Lily was about to launch into yet another interesting diamond fact, dabbing blue, yellow and white onto the canvas to create a sea of turquoise.

Tom interrupted with a smile, "No."

"That's nasty. There's so much you don't know about diamonds. Don't be horrible or I'll paint you instead." Lily picked a clean paintbrush dipped it into water and scattered it at Tom.

"I'm already a walking masterpiece – you don't need to paint me."

"I'm going to ignore that." Lily scattered more water at Tom with her brush.

"I know that it will take a better man than me to stop you." Tom dabbed at his face with his handkerchief.

"Do you know where the word 'diamond' comes from?"

"Nope." Tom pretended to yawn.

"It comes from the Greek word 'Adámas' which means 'indestructible' or 'unalterable'? I used to think that a diamond could never be destroyed but that's not true. A diamond isn't easily scratched but it is brittle. It shatters if you hit it with a hammer. Mr Saville told me about a man in Antwerp who had to cut a rough diamond and by mistake he bashed it to smithereens."

"Did he keep his job?"

"I asked Mr Saville the very same question. He said that the person who cuts the diamond is the person who adds the most value to it. He cuts it to keep as much of the weight as possible, but also to remove any flaws or blemishes. This person made a mistake but they knew that he had real talent for the cutting and so he was worth a fortune."

"What happens once they've cut the diamond?"

"They polish it."

"How?"

"With another diamond – it can take forever, years. To find a diamond you have to journey into the earth, travelling towards the centre for perhaps seventy five to more than a hundred and twenty miles. There, in temperatures over 1,200 degrees centigrade and enormous pressure, a diamond is conceived. It's like a baby. It has a possibility but not a certainty of being made. When it's formed, the journey doesn't end there, it might take anything from one billion to more than three billion years for the diamond to find its way to the surface and for someone to find it. The earth is over four and a half billion years old and so it can take nearly three quarters of the time that it has taken to make the earth to make a single diamond. So now you see why diamonds are a girl's best friend. Do you not think 'indestructible' is a good way to remember Catherine and Leo's love?"

"OK. You've convinced me. Maria can have Catherine's engagement ring on her birthday next week." Tom tickled Lily's chin. "Father Anthony can bless the ring."

"Perfect." Lily moved to the edge of Tom's chair and kissed him softly on the lips.

"You're not far off from being perfect yourself." Tom held Lily by the waist. He smelt the sweetness of orange blossom perfume dabbed behind her ears.

"Ahhhh but a flawless diamond isn't really flawless. There's always imperfection." Lily got up from her chair and skipped backwards making faces at Tom. "That makes a diamond perfectly imperfect. It's a bit like me. Shuush. Here comes Maria. Say nothing about the ring until next week."

•••

After blessing Catherine's ring and returning it to Tom, Father Anthony sat alone in his cell, a familiar loneliness settling over him like heavy clouds nestling on top of Divis or Black Mountain, promising rain and showing no signs of moving. What was the meaning of his life? He reflected on the loneliness of Christ in the garden of Gethsemane. He imagined Christ at first kneeling beside a large rounded rock embedded in hard sandy ground, beneath the swirling sculpture of an olive tree on a dark moonless night. Christ looked at what seemed to be a man in an olive tree in front of him who looked at him with panda eyes – deep, dark, sunken in a wonderful, broad sun-wrinkled face. His small nose almost hidden; his mouth surrounded by a moustache and beard. Two branches of the olive tree reached out as ears. He was wearing a crown of antlers. The man in the olive tree watched Christ watching him, calmly holding him with his gaze and a smile on his lips, pulled together like a donkey munching hay.

Christ knelt, placing his hands against the rough scaly bark, with its comforting mysterious hollows and crevices. The olive tree with the man continued to watch. The crickets sang. Their noisy call carried on a warm breeze. Father Anthony imagined Christ looking over his right shoulder seeing Peter, James and

John asleep on the grass, mouths open, snoring, untroubled. No-one awake but the man in the olive tree watching, alert, conscious with him. Thick viscous tears like blood slowly squeezed from each tear duct and rolled down his face. He now knew that he was alone. There was *no* man in the olive tree. A terrible loneliness arose in the silence. The crickets stopped singing.

"Can you not watch one hour with me?" He whispered. No-one heard. Alone – no-one listening. He slowly prostrated himself onto the ground. His nails dug into the earth, his head pressed against the spiky short grass. He moved his head to one side and felt the weight of his body settle and sink deeper into the ground. His body churned with an inescapable infinite nausea. He breathed deeply, opening himself to the sensations of disgust, despair, grief, shame, guilt, fear, anxiety and alienation. He drank from the chalice of the pain and poison of the world's past, present and future – all concentrated within his body, churning within his gut. Alone, in solitude, he stretched his arms across the earth and wept.

In the hour before Mass, sitting alone on his chair, Father Anthony bent forward, held his head in his hands and also gently wept. "It is me who is making Christ suffer. I am part of the horror he sees. I am the one who is breaking his heart – the one who can't spend one hour watching with him."

In that moment Father Anthony did not know that later that day he was going to commit the biggest sin of his life. It was a strange fact that Father Anthony was capable of having his deepest insight into love and also of being capable of betraying that love within twenty four hours.

Loneliness was the problem. Father Anthony hadn't yet realised that loneliness had a purpose. It was like a pain in his chest warning him that he wasn't well. Loneliness was the song of God singing in his heart, calling him home. Father Anthony couldn't hear the song. He didn't know where his heart was. The heart where God was singing wasn't the organ pumping blood around his body. The heart where God was singing to him was everywhere. It was the steady pulse of the Universe within and without, calling him home. When not heard, it sent the sweet sense of loneliness like the perfume from a candle in a window, lighting the way home. Father Anthony was too busy turning his ears towards the thoughts in his head and turning his eyes to imagine Maria. He could see her now – long sandy hair falling over her shoulders, kneeling at the altar rail. Her eyes closed, chin raised to receive the Eucharist. "Amen." She smiled at him before opening her mouth and sticking out her tongue. His body flooded with warmth and energy, a soft and deep connection as he looked at her closed eyes. He bent closer, his finger and thumb holding the host, touching the soft wetness of her tongue. Maria's face was shiny, like a pearl, her nose rounded like a baby's, her lips fine and smiling.

"The Body of Christ."

"Amen," Maria answered.

Father Anthony was thirty-five years old and had been a priest for thirteen years. His faith had been previously unshakeable. It was not a faith of rational beliefs. These were unimportant to Father Anthony. What was important was his sense of the presence of God who guided his steps, shaped his thoughts, informing him of what he had to do. He had a sense of the immanence of God within every cell of body, permeating his being, bringing certainty, peace and hope. It was impossible for him to imagine that there was an alternative to this – not to walk hand in hand with God in life – not knowing a God who desired him to exist, who created him and who loved him into being. This God was his real Father.

Then when he was thirty five, without warning, he realised that he no longer had that sense of faith or comfort in a God who was close to him or who cared for him. He experienced his life as shrunken within the container of his head with seemingly little or no connection to anything visceral in his body. He was like a genie withdrawn from the world unable to escape this cerebral prison. He felt a fraud. He contemplated the words of St Augustine – 'It is with the interior eye that truth is seen ... Our whole business therefore in this life is to restore to health the eye of the heart whereby God may be seen'. He couldn't see God. He couldn't feel God's presence. The memory of his previous sense of knowing God now seemed immature. It was a childish imaginary unreal God he had created. It was at best an adolescent infatuation or a projection from a feeble mind. It was nothing more than a balloon-filled idol which he now burst. He was left with dry theology, abundant ideas and beliefs about God sticking in his throat like a flaky water biscuit.

Fastening his sandals and preparing for morning Mass, Father Anthony realised that it was not Mass but Maria on his mind. He was looking forward to seeing Maria and he *felt* happy. His body felt as though it was waking up, coming alive. It felt light. He smiled at himself in the mirror, taking longer than normal to comb his curly black hair and splashing his face with aftershave. He *felt* joyful. Life away from Maria was dull, tedious and empty. His whole body longed for Maria's presence. He didn't mention Maria in his Confession with the Rector.

The Rector was a tall, athletic man of sixty-five. He was jovial and kind hearted with many years of experience as a Spiritual Director. He simply loved life and was glad to be alive. He was grateful for the gift of life. He pushed his shoulders back, straightened himself, tapped his stick on the ground as though to make the point, "It's now ...and isn't it wonderful!" His body quivered like a spring being pulled straight. Father Anthony felt himself energised by the Rector's presence. He felt an inkling of the Rector's joy. It was contagious. He only had to touch the Rector's hand and he contracted the virus of happiness for a few minutes. The Rector's words struck his eardrums, setting them tingling and vibrating with their wisdom. His gestures to Father Anthony were lightning bolts of energy splitting the air around him, smoking the room with a hazy mystery. He strode across Father Anthony's cell tapping his shiny mahogany walking stick vigrously on the wooden floor. He took a deep breath, smiled and looked through the window before sitting on a chair facing Father Anthony.

"It's a day for climbing Cave Hill. Beautiful. How do you fancy a walk along Napoleon's nose?"

Cave Hill was shaped like a giant sleeping on his back, hair streaming into Belfast Lough. Napoleon's nose a high cliff edge jutting into a clear sky.

"Maybe another day but not today, thank you."

A wintery white sunbeam highlighted three black hairs in the centre of the Rector's otherwise bald head. The Rector smiled again with an open unwrinkled face unusual for a man of sixty five years of age. Some might say even miraculous. His features were strong, angular, chiselled and polished as though from the finest cherry wood. He had the kind of face that you might imagine unfold from a life with few problems, but that was far from the truth. The Rector, on the contrary, had had more than his share of sorrows but it seemed to have affected him differently from most of mankind. He had been left an orphan at ten years of age, left in a workhouse, where he had serious health problems, suffering from a mysterious undiagnosed illness which left him lying in his bed unable to move for twelve months. Aged fourteen he was accepted to study for the priesthood. Although he walked with a stick, his body exuded vitality. He spoke with energy, emphasis and joy. He laughed his way through life in a way that left Father Anthony amazed, fascinated with a sense of awe, bemusement and bewilderment.

Where did he find his energy, his vitality, his sense of humour? To Father Anthony the Rector seemed a little too perfect. His tortured past and calm and joyful presence had turned him into a superhuman – unreal – someone difficult to aspire to – or to follow. Father Anthony couldn't imagine the Rector ever committing even the smallest of venial sins – never mind a mortal sin. In his presence Father Anthony felt obliged to hide the whole truth. By doing that he was aware that he was only fooling himself. God could not be hidden from. Yet, what had he done that needed to be confessed? Faith was a gift from God. If God took his faith away, that was not Father Anthony's fault. Had he done anything wrong? Yes. He had deliberately engaged in his fantasy of Maria.

He knew that there was nothing wrong with thoughts of Maria arising in his mind. What was wrong was his decision to hold onto those thoughts and do something with them. That was the nature of desire. Desire for Maria lured him like the call of the Sirens lured Odysseus. Father Anthony could have asked the Rector to tie him to the mast. He could have explained his weakness, his temptation. He could have begged for help. Yet he shrivelled at the thought of confessing all to the Rector. The truth was he didn't want to be tied to any mast. He was sliding down the wooden decks with no hope of return. He wanted to slide. So, he said nothing about Maria as he sat facing him in his cell.

The Rector patted his knees as the logs sparkled into life by the open fire. Father Anthony began a half-hearted confession.

What was he going to say? Being half-hearted it was filled to the brim with half-truths.

"Father, I no longer enjoy a sense of the Presence of God. It seems I have lost my faith."

The Rector slapped his thighs and leant forward on his walking stick.

"You haven't lost your faith. Faith has nothing to do with a sense of the Presence of God. A sense of the Presence of God is a consolation of faith – a gift from God and only a part of your spiritual development. True spiritual maturity takes you beyond that. You are equally happy with the sense of God's absence as you are with his presence. His absence purifies you from all feeling, from all attachment to his manifestation on earth. Faith has everything to do with what you do when you no longer feel the Presence of God. Faith is openness to the unknown, to the mystery. It's not a sense of belief."

"Why the Creed?"

"The paradox. We proclaim what we believe but at the same time we are open to the mystery of knowing the limitations of belief."

"What if I don't believe in God, in the Trinity?"

"Act as if you do."

Father Anthony shook his head. The Rector laughed.

"It's not so difficult. St Augustine said, 'Love and do what you will'. So act now with love. Let faith and belief take care of itself."

Father Anthony returned a weak smile.

"How do I know that what I do is from love rather than a selfish desire?"

"What do you think you should do? It's simple. Trust your internal Master. You know what to do. Don't lie to yourself. Be honest."

"How do I listen to my internal Master?"

"It's simple – stop thinking. Sit with your loneliness. St Ignatius advises us to absorb our loneliness as if it were drops of water falling onto a sponge. We are the sponge. Don't try to escape this loneliness. Stay awake. At such times the ego will do anything to survive. Don't allow for rationalisation. Conscience is snuffed out like a candle with rationalisation. I have seen it happen so many times before to others. Live with confusion."

Father Anthony brushed away the beads of sweat from his upper lip.

"Go to the place that hurts and stay there. Open up to the pain. It will teach you everything you need to know in the right time."

"Sometimes it feels so difficult to get from one minute to another – from one second to another." Father Anthony searched the Rector's blue eyes for some recognition of what he was not saying.

The Rector smiled as he rubbed the palms of his hands against the back of his black cassock which was warming like a hot air balloon with the heat from the logs.

"I know you feel the space immense between each moment. You want to fill it." The Rector took two steps towards Father Anthony and pulled up a chair beside him.

"You feel an unbearable emptiness of being between one second and the next – don't you?"

"Yes." Father Anthony felt his eyes stinging with tears. One rolled out of the corner of his left eye. He knew the Rector had seen it. He knew also that he had heard the tiny gasp of his in breath.

"Is it emptiness or is it angst?" The Rector leaned his head to one side and peered into Father Anthony's eyes.

"Aren't they the same?" Father Anthony found his voice a little stronger.

"No." The Rector whispered.

"They're not. One gives birth to the other. Find out which does which and you will be more than half way there." He laughed gently, tenderly ruffling Father Anthony's dark hair which felt silky beneath his fingers, like bows circling an Easter egg.

"I will try. Thank you Father."

"Don't say you will try. Do it." The Rector thumped his walking stick on the floor. "Just do it and don't think about it."

When Father Anthony said, "Your sins are forgiven. Say three "Our Fathers" and resolve never to sin again" Maria maybe should have known that something was different. Her normal penance was one "Our Father". She said, "Thank you Father."

Maria left the Confessional. Father Anthony sat in the darkness, listening to the soft tread of her shoes taking five steps to the wooden bench where she knelt to say penance. He heard the swish of her skirt against the kneeling board, the rustle of her rosary being folded into a small black leather purse which snapped closed. He heard the clickity-clack of her heels against the marble floor, walking towards the holy water font where she blessed herself on the forehead, lips and heart. The wooden door slammed shut. Father Anthony bowed his head in the Confessional. His hands throbbed. His breathing was shallow and fast. He closed the wooden shutter to his left, turned off the light before opening the confessional door, lowering his head to exit, letting the door swing gently closed behind him as he walked quickly to the back of the church. He lifted the brass latch, pulled the solid mahogany door towards him. It banged closed as he descended the steps two at a time. A silvery light from a full moon fell intermittently on the ash and oak trees. Clouds scattered, sending dark shadows into the depths of the Grove. Father Anthony took a deep breath as he jumped the last three steps onto the gravelled path.

Maria walked along the grassy verge of the path, in the direction of the monastery, turning right in the direction of the Crumlin Road. A few drops of rain trickled down her neck, snaking their way inside her warm woollen coat. She shuddered, stopping to open her umbrella, shaking it for a moment. The wind moaned softly before blowing the umbrella inside out.

Father Anthony paced quickly after her, his long coarse black habit brushing against his leather sandals. His curly black hair catching rain drops before heavily rolling down his cheeks. He could see Maria struggling with the umbrella. He needed to be with Maria. Without her he was hurtling into darkest space, catapulting into a lonely scary infinite blackness. Without Maria life was numb. It was numbness where his head and heart felt stuffed with ash. He was a walking urn that knew the slow passing of time in infinity.

At the sound of his footsteps Maria turned around. She saw his dark silhouette against the grey moonlit granite of the Church.

"Father Anthony, are you alright? Did I forget something?"

He was standing now only two steps away.

"Maria, Maria ..."

Father Anthony pushed Maria against the solid, heavy barked oak tree. Her open umbrella dropped from her hand, tumbling over and over, rolling towards the Crumlin Road. He started to unbutton her black woollen coat, two buttons shooting into the air as he pushed her onto the dampening grass.

"Please no!" Maria touched his face, pushing his lips away with her hand. He grabbed her wrist, digging it into cold wet earth, kissing her deeply. Her lack of response seemed to urge him to press his lips even more deeply against her soft, warm mouth. His teeth crunched against her teeth as his arms moved in a frenzy of undressing. He opened her coat and unbuttoned her blouse.

Maria closed her eyes, lying on the grass, her hair matted with mud. Father Anthony's hands moved towards her neck. For a brief instance he tightened his grip feeling the throb of her heart beat in his hands. He squeezed her neck gently, as though squeezing out his sin, whispering, "I'm sorry."

"Don't. Don't." Maria coughed the words as she felt his nails scratch the front of her neck. Drops of blood mingled with tears, rolled onto the spiky grass. Her breathing shallow, almost non-existent as she watched Father Anthony's face twist in pain and pleasure. "Please don't."

Father Anthony soon loosened his grasp; laying his head on her half naked body as he looked at her hand stretched out on the wet grass. In the light of moon which slithered between the spires, he saw Catherine's ring on Maria's finger. The ring glistened in the light of the moon drawing him like a magnet to her hand. He reached out, catching her hand and touching the ring with his finger, then kissing it and pulling the black woollen coat around them both, sobbing as his breathing returned to normal. The rain continued to fall; now in large drops bouncing off the gravel path – ping, ping, ping – like a small bell being struck, calling to Matins. The drops soaked into Maria's black woollen coat. Maria rolled her head to one side, seeing the moon emerge from the behind the clouds framed between the spires of Holy Cross Church.

Father Anthony sat in his cell alone before seven o'clock Mass. He prayed to the God he no longer believed in. He closed his eyes, aware of his breathing. God was not in any of his thoughts. God was not in his deep burning remorse. This was the fruit of his sin. He repeated over and over again Psalm 50.

"My offences I know them; my sin is always before me
Against you, you alone, have I sinned;
What is evil in your sight, I have done."

Then in the gap between his breath going out and before breathing in, he remembered. How pure the heart must be that bears the holy name of Jesus graven upon it. Father Anthony knew that he had betrayed God. God had been there in the Grove when he raped Maria, present in the gap between his in and out breath. There was no need to confess. His sin was known by God. Yet did he need to confess to the Rector to hear his own voice speak out aloud his sin? Did he need to make his remorse tangible in words? How else could he find forgiveness? He needed Maria to forgive him, not the Rector.

He blessed himself, crossing the room, looking at the picture of Jesus pointing to his Sacred Heart, dropping his head before opening the door. For the first time in his life Father Anthony understood the Sacred Heart not as an emotional heart but more a heart whose function was a purity of seeing. It was a heart that was able to see reality – a heart that could respond to the pain and suffering of others with compassion.

The emotional heart needed Maria as an object of desire. It was attachment which needed to be constantly refilled by the presence of the 'lover'. Father Anthony knew now that the Sacred Heart was true Love. It was Love inside of him which never needed an object to make it complete. It was infinite in its capacity to give and to receive love. It loved everyone equally without preference. Father Anthony breathed deeply, head down, bare toes curling up in his sandals as he walked along the corridor into the church and towards the main altar to say Mass. Holding the Host high the altar boy rang the bell loudly for the consecration. Father Anthony genuflected, took a second deep breath and broke the bread.

•••

In the surgery Doctor Stewart felt Maria's tummy. He took out his stethoscope and listened to her heart. He asked her to turn around and listened again through her ribs. He listened to the blood swishing back through her heart valve. There was a tinge of blue in her lips which worried him.

"You need complete bed rest. The heart valve is damaged." Doctor Stewart helped her on with her coat, saying, "You must tell your Aunt Lily and Uncle Tom. They need to know."

"What can I tell them? Maria asked.

"Tell them the truth. Tell them what happened".

"I can't. You mustn't tell anyone. You promised me."

"I won't Maria, but you should."

It was as she expected. Lily's face turned white and then red as she asked, "Who is the father?"

"I'd rather not say," Maria replied. "Please don't ask."

"I don't think you should keep it a secret," Lily insisted.

"Don't ask, I beg you." Maria shook her head.

"Someone needs to take responsibility for his actions." Lily looked at Tom.

"Let it go Lily. When is the baby due?" Tom stirred the burning embers with the poker.

Lily sighed and pushed herself against the back of the chair. "How can you say to her to let it go?" Lily asked in a perplexed voice.

Tom stacked a few more pieces of coal on the fire and wiped the marble fireplace with a wet cloth. "Maria will have her reasons. Maybe it's better if we don't know." Tom's voice was gentle, undemanding.

Maria knelt on the rug beside the fire, holding her hands out to warm them. "It will be a January baby."

•••

Maria caught the bus with Tom and Lily to the Mater hospital on the Crumlin Road to a month before her baby was due. Her heart was weakening. Father Anthony visited, bringing the Eucharistic Host in a golden ciborium. He listened to her Confession, lighting a candle beside the bed, blessing her forehead with Holy Water and praying, "May Our Lord Jesus Christ, take care of you, forgive you your sins and lead you to eternal life."

Maria closed her eyes, lying back on the pillow. She opened her mouth and stuck out her tongue to receive the Host. It was dry and stuck to the roof of her mouth.

Father Anthony blessed her forehead with Holy Water and moved closer asking, "Maria, do you forgive me?"

"You know I have forgiven you, Father. I've already told you. Forgive yourself now. You told me that God's love doesn't depend on anything you do or don't do. Stop feeling sorry for yourself." Maria nudged him with her elbow. She laughed. "Sure you know that. You don't need me to remind you. Where's all that theology when you need it?"

Father Anthony held her hand and brought it to his lips in silence. He kissed her fingers. "Thank you Maria."

He looked at her once more as he left the ward. A thin right arm, raised high into the air, waving at him. As he walked along the corridor outside the ward, her hand continued to wave at him through the window. For the first time in almost fifteen months, he smiled.

Next day, alone on the Ward, Maria cried out, "Help. Nurse. Help."

No-one heard her cries for maybe fifteen minutes. It was late afternoon, the sun streaming through the ward window when Maria, alone, gave birth to Rose. When the nurses arrived, in a panic, they forgot to scrub up. The umbilical cord was cut by Nurse Rita who wrapped Rose in a cotton blanket and passed her to Maria.

Maria held Rose, pushing her dark black hair to one side. Her face was slightly jaundiced and her mouth settled into deep smile as she slept, moving a little as though to snuggle even more deeply into Maria's arms. Nurse Rita and Maria laughed together as Rita sat on the bed and held Maria's hand. The setting sun sent golden showers of light into the ward.

Next morning Maria wakened and walked with Rose along the corridor to see an orange sun rising over the mists of Belfast. The sun changed into a steely sphere as it gained height in the January sky. Maria held Rose close to her chest feeling her own heart beating against the soft cotton rug. She looked at the empty branches of the rose trees growing outside the window, and as the mists cleared, the wintery sun warmed them both. For the first time Maria felt a part of the earth, connected, rooted. The sun warming her was also wakening the snowdrops on the dewy grass. It nudged the sheep outside the window to scramble to their feet. She had the sense of everything unfolding, coming into a perfect sense of being 'now', in this moment. Her feet touching the marble corridor were also touching the earth. She took a deep breath and kissed Rose. She had never felt happier in her life – so much at ease. She had never felt so much a sense of coming home. Her body filled with a tingling rapturous bliss. Everything had meaning. Everything was fine exactly the way it was.

On the third day after Rose's birth, Maria wakened with her forehead burning, her mouth dry and when she coughed a stabbing pain shot from her stomach towards her lungs making it hard to breathe. She shivered, pulling the sheets around her. Her breathing was rapid and shallow. She slowly pulled herself into a sitting position, looking for Rose sleeping in the cot beside her. Rose's eyes were closed. Maria lay back again on the pillow feeling a second even sharper pain in her abdomen. Something was wrong.

Sister Rita pressed her abdomen with the flat of her hand. When she took her hand away, Maria squirmed in agony.

"Peritonitis," Doctor McClelland confirmed in a low voice. By late afternoon, Maria slipped into what seemed to Nurse Rita and Dr McClelland to be a coma. However, Maria was conscious. She was aware of everything that was happening but her awareness was outside her body. She was somewhere up near the ceiling looking down at the bed where Nurse Rita adjusted a drip. She heard Doctor McClelland shout in distress, "We're losing her."

Maria watched as they struggled to resuscitate her. Her attention was then drawn to a white steady expanding light in the top right hand corner of the room. She watched fascinated as its scintillating edges continued to expand. She didn't know whether the light was drowning her as it enveloped her in deeper and deeper waves of whiteness or whether she was somehow floating into the light.

Doctor McClelland shouted in panic. "Get Father Anthony, now." Maria saw a blurred black shape of Father Anthony arrive in the room. He didn't remove his cloak. Flustered, opening his oils and the casket with the Eucharist, he fumbled to lift the Eucharist from the ciborium. He broke the Host in two and lifted both pieces. He blessed Maria with his right hand on the forehead, the lips and chest. He opened her mouth with his fingers, placing half of the Eucharist on her tongue. He took the second half and placed it on his own tongue. Maria receiving the last Sacrament of the Church felt the dry small half host sticking and then dissolving against the roof of her mouth. With her eyes open Maria gazed past Father Anthony feeling her whole being drawn once more towards the white light. Father Anthony searched Maria's eyes and recognised a look of surrender. He had seen it many times before.

She listened to Father Anthony's gasping, feeling his tears splash heavily onto her face. From the ceiling, not from inside her body, she watched him bless Rose in the cot beside the bed. For a moment when Maria glimpsed Rose, she struggled to detach herself from the light and return to her body. She made an enormous effort to push back into the body as though swimming against a deadly powerful riptide current.

The light held her back. It swept around her now like a whirlpool. The light was everywhere. Instead of rising now towards the ceiling she was falling, sinking into a white, boundless peace. Waves of light like an octopus's tentacles dragged her under the surface. She held her breath. Her arms stretched out by her side. She turned onto her back, sinking deeper. Father Anthony's body was like a surf board drifting above her – a dark pencil silhouette, hanging in the golden glow of the surface. Her mouth pressed closed. She breathed in rhythm to her heartbeat. There was enough air in her lungs. She didn't need to get to the surface. She tumbled deeper almost losing sight of the surf board. She kicked with her feet, pulled her arms strongly down by her side. She felt the pull of the water around her. She kicked again with her legs, pushing her head forward and down, opening her fingers to allow the water to move through them. Maybe for the first time she felt a sense of freedom, although she didn't know from what. She turned onto her back once more to see the board slipping even further from sight, now only an insignificant dark stain in the water. She rolled onto her front and dived deeper into the depths of the ocean, now willingly, pushing down until she couldn't see the surface at all. The light had disappeared. In the velvety darkness she did not feel alone. Where was she? Where were Rose and Father Anthony? Where was she going? For a moment she briefly quivered with fear, a final twitching movement of uncertainty in her body before she surrendered.

"No, please God. No." whispered Father Anthony.

Maria's hair scattered like ribbons of sand on the pillow. She curled up in the bed on her side like a baby in a white cotton nightdress – her face translucent. Her body seemed to have shrunk as he watched her. It was as though something working within her was undoing time, making her a baby again, taking her back, step-by-step to the womb, then back, back, back to the nothingness from which everything is born. He couldn't take his eyes away from her and from that mysterious activity which he found frightening to watch and yet entrancing. Frightening wasn't the right word. It was an awesome, terrifying, sublime activity working within her. He knew for sure that what he was seeing was the activity of God within Maria, working on her, making her perfect, making her ready for her final journey home. He knew without doubt that it was an activity of love – a love beyond any human love. Human love a pale puttering candle compared to the love of God which was like the light from a million suns. He realised that was what he had always seen in Maria – the light from a million suns.

It was not her physical body that had attracted him, not at all. He mistook that because he didn't look closely enough at this movement within her which was so beautiful. Of course she was beautiful. Why hadn't he realised that with Maria he had fallen in love with God – with the mystery of God incarnate within her? If only he had understood. It was so clear now. It made perfect sense.

He looked at Maria. Her eyes were open. He felt himself pour into their blueness. Her eyes were whirlpools drawing him in. He took a long breath, allowing himself to drop deeper into her gaze. He knew what she was telling him. How could you dare to touch a beauty of such magnitude and mystery? You don't touch God with your hands. You don't kiss God with your lips. You can't look at God and live.

"She's gone." Doctor McClelland whispered, placing his hand on Father Anthony's shoulder.

"Nooooo!" Father Anthony collapsed gently on top of Maria. "No!" His shout ricocheted into the air and was heard at the reception desk half a mile away. "No." repeated Father Anthony a third time. This time gently, almost like a "Yes."

He held her hand and pressed his thumb into Catherine's ring and then touched Maria's forehead for the last time with his thumb.

By the time Tom and Lily arrived at the Mater, Father Anthony sat at Maria's bedside, rosary in hand, gaze fixed on Maria's now solid face. He moved awkwardly to his feet. "She is at peace." Tom shook Father Anthony's hand. As Father Anthony embraced Lily, Rose coughed from her cot at the bottom of the bed. Father Anthony clutching in his hand a lock of Maria's sandy hair, walked to the cot and whispered, "She is a gift from God, like her Mother." He tickled her face, saying, "You're in good hands, Rose."

Father Anthony lifted Rose from the cot and held her in his arms before handing her over to Lily. "Let me know your plans for the Requiem Mass." He patted Tom on the shoulder, collected his ministry bag from the chair. He looked at Maria one last time, squeezing her hand, saying to Tom and Lily, "I'll leave you to have some time alone. You know where I am if you need me. I will call in with you tomorrow. God bless. Here is Catherine's ring. I thought you might like it anointed. Keep it for Rose." Father Anthony slipped the ring to Tom. He looked into Tom's eyes, "Maria blessed it with her love. Good can come with this ring. Where there is deep sorrow, there is also the possibility of deep joy. They carve each other out."

After Maria died in 1957, Rose, Lily and Tom moved into their new home at 32 Glenbryn Park. Upstairs there were two small bedrooms and a bathroom. Downstairs a small sitting room, a galley kitchen with a trolley to dry clothes which dropped from the ceiling. At the back there was an outhouse with a twin tub washing machine, a place for the cats and a door leading out into a small enclosed yard with a bunker for coal. There were fireplaces in the sitting room and both bedrooms. Lily loved to light the fire in the sitting room even in the summer. She lit the fires in the bedrooms in the winter especially if Tom or Rose had a cold or flu. Outside the backyard there was a small path lined with marigolds leading to the wild overgrown back garden where a small reeded stream bubbled over pebbles, separating Glenbryn Park from Glenbryn Drive.

Rose played in the back garden. Tom made a tree house which sat on top of a dyke separating the back gardens of Glenbryn Drive from Glenbryn Park. He wove the branches of the tree together to make a small cave. Rose would sit inside for hours watching the blackbirds sweep across the garden or the thrushes singing songs. Once when Rose was six, she ran along the marigold path, along the side of the house, without Lily or Tom seeing. She skipped down Glenbryn Park turned left at the bottom of the street and ran into the playing fields. There, Rose lay on the grass, smelling its warm earthiness, watching clouds rapidly rabbiting and dogging – watching the blue sky expanding and contracting.

"Is there enough blue sky to make a sailor a pair of trousers?" Lily asked her that morning pulling up the blind on the bedroom window.

"Yes. There is."

"Then play outside."

Lying on the grass, Rose looked at the blue sky, and then rolled onto her side feeling the tickle of golden buttercups against her face. She picked daisies and buttercups growing around her, feeling the gentle touch of the breeze on her face as she made a daisy chain, keeping one of the daisies and pulling its petals.

"He loves me. He loves me not. He loves me." She sank back into the earth feeling safe in the freckling of the sun, her blue eyes merging with the blue sky. Her eyes blinked snap, snap, snap. "This is where I end and you begin." Rose whispered to the sky.

Snap. Snap.

She didn't move, lying on the ground ebbing and flowing from the tips of her toes to the top of her head as a shiny black beetle scurried along her leg, moving north. She picked it up as it hesitated on her knee. Touching its hard shell with her right finger, she held it in her hand, looking to see how its legs attached to its body. Balancing it on her left index finger, squinting to see how its thread of a leg worked. The beetle opened its back and two semicircular wings paused for a moment before whirring into life. Rose lay back again onto the grass, listening to the whirring wings fade into the distance. She felt the hard edge of a metal crucifix inside her sock, clinking against a penny. Rummaging in Lily's bedroom she had opened a jewelry box and found a crucifix detached from its rosary. The cross was solid silver with a golden figure of Christ. On the back of the cross there was a bubble of holy water. She blessed herself with the crucifix and slipped it into her sock.

"Are you a Roman Catholic or a Protestant?" A boy asked on her way back home from the playing fields. It was 1963. His friends stood behind him hands in pockets, smirking. "Well, what are you a Papist or a Protestant?"

Rose looked at the boy through dark hair which had fallen across her eyes. She saw his red face, a rash of freckles and a cold sore on his lip. Their eyes met. He looked quickly away, staring at the ground.

"Are you fucking deaf? What are you?"

Rose felt the edge of the crucifix against her heel. She pressed it against the ground, into her worn brown boot.

"I don't know." She answered. "Nobody told me."

"Put your hand out," the boy ordered. As she opened the palm of her hand, he broke the buttercup and daisy chain on her wrist. He tossed it on the grass. Rose opened the palm of her left hand. Her fingers long and pointed, slightly curled inwards. Her right hand dangled against her blue gingham dress.

The boy took a razor from his pocket. He swiped at her left hand three times. Rose didn't move.

"Now you fucking know. That's for being a Papist." He sneered, looked at his friends saying, "Let's go." He put the razor into the pocket of his shorts, turning away as Rose stared at the blood trickling from her hand onto the ground. As the boys scattered, Rose turned right and ran across the ploughed field home with her drops of blood seeding in the playing fields.

"What's a Papist?" Rose asked Lily as she bandaged her hand.

"Father Anthony will explain when you make your First Holy Communion."

Rose searched with her toes for the crucifix down her sock. It had gone. She didn't tell Lily. She felt a terrible shame for having taken something which did not belong to her and having lost it. She retraced the steps she had taken earlier that day into Tom and Lily's bedroom. She walked over to the dresser where Lily had her jewelry box. She opened the box. The crucifix was there lying on red velvet. Rose lifted it and turned it over to see the bubble of holy water settle. She squeezed the crucifix within her small fist. The edges pressed against her flesh.

Tom encouraged Rose to play in the garden rather than to go again to the playing fields. He helped her build a set of jumps for a make believe gymkhana where Rose pretended to be a horse, calling herself 'Jellylegs', and running around the garden, jumping over each obstacle, clocking up four faults here and there and three for a refusal.

There was a small garden at the front of the house. Lily filled it with roses, lupins and lobelia. Tom built a small redbrick wall for the garden with a wooden railing and wooden gate made from pinewood. It swept up into an arch with a heavy iron lock which clicked shut. Lily made curtains for the upstairs and downstairs windows from heavy taffeta. Tom found matching white roller blinds with tassels for the upstairs and downstairs windows.

1966, nine years after moving in, Lily and Tom still had boxes of unopened wedding presents from 1941 with china tea sets and dinner plates never used. There was a tea set with six china teacups, matching saucers and piece plate, a sugar bowl and milk jug and a dinner service with six dinner plates with a jade green flower pattern, a soup tureen, two casserole dishes, a gravy boat and a ladle for serving soup. Everything packed carefully, still with cards from the people who had given the presents.

Tom bought the best quality 1950s furniture. Downstairs

there was an oval dining room table which was folded away and opened up only on Sundays, Easter and Christmas. It was then covered with a white linen tablecloth and a cream Belleek dinner set was placed on the table with silver knives and forks and Waterford crystal glasses and a jug of water. Everything was wrapped up in tissue paper after lunch and stored away in the outhouse where the kittens slept until the next week. Upstairs the two bedrooms had heavy oak wardrobes with long mirrors inside and a metal spring for gentlemen's ties. The beds were heaped with woolen blankets and an embroidered quilt. On a cold evening Lily threw a large brown fur beaver coat on top of Rose's bed.

Lily bought a heavy white Holy Bible with gold leaf trimmings on the pages which was filled with famous paintings. She kept it wrapped in white tissue in a cardboard box and opened it every day to read and to look at the paintings. She liked the 'Expulsion from the Garden of Eden' by Fra Angelico with Adam and Eve's hands to their faces full of regret, the 'Tower of Babel' by Bruegel with its crumbling walls, turquoise seas and steely white skies and the 'Sacrifice of Isaac' by Caravaggio with the terrible anguish of Isaac as his face is pressed into the earth, his father's thumb holding his head in a vice like grip as the knife glints in its movement towards Isaac's throat. Isaac can see the knife, but maybe not the angel. There was a penetrating stare from Abraham trying to understand the Angel's message and the soft peaceful look of the lamb, with its head raised looking at both the Angel and Abraham and waiting fearlessly for what will happen next. She returned again and again to the 'Kiss of Judas' by Giotto where Judas and Christ seemed to be one in their embrace, their eyes searching each other's souls, their lips moving towards one another, and something being said in the silence and in the space before their lips touched.

Lily attempted to sketch her favourite paintings at first with charcoal and pastels, then acrylics and finally oils. As she looked at them deeply, trying to follow the contour, she felt that she was sinking into the mind not only of the painter but of the object being painted. She painted the 'Tower of Babel' as a cloud floating in the sky and the 'Kiss of Judas' in oils where it was hard to tell where Jesus ended and Judas began. They were like Siamese twins.

In the conservatory at the back of the house kittens slept. When Lily opened the door in the morning, the kittens scampered across the kitchen into the sitting room, climbing and plucking the curtains. Lily sat on a chair, with two or three kittens sleeping on her shoulder or nestling into her neck. She found homes for the kittens when they were eight weeks old – when their eyes turn from blue to green. She loved the silence of cats, being in a room with them, watching them walk across the red tiled kitchen floor. There was silence in the way they sniffed each other's lips. Silence in the way they looked at her directly and kept looking without meowing.

The Glenbryn district bordering Ardoyne was a mixed district where both Catholics and Protestants lived together for a while peacefully. Lily's best friend was Anne Ramsay whose husband Sammy was a Protestant and a policeman. Anne showed Lily how to make wheaten bread, soda bread, and rough puff pastry for apple cakes and mince squares. Sammy walked Rose to the top of the street to see the bonfires being lit for the Twelfth of July celebrations.

Sammy explained to Rose, "The Orangemen march on the Twelfth to commemorate the Battle of the Boyne in 1690 when the Catholic King James and the Protestant King William confronted one another's armies on the banks of the river Boyne. King Billy won. When King William went into battle with his Dutch Blue Guards, he also had many Dutch Catholics fighting on his side. It was King William of Holland who flew the papal banner, not the Catholic King James. King William was supported by the Vatican and when his army had victory over King James, 'Te Deum' was sung in praise at the Vatican. There's not many people know that." Sammy was a regular visitor to the Belfast Library in the City Centre.

He stood with her, holding her hand as she looked into the fire crackling with life, the flames dancing high into the starry night, the logs collapsing, hissing and spitting sparks into the warm summer night. The next morning Rose wakened to hear the drums of the Orange band. She climbed out of bed, pulling back the curtain as the pipe music whistled on the early morning breeze, the drums rolled loudly into a crescendo for 'The Sash My Father Wore'. The men wore dark blue uniforms with gold braid. They carried tall orange banners with scenes of a triumphant Protestant King William sitting astride his white stallion. The bands paraded down Glenbryn Park, turning right at the bottom and right again, marching up Alliance Avenue. Rose listened until the music from the bands faded into the distance and the Orangemen made their way along the Crumlin Road.

• • •

Sammy and Anne knocked on the door on the evening of the 12th August 1969. "Have you heard?"

"It's not good news?"

"They say the UVF are assembling machine guns on the Bone. They're planning to invade Ardoyne. They're talking about a bloodbath."

"Come in."

Lily opened the box in the outhouse with the Sunday china

and placed five cups and saucers on the table in the sitting room, with the matching piece plates. She rummaged in a second box and found three candles and in a drawer in the kitchen five white linen napkins.

"I'll be back in a minute."

She lit the three candles.

"Turn the lights out." Anne asked.

"A piece of Battenberg cake?" Lily looked at Anne and Sammy as the kettle whistled.

"What about apple pie?" Shouted Sammy.

"I was keeping that for someone special." Lily got to her feet and squeezed Sammy's shoulder. She returned with an apple pie and cheese and tomato sandwiches with the crusts cut off.

Rose, Lily, Tom, Sammy and Anne looked at the candle quivering on the table and then into each other's eyes. In the silence their faces glowed and shimmered. Sammy coughed. "You know, if they make it difficult for you – you can stay at our place. We'll make sure nothing happens to you."

Lily pushed back her chair, hugging Anne and Sammy. "Thank you. That means a lot to us."

"Human beings are violent. That's the problem. It's in our nature." Sammy mumbled with apple pie in his mouth.

"Sammy, come on now. That's very negative. We can be very kind as well." Lily interrupted. "Don't generalize. Look at me," Lily teased.

"We're violent." Sammy thumped the table in mock anger. "We like being violent. We like being miserable too." His shoulders shook with laughter. "We also enjoy hurting one another". Sammy tapped his head with his knuckles and shrugged. "Pythagoras gave us the word "philosophy" meaning a "love of wisdom" and he had his house burnt to the ground for being interested in what is the Truth."

Lily brought a fresh pot of tea into the sitting room.

"Didn't they say, Sammy, that Christ's closest friends thought he was mad?" Sammy held his cup out for a refill of tea. "History is full of examples of where being wise doesn't end up well for you in this life. Look at Socrates and the trouble he found himself in for asking a few questions about what life is about."

Sammy shook his head.

•••

On the 15th August 1969 – which was the Feast of the Assumption of Our Lady into Heaven, and yet another infamous rioting day in Northern Ireland – Tom shaved in the bathroom, foaming his face with his badger hair shaving brush.

"Turn up the radio Lily," Tom shouted from the bathroom as he whipped the shaving foam on his chin with a badger bristle brush. "It's the six o'clock news."

Lily ran into the hallway and breathlessly climbed the stairs.

"Tom, the British Soldiers have been sent in. They're here. They've arrived."

"Thanks be to God!" Tom shouted from the landing with his shaving brush in hand, "We will sleep tonight."

Lily danced with Rose in the kitchen, twirling her around and spinning her across the floor into the outhouse as the toast jumped from the toaster. Lily caught it before it fell onto the floor. "It's going to get better."

The British soldiers arrived that day in Northern Ireland. At six thirty in the morning, Lily, Tom and Rose walked up Glenbryn Park on their way to seven o'clock morning Mass in Holy Cross Church. Turning left at the top of Glenbryn Park, they walked along the Ardoyne Road with the bus depot on their left and Everton School on their right.

The soldiers, rifles by their sides, lay sleeping like small green hills on the pavement, one beside the other, in combat uniforms. Two soldiers stood on guard nodding as Tom, Lily and Rose stepped over the sprawling legs.

"What have they been doing all night?" asked Rose.

"There was trouble again last night on the Crumlin Road."

• • •

Two years later, in July 1971, Lily wakened from sleep to the words, "Fuck the Pope and the Virgin Mary." Someone shouted the words a second time, even more loudly a few doors away. Lily climbed out of bed being careful not to waken Tom who lay on his side, snoring gently. She knelt on the floor beside the window and without moving the white lace curtain, peered through it. She could make out a police jeep at the bottom of Glenbryn Park surrounded by an angry mob. The street lights were out. The jeep's lights flickered to life as it moved slowly up the street. The crowd followed behind. The jeep stopped. The crowd moved around it like a swarm of bees, and then the crowd split in two with one half moving towards a house in the middle of a terrace, while the other half stayed circling the jeep. Lily couldn't hear what they were saying although it was easy to hear the rising and falling of angry voices. Then there was the sound of glass breaking. She looked at the bed. Tom was still sleeping. He had to work tomorrow and would be up early at six. Did she need to waken him? She looked again through the curtain. The jeep had turned around in the middle of the road. It started to drive slowly down Glenbryn Park, still followed by the crowd. It turned right, towards Alliance Avenue and into the Ardoyne.

The next day Tom suggested, "Should we put the milk and lemonade bottles upstairs on the windowsill?"

"God Tom, what use will they be against guns?" Lily shrugged.

Nevertheless, Rose lined five empty milk bottles, empty orangeade, cream soda and coca cola bottles on the bedroom windowsill.

"Let's get some sleep." Lily suggested.

"Rose, sleep with us tonight. You get into the bottom of the bed and Tom and I will sleep at the top. Sleep with your clothes on."

Lily pulled back the blankets at the bottom of the bed, placed a pillow for Rose at the bottom. Rose crawled into the bed and Lily blessed Rose's forehead with Holy Water before slipping into the top of the bed with Tom.

"Night, Rose, sleep tight," Lily whispered from the top of the bed.

"Don't let the bugs bite," Rose laughed from the bottom of the bed.

"If they do, bite them back." Tom pinched Rose's toes.

They slept for an hour before wakening to muffled single shot gunfire.

"Where is it coming from?" asked Lily sitting up. Her heart thumped in her chest and she felt a pulsing pressure moving into her ribs, down her back and into her stomach.

"Has to be Alliance Avenue," whispered Tom. He felt a knot of panic in his throat.

"What's happening now?"

Voices chanted "Out. Out. Out," in unison, getting louder and more insistent.

"They're in our street." Rose pulled the sheet over her face and pressed her hands over her eyes.

"Fuck the Pope and the Virgin Mary. Taigs out."

"They're coming closer." Rose pushed away the blankets sitting upright.

"Will I take a look?"

"Careful. Don't move the curtains. Look through them."

Rose climbed out of bed and slithered across the floor on hands and knees, reaching the white lace window curtain. There was a police jeep six houses away. It was followed by over fifty bobbing bodies some waving sticks in the air and cursing. The police jeep stopped. The crowd circled around it and then opened the circle to allow it to slowly advance again.

"Come back to bed." Lily shouted.

"There's a really big crowd out here and a police jeep." Rose jumped into the bottom of the bed and lay back pulling the sheet over her face.

Tom and Lily glanced at one another.

"What are they doing?" Lily asked Tom.

"We'll find out." Tom pressed Lily's hand.

A window shattered a few doors away. A burst of machine gun fire in the street outside was so close that the bedroom windows rattled. There was a menacing cheer from the crowd and then more crashing splintering glass.

"God, that's downstairs. It's our house."

Tom leapt out of bed. There was a shriek of laughter outside, more cheering and glass continued to fall onto the garden path. Tom swung open the upstairs window, knocking over a coca-cola bottle and two milk bottles into the garden below as he pushed his head out and shouted.

"What do you think you are doing? What do you want?"

"Oh, what do I want? Let me tell you. Get the fuck out of the house. Now! Do you understand or are you deaf? Get you and your fucking family out. You've got twenty four hours. If you aren't out when we come back, there is a name on a bullet for the three of you. Maybe you want to hear what it sounds like? Maybe you need a little help to get the message?"

The man wearing a balaclava, combat jacket and jeans, fired three shots into the air.

Tom stepped back, quickly closed the window and turned to Lily and Rose hugging each other on the bed. "That's it. Tomorrow we're out of here."

Lily and Rose threw on warm jumpers before going downstairs. They found Lucky hiding in a box in the outhouse. The front windows had been shot through and bullets lodged in the sitting room wall below the mirror. Lily found a brush in the outhouse and started to brush up the glass. Rose stroked Lucky. Her bushy tail only returned to normal when Tom hammered a piece of wood over the windows. There were two brisk knocks at the front door.

"Who is it?" Tom shouted. Rose and Lily stood behind him.

"Anne and Sammy."

Lily opened the door. "God love you. You shouldn't have come here with all that's going on."

"We were worried sick about you. Are you OK?"

"We're fine."

"We heard the cursing and then the shooting."

Lily touched Anne on the arm. "Come in." Lily pulled Anne gently into the sitting room.

Tom slapped Sammy on the back.

"What a nightmare." Sammy lifted Lucky who purred around his ankles and cradled her in his arms.

"Do you want a cup of tea or something stronger?" asked Tom.

"The latter."

"Take care where you sit, there are splinters of glass everywhere."

As Tom filled glasses with sherry, Sammy asked,

"Where will you go?"

"I don't know. We'll have to find out in the morning. Last night I heard that they were putting people up in temporary beds in Holy Cross School."

"Won't you stay with us until you find somewhere?"

"It would be dangerous for you if we do that. It is very kind of you to offer." Tom gulped his sherry.

"This is your home. You can't walk away from it." Sammy reached his glass to Lily for to top up.

"You walk away when you can still walk."

"Sammy, what were the police doing?"

Sammy shook his head. "I don't know."

Lily nudged Tom.

"Put a record on. We need music. Let's enjoy the next few hours. Didn't they do that when the Titanic was sinking? If we're going down, we might as well do it to music."

Tom slowly pulled himself to his feet and walked to the corner of the room where he opened the record player.

"What would you like to hear? Jim Reeves, 'I Hear the Sound of Distant Drums'?"

Lily and Anne laughed as Sammy said, "For sure we'll be hearing them in the morning."

"How about 'There Goes my Everything' by Elvis – the King himself?" Lily shouted across to Tom.

"That'll do. I've got it here."

It was after three in the morning when Sammy and Anne eventually left. Lily lay back in bed, holding Tom's hand. Rose lay at the bottom of the bed. Lily closed her eyes and images of tripods being pulled open and machine guns with belts of bullets falling from them being slotted into place appeared in her mind. She imagined the cold touch of heavy metal against soft skin of the gunman's hands, the gunman pulling the trigger and a shower of small, shiny brass metal bullets piercing someone's skin, maybe ripping through their stomach. She saw blood spurting out at high pressure like a garden hose and spilling all over the ground. She heard him cursing as he held the trigger – the curses also like bullets spraying into the air. She saw him looking pleased that he had killed someone. She watched as he walked into the pub and the same soft skin held a pint of Guinness to his lips saying, "Cheers." The same soft skin would hold someone close in bed that night, stroking her body gently, saying "I love you." Her heart raced and she breathed quickly. Rose didn't move in bed. Tom lay silently unmoving, holding Lily's hand.

Next morning Tom left Rose and Lily packing as he set out to investigate what was happening in Ardoyne and discover where they might be able to stay. As Tom turned onto the Crumlin Road, lorries flying the Irish Tricolour, stacked high with beds, mattresses and chairs raced along the Crumlin Road. Others flying the Union Jack and full with precariously placed wardrobes, tables and chairs, swerved towards the Woodvale Road. He walked up the curved road through the Grove to the monastery front door. He asked for Father Anthony.

"What do you think Father? What's our best option?"

"Do you remember the Mullan's?"

"Dr Mullan and his family?"

"Yes. They lived in 463 facing the church. They've moved out this morning. They've emmigrated to Australia. You could stay in their house. It's available."

"Can I have a look at it?" Tom edged to his feet.

"Of course you can." Father Anthony lifted the keys from a box in the bookshelf.

"I don't want to put a dampener on it but you know the downside of living on the Crumlin Road don't you? It's no Peace Line that's for sure."

"I know. But maybe even for a few months it could do until

we have time to find somewhere else."

"A lot can happen in a few months. There's many a man who has said 'Give me six months' only to find himself six foot under. You don't need me to tell you that." Father Anthony jangled the keys in front of Tom's eyes.

"Are you sure you want these? What about Rose getting to and from school?"

"There will be an army patrol for Rose and her friends going to the Convent of Mercy. Sister Anne organized that."

Tom took the keys from Father Anthony's hand and put them in his pocket.

"Well, let's have a look then."

• • •

Back in Glenbryn Park, Anne and Sammy helped Lily and Rose pack two suitcases.

"Will you be able to take furniture with you?" Anne folded jumpers into a suitcase. Lily shook her head.

"No. It will be these two suitcases, the cat and the radio."

"Here's Tom." Lily spotted Tom turning the corner at the top of the street into Glenbryn Park. She waved at him. He hurried down the street. Tom opened the gate and Lily threw her arms around him.

"We were worried about you. What's it like on the Crumlin? What's the news?"

"We've got a house. We've somewhere to stay."

"Great." Lily kissed him on the cheek. "I knew you would find somewhere. Where is it?"

"On the Crumlin Road opposite Holy Cross Church."

"On the Peace Line?" Anne shook her head worriedly.

"It's safer there than here for now Anne. It's a roof over our heads."

"It scares me you going there."

"Anne, we are not even going to be thirty minutes away from you. If anything happens you will have us knocking on your door." Lily hugged Anne.

"You know you can do that at any time of the day or night." Anne looked over Lily's shoulder straight into Tom's eyes. "Don't forget that. We mean it."

They walked up Glenbryn Park with two suitcases, the radio and Lucky the cat. Further down the street houses were on fire. The sky fomented dark grey clouds of smoke. Flames crackled and leapt furiously into the sky. Slates popped like champagne corks into the now orange tinged edges of the clouds.

As they reached Anne and Sammy's house, they stopped. They kissed each other in silence as Anne wiped a tear from her cheek and Sammy sniffed, coughed and cleared his throat.

"Don't look back. Keep walking straight ahead. We will see you again. I promise." Anne pushed Lily and Tom forward. Rose looked over her shoulder to see Anne crying.

"I told you don't look back." Anne searched in her pocket for a handkerchief.

Lucky buried her head into Rose's coat and meowed softly. Without saying a word, Lily carried the radio, Tom the two suitcases and Rose, Lucky. They walked slowly. This time they didn't look back.

As they approached the Ardoyne Road, the early stages of a riot were evident with young men gathering at the top of Brompton Park. They had to push their way through them, crossing Brompton Park onto the Crumlin Road where they spotted Mr Langley their new neighbour propped up on the garden gate like a gnome, smoking his pipe and watching rioters gathering, the way he would have watched the clouds darkening over the hills in County Tyrone as a child.

"He's from the country," Lily whispered respectfully to Rose, meaning that he was gentle and at one with nature. "I've seen him at Mass."

There was something in the way he smoked his pipe, blowing small puffs into the air, that was calming. It was as though he brought the peace from planting potatoes and tilling the earth into standing there at the gate. He never raised his voice or said a cross word. He watched it all, unflustered and at peace.

Tom opened the gate, reaching a hand across the wall to Mr Langley.

"Good to meet you again Mr Langley. Can I introduce you to Lily and my niece Rose."

Mr Langley tipped his cap at Lily and Rose, and then removed the pipe from his mouth before shaking hands and giving them a broad toothless smile.

Tom turned the key in the door. Rose placed Lucky gently onto the hallway floor where she promptly bolted upstairs, ears back. Tom guided them into the parlour with its large bay window, an open fireplace and a plaster rose in the centre of the ceiling.

"What do you think?"

Lily and Rose looked up at the ceiling, turning in circles.

"It is beautiful." Lily touched the mantelpiece. Warm golden sunlight fell onto the green carpet. Dappled light from three small stained glass windows with blue, yellow and crimson roses edged in black iron, danced on the wall.

"There's more."

Along the hallway Tom opened a second door into a sitting room, with a large window overlooking a yard. Leading off the sitting room there was a galley style kitchen with a door opening into the yard where a meat safe hung on the wall, and there was an outside toilet.

Lily took two pints of milk from her shopping bag, wrapped them in damp cloth and placed them in a bucket of water.

"One day we will have a fridge."

They climbed the first flight of uncarpeted stairs which led to a landing with a small bedroom, a bathroom and two large bedrooms. Up a second flight of stairs where there were two attic bedrooms. Rose chose the back attic bedroom as her room. Lily and Tom picked the back bedroom on the floor below.

"Let's keep to the back of the house – the rioters and the gunfire will be mostly to the front," Tom suggested.

Within an hour Tom had hammered chicken wire over the downstairs front windows to stop petrol bombs breaking the glass. He found a heavy metal bar for which he made two attachments on either side of the door which allowed him to drop the bar in place at night.

"That will give us a few minutes to escape if we need to – out of the back of the house down the entry into the middle of Ardoyne."

A few hours later, pieces of furniture had arrived from unexpected places. A piano, sofa and chairs from Aunt Mary who had decided to emigrate to Australia. Father Anthony had found a donated single bed, two double beds, a television, plates, cutlery, a whistling kettle, a teapot with cups and saucers, a mirror, a twin tub washing machine, an oak dining room table with four matching chairs, a dozen woolen blankets, eight pillows, cotton sheets and a hair dryer.

"Someone's misfortune can so easily become someone else's fortune. You can thank the McGeraghty family." Father Anthony wiped his brow pushing the twin tub into the corner of the kitchen.

•••

On 9th August 1971, internment without trial was introduced. The police were given permission to arrest people and to imprison them without the normal requirements of evidence. At two in the morning Tom, Lily and Rose heard the bin lids banging on the paving stones outside, whistles blowing to warn of the arrival of the police and army. Jeeps and Saracen tanks screeched across the Crumlin Road, blocking traffic. Within minutes rioters poured onto the streets in Brompton Park, petrol bombs crashed in flames onto Saracen tanks. CS gas hissed into the seething rioters, followed by single blasts of rubber bullets.

"You fucking cowards!" Rioters hurled petrol bombs, broken pavement stones and bricks. Tom slithered out of bed to check that the metal bar was still on the door downstairs.

Rose sat in bed in the back attic, reading with the light of a torch, listening to the cursing, the cheers when a petrol bomb exploded on top of a jeep, the blasting of rubber bullets, more cheers. She listened to it all in the way you would listen to a stormy sea and take comfort in the sound of the crashing waves against a pebbly beach. Or in the way you would listen with interest to the wind howling around the corners of a house and have a sense of peace and calm that you are inside and not outside in the storm. Rose listened to familiar angry voices, the rise and fall of the cursing, the pockets of silence before the machine guns were put into action, the rhythmic single shots from a hand gun or rifle. Even in a riot there were pockets of silence, pinpoints of peace which she developed an expertise in detecting. She listened to the silence in between the gunfire, to the brief silence before the bin lid hit the ground, or to the vanishing of the bin lid clang after it thumped onto the paving stone. She listened for the attenuated cursing with the second of silence before the furious rioters began to launch a new frenzy of expletives.

She switched off the torch. She slid into the warm sheets, slipped her feet on top of the hot water bottle and listened again to the rioters outside. She ignored what was said, only registering the rhythm and intensity of the noise as it rose and fell, became louder and faded. She listened to the disappearing curses, the vanishing of the rifle shots into emptiness before the next shot rang out. She heard the dying dull thump of plastic bullets as they hit their target. It was eventually the rhythm of the riot that lulled her to sleep.

Tom lay in bed and imagined the oak tables which he would carve the next day at work with their strong contours – the elegance of sturdiness, the touch of the silkiness of polished oak against his fingers. Beside him, Lily held his hand. The thought that perhaps the time had come for them to leave Northern Ireland had never occurred to Lily or to Tom; not until later, and even then when it flashed across Tom's mind in a momentary trajectory of possibility, it was rejected. They were rooted in the earth they trod. Tom and Lily felt a part of the community – for better or for worse. He understood the best and the worst of the people he lived with and he felt understood. The horrors of what people were capable of doing to one another only intensified the solidarity of being with them. Who would understand who they were, where they had come from, if they uprooted and went to England? Would they not be dragging themselves away from the very sinews which fastened muscle to their bones?

•••

"Where are we off to tonight?" William asked Cedric. Peter slid off the bench, pushed his hands into the pockets of his jeans and stared at the floor of the pub.

"Back to the Crumlin. They've been burning buses so the

bastards will have to walk if they're going anywhere. I'm sure they will be glad of a taxi."

Outside the Black Beetle Cedric pulled on his black leather gloves, smoothed his hair and thumped the roof of the black taxi with his fist.

"Go, go, go!"

William struggled to get the key in the lock, staggered, steadied himself placing his hand against the roof of the car, missed the lock at the first attempt and scraped the key along the door from left to right. At the second attempt he dropped the key onto the ground, making circles with his hand to retrieve it. Only at the third attempt he succeeded in opening the door, tumbling into the driver's seat. Cedric sat in the front passenger seat, straightening the fingers of his black leather gloves.

Peter sighed again deeply, slumped in the back seat, pulling a cap down over his eyes as they turned left onto the Crumlin Road at Carlisle Circus. William pushed his back against the driving seat, keeping within the speed limit and driving in a reasonably straight line past the Crumlin Road Prison, the Court House and the Mater Hospital.

It was nearly eight o'clock in the evening. Mass had finished in Holy Cross Church. The church stood on a small hill on the Crumlin Road from which streets ran into the heart of Ardoyne like arteries. You could see Butler Street, Herbert Street, Kerrera Street and Brompton Park from the grounds of the Church. There was a sweeping path from the steps of the Church to the Crumlin Road. Between the path and Tom and Lily's house across the road, was a small belt of woodland called The Grove. In the Grove the robins hid in holly bushes, the starlings rummaged for worms, and crows nested amongst the tall elm trees. To the left of the Church was the monastery and in front of this on the Crumlin Road itself the old Holy Cross Primary

School which was now used as a social club and known as the Ardoyne Hall.

Tom slid an arm through Lily's as she tucked her hands into the pockets of her camel woollen coat and slid the other through Rose's arm as they walked home along the gravel path. Dappled clouds swirled over the waning moon, hiding behind the church spires. The Crumlin was littered with the usual debris of broken glass, pavement stones, rubber and plastic bullets and empty metal cartridges from rifle fire. The shell of the earlier burnt out bus was still smouldering and half blocking the road. The burning petrol and tyres sent out a cloud of black smoke which made Tom's eyes water. He let go of Lily and Rose to wipe his eyes. Lily coughed as she held onto Rose and helped her pick her way through the broken bottles. The street lamps were out and the road was lit only by the silvery moon disappearing and reappearing from behind the clouds. As they began to run past the smoking bus, Tom took his key from his pocket to open the front door. Michael McGuckin stood in the porch waiting for a bus. The red light from his cigarette glowed in the dark.

Tom turned the key in the door and said, "Michael, I don't think the buses will run tonight. It will be tomorrow morning before they'll put them back on. They'll clear this one away first."

"I have to get home Tom." Michael glanced over Tom's shoulder as a soldier walked slowly past on patrol. Another knelt on one knee and pointed his rifle down the Crumlin Road.

"Take the bus tomorrow morning, Michael." suggested Tom gently.

"I'd rather walk. I promised Mary. It's not a good time to leave her alone with the children. I'll give it another few minutes and then I'll walk."

No-one mentioned the fact that Michael's brother had been

murdered the week before, killed in broad daylight driving a bus down the Crumlin Road, or that it was more dangerous to walk, especially at this hour of the night. The foot patrol had already passed by and there probably wouldn't be another patrol for an hour.

Nobody said anything because you couldn't be sure that if you told Michael to stay or you told him to walk which option would be the one that would kill him or save him. Maybe he would be killed if he stayed, like Bobbie McCafferty who was sleeping in bed and someone put a ladder outside his bedroom window, climbed it and pointed a tracer gun at the bed, firing several rounds and not leaving until they saw the bullets, like mini missiles, find their way to their target. There was a moment before Bobbie died when he sat upright in bed. He would have seen the bullets coming towards him because tracer bullets are like that. They light up and seem to be approaching in slow motion. To the person watching the bullet, it looks like a rock on fire. That was Bobbie's last sight – a smoking rock with fire. It seemed to be going so slowly that for a moment he maybe thought that he could get out of bed and run. But for the person who fired it, the shadowy shape on the ladder outside the window, the bullets with their marker flames were going quickly. The man on the ladder could see that there was no way that Bobbie could dodge or avoid the bullets, although he was surprised to see him sit up in bed. Was it the noise of the ladder being against placed against the window that wakened Bobbie? Or was it the voices in street as they cut the telephone lines that wakened him? Or was it an intuition that his life was nearly over that made him sit up in bed only to fall back seconds later onto the pillow dead?

If Michael McGuckin had chosen to walk up the Crumlin Road instead of down the hill he might have ended up like Bertie

O'Hare whom Rose had stumbled over on her way to the Fast Shop to buy a loaf of bread, a month earlier. Bertie lay on the corner of Brompton Park and the Crumlin Road, with his legs splayed out, his back against the wall of the bookies, eyes staring straight ahead, his body unmoving. He looked for the world as if he was in bed for the night and was only missing a candlewick bedspread to cover him. It was nine o'clock in the evening, five degrees above zero, the wind dropping rain which threatened to turn to snow or hail. Bertie with both hands on the ground, the top three buttons of his checked lumberjack shirt open, jeans soaking wet, a striped tie around his waist holding up his jeans instead of a belt, his brown boots laced with white tennis shoe laces.

"What's the matter?" Rose bent down to kneel on the ground beside him.

"I'm OK."

"Shouldn't you be going home? It's really cold. You're not dressed for this weather."

Bertie looked into Rose's eyes. His face cracked red, his moustache covered in raindrops, dark hair matted across empty blue husks of eyes.

"They got me, you see. That's what's wrong with me." Bertie said in a soft, calm, matter of fact voice.

"Who got you?"

"I don't know. They're still out there. They didn't catch them. They'll never catch them. They're clever."

"When?"

"What month are we in now?"

"December."

"Which year?"

"1971".

"I think it was this year. It was summer. It wasn't last year was it?" Bertie looked at Rose as if she would know the answer. Rose gently asked him.

"What happened?"

"They picked me up in a black taxi. I thought it was an Ardoyne taxi. They took me to a house. I don't know where. There was music playing downstairs. I heard voices. I could smell cigarette smoke. There were two of them. One of them smoked a cigar while the other drilled a hole in my head with a Black and Decker. The one who had been smoking threw the half smoked cigar on the ground, lifted a pistol from a tool box, pointed the gun into the hole in my head and shot. He shot twice. I passed out. They left me for dead. I opened my eyes and there was no-one in the room. It was pitch black. I saw a door. I crawled out of that place, pulled myself downstairs, onto the road outside. They told me in the hospital that they didn't know how I did it. I couldn't tell you how but I dragged myself out of that place. A car stopped. I didn't know if it was them.

I remembered thinking, "It's them. They've come back to finish me off." I heard the car door open. A woman screamed and kept screaming. I wanted to scream too. I couldn't. I hadn't the energy. I lay there face down on the wet tarmac with the car headlights on me. The man lifted me onto the back seat of his car. He was gentle with me. His hands were warm and soft. He said, "You'll be fine. Hang in there. Don't give up now. Don't go to sleep." The woman sat in the front seat. She kept crying and shouting, "Oh my God, look at the blood." She looked over her shoulder at me and then covered her face with her hands, shouting "He's going to die. He's not going to live." She had long blonde hair. She was wearing a black and white checked coat, I remember that. It was black and white. It was black and white. I'm sure it was black and white. The man said to her,

"Stop crying. Don't cry. It's not helping him. You're frightening him." I remember her perfume, like freesia. It was so soft and sweet. I didn't remember anything after that, until I wakened in the hospital bed with a tube down my throat. The doctor told me, "You're a lucky man." That's me, Mr Lucky. Do I look lucky to you?"

Rose wiped his face with a tissue. "You survived. There are many who don't. Where do you live?"

"Etna Drive."

"Let me take you home." Rose took Bertie by the elbow and helped him to his feet.

"Put your arm around my shoulder." Rose held onto Bertie's arm, staggering down Brompton Park, towards Etna Drive. The orange lights looked cosy behind drawn curtains. The rain fell heavily bouncing off Bertie's brown boots and soaking into Rose's coat. The drops then turned into soft sleety snow, settling on Bertie's eyebrows and Rose's hair like confetti.

No, life wasn't predictable enough in 1972 to give sound advice to Michael.

So Tom said, "God Bless you Michael. Safe home." He patted him on the shoulder and watched him walk down Crumlin Road. Michael's hands were in his pockets, his head turned down facing the ground, trying to avoid the broken glass. Tom stood at the gate watching Michael in silence, the way you might watch a ship sail out of Belfast Lough.

The silence was broken by the low whirr from a police armoured car crawling slowly up Crumlin Road, its front windows covered with wire, metal flaps like eyelids protecting the driver. Two Browning machine guns protruded through the side windows. Michael paused before crossing Herbert Street. Maybe a sniper would take a pot-shot at the jeep. Everything seemed quiet for now. Tom continued to watch. He saw him stop and then start to walk again. He watched until Michael eventually disappeared into the darkness.

Michael's heart quickened its beat and fluttered like a moth around a flame as he neared Flax Street. Anyone seeing him would know that he was a Catholic leaving Ardoyne. He stepped up his pace, pulled his blue woollen scarf around his neck and tucked his hands back into the pockets of his coat. He walked past the Mill, where Paddy used to work, increasing his pace. His right foot was sore. He had twisted it playing bowls. He wanted to go faster. The road was quiet. He needed a cigarette. He knew that he was walking too slowly and yet he stopped, took a cigarette from the packet in his pocket, flicked open the lighter with his thumb. His hand shook. He steadied it with his left hand, taking a quick puff to make sure it was lit. He fumbled the cigarette packet and lighter back into his coat pocket. It was exactly then that he saw the headlights of a car in the distance. It was maybe half a mile away and moving towards him. Was it an Ardoyne taxi? It moved slowly, only doing twenty miles an hour. He watched it turn left into a side street, do a three point turn and halt as though going to turn right and re-join the Crumlin Road. Why was it doing that? He had to keep walking. He took a deep puff from his cigarette and exhaled slowly. His breath quickened.

William waited until Michael was a few hundred feet in front of them. Fifty feet past the junction Michael thought that he was going to be okay. He took a deeper breath and tried to exhale slowly. He took another deep breath. He counted to seven breathing in. Mary had learnt that from her yoga teacher. She told him if he was ever stressed to breathe out really slowly. The taxi was stationery in the side street. Maybe they had lost their way and needed to turn onto the Antrim Road. That was more than likely what was happening.

William put his foot on the accelerator and turned right from the side street onto the Crumlin Road. The wheels skidded on the icy tarmac, hitting the pavement and mounting it slightly, a few feet behind Michael. He slammed on the breaks. The taxi shuddered to a halt. Cedric jumped out from the front passenger seat with a rifle, leaving the door open. Michael dropped his cigarette on the ground, hands by his side, he looked at Cedric who lifted the rifle high into the air behind him and swung it like a golf club, hitting Michael with the butt, whacking him in the stomach. Michael bent double, letting out a low gurgling cry. Michael could hear and feel the air exiting his body with a continuous and slow hissing noise. He couldn't breathe in. Cedric lifted the rifle a second time high into the air and brought it down with his full weight, smashing it onto Michael's back. Michael fell on the ground and Cedric kicked him in the neck. As he lay writhing on the pavement, Peter opened the back door of the taxi.

Cedric bent down and pulled Michael from the pavement, hoisting him onto the back seat. Michael's upper body lay for a minute across Peter's knees.

"Go. Go. Get out of here!" Cedric yelled. William put his foot to the floor, shouting as he stabbed the accelerator. "You stupid Fenian bastard! Not your lucky night."

Michael moaned from the floor of the taxi as Peter pushed him gently from his knees. Only Michael's head was visible if someone looked inside. An army Saracen accelerated up the Crumlin Road towards Ardoyne. William dropped his speed to thirty miles an hour. The Saracen tank passed. Michael looked up at Peter. Peter immediately turned his head, looking out of the window into the darkness as the taxi passed Crumlin Road jail. Michael tugged at Peter's jeans. Peter turned to see Michael propped up against the back door; his arms by his side, knees bent allowing his feet to rest on the floor of the taxi. Peter saw

Michael's green eyes, his thick black eyebrows, the scattering of freckles over the bridge of his nose, his wide mouth. Michael stared into Peter's eyes, now holding onto Peter's knee with his hand. Peter's felt the warmth of Michael's blood, throbbing in his hand against his leg. Michael whispered as the siren of an ambulance rushing to the Mater hospital blared as it passed.

"Save me. I know you can save me. Don't let them kill me." He tugged again at Peter's jeans. "Save me. You can do it."

Peter turned sharply to look out of the window again, into the blackness where an occasional street light flooded the taxi with light.

Peter heard Michael crying softly on the floor still holding onto his jeans.

"You're not going to save me are you?" Michael wept, his head now bent over his chest. He dropped his hand from Peter's leg and joined his hands together. Peter felt the coldness of the icy air touching his leg where Michael's hand had been keeping it warm.

When the taxi stopped at the Black Beetle, Cedric told Peter, "Get him out."

Peter opened the right hand door of the taxi. Michael tightened his grip again on Peter's trousers as Peter slid over to the right hand side of the car and jumped out.

"He's yours."

"Peter, where do you think you're going?" Cedric took two steps after Peter. Peter stopped and stared straight ahead.

"Get the wedding ring off him. You know what to do now you fuckin coward. Do it!" Cedric pulled at Peter's jacket. Peter turned to face him. Cedric lifted his hand and brought it across Peter's face. There was a moment of stillness and silence before Peter walked towards the car, bent down and reached in for Michael.

chapter 5

Tuesday 4th January 1972

Michael had been dead seventeen hours when Rose walked the last few yards home from school, on Tuesday 4th January. Her leather schoolbag hung heavily on her right shoulder. The schoolbag slipped. She pulled it back into place. Curly red haired Clara from the year above was walking in front, talking and laughing with her best friend Mary. Matt and Eddie were part of the army patrol on Rose's right, walking alongside the jeep. Max was inside the jeep. Rose kept her eyes on Clara and Mary as she moved closer to Matt – so close that her arm brushed against his. Her hand briefly touched his warm green woollen glove. No-one saw the white envelope pass from Matt's hand to Rose's as her long black hair swung from left to right with each step. She never looked at Matt as she passed Sean Graham's betting shop on the corner of Brompton Park where three men stood leaning against the graffiti covered wall, smoking, with their backs to the black taxi. Clara turned to wave at Rose.

"Bye Rose – see you tomorrow."

"See you."

Rose watched Clara turn into the Fast Shop on the corner as Mary continued walking down Brompton Park. Rose gave Matt a quick look. He looked at her with his head slightly down, smiling. She noticed the curve of his shoulders, dark hair under the beret, light blue eyes with long lashes. He walked slowly. She saw the solidity of his legs, heard the crunch of his boots, treading the earth with what seemed like the strength of a giant. She felt in his eyes his energy connected with hers and for an instant there was the sense of tension, gravity, a pressure drawing them together. Even if they couldn't touch she felt as though the edges of her being were mingled with his. The setting sun seemed to bounce towards sunset. Everything felt right. Everything felt as though it was exactly as it should be. She felt like a balloon at the point of bursting. She had never felt so intensely happy before. Matt looked at her again out of the corner of his eyes and it was as though he was reading her mind. She knew he felt the same. The jeep slowed to a halt. She had to keep walking, looking ahead as Matt jumped into the back of the jeep which then did a U-turn, heading back up the Crumlin Road with a screech of tyres. Rose turned to look as the jeep drove up past the shops, past Macdonalds fruit and vegetables, past the bakery. It felt as though Matt was an elastic band stretching away from her with infinite elasticity which would never snap. She fingered the letter in her pocket. What did he have to say to her? She couldn't wait to read it, alone, in her bedroom.

William sat in the back seat of the taxi as Cedric drove. Peter was in the passenger seat. Cedric turned to William,

"That's her isn't it? Isn't that the bitch we've seen coming out of the church after Mass?"

"That's her alright. I remember the hair. Get a closer look at her face."

Peter looked left as they drew level with Rose. She was looking straight ahead, walking with a determined step. She was singing. Not that he could hear the words but her lips were moving in slow motion and she was smiling. The wind tossed her hair over her face. She brushed it back with a sweep of her hand, hitching the satchel back into place. She looked to the right as though she knew they were looking at her. Peter stared into her eyes. She smiled at him as Cedric dropped his speed to twenty miles an hour. For Peter, it seemed as though time slowed down. It was as if the taxi was idling at four miles an hour – at walking speed. He saw her long thick black eyelashes, fine eyebrows, high cheekbones. His heart didn't thump but was strangely still. Rose continued smiling at him as the car overtook her, moving past Kerrera Street, picking up speed as it reached the Mater Hospital. Peter caught the last few words of a conversation Cedric and William were having,

"So, that will be easy. Let's make sure we have one more child-bearing Fenian who won't have children." William laughed.

"What's going on?" asked Peter.

"That long-haired bitch, she's for the chop. We only need to have a look in the diary and see when." Cedric hit his hand against the steering wheel, laughing. He wiped a few tears with the back of his hand and put on a posh voice,

"William, can you tell me what the diary is looking like? When is the next available date?"

William snorted. "Give her a day or two to pray for her soul. She'll need it."

•••

Clara opened the door of the Fast Shop on the corner of Brompton Park. A bell tinkled. Mr O Grady from the Fast Shop was on his knees behind the counter. He slowly got to his feet.

"Can I have a pan loaf please Mr O Grady?"

While Mr O Grady fixed his dentures in his mouth to reply, Clara surveyed the jars of sweets on the counter – pineapple chunks, lemon sorbets, rhubarb and custard, midget gems, wine gums, coconut mushrooms, liquorice allsorts and blackjacks.

Mr O Grady shuffled towards the counter with the pan loaf. He stared at her from behind thick rimmed glasses.

"How was school today Clara?"

"Great. Miss Donovan the Spanish teacher said if I wanted to do Spanish 'A' level, it would really be a good idea to try to get an au pair job in Spain this summer. I would need to save money for the flights. I am here to ask if you have any work."

"Well, you've asked at the right time. I'm opening up a second shop in Andersonstown. I need to find someone to help out here. Why don't you come round on Friday after school and we can talk. If you like what you hear you can start on Saturday." Mr O Grady looked around to make sure no-one was listening. "I need you to hide the money from the till every hour in case they come in to rob you. It's happened twice in the last month but they only got ten pounds."

"Sounds like a good plan Mr O'Grady. Can I have a quarter of pineapple chunks and a quarter of liquorice allsorts?"

"You're not going to eat me out of my profits when you're here are you?" Mr O Grady chuckled, pushing his glasses back up to the bridge of his nose.

Clara blushed.

"Only joking. You can eat anything you want. You don't want to put on too much weight though if you're off to show your figure in Spain in the summer."

Clara blushed again. She did have a sweet tooth.

"How much will I earn?"

"50p an hour."

"Perfect."

Clara imagined – two whole months without any rioting. Two months of not being afraid that someone would spit in your face or throw a brick at your head when walking home from school. She wondered what it would be like to able to go to bed at night without worrying that you might be killed in your sleep. Maybe those dreadful nightmares would stop too. The ones where she was lying in bed and someone broke down the front door and she heard heavy boots climbing the stairs. Clara would jump out of bed and straighten the sheets, and smooth the eiderdown to make it look as though no-one had been sleeping there. Then she would hide in the wardrobe and listen to whoever it was walk towards her father's room.

She knew that the first place they would look would be under the bed. She sat on the floor of the wardrobe in the dark with the hanging jackets and trousers crumpled on top of her head. She held her hands over her face, pressing them into her eyes. When she loosened her fingers, the smell of the damp and mothballs surrounded her like a cloud of soggy mist. There was nowhere else to hide. She heard them turn the door knob of her bedroom. It squeaked. They clumped towards the wardrobe without even looking under the bed. Maybe that's where she should have hidden there after all. The wardrobe door opened, light from the streetlamp outside shone on a black gloved hand and a parka. She woke up.

•••

Ciaran McCann, Clara's father, headed up the IRA in North Belfast. He read about Paddy's and Michael's murders in The Irish News while having a drink with Danny and Sean. The Easter Rising Club was dark inside, with no natural light. There were smelly drink-stained carpets which caught your feet slightly as you walked to the bar, and there were chipped tiled floors which occasionally crunched when Ciaran walked by onto fragments of broken glass. An Irish Tricolour hung from the wall near a small stage.

Ciaran had three children – Conor aged nine, Frances eleven and Clara sixteen. He fed them history, including the history of the Irish Famine, sitting around the dinner table for Sunday lunch. Poor Irish families depended upon the humble potato to survive during the early nineteenth century. On the banks of Lake Titicaca between Peru and Bolivia, in 4,000 BC, Peruvians spread the 'Chuño' or potato on the ground during frosty nights. When the sun rose the potatoes were covered with straw to protect them from the harsh radiation of a relentless sun. Later children trampled the potatoes to remove their moisture and peel, they were placed in a running river to remove any bitterness and lastly, they were dried for fourteen days and stored for up to four years. For the Peruvians the gormless potato was a God. The Incas counted units of time by the length of time it took to cook a potato into various consistencies. Potatoes were used to divine for Truth and to predict the weather. There were more than one hundred varieties of the potato in a single Andean valley.

For Ciaran, 1845 was a good enough starting point not only for the potato but for Irish history. In 1845 the potato blight hit Ireland. 'Fungus phytophthora infestans' arrived, evidenced by dark blotches appearing on the tips of the potato leaves and plant stems, and white mould under the leaves. More than one million people in Ireland died from starvation between 1845 and 1851. Another million were forced to leave, many dying on the coffin ships on their way to find a new life in America.

Ciaran told his children how the freezing winds from the Atlantic battered the frail frames of starving women, babies and children, struggling through the bogs of Connemara to walk north looking for food. Meanwhile on the East Coast carts carrying corn rumbled over uneven ground heading for Dublin where they were loaded with fattened livestock to be shipped to England.

Ciaran left The Easter Rising Club on the 4th January, and walked down Strathroy Park about two hundred feet behind Margaret Mulvenna. He noticed without much interest her frizzy curly brown hair, shopping bag, beige duffle coat (which looked a size too big), wrinkled woollen tights, purple skirt and flat black leather shoes. He saw her struggle with the weight of the shopping bag moving it from her left hand to her right. He didn't see that she was carrying two pints of milk, half a stone of potatoes, six Paris buns, a plain and a pan loaf. He was more interested in what was happening ahead of Margaret.

Margaret was a small, slim-built mother of five. She had been born a Protestant but had converted to Catholicism ten years before when she married her husband Joseph, who was Catholic. Aged thirty-six, Joseph died unexpectedly from a brain haemorrhage while lying asleep in bed with Margaret on the 5th March 1970. A week later, she was burnt out of her house in the Protestant Glencairn District and moved for security into the inner district of Ardoyne with her five children. She was thirty years old. Her youngest child was five. Every morning she wakened with a sense of dread about what the day would bring. Every day she said 'Thank You' to God for being alive.

Ciaran glanced at his watch. Danny and Sean should be in position. He wondered for a moment if Margaret was going to walk straight into the line of Danny's fire. A burst of machine gun fire rattled for about thirty seconds only a hundred yards in front of Margaret. Ciaran stopped, took a packet of Benson and Hedges out of his pocket, lit a cigarette, watching to see what would happen next.

At Margaret's gate, a young British soldier lay shot on the ground. One of his comrades held his head with the helmet still on, as another ripped open his green jacket. Margaret dropped her shopping bags on the ground, ran towards him, and knelt on the ground beside the soldiers.

"Can I help?"

She looked into the boy's white waxen face. He was eighteen. He stared back at her, more resigned than frightened.

"How bad is it?" he asked.

Margaret, put her hand on his shoulder and leant forward. She removed his helmet, smoothing his fringe back off his forehead. She remained silent.

"You'll be OK. Hang in there. We'll get you to hospital." One of his friends whispered, patting his hand.

"Let me get some towels." Margaret clambered awkwardly to her feet, feeling dizzy. One of the soldiers helped her to steady herself before she ran down the garden path, past the tall oak tree growing in the middle of the garden. She turned a key in the lock, ran upstairs, tripping on the top step and banging her head against the landing. Pulling herself to her feet she searched for a basin of water, clean towels and a pillow. She ran back down the garden path with the warm water splashing from side to side. She lifted his head gently to place the pillow on the ground. The soldier's head was heavy and wet in her hands. Then she realised that it was not so much that his head was wet but that her hands slippery and smeared with his blood. He must have hit his head hard when he fell to the ground. He smiled weakly at her.

"Thank you."

She passed the towels to his friends and moved the basin closer. She saw the small black hole in his chest. There was blue bruising spreading around the hole with only a small trickle of blood running down his body towards his trousers.

Margaret soaked a towel in the warm water and pressed it to his chest.

"There may be internal bleeding, " one of his mates whispered lifting a second towel, dipping it into the water and ringing it out for Margaret.

He moved onto all fours and put his lips close to his mate's ear.

"Don't give up. Stay awake. Don't go to sleep." The wounded soldier's eyes rolled back in his head. He took one large breath before his head moved and fell to the left of the pillow.

"You know you can't sleep." The soldier shook his shoulder gently.

Margaret held the boy's hand and searched for a pulse. She bit her lower lip and shook her head.

"He's dead?" His friend knelt on the ground, resting his head on the pavement, his arms stretched out in front of him.

The silence was only broken by the almost inaudible sobbing of his friend.

"Will someone say a prayer?" Margaret whispered.

"Will you? He's a Catholic." His friend knelt beside the dead boy with his hands joined.

Margaret, blessed herself and then blessed the dead soldier's forehead with the sign of the Cross as she said, "Oh Angel of God, my Guardian dear, to whom his love entrusts me here, ever this day, be at my side to light, to guard, to rule and guide me home."

Ciaran lit a second cigarette, watching Margaret bend over the soldier in prayer. He lit a third cigarette as a soldier arrived with a stretcher and he saw the body being trundled into the back of a Saracen tank. He watched Margaret rest her hand on his friend's shoulder before he handed her the white towels covered in blood, the pillow and empty basin. Ciaran lit a fourth cigarette, leaning against the railed garden of the house facing Margaret's. He didn't notice the bare oak tree. He didn't see Smokey her white and grey cat sharpening his nails against the lower bark, or Dennis's bike on the ground under the window sill. He didn't see Margaret walk slowly up the path towards the front door with her head buried in the pillow. Ciaran kept his eyes on the Saracen tank until it turned right at the bottom of the street.

●●●

That same afternoon, Peter sat in his bedroom in a terraced house off the Shankill Road, strumming Van Morrison's 'Tupelo Honey'.

"She's as sweet as Tupelo Honey. She's an angel of the first degree." The walls of his bedroom were papered with woodchip painted deep primrose yellow and orange hopsack curtains hung from the windows. His bed was covered with an orange and cream crocheted quilt made by Eileen for his sixteenth birthday. As he strummed, Peter searched his mind for a strategy to save Rose.

"Are you coming for a pint?" asked William, peering through the open door, expecting 'No' for a reply.

"OK. Give me ten minutes."

Peter looked at himself in the mirror in the bathroom. He hadn't shaved that morning. He had a stubbly gingery blonde beard, long and bushy sideburns, almost non-existent eye lashes and eyebrows. He looked as though seeing himself for the first time. He saw a broad face; square shaped with wide elongated eyes. He moved closer to the mirror, peering intensely as though trying to find out who was behind the face that looked back at him.

"You're an ugly looking sod. Why would she look twice at

you? She deserves better." His intense blue eyes looked back at him. "Save her life you ugly brute. Do something to make up for the disaster of a life form that you are."

•••

"What are you having?" William asked, scratching at a spot on his chin.

"A pint of lager." Peter slid onto the bench beside the window.

"Why do they call it the Black Beetle?" Peter rubbed his hands on his jeans.

Cedric wearing a navy blue polo neck jumper and jeans threw his hands into the air and spluttered.

"The cockroaches."

"Are cockroaches not brown?" Peter shuffled on the bench.

"Who bloody cares whether they're black or brown or what they call this place. It's a drinking hole, isn't it, not a fucking art exhibition of brown and black cockroaches. Make mine a pint of Guinness with a whiskey chaser."

"Cheers." There was a few seconds of silence before Peter lifted his pint and gulped half of it down without speaking.

Cedric nudged William with his elbow. "He's getting the hang of it at last."

Peter placed his glass on the table, wiping his lips from left to right with the back of his hand.

"I've been thinking about what you were saying about that bitch on the Crumlin. She's a bit of a lightweight, don't you think? Why don't we go for one of the big boys, one of the big hitters in Ardoyne?"

"Who do you have in mind?" asked William, raising an eyebrow to Cedric.

"Well, what about Ciaran McCann? We could go for him."

"Could we now," Cedric drawled sarcastically. "You're an expert now are you? You've been on two jobs and now you're ready to give orders. That's a good one. We couldn't get you started but now you want to take over. Let me tell you something," Cedric leant across the table, pointing his right index finger at Peter's right eye, "Just in case this isn't clear, you do what you're told. You're only a fucking apprentice. You're not telling the professionals how to do their job. When you've earned the right to do it, we might listen to you or we might not but you will still do what we tell you to do. Do you get it? Or do you need to hear it in a different way?"

"I'm not telling you what to do." Peter insisted, "I'm only saying that if we go for one of the big shots, we'll make an impact. It's the same effort. Who cares about whether we kill that bitch. She's nobody."

"How come I'm not convinced?" William nudged Cedric knowingly. "Somehow Peter, I get the feeling that you're not committed to this – if you know what I'm saying. Maybe we need to sharpen up your commitment a little. Fancy a drive?"

William stood up, leaving half of his Guinness unfinished and downing the chaser in one. Cedric hit Peter, who was still sitting, across the head.

"After you."

Peter slid out from the bench, stood beside William who grabbed him by the elbow. Cedric took his other arm.

"Let's go."

William drove the taxi in silence up the Crumlin Road. A black cat ran in front of the car from an alleyway. William hit the brakes. The cat scampered into the Grove. He muttered under his breath.

"If that cat had been a dog, it would have been a dead duck."

"Shut your mouth." Cedric snapped at William.

"Why didn't you kill the bloody cat anyway?"

William shook his head. "I've told you before that cats are honourable creatures."

Cedric turned to Peter. "We're going to show you something that I think will make you wise up." He moved his lips close to Peter's ear. "Brother or no brother, you're going to play the game the way we play it."

The black taxi turned left off the Crumlin Road, into the street parallel to the Grove. William parked on the left hand side of the road, opened the driver's door, climbed out and walked towards a small metal gate leading into the Grove. Cedric and Peter followed behind. The light was failing. Rain began to fall, gently at first and then as the wind increased it swept horizontally through the trees, whipping the empty branches and stinging the faces of William, Cedric and Peter. Peter pulled his Parka hood over his head; his jeans darkened with the heavy rain.

"Of course maybe you were only joking about us not killing the bitch." William pinched Peter's face. They walked in single file along a small overgrown pebble path winding its way towards Holy Cross Church. The trunks of the trees were steady, unmoving, as the branches continued to sway in broad circles. Peter walked slowly with his head down. Cedric pushed him forward jabbing his hand into his back.

"It's here." William limped more quickly a few steps ahead. He stepped onto the wet grass, making his way determinedly towards a holly bush. Peter could see that to the left of the holly bush was a rectangular hole in the ground. It seemed to be an empty grave with a pyramid of mud beside it.

"Get in." William ordered.

Peter raised his head. "You can't be serious?"

"Get in." William repeated. Cedric pushed Peter towards the grave.

"Do as he says. We were keeping this for one of the priests. We thought they might like to be buried on Holy Ground."

Peter looked at Holy Cross Church in the distance. The sky was clearing of clouds. The twin spires pushed towards the moon. The door of the Church opened. There was a warm light falling on the steps. Peter saw the silhouette of a tall man dressed in black. His cloak fluttered in the wind. He seemed to register them. Pulling a torch from his pocket he shone it in their direction, the light swallowed by the darkness of the undergrowth. William and Cedric, with their backs to the church, didn't see Father Anthony. Peter knelt on the wet grass and lowered himself into the grave, swinging his legs over the edge and jumping into the pool of water at the bottom.

"What next?" Peter shouted.

Cedric pulled a revolver from his inner pocket. "Turn around."

Peter turned his back on his father and Cedric. He felt the cold metal press against the nape of his neck.

"Remember what this feels like. Take a good look around you. This will be your last view if you don't do as you're told. You're not giving any orders."

Peter rested his chin on his chest, he breathed deeply.

"OK. That's enough!" William barked at Cedric. "He's learnt his lesson. Let's go."

"What are you talking about? Have you gone soft? Let's hear him." Cedric pushed the pistol hard against Peter's temple. "Tell us what you have learnt Peter?"

"For God's sake Cedric wise up. Get a grip."

William leant over the grave and reached a hand down to Peter. Peter felt an unfamiliar softness in his father's hand.

"Quick, give me your hand. Let's get out of here."

"Cedric, hold onto me." William shouted as he slid on mud.

Cedric put the gun in his pocket and held William around the waist as Peter, gripping William's hand, scrambled out of the grave.

Peter looked towards Holy Cross Church. The priest had gone. The doors were closed, the lights out.

They walked in silence along the pebbled path to the gate. William opened the back door of the car. Peter climbed in and lay on the back seat. As they turned right onto the Crumlin Road, an unmarked police car, its siren blaring, swung left, heading for the Grove.

"I wonder where they're off to in such a rush?" Cedric looked at William. "Do you want to follow them and see what the craic is?"

"Eileen will have dinner ready. Let's go home."

•••

Father Anthony sat underneath the picture of the Sacred Heart of Jesus in the reception area of Holy Cross Monastery with Inspector Quinn sitting beside the white marble statue of the Virgin Mary and Police Constable McGuigan beside a statute of The Little Flower.

"Would you like a cup of tea Inspector?" asked Father Anthony.

"No thank you."

"So you found no-one in the Grove?"

"We found an empty grave. There were recent footprints around it and in it. It appeared to be three men which confirms what you saw."

"It looked as though they were about to kill him."

"They may have seen you and taken him elsewhere to execute him. That's a possibility."

"Is there anything we can do?" asked Father Anthony.

"I don't think so. We'll keep a few soldiers around for a few days."

"Thank you for that." Father Anthony stood up and walked slowly to the main monastery door and pulled back the heavy lock. "Do you think the footprints will help you to identify who they are?"

"The footsteps are distorted with the mud and rain. Unlikely I'm afraid."

• • •

Cedric opened the door for Jenny as he guided her into the Queen's Head. She walked ahead of him and he took a deep breath. She wore a flared pink velvet skirt with blue silk bows around the hem and a long pink angora jumper with a flowery blue and pink silk scarf. Her hair was tied up in a ponytail. She carried a cream duffle coat on her right arm. His heart pounded. He followed her into the bar, pulling out a seat for her sit.

"They do a great lasagne." He noticed the softness of her skin on the nape of her neck, the curly golden downy hair above her scarf. He hovered a moment, breathing in the fruity sweetness of her hair.

"Are you warm enough?" Cedric hung the duffle coat on a stand in the corner.

"Yes thank you. I've got four layers on and these." Jenny pointed at the furry boots and leg warmers.

"What would you like to drink?" The waiter handed out the menus.

"Orange juice please." Jenny twiddled with a small golden cross around her neck.

"Me too." Cedric then pointed to the specials on the blackboard. "There's no holding back. You can have anything you want. Don't pick the cheapest."

As Jenny studied the menu, Cedric watched her. Her face seemed to change constantly in front of him like a waterfall where the water dropping so rapidly gives the impression of staying in the same place.

"Don't rush. Take your time."

"I've decided." Jenny set the menu to one side. "Now you have to tell me all about yourself. All I know is that you have a taxi business with William."

"I have other plans."

"What kind of plans?" Jenny looked into his eyes. He stared at her without breathing for a few seconds.

"Dreams. You know. Dreams."

"Don't be so mysterious. What kind of dreams?"

"What kind of dreams do you like?" Cedric laughed and took a deep gulp of orange juice.

Jenny curled a strand of hair around her finger and it fell into a ringlet on her shoulder.

"Wouldn't it be wonderful if the Troubles would end and we could enjoy a normal life – like being able to go for a walk along Portstewart beach."

"You can go for a walk on Portstewart beach. What's more I know a highly recommended taxi driver can you take you there for a good price."

Jenny smiled weakly, feeling slightly uncomfortable and not knowing why. Maybe it was because Cedric seemed to not so much smile at her but rather to leer at her. His voice was unusually sugary sweet. She began to wish that she hadn't said yes to this date.

"You haven't told me about your dreams. Tell me more."

"I'd like to take care of Eileen, find a house in the countryside, maybe by the sea. Eileen's a good person. She deserves better than Elmwood Terrace. You remind me of her."

As Cedric looked at Jenny he felt his heart thumping wildly. He wanted to reach across and take her hand. His face flushed. 'Don't do it' – he repeated the words silently as he dropped his head to stare at the menu.

"In what way do I remind you of Eileen?" Jenny tried to sound more relaxed than what she felt.

"She's different from most people. She's a kind person. You seem a kind person. She wouldn't hurt a fly."

"She doesn't come with you to the Black Beetle?"

"No. That's not her scene. She's an artist you know." Cedric searched in his wallet for a photo. "That's one of her paintings. She has her first exhibition on Saturday."

Jenny took the photo and looked at it closely. It was a painting of a woman holding a baby. The woman wore a green skirt, a flowery blue, pink and white patterned blouse. It was hard to see the features of her face apart from a small rose titian mouth, a broad nose and very little hair – more a shaved head, or an African short tight curl. It was hard to tell from her eyes in which direction she was looking. At first Jenny thought that she was looking over her shoulder to her right towards a threatening shape – only slightly defined in purple against a blue background. You couldn't tell if the shape was of a man or of a woman or even if it was human at all. A second look suggested the woman's eyes were looking to the left as though she was anticipating danger and was protecting the baby. Her arms were holding the child tight to her chest.

"Who is the baby?" Jenny stroked the image as though trying to feel the textured paint of the original.

"Don't put your fingers over it. Hold it by the edges." Cedric grabbed the photo back and held it between his finger and thumb. "Hold it like this." He showed it again to Jenny.

"Sorry." Jenny shrugged her shoulders. Cedric replaced the

photo in his wallet. "Who is the woman?"

"I don't know."

"The baby?"

"I don't know." Cedric wished he hadn't shown Jenny the photo. He closed the menu and looked around for the waiter.

"The painting is a bit scary."

"Life's scary, isn't it?" Cedric put his hand in the air to attract the waiter's attention. "How about Thursday for Portstewart Beach? I've a day off." Cedric loosened his pink silk tie and opened the top button of his blue cotton shirt.

"I haven't been to Portstewart since I was on holiday when I was six." Jenny finished her orange juice. "I loved it. It would be good to see it again. I'm working Thursday evening. I would need to be back for around three o'clock. Would that be OK?"

Jenny didn't know why she was making this happen. As soon as the words were out, she wanted to gobble them all up.

"There's still time to have a day to remember." Cedric played with a gold ring on the little finger of his left hand, twisting it clockwise.

"Why not bring Eileen along?" Jenny asked quickly.

"She is busy getting ready for the art exhibition. There will be another time." Cedric closed the button on his shirt and tightened his tie.

"Here are the starters." Two prawn cocktails slid onto the placemats with wedges of lemon hanging precariously over the edge of the glasses.

"I'm famished." Cedric dropped his hands onto his lap and waited until Jenny picked up her fork before he took a mouthful with his hand shaking slightly. Jenny didn't notice the shaking only the way he wiped the mayonnaise off his upper lip with his left hand rather than with the paper napkin.

"You don't work full-time at the Black Beetle do you?"

"No. I'm a student." Jenny relaxed a little.

"What are you studying?" Cedric's lips tightened into a straight line, his cheeks were still flushed.

"Nursing. I'm in my first year." Jenny leaned forward for the pepper pot.

"Let me help you." Cedric passed the white ceramic salt and pepper pots.

"What's Peter going to do when he finishes his 'A' levels?" Jenny looked into Cedric's eyes without blinking.

"Why do you want to know about Peter and his 'A' levels?" Cedric couldn't stop his voice sounding slightly irritated or his lips drawing into a tight straight line.

"It's interesting to know about other peoples' plans. What does he want to study at university?" Jenny looked quizzically at Cedric.

"Medicine at Queen's," Cedric blurted out without being able to avert his gaze from Jenny's green eyes.

"Lucky man. I would have loved to do medicine but didn't get the grades. He must be clever."

"There's more to life than getting good grades." Cedric scraped the prawn cocktail glass clean and continued scraping.

"What would that be now?" Jenny laughed and sat back in the chair. "We're back to those dreams again, aren't we?"

• • •

Later that evening, as Margaret lay in bed listening to the rioting on Etna Drive, she didn't know that she was living her last forty eight hours. She would continue to watch the minute hand of the clock move forward slowly until day break. That's what she did every night. Only when the sun rose over Belfast Harbour did she eventually fall into a deep, heavy sleep for an hour or two before breakfast.

chapter 6

Wednesday 5th January 1972

In 18, Elmwood Terrace Peter pulled a chair up to the breakfast table.

"What have you got on today?" Eileen asked sipping on her tea, passing a slice of toasted wheaten to Peter.

"History, English, Biology and Chemistry."

"That's a busy day." Eileen filled Peter's mug with tea. "You'll have Mr McCabe today for History and English?"

"Yes. Can I ask you a question?"

"Of course you can. What is it?" Eileen lowered her voice.

"Did you love Dad when you married him?"

Eileen pulled her chair closer to the table. She cradled the cup of tea in both hands. She looked into the teacup before raising her eyes to look at Peter.

"That is a question I wasn't expecting. What makes you ask?"

"I've wondered for a long time why you married him."

Eileen looked away from Peter through the window into the darkness outside.

"I don't think I loved him."

"Why did you marry him then?"

"I was young. I didn't know what love was about. He was quite a bit older than me – thirteen years. I was only sixteen when we met. William worked in the Royal Victoria Hospital. I met him when my mother was in hospital. My father died when I was four. When mother died in 1939, the only family I had left was Uncle Roy. I moved in to live with him. He was a kind man but it wasn't the same as having mother alive. With mother I could sit with her in silence – neither of us saying a word – and I felt deeply happy. With Uncle Roy when we sat in silence, I only felt an enormous loneliness. When we looked into each other's eyes it was as though the ghost of mother was seen by us both. We couldn't see each other; only feel the pain of memory of the person we had both loved and lost. The war had started and William stayed in touch and seemed strong, as though he knew what to do with his life. He knew his own mind. He had been kind to my mother during those last months. I didn't forget that. I felt protected, safe. He asked if I would go out with him. I said yes."

"You said that you didn't think that you loved him. What did you feel for him?"

"It was a kind of neediness. I needed someone to fill the gap left by mother's death. I knew in the week before we were married that I shouldn't marry him."

"What happened? Why did you marry him then?"

"The week before we were due to be married, I spent three days thinking about how I could tell William that I didn't want to marry him. I wanted to call the wedding off. It was a Wednesday evening. He was due to visit and take me to the Plaza. I didn't bother getting dressed up or putting on any make up. I had decided that as soon as he knocked on the door, I would invite him in for a cup of tea and tell him that the wedding was off. That night, he arrived early. He wasn't dressed for going out dancing either. He was still wearing his hospital clothes. He told me he had to work late. He described how injured soldiers had been brought home and how he had worked a fourteen hour day helping re-arrange the beds and cleaning two storage rooms to make room for new beds. He came into the kitchen and kissed me on the cheek. It was a different kind of kiss – soft, gentle, not rushed. I stepped back in surprise and watched him limp from the kitchen into the sitting room. Seeing him, I felt a new, different emotion, a kind of painful sweet sadness. It seemed that his kiss sealed our destiny together. It awakened something which meant that I could never leave him, even if it wasn't love. We were meant to be together. It was fate. It was as though he had read my mind. He sat on the sofa in the sitting room drinking tea. He said, "You know Eileen, I've never known what it is to love anyone. I think you should know that. I don't think anyone has ever loved me. I don't think even God loves me. I don't think anyone could love me. I understand if you want to call the whole wedding off. I'm not good enough for you."

"Are you saying that you don't love me William?"

"I'm saying that I don't know what love is. I would like to take care of you but I don't think that is good enough for you. You can do better than that. You can find someone who knows what love is and who knows how to love you."

"That was when I should have said yes, he was right, and that the wedding was off. I didn't. I remembered his kiss. I felt that I wanted to learn how to love William. I thought that it was sad to live and never to have known that you're loved or never been able to love. I thought that I could be the person who could help him to know what love was, given time. I could learn how to love him and learn how to be loved by him. I told him nobody is perfect." Eileen laughed. "When I look back now, I don't feel that I made the decision to marry your father because I loved him, it was more that I knew that I couldn't leave him."

"Wouldn't you want to leave him now? You could meet someone who would be more like you and who would appreciate you."

"If I made a mistake in marrying your father Peter, I could do it again. No. I learnt to trust something else inside, something much more dependable. Knowing that my thoughts and feelings were so uncertain, unstable and unpredictable, I found something else inside which guided me and continues to guide me. I don't need anyone. Not you, not your father or Cedric, or any other man, to be happy and to find peace."

"What is it that you found to guide you?"

"I can't really describe it. It's like finding a way of listening to your heart rather than to your head. As I said I learnt not to trust my thoughts or feelings. I knew instead how to listen to my heart. Everybody eventually has to find out how to do that. No-one can teach you. It's not easy because the heart speaks in a soft voice. The head has a much brasher voice that bullies you into doing what it wants. The heart whispers to you. It's more like a kitten turning over on its back and allowing you to stroke its tummy. It doesn't force you. It gently opens you up to see what you need to see. I found that it led me to a peace that I never expected."

Peter wiped crumbs away from his lips. "I still don't know what you mean? How can I do that?"

"I don't know either Peter. If I knew, I would tell you. I would want you to know."

As Peter closed the door of 18, Elmwood Terrace, the sky billowed with grey clouds tinged with orange, threatening a fresh fall of snow. The day had an ancient feel to it as though Peter was stepping into a Turner or a Constable painting. Temperatures had fallen below zero. The cold wind now carried small hailstones that hit Peter on the face. He buried his chin into his woollen scarf, wishing he had remembered to wear a hat. He hummed Van Morrison's 'Tupelo Honey', trying to remember Rose's face, imagining what she would be doing right now. Would she also be walking to school? A dog barked in a backyard – a hollow repetitive bark which followed him all the way to the school gate.

• • •

At eleven thirty on the morning of 5th January as Peter moved into his History class with Mr McCabe, Ciaran gave orders for Margaret Mulvenna to be murdered.

"Can I have a word?" Peter asked Mr McCabe at the end of the History class as the rest of the class filed along the corridor to Geography.

"Of course dear boy, do sit down."

Mr McCabe waved at a chair behind the first row of desks. Peter sat down and leant forward, holding his head in his hands. He raised his head and stared into Mr McCabe's grey eyes.

"Mr McCabe, do you think it is possible for people to change their mind, if they have strong opinions or a strong desire to do something? Is there evidence in history of people changing for the better?"

Mr McCabe buttoned up his waistcoat and perched on the edge of the table at the front of the room and rested his hands on his thighs.

"Well 'for the better' is perhaps difficult to define. What one person perceives as being 'better' may not be the same for another. However, if we look at Saul on the road to Damascus, he is an interesting example of what perhaps you are asking about. He persecuted Christians and then became one of their strongest advocates. History is full of examples of people who dramatically changed their perspective and then acted differently and changed the world."

"What would make someone change their mind, their way of seeing?" Peter leant back in the chair, pulling on his left ear lobe.

Mr McCabe stood up and pulled a second chair from behind the desk to sit side by side with Peter. He took a deep breath.

"Let's look at the process of forming a perspective or opinion."

Mr McCabe walked to the blackboard and quickly drew a flow chart, scraping the chalk across the board to form four boxes. He then drew five arrows at the top of the blackboard pointing into the first box, an arrow pointing to a second empty box, another arrow pointing to a third empty box and a final arrow pointing to a box at the bottom into which he wrote the word 'actions'. He drew two lines out from this box – one to the right where he wrote 'what we say' and a line to left where he wrote 'what we do'.

"It's as simple and as complicated as this. What we say and do is our activity in the world. We can change what we say and do, but we need to understand the process of learning. What happens before you say or do anything?"

Peter thought for a moment. "I'm not sure."

"What was happening before you answered?"

"I was thinking about your question."

"Wonderful." Mr McCabe wrote 'thinking' in the box above 'actions'.

"What happens before you think?"

"I'm trying to make sense of the question. Is that not still thinking?"

"Let's imagine that you are lying in bed. You hear a loud noise in your bedroom which wakens you from your sleep. What happens?"

"I wonder what the noise is."

"That's right. What else?"

"I wonder what I should do. Should I get out of bed or not to investigate?"

"That's still thinking isn't it?"

"Yes. What might make you get out of bed?"

"I might feel curious or afraid."

"Absolutely. Emotions tend to be triggered before conscious thinking. There are exceptions to this but for now let's keep it simple."

Mr McCabe wrote the words 'emotion/feeling' in the box above 'thinking'.

"We've only one box left. What happens before you have an emotional reaction to anything – for example before you experience fear, interest, confusion or humour?"

"Well, if I think back to the bedroom and hearing the loud noise, I'm trying to work out what the noise is, my brain is trying to understand it. Has a balloon burst or is it a gunshot? Is it in the house or outside?"

"Exactly. Let's call that an unconscious struggle for perception or understanding of the world. It is a type of unconscious thinking. The brain is trying to make connections between what you already know and what is happening now. The five lines up here represent the five sense gates – hearing, touching, tasting, smelling, seeing – your brain is mapping over in less than a second what you are experiencing with what you already know. All learning is about changing this unconscious pattern, which will bring with it an emotional reaction, triggering new thinking and bringing new actions."

Mr McCabe returned to his chair, still holding the chalk in his hand.

"There, dear boy, on that blackboard is the answer to your question and much more. In that simple flow chart is a pointer towards enlightenment and wisdom. Einstein said, 'Take things to their simplest and no simpler'. The external trigger of the senses activates this process which is completed in less than a trillionth of a second. Internal thoughts can be considered as external sound and they also trigger emotional reactions. Yet we are capable of changing our response. We can learn. We can make the process more complex and interesting. Buddhists would say that none of this really happens in a linear way such as I have described but is more a simultaneous arising and collapsing moment by moment. We can search out parallels in quantum physics or we can look at the work of the great philosophers – Hume, Kant, Schopenhauer, and Wittgenstein – but I have found it most helpful to simplify and to work with what we can observe and change. We can observe our emotions and our thoughts. We can change what we say and do. We don't have to be driven by what we experience if we can develop the skills of being able to observe our experience, being able to stay with what we are observing – concentration and equanimity."

"What do you mean by equanimity?"

"An unconditional acceptance of whatever is happening – a matter-of -factness or a detachment in seeing what is – neither liking or disliking what is and therefore not pushing it away nor trying to hold onto it. The Greeks called it 'apatheia', which is not the same as apathy. It's a kind of 'hands off' loving attention. In Ignatian Spirituality it is called 'indifference'. You don't care what you do – only that you can discern God's will and do it."

Peter sat upright in the chair,

"What happens if you have someone like Hitler? Do you let him murder? Do you try to stop him?"

"You act. Apatheia doesn't mean that you are passive. You act but without being driven. You act from what you see. You are not violent."

"What might you do?"

"You might say something to help them change. You might do something. Maybe you say or do nothing. I can't be prescriptive. It depends."

How do you help him change?"

"People change because they want to change – or because the scales fall from their eyes."

Peter examined the flowchart scrawled on the blackboard. He leant forward in his chair. "If a person has strong emotions, it could be difficult to change their thinking."

"Yes if desire is strong, it can be difficult to change thinking. Desire is a problem – along with hatred. So we have to go beyond desire and for most people this is a challenge. Impossible it is not but neither is it easy. Think for a moment about the experience of going beyond desire, what it might be like. If we were able to experience without thinking, without judging – neither liking it nor disliking – what would that be like?"

Peter held both hands over his face pressing hard against his eyes before replying. "I don't see how you could comment on it. Wouldn't it be the same as not seeing, tasting, feeling anything? Wouldn't that seem like a kind of death or non-existence?"

"Perhaps, but it could also be seen as a new life. But I am digressing. Let me return to your question – if it is possible for the hardened killer to be influenced to have a change of heart and to therefore let go of the desire to kill, to murder, to torture. That was your question, wasn't it? Well, let me ask you one more question. How is hatred different from desire?"

Peter threw his hands into the air and rocked the chair back onto two legs. "Are they not completely different?"

"I would suggest that they are more similar than different." Mr McCabe tapped at the emotion box on the blackboard. "How are they created? Are they not both created through the mind which we simplified here?" He pointed to the 'filter/ perception' box on the blackboard. "If we take the case of Saul, when he fell blinded to the ground it was as though Nature had wiped out his previous mind-set. He could no longer see as he used to. In his situation, it appears that Saul did nothing to provoke the change; it seemed to have been a spontaneous inner restructuring of his mind. For most people our learning is less dramatic, more organic, with subtle changes happening from day- to-day based on our capacity to reflect, to learn from what we have done and to change on the basis of that reflection. We come to the rather fascinating questions of who is aware, who is reflecting and who changes."

"You said that there is the question of 'Who is aware?'

"Yes. Who do you think it is?" Mr McCabe took a cotton handkerchief out of his pocket and blew his nose. "You're an intelligent chap."

Peter looked again at the flowchart on the blackboard. "If I am watching my thoughts, I cannot be my thoughts. If I am aware of my emotions, I cannot be my emotions. It seems that the space around thoughts and emotions is what is watching – and that space is who or what I am."

Mr McCabe nodded vigorously. "Perhaps we might call that space 'Awareness'. That space is a vibrant, intelligent, loving Awareness." Mr McCabe smiled broadly, wiping a trickle of sweat which ran down his forehead with the handkerchief.

The bell rang outside for break. Peter jumped as the radiator beside his chair gurgled into life. He looked at Mr McCabe who was holding his index finger against his lips, his eyes soft and questioning. "Who is it, Peter? Can you tell me? Who is it who is planning a murder and who are they planning to kill?" Mr McCabe leant forward and put his hand on Peter's shoulder. "I'm all ears."

Peter told Mr McCabe the whole story after school in a tea shop near the City Hall. Donald McCabe munched angel cake and sipped tea. Peter sat across the table, his face whiter than the tablecloth.

"Peter, this makes you an accomplice to murder."

Peter breathed heavily. "I know, but I never wanted to be involved. I couldn't say no. I've told you what they did. They wouldn't think twice about killing me. I know it."

"I believe you, Peter, but where is the evidence to show that you weren't willingly involved?"

"Paddy and Michael knew but they're dead."

"Let's not think of that now. We will convince the police Peter. They will understand, I promise. Let's think now about what we need to do to stop them murdering Rose or anyone else."

"I've tried to do what I thought might work but I might have made it worse. They're now watching me, suspicious of me."

"There is always a way." Mr McCabe patted Peter's hand. "What would they not expect you to do?"

"Maybe they wouldn't expect me to speak to Mum?"

"What about talking to your Dad?"

"I have never talked to Dad. I don't think now is the best time to start."

•••

William turned the corner onto Elmwood Terrace. Everything in his body hurt. He was aware of how difficult it was to move his left leg. It was stiff and dragged behind him like a leaden weight, daggers of pain in his knee and ankle. The wind pummelled his face with small rounded hailstones. He closed his eyes as he tugged his woollen scarf into a knot to try and stop it slipping free. As he did so he heard the sound of a small motorbike starting up at the end of the street. It wasn't that particular noise that made his heart beat faster, sending fear flooding through his body. It was the sound of laughter – the laughter of two teenage boys.

He opened his eyes. On the left hand side of the road a small motorbike was making circles in the road. There were two skinny boys riding it. William didn't really look at them. He heard them laugh even louder. They were cheering as though riding a bucking bronco. He could make out that they were maybe twelve or thirteen, too young to be riding the bike legally. He didn't spend too long looking at them.

They straightened their circle and approached. He turned his attention to the six feet of rope attached to the exhaust pipe of the bike. On the end of the rope a shape a little more than a foot long was rolling and bouncing along the road towards him. William rubbed his eyes with the back of his hand, not sure he could trust his vision. It was easier to make it out now. It was a ball of fluff, rolling from left to right on the end of the rope, occasionally catching on the pockmarked tarmac which sent it sailing high into the air before crashing back onto the surface. The ball of fluff screeched rasping hopeless cries as it was dragged.

William threw himself in front of the bike as it drew parallel to him, the boys falling off and the rider screaming. "What are you're doing, you fucking idiot? Do you want to kill us?"

William crawled onto his knees. On all fours he felt his way to the end of the rope, patiently and delicately undoing the knot attached to Bouncer's collar.

He cradled Bouncer in his arms. For five minutes he was unaware of anything other than feeling the faint heartbeat which still moved within Bouncer's chest. Blood from Bouncer's mouth and broken teeth seeped into William's beige raincoat. William didn't notice the boys jump over the wall at the end of the road as he buried his head in Bouncer's long stripy coat of winter fur.

"Don't die on me. Please don't die." William lifted his head and stroked Bouncer with his finger on his favourite spot behind his left ear. Bouncer moved his leg an inch and a small pink tongue with a nail file finish licked William's hand.

William felt the roughness of the tongue and heard a small purr start around Bouncer's heart. He kept looking at his closed eyes. Bouncer slowly opened his eyes and looked at William. William bent closer. He heard the small purring noise get louder as Bouncer slowly lifted his paw and tapped him gently on the nose.

William leaned back against the wheels of the bike and took a deep breath. He gathered Bouncer to him in a circle of fluff, pulling his tail neatly around him as though Bouncer was curled up on his knee on the sofa.

Holding Bouncer on his knees and caressing him William rocked backwards and forwards. His body started to vibrate with Bouncer's purring. He felt a deep peace move through him. He kept rocking gently, squeezing Bouncer to him, occasionally dropping his face into Bouncer's fur and shaking his head deeper into its wetness. He didn't notice his face covered in blood.

It was only when a car turned onto Elmwood Terrace and the driver got out to help William to his feet that he thought of moving. He refused to hand over Bouncer. Instead, he walked the remaining few steps to his front gate, Bouncer still purring in his left arm, walked past the cherry tree, and heard Eileen's feet running along the hallway as sank to his knees on the doorstep.

chapter 7

Thursday 6th January 1972

Cedric zipped up his leather jacket before opening the passenger door of the taxi. He reached out a hand. "Madame."

Jenny placed her hand in his. She was surprised how warm and soft it felt. Yet she still wanted to shake her hand free. She looked into Cedric's eyes. He glanced away as she slid her legs out of the taxi. She wrapped a multi-coloured scarf around her neck and tucked it into the duffle coat.

"We can pop into the golf club later for a hot drink if you like."

Jenny tied a loose lace on her boot. She pulled her pink pom pom hat down over her head. "Sounds good."

"If you don't mind, I'll leave the taxi here. If I drive it onto the beach there will be sand everywhere." Cedric locked the door.

"That's fine." Jenny stuffed her hands into her duffle coat pockets. "It's freezing. Let's walk quickly." Jenny started to run towards the beach.

Cedric walked quickly behind pulling on his leather gloves.

There was a strong gale blowing from the North whipping up the waves into foamy white tops. The wind then snaked its way across the sand, carving deep rhythmical curves as far as the eye could see. To the right Jenny watched gannets plunging into the waves in search of food. There was a moment of stillness when the gannets pointed their heads straight down and then almost hovered over the waves in a way that seemed timeless.

"It must be cold in there." Jenny turned to Cedric. "There must be easier ways of finding a bite to eat."

"Like driving a taxi?" Cedric laughed.

Sandpipers and wagtails raced ahead of them towards the Barmouth. The sand was soft underfoot near to the water's edge which made walking more difficult.

"Over here is easier." Cedric headed towards the sand dunes where the spiky grass shivered in the wind.

"I can't believe that there's no-one here. It's so beautiful." Jenny buried her face into her scarf.

"It's better that way, don't you think?" Cedric moved closer to Jenny. His shoulder bumped against hers. Jenny took a few steps to the right.

"I like having people around." Jenny pushed her hands more deeply into her pockets. "Don't you?"

"Depends. Are you warm enough?" He rubbed his hands together. "Freezing isn't it?" Cedric watched the tip of Jenny's nose turn red.

"Maybe we could walk faster. Race you to the Barmouth."

Jenny started to run with her hands in her pockets, her head down looking at the sand, fighting against the strong wind whipping sand into the creases of her jeans. Cedric followed, gasping deeply. His body felt heavy, solid and unwilling to move.

As they reached the end of the beach they scrambled onto the slippery rocks to see the river Bann sweep into the Atlantic like an artery releasing blood into infinity. White luminous clouds billowed high above them. Strong waves dashed against the rocks at the end of a rocky pier. A black cormorant watched regally as foam from the breaking waves stuck like candy floss to its feathers. Cedric felt his cheeks turning numb as he licked salt from his lips.

"Careful!" Cedric shouted as Jenny made her way slowly over the rocks towards the edge of the pier. "It's dangerous. You could slip."

Cedric got onto his hunkers and followed Jenny, trying to balance by grabbing hold of the rocks in front of him and using his knees and lower legs to slide over them one by one. He glanced into the river to his left. The water dashed against the rocks and then jettisoned back into the powerful currents which propelled it towards the Atlantic. He felt his head beginning to swirl. He couldn't think. He could only feel this nauseating movement which didn't allow a single thought to settle into awareness. His stomach lurched as though he had dropped several floors quickly in an elevator. He kneeled upright, rubbed his hands together, spotting a rock a few feet in front of him. It was flat on top. Keeping his sight on the rock, without looking into the river or into the sea, he tentatively edged forward, reaching the flat glazed surface and sitting down, not caring that the cold water seeped into his jeans. He closed his eyes briefly, smelling the seaweed, hearing the seagulls crying overhead, rubbing his eyes with the back of his gloves.

He opened his eyes to see Jenny standing on the last craggy rock looking out into the Atlantic. She removed her hands from her pockets and held onto her hat. Cedric looked out to sea. There was a series of three magnificent waves approaching, the last much higher and stronger than the others in front. They were like glorious cavalry horses charging fearlessly into battle. As he stared into the turquoise green depths of their curves, he saw them gain in height, pulling the water up into the sky where the curled white tips almost appeared to vanish into the scudding clouds. The third wave advanced at a faster pace, gobbling up the second wave, and rearing itself higher into the sky before the last two waves pulled together and became one.

Jenny had her back to the sea, watching Cedric scramble to his feet. Her hands were over her ears, still holding onto her hat. She couldn't hear what he was shouting but saw his lips twist into a scream. He shook his arm vigorously pointing with his finger towards the sea. Jenny turned slowly. She twisted her head slightly to the right when the wave struck. Jenny felt the full force of the water hit her like a slap from a whale's tail. She lost balance. Cedric, trepidation lost in a paroxysm of fear, leapt across the last three remaining rocks as Jenny disappeared from sight.

Jenny was aware of her body turning over and over. There was nothing she could do to stop it. She was enveloped in an energy which tossed her at its whim like a killer whale playing with a sea lion. There was a heavy thump as her body hit the hard sand. She heard the air leaving her body through her mouth. She knew that she had to breathe in but the air kept pushing out. Then, there was the sound of waves dragging the sand and small pebbles out to sea. She was alone for a moment. She lifted her head and saw a wall of water above her. She managed to take a deep breath. The wave collapsed, pulling her again further out to sea. She turned over three times, instinctively holding her breath before again being dashed onto the sand. Once more she heard the familiar sound of the rasping, dragging of sand and pebbles. She tried to get to her knees in an attempt to crawl towards the shore. She knew time was limited. She had to move quickly before the wave returned. She moved only a few inches before being whipped away again and being pulled into the bowels of the sea, turning and tumbling over and over, lips tightly closed, open eyes seeing a dark shape moving towards her through the murky sand. She instinctively reached towards the blackness and grabbed Cedric's thick black leather glove. As the wave receded Cedric lifted Jenny into his arms. She spluttered and gulped for air. He felt the weight of her presence in his arms like the constant steady pulse of his heart beat pulsing within him. Jenny lifted her arms and placed them both around Cedric's neck.

"Thank you."

She kissed his cheek, tasting the salty grains of sand against her lips, feeling his prickly stubble send quivers of bubbliness to her toes.

"You're going to be OK." Cedric pressed his head against her, nudging her gently the way cats do when they're pleased to see each other.

"You saved my life." Jenny shivered as the strong wind pressed the sodden jeans against her thighs.

"We'll have you warm and toasty in no time." Cedric held his head high in the air and although Jenny was a dead weight in his arms, he was determined to walk the length of the beach without stopping, without dropping her. "You owe me a pint in the Black Beetle. I'll have you there for 3pm no problem."

Cedric felt lightness in his heart which was new. He felt a smile spreading across his face. He didn't feel the cold, only a soft warm flame in his belly as Jenny pulled him tighter. Then his body quivered and his heart sank as she whispered, "What will Peter say? He will never believe what happened."

The sand under foot felt softer now under Cedric's heavy black boots. He kept looking straight ahead and tried to keep part of his attention on the feel of Jenny in his arms. He blotted out any memory of Peter looking at Jenny, listening to her telling her story. Instead he concentrated on the softness of the curves of her thighs, the tug of her arms around his neck.

"Peter mightn't be there tonight. He sometimes has rugby practice."

•••

While Cedric helped Jenny out of the taxi parked near Portstewart's Golf Club, Tom cycled towards Downpatrick. Since Rose had been born, he made the journey to Castle Ward each year to give thanks for the year gone by and to think about the year ahead. He loved hearing the squawks of the ducks on the Lough and the high pitched screams of seagulls overhead. Making this annual pilgrimage to Castle Ward allowed him to nestle into the rhythm of the lapping waves, feel the touch of the breeze on his face, smelling the sodden earth and tasting the harmony of being at one with nature.

He turned left at the roundabout a mile from Downpatrick town centre and cycled the remaining seven miles along a fairly flat road towards the estate. There was an hour of sunlight left before he would need to return home. He arrived at the main entrance beside Ballycutter Lodge, dismounted his bike to walk along the path, frozen solid with patches of black ice. It was difficult to hold onto the bike handles as he slipped walking downhill past Castle Ward House, further down past Old Castle Ward, heading for the old Boat House on the edge of Strangford Lough. He walked along the edge of the road where the frozen grass crunched under his boots. The sun sparkled on the snow on the path in front of him like stars exploding in micro bursts of glitter. Slipping again on the ice, he took a few faster steps, with his woollen gloves gripping firmly to the handlebars. His bicycle clip bit into his right calf. He stopped, rested the bike against the grey stone wall, bending over to pull his woollen socks into a more comfortable position, adjusting the bike clip, his eyes watering with the cold. He coughed deeply, the phlegm tasting a little bit bloody on the back of his tongue. He felt slightly feverish as he coughed a second time. This time the cough rattled around his heart, straining muscles at the back of his throat which seemed to almost close over. He grasped hold of the handlebars again and pushed the bike past the Farmyard, past the Clock House, turning onto the narrow path leading to the Boat House.

The trees were empty of leaves, reaching into the blue sky with fine dendrites making their connection with an infinite universe, sending messages and information into eternity. A blackbird swooped over the frozen grass, back glistening in the golden light of the winter sun. He finally reached the Boat House on the edge of the Lough, leant the bike against the green wooden door and opened the rucksack to remove a bag of twigs. He scattered them on the ground. He struck a match and with the help of two firelighters the twigs crackled into life. Tom watched a heron lift heavily into the air and swing into a low flight towards the Deer Park. A small plume of blue smoke rose like incense into the blue sky, swirling into tangerine tinged clouds. He prayed.

Firstly he prayed for Rose and Lily that they would be safe and happy. Then he then prayed, as he always did, for his ancestors. It seemed easy in Castle Ward to hear them calling him. Listening to the silence on the shore, Tom heard them calling from the depths of Strangford Lough. Their voices were at times gentle, soft, faint and apologetic – not at all demanding. It would have been very easy to miss what they were saying as he tended the fire, throwing twigs onto the orange embers. They were whispering to him in the blue pine scented smoke twisting into the air. Tom stood beside the fire, staring over the Lough's turquoise shimmer, watching a boat bob close by. It was when his thoughts stopped and he listened in the silence and stillness that he felt connected to everyone who had ever walked a path on this earth ahead of him. He was at one with them. That was when Tom felt that he was really praying – when all the words dropped away.

What did break that sense of peace was a sense of discomfort in his gut. Tom felt suddenly strangely uncomfortable. A kind of anxiety gripped him, tightening into a knot in his stomach. He had a premonition, an inkling, an intuition that something extraordinarily dreadful was about to happen. It was as though his body reached feelers out into the space beyond him. His body knew – not his head – what was happening and what was about to happen. He knew that if he stayed in his head he would feel safe – but to do what he had to do he need to be in tune with his body. He breathed deeply and felt fear arising in his throat, stirring in his stomach, circling in his heart which thumped erratically. His heart then fluttered as though trying to escape his rib cage, pounding against his ribs the way a bird in a cage panics as the cat circles it.

He looked to his right where the wall of clouds stretched out not only in front but also to his right, rolling into the distance towards Downpatrick. He knelt on the ground and breathing deeply he leant forward and carefully placed a handful of twigs into the crackling smoke. The damp twigs threw a larger billowing cloud into the sky. He shivered and the coughing returned as he buttoned up his tweed jacket and tucked his scarf into his v necked jumper. Clasping his hands together he stared at the jumping flames, not noticing that the sun was setting and that the moon was cutting its way through the velvet darkness. A robin settled onto the handlebar of his bike, cocking its head to one side, looking at him inquisitively. It then hopped onto the stony path, stopping at his rucksack, jumping deftly onto his left strap and stared with Tom into the orange and cadmium yellow flames.

"Don't let it happen." Tom prayed, watching the flames collapse into the fire's final embers, burning a small hole into the thawing circle of earth. He looked at his watch. He was going to be late home. Lily and Rose would be worried. It was six o'clock.

• • •

At five o'clock in the evening of the 6th January, the Feast of the Epiphany, Margaret laid the table for dinner – cod poached in milk, boiled potatoes with peas and a pot of tea. Danny knocked at the front door. Dennis, Margaret's oldest boy aged fourteen, opened the door. Danny, Sean and two women pushed Dennis against the wall, forcing their way inside. Danny and Sean watched Margaret finishing pouring white parsley sauce over the cod in a Pyrex serving dish. Margaret swung around, saw the guns and screamed. Danny lunged at Margaret, dragged her away from the serving dish which fell onto the floor, the milk splashing onto her legs and the dish shattering into tiny jigsaw pieces. She was pulled from the kitchen into the sitting room. Thomas and Dennis grabbed hold of both her hands and screamed, "Don't let them take you Mummy. Don't go." One of the women put a gag into Margaret's mouth although Margaret hadn't said a word. Dennis tried to pull the gag out of his mother's mouth, "Leave her alone. Leave her alone. Get out of here. Don't hurt her. She hasn't done anything."

Margaret's small frail body now started to shake uncontrollably. The woman who gagged her, spat into her face. "Soldier lover!"

Margaret felt the spit on her face as Danny pulled her hands behind her back, to allow Sean to bind them together with thick twisted cord. The two men then marched her into the hallway. The front door was open. Margaret stumbled down the garden path, past the oak tree towards a waiting green Vauxhall Viva. Ciaran was inside the car. Danny opened the back door and pushed Margaret inside, bending her head with his hand and nudging her over on the seat with his thighs.

Ciaran drove towards Downpatrick. He parked in a lay-by half a mile from Ballycutter Lodge. Frances got out first and took Margaret's arm, this time gently, helping her from the car. He removed the gag from her mouth. She took three deep breaths as though tasting the air for the first time. The coldness made her cough. Sean and Ciaran walked ahead through the gateway. There was no-one in the Lodge. Danny turned right walking along a path through the small woodland. Margaret staggered beside him, her hands still tied behind her back, shivering in her thick brown woollen tights, her swing purple woollen skirt catching in the thorn bushes along the path. Danny kept pulling her on, ignoring the fact that her skirt was getting plucked around the hem.

Margaret was wearing the brown Pringle cashmere turtle neck jumper which Dennis had saved up for as her Christmas present. She felt its softness against her neck. She struggled to stay on her feet as her flat black leather shoes slipped on the ice at the edge of the Lough. She went over on her ankle. The temperatures were now barely above freezing as she listened to the gentle squish of the waves, feeling the spray touch her face, her lips tasting its saltiness. She noticed the ivy creeping around the trunk of the lime trees reaching high into the darkening sky. She saw the evening star appear in the sky as Danny guided Margaret to the small frozen lake where the slithered moon shone on the frozen surface. She compulsively took another three gasps of cold air, seeing for the first time a tree sticking out of the water like a petrified swan.

Danny and Sean took a few steps towards the lake. She heard them muttering to one another. Were they changing their minds? She heard a heavy tread and crunch of boots against the frozen pebbles. She glanced again at the petrified swan, with its wing half open. She was aware that her breathing was becoming deeper. She felt the cold air enter her nostrils, her chest expanded, her stomach pushed against the elasticised waist of her skirt. She felt a trace of warm air at the tip of her nose. She took another cold breath of air, hearing Ciaran move closer. Margaret turned around and stared at the Lough and twinkling stars over Ciaran's shoulders, hearing him take several deep breaths. She heard again the tread of Ciaran's footsteps on the frozen grass. Ciaran walked towards her, a knife in his right hand, his beard jewelled with droplets of water from the spray of the Lough. He looked directly into Margaret's eyes.

"I don't want to die." Margaret whispered quietly. "I would like to be brave, but I'm not. I'm afraid. I'm terrified. I don't want to die. Do you know what it feels like to be scared out of your mind?"

"This is a war. You shouldn't have done what you did. You know the consequences. You helped the enemy. This has to be a lesson to others." Ciaran replied.

"Don't you want to see your own children grow up? I want to see my children grow up, get married. I want to see my grandchildren."

"You interfered with a military operation."

"I helped a man who was dying. How will it help Ireland to leave five children without a mother?"

"You brought this on yourself. You are a traitor to Ireland.

Why didn't you think about your children before you helped the enemy?"

"Do you have children?"

"I do. I am fighting for them, for the future of the children of Ireland."

Ciaran, held her wrists as the knife sawed slowly through the rope.

Margaret looked down at her hands now hanging by her side, mottled blue with the cold. She felt the cold air moving again through her body. Her feet were freezing as the melting snow seeped into her shoes.

Ciaran passed the knife to Sean who had taken a few steps closer. Sean handed him a pistol.

Margaret straightened her back and rubbed her eyes with the back of her hand for the last time. "Will you do something for me? Tell my children that I love them. Tell them to be kind to each other and to take care of each other. Tell them to be gentle and to forgive you. Tell them that I will look over them and love them always. I'll never leave them. Will you do that for me?" Margaret asked, looking deeply into Ciaran's brown eyes. She then looked beyond Ciaran towards the Lough, where the moon hung low on the horizon with a silvery halo and a mist skidded across its surface. She brought her hands together, bowed and turned to face the petrified swan in the frozen lake as the cold metal of Ciaran's pistol touched the nape of her neck.

"May God forgive you." Margaret whispered. "You call yourself a Christian? It's easy to kill an unarmed woman isn't it soldier?" Margaret's voice was low yet confident.

"It's war. You follow orders." Ciaran's voice for the first time trembled.

Margaret questioned again. "Whose orders? Isn't it you who gives the orders around North Belfast?"

Ciaran pressed the pistol deeper into Margaret's neck. "Shut up. Save your words for your bloody prayers."

•••

Tom had packed his rucksack when he heard footsteps to his left. He saw the black outline of Margaret, Danny, Ciaran and Sean walking two by two along the path passing Potter's Cottage. He saw Margaret stumble, and being caught by Danny before falling on the ground. He watched Danny and Sean talking together, while Margaret stood alone and Ciaran took a few steps towards her. The moonlight glistened on the barrel of the pistol in Ciaran's hand.

Tom dropped the rucksack on the grass and ran towards Margaret. Ciaran swung round and pointed the gun at the approaching stumbling shape while Danny and Sean remained motionless beside him. Ciaran pulled the trigger. A loud crack of gunfire rang across the Lough. Tom fell to the ground. A second shot followed. Margaret collapsed face first into the frozen lake, the ice cracked open and the dark water below swallowed her.

From the ground, Tom saw Ciaran, Danny and Sean run towards Potter's Cottage. He tried to move into a sitting position. A stabbing pain shot down his right arm. He could see a hole from the bullet in his overcoat. He unbuttoned the coat. There was a hole in his green woollen jumper but no blood. The bullet had deflected off the medal of Our Lady of Mount Carmel. Tom fingered the medal. It was slightly dented and his chest was bruised, but the skin on his chest hadn't been broken. He staggered to his feet and walked quickly towards the side of the lake. Margaret's body had surfaced and was bobbing face down in the water with arms are outstretched. Tom jumped into the icy water. He only needed to swim a few feet to reach Margaret. He pulled first on her woollen skirt and then was able to grab her shoulders, turning onto his back, swimming, kicking his feet into the air, Margaret now on top of him. As he reached the edge of the lake, he pulled Margaret onto the grass. Margaret's eyes were open. She stared at him, a steady unblinking stare, and blood trickling from the corner of her mouth. He felt for a pulse. Nothing. He took a deep breath and breathed into her bleeding mouth, pumping her chest with his hands one on top of the other. Tom stared into Margaret's eyes for a minute before closing them gently with the tips of his fingers.

•••

"Can you give me a description of the men involved?" A policeman asked Tom in Holywood Barracks.

"Sorry. It was dark. I saw a gun and a woman. It all happened very quickly."

"There were three men?"

"Yes. One had a gun. He pointed the gun at the woman. When he heard me, he swung around. I took him by surprise. He shot at me first and then he shot the woman."

"What were you doing in Castle Ward?"

"Trying to find peace and quiet." Tom held his head in his hands. "Is it alright if I go now?"

"If you remember anything else – ring this number. It's confidential." The policeman passed a piece of paper to Tom. "You can speak with Sammy if you feel easier."

"How do you know about Sammy?" Tom folded the paper and placed it in his trouser pocket.

"It's a small world. It's hellish at times, but small."

chapter 8

Friday 7th January 1972

" I'd love to know who that fuckin' bastard was who nearly messed things up." Danny rolled a cigarette, licking the paper before sticking it, saying,

"How the hell did you miss him?"

"Don't know. I aimed straight at him."

"Let's hope that you do a better job than that this afternoon."

"Have you got the machine gun?"

"It's in the car."

"The tripod?"

"Yes. Let's go."

• • •

Rose opened the gate and as she pushed the key into the front door lock she noticed an unfamiliar shape behind the lacy curtain. A hand moved towards the snib and the door slowly opened. Rose glimpsed dark brown eyes staring at her from inside a green balaclava.

"Get inside now."

Rose's heart beat quickly as she hoisted her schoolbag onto her left shoulder and walked slowly along the hallway. On her left the parlour door was open. She saw two men also wearing balaclavas assembling a machine gun onto a tripod. The metal slithered, slid and clicked into place. Danny and Sean glanced quickly at her and continued.

"Upstairs. Your aunt is in the attic." Ciaran instructed.

Rose ran up the first set of carpeted stairs. She walked quickly past Lily and Tom's bedroom.

"Upstairs. The attic." Ciaran repeated behind her.

She slowly climbed the second set of uncarpeted stairs to the back attic. She opened the bedroom door. Lily was sitting on the bed. She jumped to her feet as Rose ran towards her and threw her arms around her.

"Oh my God, Rose. I'm so glad to see you."

Ciaran was watching from the door. "Stay here until it's over. Tom has fifteen minutes to get home. After that we're going ahead whether he is here or not."

"Please don't." Lily moved towards Ciaran. "Don't do it."

Ciaran closed the door heavily. His boots clunked noisily as he descended the first flight of stairs, fading to more muffled tones as he reached the first floor landing.

"They arrived half an hour ago." Lily sighed deeply. "I shouldn't have opened the door."

"You couldn't have known who was there." Rose took off her blazer and hung it over the back of the chair.

"I could have asked who it was."

"They could have told you a lie and you would have opened it anyway."

"There must be something we can do."

"What?"

"I could pretend to have a heart attack," suggested Lily.

"If you go downstairs they might shoot you. They're going to be nervous and trigger happy. You heard them say that they'll do it in fifteen minutes."

Rose dragged the chair from beside the bed over to the skylight window and climbed onto it. She could see into the back yard. The back yard door leading into the entry was open.

"They've set it up to escape through the back door into the entry."

"Is that Tom now?" Lily asked, hearing new footsteps on the stairs.

"What's happening?" Tom's question could be heard in the attic.

"It is Tom." Lily held Rose's hand and squeezed it tightly.

"What's he saying?" Rose whispered.

Ciaran mumbled something in reply which Rose couldn't hear.

Heavy footsteps climbed the last set of stairs.

Ciaran threw open the attic bedroom door. Tom stepped inside.

"I think I'm having a heart attack." Lily threw herself onto the lino floor and started breathing heavily, clutching at her chest.

"Get an ambulance. You don't want another death on your hands." Lily whispered hyperventilating. She stuck her tongue out and shook her head from side to side. "Aaagh. This hurts." She clasped her right fist against her breast. Tom dropped on his knees beside her.

"Are you OK, Lily? Speak to me."

"Would you stop fuckin' about? None of you move from here." Ciaran said firmly, slamming the door closed.

The room was silent as they strained to listen to what was happening. In the distance, they heard the unmistakable although faint sound of a Saracen tank rumbling at its slow familiar pace up the Crumlin Road. Lily and Tom sat on the bed, Rose on the chair, and Lily started praying the Rosary.

"Our Father who art in Heaven ..." Tom and Rose joined in, "Hallowed be thy name. Thy kingdom come. Thy will be done on earth as it is in Heaven."

The sound of the Saracen tank was louder now. It was only a few doors away, then one door away.

"Holy Mary, full of grace, the Lord is with thee; blessed art thou among women, and blessed is the fruit of thy womb, Jesus."

As the Saracen drew parallel with the house Lily, Tom and Rose stopped praying. The thick silence ruptured by heavy machine gun fire, smashing glass, single deliberate return fire ...poom...poom...poom. There was a second blast of machine gunfire and a loud piercing scream from a girl filling the room, hanging in the air before it too disappeared into silence.

It is hard to say how long it was before Tom, Lily and Rose opened the door and made their way downstairs. All sense of time disappeared. Tom made the first move, drawing himself wearily to a standing position from the bed, running his hand slowly up and down Lily's back, patting Rose on the head before opening the door and descending the stairs. Reaching the parlour, he could see that the gunmen had gone with the machine gun and tripod. The net wire on the windows was blasted with large holes. Glass was shattered on the carpet, together with twenty spent cartridges. He joined Lily and Rose in the hallway and opened the front door. On the other side of garden wall there was a large pool of blood and long strip of blood-soaked white cotton wool. There was no-one around – no body, no ambulance, no soldiers, no police. Everyone had gone, vanished, disappeared. How long had they been upstairs after the shooting?

Mr Langley, who had been watching from behind the curtain, opened the door.

"Are you alright?"

"Yes, but someone has been hit. We heard a scream. Who was it?"

"Clara McCann. She's dead. She got caught up in the crossfire." Mr Langley pointed up the road. "She turned the corner from Brompton Park onto the Crumlin Road and walked straight into it. She didn't stand a chance."

"She was in the class above me at school." Rose whispered.

"She was Ciaran's eldest girl." Mr Langley shook his head. "Just on her way back home after buying a loaf of bread."

The police arrived ten minutes later, pulling up outside the front door in a grey jeep.

"We need to take a statement."

"Let's talk in the kitchen. Would you like a cup of tea?"

The two policemen sat on the battered green sofa in the parlour. One pulled out a small notebook and ballpoint pen and started taking notes.

"Did you see their faces?"

"No. They were wearing balaclavas."

"Did you recognise any voices?"

"No." Lily replied. Tom was silent. He crossed his legs and scratched the back of his head.

As they talked over tea, Rose couldn't forget Clara's scream. It kept repeating in her head. A scream rolling on and on and when it was about to end, Rose imagined it starting over again. She didn't hear what the policemen were saying. She didn't see them place the empty mugs of tea and the untouched plate of biscuits on the small table, straighten their caps and leave the room.

"It mustn't ever happen again." Rose said as they sat together again on the sofa, later that evening, sipping tea.

"Maybe I could have tried to talk them out of it." Lily whispered again. "I was with them for more than half an hour on my own. I tried but I could have done better."

Tom put his arm around Lily's shoulders. "You know Lily, I think it was Ciaran McCann who took the house over today. He also killed Margaret last night in Castleward. I wasn't sure but today I recognised his voice."

"God Almighty. Are you going to tell the Police?"

"I don't know. Look what they did to Margaret Mulvenna. They would stick a bullet in your head or Rose's without even thinking about it."

"Tom, we have to do the right thing – don't we?"

Tom held his head in his hands, staring at the emerald green carpet. Lily saw his shoulders heave. Tears rolled along the inside of his glasses gathering into a pool before cascading over the gold edge rim and seeped gently into the carpet. "For God's sake, Lily, how do you know what's the right thing to do. If I had only told the police about my suspicions that it was Ciaran who killed Margaret last night, Clara might still be alive. If I tell them now you and Rose could both be killed. It's not what happens to me that matters but it's what could happen to you both."

Lily squeezed Tom's shoulder. "Let's sleep on it."

That night Rose lay in bed, her heart thumping, placing her fingers in her ears in an effort to blot out the noise from the cursing and stoning, the blast of the rubber bullets, the single sniper shots and machine gun fire as the riot intensifies. That night she couldn't find the space between the shots, or listen to the contour of the noise. All she could hear were the sharp punches of rubber bullets into the air, the piercing narrow replies of arrow like rifle fire, the shattering of glass, the swishing of petrol bombs. Her throat closed over. She struggled to breathe.

Her stomach felt as though she had swallowed a ball of fire. She was conscious of the breath entering her nostrils, fine and smooth, but there was not enough oxygen. She panicked, opening her mouth and gulping at the air. Her heart alternately fluttered and thumped against her breast bone like a butterfly in a jar.

In the darkness she felt a presence, a shadowy essence, as though someone was looking at her, standing over her, watching her. She turned her head on the pillow to look. She could make out the faint outline of a bookcase, a table with a statue of Our Lady, on the wall a picture of the Sacred Heart and beside the table a small white wicker chair. There wasn't anyone in the room. She sensed – didn't see – an invisible outline which seemed to be of a man, bending over, watching her. Then she sensed him in the bed beside her. He pulled back the sheets back slowly on her left and slipped gently into the bed beside her. As he rested his head on the pillow, her heart beat slowed down, her breathing became more regular, and she felt waves of peace flow over her.

When she did fall asleep, she had a dream. She dreamt that she was looking into space, into a deep blackness into which emerged a huge planet. It was dark blue and studded with jewels of different shapes, sizes and vibrant colours – orange, crimson, emerald green, violet. It sparkled radiantly, spinning slowly in a velvety blackness. It drew closer and closer and was embraced and then absorbed into Rose – nothing existed except the glittering planet revolving gently within Rose's darkness.

When Rose awakened it seemed as though for a few seconds everything had reversed and she was now the planet, swirling within the darkness of her bedroom. She was a deliciously peaceful being turned and turning, shining in the dark. Rose didn't need to understand the dream. It was how the dream made her feel that mattered more. She knew that this feeling of peace and calm could fill the sense of fear she felt, alone in her bedroom listening to the cursing in the street or shuddering as yet another bomb blasted apart sending nails screaming through the air. She thought of Matt as she lay in bed and the darkness began to lighten, allowing the familiar shapes of the dressing table, the oak chair, to re-emerge. She knew what she had to do. She had to see Matt. Fear shouldn't stop her from seeing him. Fear should never stop you doing what you know is the right thing to do.

She opened the drawer beside her bed and removed Matt's letter. She crawled back into bed and read it again in the fading silvery moonlight. She placed it beneath her pillow and buried her head deep into the pillow's feathery softness. It was comforting to feel the heavy blankets on top and she turned on her tummy, stretched her arms out to both sides and pressed herself into the mattress as though she was rooting herself in the solid earth. The rioters had gone home. There was silence in the room and outside on the Crumlin Road, not a whisper. There was only the weekend to get through and then she would see Matt on Monday.

chapter 9

Saturday 8th January 1972

On Saturday 8th January Eileen woke with a sense of anticipation. It was the day of the inauguration of the art exhibition. She pulled back the floral cotton curtains in the bedroom and looked out into the dark January sky. Three sparrows chirped loudly to each other on the empty branches of the cherry tree. William slid from the pillow like a slug down the blankets. He rolled onto his right side, his head no longer visible and his snoring muffled. There were a few grunting noises before he wriggled back up onto the pillow, swung his arms to the left and heaved his body towards Eileen's side of the bed. The acrid smell of stale lager hung like a cloud over the bed. Eileen picked up the alarm clock from the bedside table as William's hand moved closer towards her. She inched towards the edge of the bed. It hadn't gone off yet. It was quarter to seven. She quietly slid from beneath the sheets, her feet touching the sheepskin carpet beside the bed. She pulled the sheets over William, shivering slightly in her pink brushed cotton pyjamas. What to wear? She opened the wardrobe door slowly without waking William and removed a hanger holding beige polyester trousers. She rummaged for an orange Pringle jumper from the shelf and extracted black boots from the floor of the wardrobe. She tiptoed to the bathroom.

Eileen looked in the mirror. She liked doing that each morning and trying to spot what had changed from the day before. Today her eyes looked slightly baggier. She leaned forward to make sure. Her eyes were definitely baggier. Not surprising, it would be her fiftieth birthday in May. Her hair was greying at the temples but still quite blonde. She hadn't resorted to the help of a dye. She couldn't make up her mind if she should go grey gracefully? She was undecided. Her skin was still light and translucent. She was little bit overweight but people told her that 'it favoured her'. Her face was plumped out and hydrated rather than shrivelled and wrinkled, which made her look much younger than forty nine. She poured the almond beige foundation onto her left hand and patted it over her face before smoothing it in. With a tissue she removed the foundation from her hairline before brushing on a salmon pink blusher over her cheeks, drawing black eyeliner along her eyelids, smudging a light green eye shadow and thickening her lashes with mascara. She caught her fine blonde hair into a ponytail. Tiptoeing back into the bedroom in the bottom drawer she found a silk scarf with exactly the right shade of orange, a hint of beige and a scattering of cornflowers. She tied it loosely around her neck. She glanced at William still lying on her side of the bed, now with his back to her. She opened a jewellery box beside the bed and removed the diamond solitaire which Cedric had given her a few days before. She placed it on the fourth finger of her right hand.

Walking downstairs to make a cup of tea, Eileen looked at the ring as her hand slid along the banister. It was dark outside with at least another hour to go before sunrise, but the light from the hallway caught the diamond and it glowed rather than glittered. As she sat alone at the kitchen table gazing at the diamond, she wondered if it was it a bit flashy to wear with the Pringle jumper and polyester trousers. Was her hand too old and wrinkly for a solitaire? Forty years of scrubbing, hand washing clothes, washing dishes, planting flowers in the garden, had left them looking decidedly more worn than her face. She removed the ring, rubbed Nivea cream into her hands and replaced it. The ring sparkled brightly under the kitchen light.

She sipped on her tea and planned the day. At nine o'clock the art exhibition would open in a small gallery in Bedford Street, not far from the City Hall. Eileen's painting 'Sunrise over Belfast' was now hanging with over two hundred and fifty exhibitors from all over Northern Ireland. Shankill Arts were exhibiting her work along with nearly twenty other art groups throughout the Province. The Belfast Mayor would be there to open the exhibition. They were going to be serving coffee, tea, biscuits and a glass of sparkling wine from nine o'clock. Eileen laughed when her art teacher told her that. Who in the name of heavens would drink wine at nine in the morning? They were expecting more than five thousand visitors. Would she sell her painting? What would she do with the money? It would be useful for Peter going to University next year. There were lots of books he would need to buy.

Eileen laid the table for breakfast. Peter would be up soon. He had rugby this morning. William and Cedric probably wouldn't waken before lunch-time. She changed the water in a vase of roses before gently closing the door and walking to the bus stop to catch the eight thirty bus for the city centre.

As she walked down the garden path the sky was brightening. Three crows flapped against each other in silence overhead. The wind growled around the empty branches of the lime trees in the neighbour's garden. A wind chime placed in the cherry tree in the garden tinkled, first gently and then louder. The wind dropped. The chime was silent. As Eileen stepped onto the bus for town, she failed to see Mr McCabe struggle with the lock on the garden gate, pull his cap over his eyes, wrap his scarf tightly around his neck and walk briskly to the front door of 18, Elmwood Terrace.

Peter opened the door, still in his pyjamas, rubbing his eyes. "You're early. You nearly bumped into Mum."

"I saw her leaving. I discreetly stayed out of sight. She seems a charming woman. Have you spoken to her yet?"

Peter whispered, as they walked into the kitchen, "Not yet. I have a two part plan. She gets told after part one." He pulled out a chair for Mr McCabe. "What will we say to explain why you are here, if Dad or Cedric come down?"

"Don't worry. Leave it to me. Your father doesn't frighten me. I'm used to dealing with bullying types." Mr McCabe put his elbows on the table and leaned towards Peter. "Let me update you. I have spoken to that friend I told you about in Portstewart. He has agreed that Tom, Lily and Rose can stay with him in a safe house for a while until we tell the police and stop the killings, if that helps. It's immediately available. It a beautiful house down by the sea – a few yards from the golf course. They will be safe there. We need to speak to Rose and her family as soon as possible."

"Did you see the news last night?" Peter asked in a low voice.

Mr McCabe shook his head. "I've given up watching the news."

"The IRA took Rose, Tom and Lily hostage. They shot from the house and there was a girl killed."

"Rose?" Mr McCabe pushed the chair back.

"No. It wasn't Rose. They said that it was the daughter of Ciaran McCann. She walked into the cross-fire."

"It's out of control. We are spiralling into greater insanity. It's even more urgent that we talk to Rose." Mr McCabe held his two hands together and allowed Peter to continue.

"I will talk to Rose. That's part one of the plan. Part two is that after talking to Rose I will talk to Mum about William and Cedric. She is the only person I know who can persuade them to stop the killing."

"When are you planning talk to Rose? Tell me exactly when. You can't do this alone and it needs to happen now. The police can be here in fifteen minutes. William and Cedric can be safely behind bars by lunch-time today." Mr McCabe's fingers pressed into his hands creating four small indentations as though his skin were made of putty.

"You don't understand, Mr McCabe." Peter rubbed his face. "They can still have Rose killed from behind bars. We have to make sure she is safe. I will talk to her next Wednesday. Afterwards I will talk to Mum." Peter looked anxiously over Mr McCabe's shoulder towards the door.

"Why wait until next Wednesday? Why not tonight? Every minute counts in a situation like this. Wednesday is a long way off." Mr McCabe spoke in a calm soft voice but there was no mistaking his sense of urgency.

"Cedric has met someone. He was talking about her last night. She's a student nurse and she starts back to her nursing next Wednesday. He won't do anything before Wednesday. I know from the way he was talking to William. Next Wednesday he will drive Jenny down to Lurgan. That has to be the best time to see Rose. There is no chance that he will go to Ardoyne. It's perfect timing."

"But if he is going to be so taken up with Jenny between now and Wednesday, it would seem to me dear boy that you can act now not later." Mr McCabe's cheeks were slightly rosy but his voice was even more gentle and tender.

Peter glanced again at the kitchen door. "Don't you see that I have to be certain that he isn't around? I don't know what he is doing between now and next Wednesday but I do know for certain what he is doing on Wednesday. That's when I can visit Rose and know that he won't turn up."

"Your logic eludes me. If Cedric is going to be with Jenny between now and next Wednesday – why would he suddenly turn up?"

Mr McCabe stroked Bouncer who had jumped onto his knee and who was curling around and settling down with a continuous purr.

"I don't trust him, you see. He might follow me if I go to see her before Wednesday. I know the way his mind works. He would like me to look over my shoulder and see him standing where I am not expecting him. He's not in a killing frame of mind when he is with Jenny. But he still could stop me talking to Rose. So I have to act normally in order not to give anything away. I will only have one chance to get it right and so … Sssssh. Footsteps. Someone's coming."

Peter pushed back the chair, jumped to his feet and reached for the radio sitting on the shelf as William stuck his head around kitchen door. A long strand of black hair had fallen down the right side of his head reaching his shoulder. His eyes were bloodshot; his face had a jaundiced look to it. He gave a forced smile.

"Who's this then?" He pointed at Mr McCabe before limping into the kitchen in his pyjamas, heading towards the table.

Mr McCabe stretched out a hand, continuing to stroke Bouncer with the second hand. "Pleased to meet you Mr

McManus, I've heard much about you. I'm Donald McCabe, Peter's history and English teacher."

Peter turned the radio on behind William's back and shook his head vigorously to discourage Mr McCabe from saying more.

William looked over his shoulder at Peter. "What is he doing here on a Saturday morning? It seems an odd time to get help with your history?" William slithered uncomfortably in his seat. "Where is Eileen?"

"She caught the bus into town for the art exhibition. You remember the exhibition, don't you?" Peter looked at his father in disbelief.

"Of course I do. Didn't I bring the painting over to the exhibition for her yesterday?"

Peter filled a kettle with fresh water. "Mr McCabe offered to drive me to rugby training this morning. We're collecting Bryan and Simon on the way. Is that not right Mr McCabe?"

William sniffed, wiping his nose with the back of his hand. He looked at Mr McCabe and then Peter, pointing to the teapot. "Be Mother – pour me a cup of tea."

Peter filled William's cup and passed him the milk jug, looking nervously at Mr McCabe. "Sorry, Mr McCabe, I forgot to ask. Would you like a cup of tea?"

"Delighted, my boy, and then we had better be off. You need to get dressed I imagine or we will be late."

"How's history going then?" William heaped a spoonful of raspberry jam onto the wheaten bread and pulled a long strand of dark hair across his bald spot.

"If he doesn't get an 'A' I'll be very surprised." Mr McCabe removed his cap and sat it on the table. "More than surprised – I would be astounded. He has the brains for Oxford. He has a great head on his shoulders. You should encourage him."

"I'm always pushing him. Has he not told you that?"

"Indeed. Indeed. This is a marvellous cup of tea Peter, if I may say so. You can tell a lot about someone in the way they make a pot of tea and even more in the way they pour it. You excel on both counts."

"It doesn't take much to impress you." William munched on wheaten bread. "I'll have Bouncer over here if you don't mind." William's chair screeched on the tiled floor as he pushed it back and then shuffled towards Mr McCabe, lifting Bouncer from his lap. Bouncer didn't resist. His legs floppy, his large tiger head turned towards the floor, eyes opened and tail curled between his legs.

• • •

At nine thirty, Lily ran up the steps leading into the gallery. Her fake leopard skin coat flapped in the breeze. Following the takeover of the house and Clara's murder, she had no desire to go to the opening of the exhibition but Tom and Rose had insisted.

"You have to go. It's important to keep a shred of normality alive," Tom said as he helped her on with her coat. "Rose and I will be along later."

Outside the gallery scrolls announcing 'Exhibition Inauguration' quivered in gold. As Lily reached the top step she almost collided with Eileen as they simultaneously made for the revolving door.

"Sorry, after you." Lily waved for Eileen to go first.

"Thank you. Are you exhibiting?" Eileen asked, removing her silk scarf as she entered the hallway. Nobody else would be here so early."

"Yes", I'm here with Ardoyne Arts, what about you?"

"I'm with the Shankill Group."

The Art Teachers from Ardoyne and the Shankill stood side by side at the registration table.

"Good to see you, Lily. Who have you brought with you?"

Lily turned to Eileen. "I never asked your name?"

"Eileen McManus." Eileen shook the Art Teacher's hand.

"Good to see you. Vincent Thomas."

The Shankill Art Teacher smiled and shook Lily's hand.

"Peter McGrath." Lily shook it firmly.

"A pleasure."

"The pleasure is mine. The cloakroom is down the corridor on the left hand side. There are refreshments in the room off to the right."

"Would you like us to bring you something?" Lily asked.

"We'll be with you in a few minutes when reinforcements arrive. Help yourselves."

"Let's get our coats off and have a look at the paintings." Lily had already pulled one arm out of her coat.

As Eileen hung her coat on the cloak rack, Lily noticed the diamond ring.

"What a beautiful ring."

Eileen held her hand out.

"Cedric gave it to me a few days ago. It's the first time I've worn it."

"It's unusual."

The light from the chandeliers sparkled on the heart shaped stone. It flickered with roses, blues, greens and silver.

"Would you like to try it?" Eileen asked.

"I would love to. I work in a jewellery shop not far from the City Hall. Diamonds are my passion – after my husband of course." Lily laughed as Eileen slipped the ring from her finger.

Lily brought the ring close to her face. The heart shaped solitaire was mounted in gold with four small fingers holding it in place and a small 'V' at the bottom of the heart. The facets were edged like Mont Blanc – sharp, precise, angled to capture light and colour. The edges pulled Lily into a kaleidoscope, of light and colour. The heart shaped solitaire's straight lined facets appear to move and wave like poppy petals swaying in a gentle spring breeze.

"It's hypnotic." She handed it back to Eileen. "It's engraved." Lily pointed to the inside of band of gold.

"I know. It's not brand new." Eileen slipped the ring back on her finger. "It says 'P to M with love'. I would like to know who owned it before." Eileen twisted the ring to allow the diamond to sit in the middle of her finger.

"It's stunning." Lily held her hands together as though in prayer. "It will have a story behind it for sure. Talking of stories, let's go and see your painting and you can tell me all about it."

Lily studied Eileen's 'Sunrise over Belfast', painted with acrylics. It showed Belfast Lough with a long sweep of turquoise sea, tangerine clouds and dark mountains waiting to awaken.

Eileen explained, "My favourite time of day is early morning. I like to waken at five most mornings although today I was late. It was nearly seven before I got up. Normally I make a cup of tea and go out into the garden and listen. Sometimes, the birds haven't even wakened. There is a cherry tree in the middle of the lawn. In the morning, I stand beneath the cherry tree and listen to the wind moving through the branches. In those early moments the day seems full of hope."

"I love it." Lily stepped back to see it from a distance. "It has lots of atmosphere. It captures a sense of peace."

"Where is your painting?" Eileen asked.

"It's over there." Lily pointed to the back of the room.

They stood beside it,

"Careful. It still might be wet."

Lily's painting had thick oil brush strokes, a swirling moon and a tree in the foreground with dark branches reaching into the sky. There were orange and yellow splashes of light sprinkled over the foothills of Cave Hill.

"It's vibrant. How do you like working with oils?" Eileen asked. "I've never had the courage to try them."

"The first time I used oils, I fell in love with them." Lily explained. "I mixed the colours and – Prussian blue with cadmium yellow and a dash of white and I couldn't believe how transparent the turquoise was and I found myself mixing and mixing without even thinking. Vincent said he had never seen anything like it. I must have painted with oils in a previous life! I couldn't go back to acrylics. But you do need patience. I normally have three or four paintings which I work on at the same time. I love capturing the contrast between the sea and the mountains. The mountains are solid, unmoving, strong and dependable. The sea is always changing, moving, never totally still even on a calm day. In the evening, when the sun is setting, there's a special silence which falls over the land, a silence you don't get on the Crumlin Road, but I know it's there somewhere in the Lough and in the mountains. Painting this reminds me of that silence and beauty, of the strength and stability of the mountain and power of the sea."

"I really like it." Eileen moved closer to look at the brush strokes. "You're not shy about using lots of paint."

"I keep painting over the top of what I've already done. Then eventually I decide that it is time to stop. I quite like the idea that there are several layers of painting beneath the one you see. It's a bit like the earth's strata – you have several layers lying on top of one another made up by natural forces. I am a natural force of a certain kind." Lily laughed. "What you see on the surface isn't everything. The technique works well for creating texture in the sea." Lily pointed to the rough choppy brush strokes close to the setting sun.

"There's lots of spontaneity in it and no fear." Eileen took a few steps back and turned to Lily with a smile.

"How do you fancy a cup of coffee before we see more?"

Over coffee they discovered that they were both born in 1923 and were married during the Second World War, Eileen in 1940 and Lily in 1941.

"We married young." Lily commented. "We were babies. You mentioned that you have a son who gave you the ring. Do you only have the one?"

"No. I've two boys. Cedric is my thirty year old. I still think of him as a boy. There is a big gap between him and my second boy, Peter. Peter is seventeen. He's still at school, at Orangefield. He's more quiet and serious. The age gap means they're not really as close as I would like them to be but I suppose that's to be expected. Peter goes out with his brother and father from time to time, but mostly he stays at home playing his records and the guitar in his bedroom. He loves music. He wants to be a doctor. What about you, Lily, do you have children?"

"No. We would have loved children but it didn't work out that way. I always imagined a family of five. There's nothing I like more than everyone sitting around the table laughing and crying at life over a never empty pot of tea. However, that wasn't to be."

Eileen pushed her coffee cup to one side. "I'm sorry, I didn't mean to pry." She reached for Lily's hand.

Lily squeezed her hand. "No, it's not you. It's not even about not having children. It's only the memory of what happened next. We did have two children, not our own – Maria and Rose. Maria died and now there's only Rose."

"Did you adopt, then?" Eileen asked sipping her coffee.

"No. Tom's sister Catherine died shortly after giving birth to Maria. We then took care of Maria." Lily took another sip of coffee and patted the corner of her mouth with a handkerchief. "Catherine was murdered actually."

Eileen opened her mouth to say something but nothing came out.

Lily looked at her and nodded. "I know. You don't need to say anything."

"I'm sorry." Eileen whispered.

"It's OK. It was a long time ago. The pain eventually gets buried somewhere within you. I can talk about it now. Catherine was murdered and then sixteen years later, Maria died after giving birth to Rose."

Eileen nodded. "That makes Rose very special for you."

Lily's eyes lit up. "Yes indeed. She is our beautiful Rose."

Lily spotted a waiter dispensing champagne.

"Do you feel naughty? Like a small glass of wine?"

Eileen hesitated. "I don't normally, but why not." She reached for a glass.

"Does your husband like art? Will he come along to the exhibition?"

"I don't think it's his scene." Eileen shook her head.

Peter and Vincent walked towards them laughing out loud. "I'm not sure if this is allowed Lily." Vincent pointed to the glass. "But then again it might be the best idea of the day." He walked over to the waiter and returned with two glasses.

"They've sold the first two paintings. Not either of yours yet but I think they'll both fly off the walls. Cheers to both of you and congratulations for making the exhibition." Peter raised a glass.

"Cheers everyone."

Vincent leant forward and clinked a glass against Eileen's.

"You're welcome to join us for our art classes. They're very informal. We hold them on a Saturday morning."

"Thank you." Eileen took a sip of champagne. It was cold and the second it touched her lips, she felt her whole body warming with tingling energy. Even her toes buzzed the way they do when you've been walking on snow and come home and pull your boots off and sink your feet into a basin of hot soapy water. She looked into Vincent's eyes which were smiling back at her. "That might be possible. Peter has rugby on Saturdays and I am sure that I could come from time to time."

Lily opened her handbag and pulled out a small address book with a pink and blue flowery cover. She passed it to Eileen. "Write your telephone number down and I'll give you a ring and explain where it is. Maybe you know it – on the Crumlin Road – the Ardoyne Hall? Does that ring a bell?"

Eileen shook her head. "No. But I'll find it I'm sure."

Peter dabbed his moustache with a napkin and added,

"Lily you're also very welcome to come to our Centre. We also hold classes on Saturdays – maybe you can find time?"

"Not a bad idea. Why not?" Lily slipped the address book back into her handbag.

She heard footsteps approaching and glanced up to see Tom, Rose, Sammy and Anne approaching. "I don't believe it – and Sammy and Anne. We haven't seen them in months. Let's get you introduced. You'll love them."

"Look who we found on the number 57 bus." Tom placed an arm around Sammy's shoulder, "The Philosopher and his lovely wife."

While Rose, Lily, Eileen and Anne were looking at the paintings in the third exhibition room, Tom took the opportunity to stay at the back with Sammy, at first catching up on what was happening in Glenbryn. Then when he was sure that the others were out of earshot, he pulled Sammy by the arm and whispered, "Sammy, I need to talk to you. It's about Margaret Mulvenna and Clara McCann. I know who killed them. I need some advice from you about what to do about it, if you don't mind."

•••

Mr McCabe pulled gently to a halt on the corner of Bedford Street near the City Hall. The city was quiet with people tired from the Christmas festivities and New Year sales. It was cold with a strong wind whistling from the north. A few seagulls glided overhead into a sky which was steely grey and threatening snow.

"Are you sure you want me to leave you here? It's quite a walk for you." Mr McCabe leant his head to one side like a pigeon curious about what it was seeing. He even pecked at his hand with his mouth catching the edge of his leather gloves to remove them and shake Peter's hand.

"I'm sure. I'll find somewhere for a coffee and then I'll go and see Mum at the exhibition." Peter shook Mr McCabe's hand. It was warm. He found himself holding it with both hands.

"Thank you for everything. You didn't need to get involved in my mess."

Mr McCabe patted him on the shoulder. "You have my telephone number. Ring me without hesitation – at any time – if there are any developments. If I don't hear from you, we will see each other on Monday at school. Whatever happens, stay calm."

Peter watched the white MG slide smoothly into the distance when he felt a tug on his arm. He turned to see Jenny standing beside him, her pink pom-pom hat pulled down over her forehead. She pulled up the collar of a navy blue coat and stared in an amused way into his eyes. He remembered that Jenny always seemed slightly amused at whatever was happening.

"I didn't expect to see you here." Jenny dug her hands into her pockets.

"Me neither." Peter laughed. "What are you up to?" Peter hadn't noticed before quite how attractive Jenny was. Somehow the dim lighting of the Black Beetle didn't do her the same justice as seeing her in the fresh air. The freezing breeze brought a healthy rosy glow to Jenny's face. Her fringe curled over the pink pom-pom and today she had her hair in two plaits which made her look even younger.

"Do you fancy a coffee?" Jenny pointed to the small tea shop they were standing outside which had enormous scones in the window and even more enormous doorstep sandwiches spilling salad, mayonnaise and tomatoes onto circular plates. It was the same place that Peter had been to a few days earlier with Mr McCabe.

"The German biscuits here come highly recommended." Peter opened the door of the café and made a sweep with his arm letting Jenny pass.

"I've had my twenty minutes of sunshine. They say you need twenty minutes a day to make Vitamin D, it protects against heart disease." Jenny pulled off her woollen mittens. "Well not quite sunshine but it's as good as it gets in January. It's a little safer than earlier this week on Portstewart beach."

"I never thought of Portstewart Beach being dangerous." Peter raised an eyebrow.

"Did Cedric not tell you what happened?"

"No." Peter leaned forward.

"I slipped into the Atlantic with the help of a hurricane force gale." Over coffee and scones Jenny told Peter about how Cedric had rescued her. As she was telling the story and pulling the cherries out of her scone to eat separately, Peter was surprised to find that he was strangely relaxed in Jenny's company, as though he had known her a long time and didn't need to make an effort to talk. He tried to work out if Jenny was doing anything special to make him feel so good but the only observation which came to mind was that Jenny was natural. She was bubbly, spontaneous, funny and easy to be with. Before long her stories turned to nursing.

"Strange things happen with people when you're nursing them. But you'll most likely find that with medicine too. You are able to go deep in relationship very quickly. It's as though all the superficialities of small talk drop away and you connect with the person's soul. You know who they are in a way which words would never explain. You hold all these faces in your heart. It's like they're a part of you. Not only their faces." Jenny winced. "I remember when I started on the surgical ward, this young guy was admitted who had fallen from his motorbike onto a metal railing. I had to get him ready for theatre and he was totally conscious. As we talked, I pulled off his shirt to see that he was pierced like a sausage from front to back. He looked at his stomach and I looked at his back and then we looked at one another and somehow it felt as though I was him. I knew what he was feeling, I knew what he was thinking. For a moment the two of us become one. I suppose it must be like that falling in love."

Peter sipped on his coffee. "It sounds as though you can fall in love with anyone then."

Jenny pulled her pom-pom hat off and threw it onto the empty chair beside them and shook her plaits as though to loosen them with her hands. "I think so, if you just keep looking at anyone closely enough. That's what you do when you're a nurse. You keep looking. I remember an old man who was dying from cancer. He didn't want to die. It felt as though death was happening too quickly for him. He was all tubed up because he couldn't eat any solid food. I shaved him because even then when you're only two days away from death, there's still a sense of dignity in a human being. I shaved all around the tubing going up his nose and over to his ears. I did it as best I could but there were some difficult bits and I went very slowly around those. He kept looking into my eyes. His eyes were deep blue. He kept looking and he didn't say anything. I felt all of the sadness of his life coming to an end and how he didn't want it to happen so fast. The cancer was eating him up. It wouldn't slow down for him. But when I looked into his eyes and we kept looking at each other – falling into each other – it felt as though time slowed down if only for a few moments. I can never forget him. It's like that with everyone. They become a part of you and even their pain doesn't matter because somehow you become so big, that you can hold it all."

"Do you think you will keep seeing Cedric when you return to nursing on Wednesday?"

Jenny dropped her eyes and patted the red and white gingham tablecloth as though she was playing a small drum. She raised her eyes and looked again at Peter.

"Cedric is different. He is the first person that I've looked at and have not felt that I know him. Whatever is inside him is scary. For the first time with him, compared to everyone else I have met, I don't know if I am big enough to hold who he is. I don't know if I want to. But you must think that's an awful thing to say – after all he is your brother."

Peter took a teaspoon and scooped out the milky foam holding to the edges of the coffee cup. He raised his eyes to Jenny. "He may be my brother but I think you know him better than I do."

Jenny looked back at Peter. His face was so relaxed, so calm, she felt an overwhelming desire to tell him what had happened at Portstewart. Not falling into the sea, nor Cedric rescuing her but what happened when they got back to the taxi. How Cedric had put her gently on the pavement and opened the taxi passenger seat door. He opened the boot of the car and brought her a red, yellow and black tartan woollen rug. He helped to remove her duffle coat and then as he wrapped the rug around her shoulders, he moved closer as though sniffing her face for something the way a dog might sniff for a buried bone. He stopped at her lips which were still salty and he pressed his lips against hers.

She didn't know why she did it but she found herself responding to his kiss, even though her stomach churned as though she had eaten something revolting like half cooked onions or the slimy fat on a piece of beef floating in an insipid Irish stew. Her heart and stomach wanted to push him away but something stopped her, even though she knew that what she was doing was wrong, very wrong and that the consequences of not acting now could be serious.

She looked again at Peter and swallowed and said nothing. Her heart burnt with the desire to explain. It thumped wildly. Maybe it was a different kind of a mistake compared to going out with Cedric the one that she was going to make now – but it was definitely a mistake not to be honest with Peter. She ached to hold his hand and tell him everything, yet she stayed still and silent. If she told Peter, she knew that would take away this nausea which churned within. She wanted to tell him that last night when Cedric drove her home after work, he had kissed her again. She wanted to explain to him that she felt drugged, incapable of resisting whatever he would do. She had let him continue kissing and caressing her even though her soul quivered in her body and pleaded for her do something. Instead of pushing Cedric away, she had gone even limper in his arms. Then she had noticed a curious sensation that her body responded to his kiss, not her soul. Her body had enjoyed it, some primal urge that was not hers had stirred within her, urging her to procreate. An instinct stronger than the gentle beat of her heart, or the quivering whisper of her soul.

Jenny sighed and rolled a cherry around the plate with her fingers. Why couldn't she tell Peter? If she said nothing, maybe after Wednesday when she returned to nursing, she could imagine that what had happened with Cedric had never happened at all. She could return to a state of innocence. She would never need to see him again – never need to think about him again.

"That's the first time that I've seen you look serious." Peter stared into Jenny's green eyes which looked back at him with a glazed stare. "Are you OK?" He waved a hand in front of her eyes.

Jenny laughed and pointed to the counter. "More coffee please with lots of milk and one of those German biscuits you recommended."

"What a good idea." Peter removed his parka jacket and hung it on the back of the wooden chair. "We're not in any rush."

"No we're definitely not." Jenny removed her navy coat and also hung it on the back of her chair.

chapter 10

Sunday 9th January 1972

Eileen sang 'I'll Tell Me Ma' as she cleaned the kitchen after Sunday lunch. She looked forward to sitting down and watching Bing Crosby, Bob Hope and Dorothy Lamour a little later in 'The Road to Bali'. Now she was enjoying the peace and quiet with time to tidy up and to think back to yesterday. Peter was out with his rugby friends taking a train to Bangor. Cedric was having lunch with Jenny somewhere along the Coast Road. He had mentioned going to Carrickfergus. She was glad about Jenny appearing into his life. She could already see the seeds of change sprouting in him. He seemed less sour, opinionated, and arrogant. He normally scowled over breakfast and argued with Peter but this morning, he had wrapped a present for Jenny and ignored Peter rather than start his normal aggressive banter. It was good to see him thinking of someone else, turning away from self-obsession to explore Jenny's world.

William had taken Bouncer to the Vet for an emergency check-up – even though Eileen thought that Bouncer had recovered remarkably well from his ordeal on Wednesday. William, however, insisted that he was a little quiet and was demonstrating new concerning behaviours. It was true that he had untypically peed on the sitting room carpet rather than miaowing to be allowed outside. He had started to howl, long soulful cries which he repeated all night for no apparent reason. He had taken to hiding behind the sofa when anyone walked into the sitting room. Eileen didn't consider any of these behaviours to warrant the category of 'emergency' and the need for a visit to the vet on a Sunday. But she thought, if it put William's mind at ease, better to do that than a visit to the Black Beetle.

Eileen remembered with a thrill of pleasure that she and Lily had both sold their paintings. Not only had red dots being placed on both paintings to indicate that they were not available for other hopeful buyers, but they had even received the money – twenty five pounds each. She would have been quite happy to give the painting away for free but it was exciting to sell your first painting. It felt like a stranger looking into her soul, liking what he saw and paying her to reveal a little more. There were many more paintings where that one had come from and so she felt the future full of possibilities for her art.

"I think Van Gogh only sold one painting in his life. He sold it to his brother who bought it because he knew he had no money." She joked with Peter the night before.

"You've a whole lot more upstairs in the attic. You may get them out and shake the dust off them, apart from that scary one which I would leave well hidden." Peter shook a finger to emphasise "Don't do it."

"Which is the scary one?" Eileen laughed.

"The one with the woman holding the baby with that Devil looking over her shoulder. She looks terrified about what is going to happen next."

"That's a painting of me holding Cedric when he was a baby." Eileen playfully hit Peter over the head.

"Who or what is the big black shadow on your right then?" Peter raised his hands in the air.

"I painted what I painted and only afterwards saw this shadowy shape. It could be a 'Protector'. I wouldn't deliberately paint someone evil." Eileen went quiet.

"I'm telling you, it looks as though you are protecting the baby from the Evil One." Peter yawned.

"Stop it." Eileen twiddled with her hair, sighed deeply and sipped on her tea.

After cleaning the kitchen floor and washing the windows first with vinegar in water and then polishing them with Saturday's newspaper, Eileen enthusiastically took a step ladder up to the attic, to select paintings which might sell in the next exhibition. She thought about how she could paint over the ones she didn't like and create a more textured looked like Lily did with her oils.

She found the step ladder and struggled up the stairs to the landing. Leaning the step ladder against the flowery iris wallpaper, she slowly climbed the wooden rungs until it was possible with both hands to slip the cover to one side allowing access into the attic. She took another two steps up the ladder and then grabbed the two wooden handles which Cedric had made on the inside to allow for easier access to the storage space. She pulled herself forward, awkwardly raised one knee and with another pull she was there, kneeling for the first time in the attic. The only people who had been in the attic before were William and Cedric. Peter and Eileen were ordered to leave any items which they wanted to be stored in the attic, on the landing. William and Cedric made sure that they were removed from sight within hours.

Eileen reached forward to lean on the arm of a sofa which sat on the right, covered with a white cotton cloth. It was difficult to see what else was there. She should have brought a torch. She looked down at her legs – her tights had two long ladders stretching from the knee and whizzing down as she looked towards the toes of her shoes. She should have worn trousers. It was starting to look like an ill thought out plan. She remembered that Cedric and William used to shout at each other to stand on the wooden beams and not the plaster floor. She edged forward, sliding her right foot along a beam followed by her left foot. She could make out the shape of the paintings at the very back of the roof space but it was clear that there was no way that she could lift them all the way back and balance on the beams. There was even less likelihood that she could get them down the step ladder. She would need Cedric or William to help.

However, now that she had made the effort to get into the attic, she was curious to investigate what was there. There was an old dresser to her left. Didn't that belong to William's mother? Even with the little light which entered from the landing, she could see dark golden wood, streaked and circled with black. There were four drawers each with amazingly bright brass handles. Who had been polishing them? Didn't William or Cedric have better ways to spend an afternoon than polishing the handles of a dresser which never would see the light of day?

It was easy enough to step across the beams, holding onto the roof to balance, it was like sliding across rocks in a river to navigate a gentle current swirling around her feet. It took only four steps before she could rest her hands on top of the dresser. She opened the first drawer holding both handles. It stuck on the runners. So she had to close it again and then even more gently tug it open. She looked in. It was empty. She put her hand in and felt towards the back of the drawer. There was nothing. She slid it shut and this time it didn't catch and clunked close.

She moved to the second drawer which opened easily. Almost too easily, or perhaps she had pulled too strongly. It nearly landed on the floor but she caught it before it left the runners and eased it slightly back. She coughed, noticing that her movements were stirring up a small cloud of dust. She bent to peer into the drawer. It wasn't empty. There was a rectangular shape about a foot long by six inches side and six inches deep, covered with a white silk cloth. It was definitely silk. Eileen felt the smoothness of it slip between her fingers. Was it one of her scarves? She pulled it free from what she could now see was a wooden box. It was one of her scarves – a white silk headscarf which she thought she had lost years ago. Her mother had bought it for her in the year before she died. Eileen had looked for it when she moved after marrying William and couldn't find it anywhere. She brought it to her nose and smelt it, pressing it against her face. Her mother's hands had touched it. She had never washed it – she couldn't wash it – it would have been like washing away the scent of her mother. She breathed in and tried to remember the smell of her mother. Maybe she only imagined it but it seemed as though she could smell a floral sweetness, a musky warmth that was her mother's smell.

Still holding the scarf in her hand, she lifted the wooden box. It had two brass hinges on the back which were also shining and a brass metal clasp on the front which she pulled to one side, opening the box. By now her eyes were accustomed to the darkness and so she could see the contents. They were rings – what seemed to be mostly wedding rings tagged with a fine piece of white cotton thread and a small white label the size of a fingernail. She lifted one out – it had the name – only a first name in tiny letters – James, September 1941. Eileen counted the rings on the palm of her hand. There were fourteen in total – three with dates in the 1940s, four with dates in the 1950s, four in the 1960s and one in the 1970s – January 1972 with the name Michael.

Eileen dropped Michael's ring back into the box with the

others. They made a dull thud rather than a tinkle as they hit the red velvet lining the bottom of the box. She slammed it shut, fastened the catch, wrapped the box up again in the white silk scarf and pushed the drawer closed with unnecessary force. She turned back towards the light which was shining upwards from the landing. The way back seemed more difficult. She felt dizzy and wobbled on the beams. Her hands no longer felt that the roof above supported her, neither did the beams below. She knew that she must not, at all costs fall. She needed to avoid putting her foot through the ceiling.

Eileen descended the wooden ladder, gripping the sides and then sat on the landing floor with her head in her hands. A few miles away in Ardoyne, Ciaran McCann sat beside the open coffin of Clara who was to be buried the next day. Party-like noise drifted in from the kitchen where Conor and Frances were eating ham sandwiches made for them by their Aunt Mary. Ciaran listened to Conor laughing. There was a sense of reality in Conor's laughter – an awareness that life would continue without Clara. This gave him a sense of comfort. There was still hope for Conor and Frances. Maybe there would be more hope for them if he was out of the way. Not for the first time in his life Ciaran wished that he had never been born. He felt like a pinball hurtling through life with someone else pulling the lever, bashing him against unpredictable circumstances, hurtling him to meet unexpected situations, propelled at speed into the next encounter.

He heard a guitar playing 'Down by the Sally Gardens' accompanied by a tin whistle. He smiled to himself – it had to be Sean and Danny. There was more laughter from Conor. He heard voices joining in singing the words. It could have been Clara's birthday party rather than her wake. The notes from the tin whistle silenced his thoughts for a few seconds. He looked again at Clara in her coffin. She wore her school uniform – a white blouse, blue and yellow striped tie, a pleated navy skirt and a blazer. He pulled his chair closer to the coffin and touched her forehead. It was cold, hard, and waxy like an uncooked potato. Her eyes were closed and the undertaker had rubbed tan make up on her face and light pink lipstick on her lips. Clara had never worn make up before. Her face wasn't recognisable to him – not in the way he wanted it to be. He could see her features – her straight nose, fine arched eyebrows, long blonde eyelashes, lips all of these were in the correct places like pieces of a jigsaw puzzle. There was a small rogue black hair growing above her upper lip which he remembered wanting to remove with tweezers but didn't say to Clara. It should have been her mother Dana who would say that kind of thing but she had left them five years ago. She had run away with a married policeman and was living somewhere in the North of England. In that moment the one small black hair symbolised everything that was Clara – everything that made her different. For Ciaran the reality of Clara had become this one small curved black hair above her lip, only half an inch long.

He had wanted Clara to look beautiful in death so that people would say that she looked as if she had gone straight to Heaven. She didn't look beautiful in the coffin. Her blonde hair fell back on the white satin pillow like a wig. Her face was pulled in like an old woman sucking in her cheeks. Her lips were held in a straight line never to curve again into a smile. The bullet wound was lower down in her chest hidden by the white blouse. He imagined how it would be, probably the size of a coin in the centre of her chest with bruising all around it in circles like Saturn.

He could hear Frances now singing to Sean on the guitar in the room next door. She sang a 'Song for Ireland':

"*Living on your western shore, saw summer sunsets, asked*

for more. I stood by your Atlantic Sea and sang a song for Ireland."

Her voice was strong and gentle. It filled the room with an ephemeral softness. Frances's voice strengthened with the last verse.

"Dreaming in the night
I saw a land where no man had to fight,
Walking in your dawn,
I saw you crying in the morning light,
Lying where the falcons fly,
They twist and turn all in your air blue sky.
I stood by your Atlantic Sea and sang a song for Ireland."

Ciaran held Clara's hand and wished that he would hear three loud knocks at the front door and that he would be bundled into a Saracen tank, pretending to struggle on the way down the hallway but really wanting to be taken away, interned in H-Block as so as he wouldn't have to look into the eyes of Conor and Frances when they discovered who killed their sister. They would discover eventually.

As Frances finished her song, there were three gentle knocks at the front door. Ciaran dropped Clara's hand, wondering if he had created this reality. Like King Midas whose touch turned everything to gold, maybe Ciaran had made this real by thinking about it. The army had come for him and he was ready to go. His time had come. The kids would be better off without him. He had filled their heads with a pack of lies. His sister Mary had more sense. She would make sure that they were well taken care of.

Sean tapped gently on the door of the bedroom. "Tom Martin has called to have a few words with you. Are you OK to see him?"

chapter 11

Monday 10th January 1972

Rose didn't go to school on Monday. The night before, Tom had asked if she wanted to go to Clara's funeral and she shook her head. He looked at her in a mystified way but didn't pursue the matter. He removed his glasses and wiped them clean with his cotton handkerchief in the way he did when he was confused. Lily held Rose's face within her hands and gave her a big kiss.

"You don't need to go to the funeral. Try to get a good night's sleep."

Rose held Lily tight, squeezing her, pressing her cheek against Lily's soft skin. She kissed her before letting her go and giving Tom a kiss, feeling his stubble against her lips. Kissing Tom on the cheek before going to bed always sent ripples of pleasure throughout her body – small jolts of liquid electricity. Kissing Lily's soft cheek was different. With Lily the kiss brought stillness and peace – like contact with a fragile petal whose beauty was empty of fear, empty of the churning and stirring of emotion.

"Good night. Sleep well." Rose closed the sitting room door

behind her and heard Tom and Lily murmuring together as she climbed the stairs to the bedroom. There were no rioters outside on the Crumlin Road. The house was filled with an uncommon quiet which gave Rose the feeling that the very walls were watching her as she climbed the stairs – watching her with love.

Next morning, before getting out of bed, she opened the bedside table drawer and searched for the white envelope from Matt. She read his letter once more. She pulled on her navy skirt, white blouse, blue and yellow striped tie, pullover, and blazer with the Convent of Mercy emblem – a cross with the word 'Mercy' and the motto, 'Truth in our hearts'. She read the letter twice. She didn't say a word to Tom and Lily over breakfast about what she was going to do. Instead she put on her navy raincoat, closed the front door as normal and walked quickly up the road to a different bus stop where she joined the queue waiting for the number 57 bus headed for the City Centre.

Rose paid the fare and climbed the spiral staircase to sit upstairs in the smoking area. The bus trundled down the Crumlin Road, stopping to pick up three passengers outside 463. Mr Langley got on board. Rose's heart beat faster. Mr Langley liked to smoke a pipe – maybe he would come upstairs. She quickly left her seat at the front of the bus and moved to the back where there was still an empty seat beside a woman wearing thick glasses. She need not have worried as Mr Langley stayed downstairs. She took a deep breath and settled comfortably back in the seat, feeling even more relaxed when Mr Langley got off the bus at Carlisle Circus. She watched him light his pipe and limp slowly towards the Antrim Road. She took off her school tie, hid it in the satchel and buttoned up her raincoat to hide the badge on her blazer. She took out Matt's letter.

"Dear Rose,

On Saturday 8th January, Eddie, Max and I have been commissioned for a special surveillance assignment which might give us a chance to meet – if not to meet alone, at least to we will be able to talk. At last! There are so many questions I have to ask you and so many things to tell you. More than anything, I want to be with you, to be able to look into your eyes for more than a few seconds without worrying that someone will see us. I want to hold your hand – to feel its softness which I can only now imagine. Believe me, I do imagine it constantly. Don't mention to anyone where I am. Promise – not even to Tom or to Lily. I've drawn a map of the house we will be staying in for four days from Saturday. Try to come on Monday 10th January. I know we will be inside that day. Get in by the downstairs window to the left of the front door. I'll leave it open. If you can't make it – don't worry – I'm back on school patrol again on Wednesday 12th. I have been told that at long last I will have leave in April. I'll go back home to Cardiff. Maybe you will find a way to visit my family in Rhiwbina? We can see if Tom and Lily would be OK with that. I don't see why not. I hope that you Tom, Lily and of course Lucky keep safe. See you Monday if not Wednesday. Love always from Matt xx".

Rose studied Matt's map, tracing the direction with her finger along Matt's line dotted from the cemetery to the house marked with an 'X'.

When the bus arrived at Belfast City Centre, Rose caught a second bus heading for the Falls Road and got off fifteen minutes later at the cemetery. Rain started to fall heavily, bouncing off the pavement and the tops of the armoured police jeeps parked in a line outside the main cemetery entrance. Two women huddled under umbrellas and then linked arms and staggered through the metal gates. They pushed their way through the middle of a large crowd of mostly black coated mourners, flowing together like a slick of tar towards the graveside of Mickey Hannah. Mickey had been shot dead for not stopping at checkpoint Charlie a few days earlier. Rose skirted the edge of more than a hundred mourners. She glimpsed an oak coffin draped in an Irish tricolour carried by four men wearing balaclavas, camouflage green uniforms, black berets and gloves. It hadn't been Rose's intention to stumble across Mickey's funeral but now that she was here, she stopped as ropes were laid on the ground, the coffin placed on top of the ropes and the four men lowered the coffin into the hole.

Two IRA men standing beside the grave raised rifles into the air and shots crackled into the grey clouds. A helicopter rumbled into sight, dropping lower to take photographs of the mourners. The coffin inched its way into the hollow blackness. A handful of mud thrown on top clunked in a muffled way against the wood. A small girl wearing an emerald green woollen coat, yellow gloves and a black knitted bobble hat walked to the graveside. She looked around, reached a hand towards a thin faced woman approaching in a long black coat. The two stood side by side as the girl threw a worn brown teddy into the grave.

A pink rose toppled from the mother's hand into the darkness. The priest opened the prayer book. The wind turned three pages which he turned back. "Dust thou art and onto dust thy shalt return." His words were carried away on a stronger gust of wind, disappearing into the heavy rhythm of the helicopter propellers slicing at the low clouds.

The crowd started to quietly disperse, with Rose following those who turned left along a pathway leading out of the cemetery into a side street. The rain continued to lash against two yellow and black spotted umbrellas which turned inside out ahead of Rose who tucked her hair into her coat and turned up her collar. With rain streaming down her face and then trickling down the back of her neck she pulled on a pair of navy woollen gloves. Then, lifting her head, she spotted the derelict building on wasteland about one hundred yards ahead on the right. She pulled Matt's map from her pocket. It had to be that house. She stopped for a moment to check.

Two men ahead of her, hands in pockets, bumped into each other from time to time as they stumbled across the muddy rough ground. They were heading in the direction of the derelict buildings. Rose watched a gust of wind lift two tiles from one of the houses. The tiles flew through the air like clay pigeons before crashing and splintering onto the ground. The upstairs windows were surprisingly clean. The house which Matt had marked with an 'X' was the middle house. She saw the splintered front door and the slightly opened downstairs window banging gently in the breeze.

A woman with a spotty umbrella, wearing a red woollen coat, unexpectedly turned around and looked at Rose. She then looked in the direction in which Rose was looking. Rose crumpled Matt's letter in her pocket. As Rose looked at the house, the sky suddenly cleared and the sun burst through the clouds sending a broad ray of sunshine into the upstairs window of the middle house. It glinted for a moment on what seemed to be a silvery object. The woman in red looked at the glinting light and then grabbed the arm of her friend and she shrieked at the three men walking ahead of them, "Have a look over there. They're in there."

The helicopter dropped height as if the soldiers on board had heard the woman's words. The wind from the rotor blades swayed the tips of the tall Poplar trees edging the wasteland. Someone shouted.

"Get them."

Taking his hands out of his pockets, a short legged man with broad shoulders ran towards the house, closely followed by others, women stumbling in high heels, tripping over the broken bricks and splashing through the pools of rainwater. One man threw a brick into the air, breaking the upstairs bedroom window. Rose started to sprint, overtaking the women and catching up with the men. She reached the front door as the first man threw himself against it with his right shoulder. It didn't move.

One of the women shouted. "The downstairs window is open. You can get in the window."

Two men turned left, towards the window. The smaller of the two joined his hands together and bowed towards his friend who stepped onto the joined hands and hoisted himself through the window.

Rose, clutching her satchel, reached the front door as the two men now both inside opened the door. She threw the satchel to the ground. A man wearing jeans and a loose white tea shirt which fluttered against his torso like a flag screamed.

"The fucking cowardly bastards are upstairs hiding. Get reinforcements." He looked at Rose who ignored him; instead she squeezed into the hallway, past a smaller man with a varicosed face, while two women staggered in high heels across the wasteland into a nearby road and turned left out of sight into a terraced street. The helicopter hovered directly overhead, dropping closer to the roof of the terraced building.

Rose panted as she climbed the stairs behind three men and two women. Rivulets of sweat ran down the sides of her face. She felt as though she was going to vomit. The men reached the bedroom on the left ahead of her. Her hands visibly shook as she approached the open bedroom door. The short legged man, flanked by his two friends, walked briskly towards the three soldiers, cornering them in the way a sheep dog presses sheep into a pen. The short haired men were unmistakably British soldiers in plain clothes with short hair, one wearing a tweed jacket and jeans, the other two wearing blue anoraks and jeans. Rose watched Matt in his tweed jacket scan his pistol across the three men.

He hadn't yet seen Rose.

"If you come any closer I'll fire. I don't want to do that. If we leave the building now no-one gets hurt."

"Who the fuck do you think you are giving orders you fuckin' British bastard. You drop your fuckin' gun on the floor."

Max and Edward pulled pistols from inside their anoraks as Matt shot a warning shot into the ceiling. "We're not joking. We leave here and no-one will be killed."

Two more men pushed past Rose into the bedroom, rugby tackling Max and Edward to the ground. Matt watched for a second, his hand raised in the air, the pistol pointed again at the ceiling. A third man lunged forward, grabbed Matt's arm and within seconds the three soldiers were disarmed, lying face down on the floor, hands clasped on top of their heads. Two men strode into the bedroom with pick axes and rifles. There were now seven men and two women in the room with Rose, Matt, Edward and Max.

Matt, Edward and Max lay on the floor. One of the women offered the men perched on the windowsill a packet of cigarettes. A path was opened in the room to allow the two newcomers to walk slowly towards the soldiers. They stood on either side of Matt and Max with Edward in the middle. The room was now silent. There was a pause as one man with a squint in his eye lifted the butt of his rifle and brought it down on top of Matt as though he was tenderising a steak. The second man thumped Max with edge of the pick axe which he then threw on the carpeted floor. There was another pause, unbroken silence filling the room, mingling with an almost tangible aroma of anger and fear akin to the acidity and bitterness of CS gas. Before the silence shattered, Rose hurtled across the room, finding a gap between the two men and throwing herself on top of Matt. She placed her head on top of his head, her arms around his shoulders, each of her legs on top of his legs.

"Oh my God Rose. Get out of here. " Matt whispered. "I was insane asking you to come here."

"Don't be stupid." Rose squeezed his hand.

Rose lifted her head into the air like a snake as she coiled her lower body around Matt. "Stop. For God's sake stop."

The man with the rifle indicated with a nod to his friend to retrieve the pick axe. Edward had turned on the floor to lie on his back. The head of the pick axe caught him mid stomach. He squealed, curling onto his side.

"Get out of the way or you're dead meat. There's no place for a soldier lover here."

"Don't you see what you are doing?" Rose slid off Matt onto the floor.

Edward clutched his stomach and started to sob. Max lay unconscious, unmoving on the floor. Matt moved his hand to try to touch Rose's hand. Rose rolled onto her knees and from there got shakily to her feet and approached the man closest to her who was holding the butt of the rifle with his two hands. He was only in his twenties with thick dark hair falling over his eyes. Rose lowered her voice and almost whispered in a trembling stutter, "How does a country which wins freedom in blood know what freedom means?"

"Who do you think you are, you bitch? Mother fuckin' Theresa? This is a war. These are soldiers. Didn't we only an hour ago bury Mickey Hannah? Did they give him a chance when they opened fire on him? He wasn't even bloody armed. It's easy to be brave when you have a gun in your hand. Let's see how brave they are now. They knew when they joined the British army what it's all about. Get her to fuck out of here. I don't care what you do with her. We'll finish here what needs to be done."

Rose knelt on the ground and took hold of Edward and Matt's hands. Edward squeezed Rose's hand in silence. Matt rubbed the inside of the palm of her hand with his thumb.

"If you want to kill them, kill me first."

"Be careful what you ask for – you know they say that you might just get what you ask for."

One of the men pushed forward to pull Rose's hand free from Edward's grip. Edward struggled to hold on, pulling himself into a sitting position as Rose was dragged away by her feet. Matt let her hand go gently. A man raised a rifle, pointing it first at Rose and then slowly moved it to the left and aimed it at Edward. He pulled the trigger. Edward's head thudded against the bedroom carpet. His navy blue anorak, dripped with crimson blood onto the ground. Matt crawled onto his knees and attempted to stop the bleeding from Edward's neck. A rifle butt lifted high into the air, swung like a golf club, clacking Matt directly on the left ear. Matt fell heavily on his right shoulder. Max wriggled on the ground towards Matt.

"Aaaaaaaagggghhhh!" A woman jumped from the windowsill, lifted the pick axe from where it had been thrown on the ground and hit Max across the back with the blunt side.

Rose closed her eyes as she was grabbed by the collar of her raincoat, then lifted like a cat and pitched onto the uncarpeted landing floor outside the bedroom. She fell hitting her head on the wooden flooring. Edward's blood had mingled with hers seeping now into the unvarnished wood. A hand clutched at the roots of her hair. Her head was lifted six inches of the floor and then banged again onto the wooden floor.

"Maybe that will knock some sense into you."

Rose couldn't see what was happening now. Everything was blurred as she squinted to see who was now beside her.

"Come with us, you fucking soldier lover." A woman hissed into her ear pulling her again by hair into a sitting position. Rose didn't know how she got downstairs. She remembered her body thumping against the stairs and the banister. She had no idea how many women there were or how many hands pulling at her raincoat. One of her shoes came off and bounced downstairs, lying on its side near the open door. Three buttons burst open on her raincoat, scattering like sparklers left, right, one hitting the ceiling.

The next fully conscious moment Rose had was of stepping onto broken glass with her shoeless foot as she was dragged across the wasteland. Two women carried her by the arms. Her legs dragged behind. They let go of her arms and she fell heavily onto the frozen mud. "Walk, you bitch. We're not carrying you." A hand dragged her to her feet. She took a few steps and fell. She opened her eyes slowly and through a haze she vaguely saw two women looking at her.

"Give me a fag. We'll be here all day waiting for her." She saw a woman with peroxide hair, flared jeans, a long Afghan jacket, puffing on a Benson and Hedges cigarette. Rose struggled to her feet. The helicopter blades rattled overhead.

"That one on the corner will do." A second woman wearing high black paten stiletto shoes with a pink bow on the front and no stockings, pointed to a lamp post on the corner of the street.

Rose raised her head to see where the woman was pointing. She saw the lamp post and sighed in relief. They are going to tar and feather me; not kill me. She struggled to her feet.

As she approached the lamp post, she couldn't help herself falling again and as she fell she managed to steady herself catching hold of its thick metal trunk. It felt strangely comforting, solid and steady. She held it with two hands, breathing deeply as a dwarf sized, thick bellied woman, pulled a thick rope around Rose's waist. The peroxide woman helped her to roll it higher around Rose's chest and neck. Rose's arms were at her side. Her head fell to one side.

"Scissors," the dwarf woman demanded, taking a pair of large dress making scissors from the peroxide woman.

Rose heard the helicopter again hovering closer overhead. By turning her head only a few inches to the left, she could see it hovering closer and closer to the roof of the house. A soldier descended like an ant on a rope towards the roof.

The dwarf woman took the scissors and pulled at Rose's black hair. She caught the few strands of hair from inside her collar and began hacking at the shiny black mass as the smoke from her cigarette wafted over Rose's face. Rose felt the pointed tips of the scissors piercing her head as she watched handfuls of hair falling in clumps onto the pavement.

"The tar."

Silence as a bucket of warm tar poured over Rose's head. Rose closed her mouth and eyes, holding her breath as the tar slid down her face. She felt the edges of the plumes of the feathers smothered in tar gently slither down her face almost as a caress when two high velocity shots rang out from inside the derelict building. There followed a splattering of machinegun fire.

Rose dropped her head onto her chest as the shots faded. She moved her head slightly to the left, coughed, spitting tar into the air as the helicopter landed. She took a deep breath.

The peroxide woman shouted "Good on you boys." She spat at Rose's face. "Job done – no thanks to you bitch. The next time there will be a bullet with your name on it if you don't wise up."

Rose closed her eyes feeling the tar cooling on her head and face. Crow's feathers crawled along her neck. The crunch of the women's steps on the gravel path grew fainter. Her heart thumped. She tried to swallow but could only cough, her chest quivering, then in spasm projecting tar and feathers into the air as her shoulders shuddered and her hands mottled blue. Rose consciously took a breath. The air felt pure, cold, and clear, like the first breath of her life. Her body started to shake more than quiver. It scared her how this body, which no longer felt like her body, would react to the next second, minute, hour. She could feel the air now entering her nostrils – finding itself a small pinprick of access to her throat. She focused on this point of contact, then the movement of the air and its rhythm rather than the sense she had before of being drowned in tar. The fact that she was breathing and could find this tiny path of access to air was a lifebelt.

Rose's head hung forward, her arms tied behind her, her body roped to the lamp post. She was alone. She felt the coldness of the air congeal once again the tar around her nose. She struggled to breathe. She kept her eyes closed and heard the familiar drone of a Saracen approaching. Rain lashed against her head, sinking into the rain coat. The rain turned to sleet. Eyes closed, Rose felt a strange heat within her stomach, as though someone had lit a small fire from tinder in a rain forest.

A breeze passed over her as the rain withdrew. She was exposed kindling tinder. The flame from the tinder burst into an immense penetrating flame. She burned inside with a sweet, intense fire. Her body felt on fire. She didn't care. She was no longer aware of breathing – the burning was her breathing. In the midst of the fire within, she felt the touch of peace, a cool, smooth, round pearl of stillness forming in her stomach. It grew and spread throughout her body – with a shiny, silk, white, beauty – a stopping of time within a pearled peace.

A Saracen tank screeched up beside her. A soldier jumped from the tank, cutting the ropes. Rose slid to the ground. "Thank you."

He caught her hand. She noticed that his hand was gloveless, soft and warm.

"Did you know them?"

"Yes."

Rose could hardly breathe never mind explain how she knew Matt, Max and Edward. How they called themselves the Crouch Brothers because they spent more time on their knees than walking. Matt the tallest with dark black straight hair, blue wide eyes, a wide nose, thick lips, broad shoulders, square hands. He radiated solidity and strength. Max, at least six inches shorter than Matt, with light brown hair, green eyes, always a little bit nervous, with a slight stutter. Edward was the smallest, fine boned, frizzy blonde hair, hazel eyes with a trace of blonde eyelashes and a delicate small mouth. He had the best sense of humour of them all. He had a way of looking at you with eyes that stayed so still, unblinking, that seemed to grow larger with every second of watching. He smiled at Rose with those wide open eyes which Rose couldn't help laughing into. Her laugh was infectious and before you knew it Max was holding his stomach and Matt patted Max several times on the back, as though he was a horse who had won a first place rosette.

The first time she had seen the three of them had been only three months before, yet it seemed a long time. They were on duty for the first time on the school patrol run, guiding the girls from the Convent of Mercy as they walked down the Ballysillan Road onto the Crumlin Road into Ardoyne. They were having fun with each other and it was infectious – Rose laughed out loud and Matt turned and looked at her and winked. Rose remembered that her face blushed crimson and she looked at the pavement for at least ten minutes before she looked up again. Matt hadn't stopped looking at her. He winked again. Rose was careful that Clara and the others walking in front didn't see her smile back at him. From that day she had always walked the first stretch of the journey home at the back of the group. Matt and she learnt to communicate without words. They looked at each other the way horses do. They didn't talk, didn't tell lies, didn't cheat but saw something in each other below the surface which was real. Rose's heart pounded in her chest in anticipation of seeing Matt when the last school bell was rung each day. Sometimes, as they neared Ardoyne, Rose would give Matt a knowing look and move forward to have a few words with Clara so no-one would guess what was going on. By the time she crossed Brompton Park, onto the Crumlin Road, she rarely looked back at Matt, but looked straight ahead, more often than not finding herself singing.

"One survived." The soldier lowered his eyelids and dropped his chin onto his chest.

"Who?"

"Matt." The soldier rubbed his mouth with his glove.

His face went hazy in front of Rose. He reached forward, grabbing Rose by the elbow as she fainted. When Rose opened her eyes, she saw the soldier holding a bottle of water to her lips. She sipped, closing her eyes, listening to him.

"We need to get out of here. Emotions are running high. They will bring the snipers out." He shook his head as though he could read her thoughts. "It was never straightforward. There were too many civilians. We did our best."

Rose climbed into the Saracen tank and a soldier handed

over her abandoned schoolbag. "We found it by the front door. Matt said it was Rose's. You are Rose, aren't you?"

"Yes. I am."

"Where do you want us to take you?" The driver asked.

"To Holy Cross Church. The Woodvale Road side. "

A young eighteen year old soldier with thin lips, wide open blue eyes, holding his rifle between his legs, looked steadily at Rose as the Saracen moved along the Falls Road.

"Thanks for what you did. Matt talked about you. He was right about you."

The Saracen tank moved slowly up the Shankill Road, passing the Black Beetle, then along the Woodvale Road, to pull to a halt at the back of Holy Cross Church. Rose stared at the floor, only moving her eyes to the soldiers' boots which didn't move an inch in thirty minutes.

Before she stepped down from the Saracen, a soldier handed Rose a white cotton towel to cover her head. She turned it into a turban, took off her coat and folded it over her arm and then jumped from the back of tank. She watched for a moment as the Saracen moved slowly around the roundabout, turning onto the Crumlin Road. She quickly climbed the stone wall with its iron railing into the grounds at the back of the church. She had never been so far back in the Grove before. It was easier than she thought to push through the brambles, the lime and oak trees, to emerge close to the front door of the monastery. There was no-one round. Once she reached the familiar pathway leading towards the Crumlin Road, she ran. There wasn't anyone at the bus stop. As she opened the gate, she rested her gaze momentarily on the Saracen waiting outside the bookies, before fumbling in her pocket for her key and twisting it in the lock. She slammed the door shut behind her. The towel dropped to the floor.

"Lily. Lily. Are you home?"

She ran along the hallway opening the sitting room door.

Lily sitting on the sofa dabbed Prussian blue oil onto a canvas. She was absorbed in filling the upper left corner with gentle brush strokes creating an evening sky. She leaned forward and touched the canvas with her right hand, making circles in the paint, breathing gently as Rose threw open the door. Lily jumped to her feet, leaving the canvas quivering on its easel. The paintbrush fell from her hand. "Mother of God, what on earth happened to you?"

•••

Tom lay in bed listening to Lily's gentle breathing. The wind howled outside the window and the tarpaulin flapped agitatedly trying to free itself from the roof. He hadn't yet managed to have the slates replaced on the roof after the car bomb attack on New Year's Eve. He shivered, turning on his side to curl up beside Lily, stretching his arm across her to gently grip her shoulder. She didn't waken. He pressed his face into her back and then moved his head to the right so that he could hear Lily's heartbeat. The rhythmic thump of her heart and the occasional gurgle of liquids within her body comforted him. Yet they couldn't quite calm the anxiety which flooded his stomach, rising to his heart and attempting to surge into his head. It was a sensation of nervousness and uncertainty which gripped him – like a thirsty wasp attempting to drink water from the frothing waves of a stormy lake. Or the way a fly buzzing with friends might feel when trapped in a spider's web it watches the eyes of the spider rapidly approach.

For the first time in his life Tom felt afraid. It wasn't only in his stomach and heart that he felt afraid, but in his mind. It felt as though everything that had held him together in his head had snapped. Everything that had kept him sane had gone. Ping.

Ping. Ping. His sanity snapping like an elastic band pulled to its limit, breaking, of no use anymore. He was disintegrating, falling apart. There was no ground beneath his feet – yet he had to walk. He had to act, to do something. His body shook uncontrollably but gently, a vibrating rhythm matching Lily's heartbeat. What would happen to Rose? What should they do about Matt? If the IRA found out about Matt, Rose would be killed. It was of no comfort to know that Ciaran wouldn't kill her, not after his conversation with Tom on Sunday. But there were others who would kill Rose without a second thought. In one hour he would be expected to get up, get dressed and be good old Tom. He didn't know who that was any more.

He knew what Tom did. He cut wood. He polished it, shaped it, smoothed it and turned it into tables and chairs. He remembered the touch of the wood – the feel of it against his fingers, the warmth of it against his body as he held it close. More than anything he wanted now to have the trunk of pine or an oak tree resting in his arms. He wanted to smell the incense of branches on a fire, to hear the crackling of wood in the heat of a burning flame, to see the smoke rise again to the heavens in a cloud of blue and to soar with his spirit upward, to infinity beyond the pull of earth.

Over tea and toast Tom declared that Rose shouldn't go to school.

"We need to get your hair sorted. It has to look like you've decided to cut it short, not like you have been tarred and feathered."

Lily ruffled the hair on the top of Rose's head. "Well we have managed to remove the tar. But you are right, it needs a proper cut. I will ask Susan to come to the house and give you a decent haircut. We can trust her not to say anything."

"Please can I go to school tomorrow? I need to see Matt."

"Tom, we have to get back to normal as soon as possible. People will ask questions if Rose doesn't go back to her old routine." Lily brought a fresh pot of tea to the table and put her hand over Tom's noticing how wrinkly and old it looked, like a crumpled paper bag beside the toast. She lifted his hand and kissed it gently and sat it down on the table again.

Tom was motionless. He gazed at Lily. She was smiling at him the way you would smile at someone in a hospital bed who you knew couldn't help themselves – a tender, warm smile. She wore navy blue slacks and a long white and navy blue striped tunic with flat pumps. She had pulled her hair into a ponytail and her face was radiant. To Tom she seemed very far away although was sitting beside him. He felt he would have to shout to her to be heard and so although he whispered to Lily he thought was shouting,

"Why don't you give Rose Catherine's ring? It's her birthday on Thursday. It has been blessed by Father Anthony. "

Lily looked at Rose. "Would you like Catherine's ring? It was your mother's also."

Rose felt her eyes prickling with tears as she nodded. "Yes, thank you. On my birthday."

...

Father Anthony opened the curtains of his bedroom and watched the branches of the oak tree sway in gale force winds. It was still dark and the stars could be seen twinkling overhead. The moon was hidden behind a puffy grey cloud. It was going to be a lovely day. A thunderstorm was forecast for the afternoon. Father Anthony loved thunderstorms. As a child he had frightened his parents by dangling his legs from the second floor upstairs bedroom window to get a better view of the storm approaching their farmhouse in the country.

He watched black rolling clouds get closer as the wind picked up and announced the proximity of the storm. His parents shrieked with fear that he would either fall from the window or be struck by lightning. He had only felt exhilarated by the whole event.

Before getting dressed he sat on the bed, closed his eyes, resting his hands on his knees. He felt deeply peaceful, triggered by a sense of gratitude for life. He realised that he had felt this way for quite some time – peace and gratitude for life. With his eyes closed all he could see behind his eyelids was a peaceful blank screen. There was no internal chatter in his head and his body was empty of emotion. He realised that this was peace this absence of emotional hurly burly in his body.

As he sat opening himself up to a sense of contentment he felt his body beginning to flow like waves in the deep sea and the restful screen behind his eyelids also started to flow into waves of increasing brightness. He was aware of his breathing – deep and slow – until that too disappeared. He was flowing like a river. "Peace is flowing like a river."

Time had disappeared. When he opened his eyes and became aware of the room once more, the sun had come up and the room was lightened by the softest glow. Sparrows were chattering outside, crows turning in the air and caw-cawing. Never had he heard a more beautiful sound. He remembered the words of the Rector from many years before when they were talking about Father Anthony's crisis of faith.

"Is it emptiness or is it angst?"

He remembered the Rector laughing and then saying, "One gives birth to the other. Find out which does which and you will be more than half way there."

Father Anthony thought that he now knew. "Angst leads to emptiness."

He thought that the other half of the truth which the Rector wanted him to learn was emptiness leads to angst.

He smiled to himself. It was all OK. Angst could be purified in the emptiness of love. It could be burnt up in the flame of emptiness.

He looked through the window to find someone to share this moment with and a large black crow fluttered awkwardly onto the small windowsill. It turned its head to one side. It lifted one leg, falling off the window sill and flapping left towards the oak tree with a loud caw-caw-caw.

chapter 12

Wednesday 12th January 1972

On Wednesday at two thirty in the afternoon, William and Cedric were in the Black Beetle watching Sammy P play cards. "We'll leave you to your cards, Sammy P, but don't forget tomorrow's plan. We need you. What'll you be having?"

"Make it a double whiskey."

Sammy P slowly separated the cards into four bundles of fourteen – spades, diamonds, clubs and hearts. He shuffled them, his foot tapping on the ground, biting his lower lip, turning the first card face up – the ace of clubs – the remaining six cards he placed face down in a horizontal line. He quickly slapped another row on the table, one face up and the remaining five face down. A peat fire smoked in the corner, struggling to spark into life. Jinny was the favourite to win the two-thirty at Newbury. A cheer went up from three bobbing heads beside the TV in the corner when Jinny won. Alex limped across the bar from the toilets, slapped Sammy P on the back.

"How are you getting on, Sammy P? Are you winning?"

Sammy P looked up and stared at Alex, deck of cards in his right hand.

"I'm telling you now, I'm warning you, don't talk to me when I'm playing cards. Do you get it? Never talk to me when I'm playing cards."

Alex patted him again on the shoulder, "No harm meant, Sammy P."

"Don't speak to me. I've told you once. Now I'm telling you a second time, don't talk to me when I'm playing cards. If I have to tell you a third time, you'll be hearing from my lawyer."

Alex winked at Cedric and William, making a sign with his right hand to say that he had zipped his mouth and hobbled to the counter to order a drink.

"A pint of Harp, Billy."

William leant on the counter beside him.

"Make it a double whiskey, two pints of Harp and an orange juice. Cedric's on the juice today. He's driving Jenny back to Lurgan."

William pulled his trousers up over his small paunch and pulled his v-neck jumper down over the trousers. He limped back to the table.

In silence Alex set the two pints of Harp on the table, the orange juice in front of Cedric and the double whiskey beside Sammy P who dealt his cards. Sammy P lifted three cards, turning the third face upwards. It was a red seven. He looked carefully at the cards turned face up. His hand moved to place the seven of hearts on top of a red eight of diamonds. Alex slid onto the bench beside William and Cedric, clutching his pint of gold.

"Now you know you can't do that, Sammy P. I know you're playing on your own, but you can't cheat."

Sammy P raised his eyes to look at Alex, who smiled at him, taking a sip of his beer.

"I warned you once not to talk to me when I'm playing cards. I told you twice not to talk to me when I'm playing cards and I warned you that if you did it a third time, that I would have to get my lawyer."

Sammy P gathered all fifty two cards together, placed them into a neat pile, squashed free from the table and walked slowly to the back of the pub. Alex winked again at Cedric, or was it a nervous twitch? Three minutes passed without any sign of Sammy P. Three and a half minutes later Sammy P appeared, running towards the table wielding a black Shillealeah – a black shiny stick of oak, rubbed in butter and cured in a chimney for two months – used for settling disputes in what was called a gentlemanly manner. On reaching Alex's table he swung the Shillealeah like a golf club and cracked it into Alex's ribs. Alex threw himself onto the red tiled bar floor but Sammy P made a second connection with Alex's ribs.

"Don't talk to me when I'm playing cards! Now do you get it?"

"Right, Sammy P! Leave Alex alone and let's talk about tomorrow's plan." William patted the bench. "Sit. If we don't organise tomorrow properly you'll be getting a little bit of what you dished out to Alex, if not more. Do you get what I am saying? I think Cedric and I have the advantage of imagination over you. We're creative you know?"

Sammy P nodded, sliding onto the bench beside William and Cedric. Frank and Richard helped a groaning Alex to a quiet booth towards the back of the bar.

"What time will you have the car bomb ready?"

"Around five."

"Good. We leave here at six. That gives us plenty of time. You drive in front. We follow. Anything you don't understand?"

Sammy P shook his head. William patted him on the shoulder. He lifted what was left of Sammy P's whiskey and drank it.

"No drinking and driving Sammy P."

"I'm off to see Jenny." Cedric slid back his chair. "See you later William and see you tomorrow, Sammy P." He waved at Frank who was still tending to Alex at the back of the bar, mopping his forehead with a damp white cotton facecloth.

•••

Fifteen minutes before they arrived at the Nurse's Home in Lurgan, Jenny told Cedric that she no longer wanted to see him.

"This has something to do with Peter, hasn't it?" Silence. "What's changed?"

"We're too different. I don't want to waste your time. You will find someone else. You need to work out what your dream really is and who would be best to be in it with you. It's not me." Jenny stared straight ahead, feeling her stomach tighten and her breathing quicken. What else could she say? How could she tell him it was all a mistake right from the start?

The top of Cedric's lip was white, the black bristles even more pronounced, his lower chin glowed red. He stepped hard on the accelerator. Jenny wished that she had waited until she had arrived before telling him, had got out of the car and had Sister Maureen standing watching her at the doorway of the home.

The car jolted to a halt outside the red bricked building as Cedric stabbed on the brakes. He swung the driver's door open, walked briskly to the back of the car where he removed her case from the boot before slamming it shut.

"Can we still be friends?" Jenny whispered as he stomped away from her.

Silence. He didn't look back as she climbed the steps to the entrance. Sister Maureen appeared at the front door and gave her a hug as she heard another long screech of tyres and turning around, saw his car take the corner on the wrong side of the road.

•••

On Wednesday afternoon, in his bedroom, Peter wrote a note for Eileen.

"Back around nine this evening after rugby practice."

He folded the note in two, writing 'Mum' in capital letters and placed it behind the clock in the sitting room. He climbed the stairs to Eileen's bedroom and, walking over to the bedside table, opened the drawer. He searched for the jewellery box. He lifted out the box holding Eileen's ring, opened it and examined the heart shaped solitaire for a few seconds before pulling it free from the plastic packaging and slipping it into his pocket. He placed the empty box back into the drawer. He pulled back the curtains in the bedroom. It was a grey rainy afternoon.

Clouds moved slowly across the sky. Thunder growled in the distance. The rain fell at a steady pace, bouncing off the paving stones outside. He rummaged for his anorak in the bedroom and after finding it, closed the bedroom door as lightning crackled through the smouldering grey clouds and flashed into the mirror on the landing. He stared at himself in the reflection. He hardly recognised himself. His face seemed white and stone-like. His lips were in a straight line and blue. He listened until the last rumble of thunder died into silence. The hallway was almost in darkness as he pulled up his hood, and pushed his rugby gear into a duffel bag. He gently hoisted it onto his shoulder and jumped downstairs, two steps at a time, slamming the front door as he left. Thunder cracked louder, ripping across the sky as the rain fell heavily, yet everything it touched stayed almost still, unmoving.

The leaves from the hedgerow were steady, the empty twigs of branches on the oak tree shivering in the lightest breeze.

Peter got off the bus at Holy Cross Church below the main gates. He pulled the hood of anorak over his head. It was seven-fifteen. Mass was half way through. He turned left and walked up the driveway with his rucksack on his back. The monastery with its soft orange lights was on his right. He breathed quickly. Someone shouted on the Crumlin Road. What were they saying? He quickened his pace. In front of the monastery there was the dark shadow of a statute to Saint Paul of the Cross which marked the site of the original church. He climbed the front steps, opening the heavy oak door. Several hundred heads were bowed in prayer. A bell rang. The heads bowed again in unison. He walked slowly to the last bench which was empty and sat with his hands on his lap. Where was Rose? He started to scan the benches beginning on the right. At first he didn't recognise her. She was sitting half way down on the left hand side. What had happened to her hair? It was her wasn't it? It was in the angle of her chin as she looked right that he recognised her.

The congregation stood up to pray together. Yes, it was definitely Rose. The priest held a small white flattened piece of bread in the air, his eyes raised towards the ceiling. The altar boy rang a bell, three times. Everyone bowed again. Peter bowed his head looking at the row on front. He then knelt on the cushioned kneeler. As everyone stood up he stood and joined them in saying the 'Our Father'. An elderly man with twinkling blue eyes turned around in the bench in front and reached out a hand. "Peace be with you". Peter shook his hand. "Peace." He reached a hand to a woman muffled in a scarf, "Peace be with you."

The congregation filed from the benches, walking up the aisle towards the priest who waited for them at the altar. They knelt down. The priest said "Body of Christ" and Peter heard "Amen". He watched Rose hold her hands out and then place the communion into her mouth. She walked away from the altar; her hands joined together, her gaze on the floor. It was definitely Rose. The dark haired priest wiped the communion goblet clean, placed a white cloth on top and then a gold plate. He said the prayer after communion.

"The Son of Man came to serve, and to give his life as a ransom for many. Alleluia." He then gave a final blessing. "In the name of the Father, the Son and Holy Spirit, go in peace to love and to serve God. I would like to remind you all that there will be Confession this evening from eight o'clock until nine. Have a safe evening everyone."

Peter, breathing heavily, bowed his head as people started to leave the church. He took a deep breath of frankincense mingled with the heavy musk of extinguished candles. He looked up after a few minutes to make sure he didn't miss Rose. Marble pillars stretched up to the ceiling where they disappeared into angels and chubby babies flying through the air. Rose sat alone. The remaining congregation gradually left, genuflecting at the end of the aisle and walking silently towards the back of the church. A few gathered around a statute to light candles. Peter stood up and walked slowly to the bench where Rose was sitting. He sat beside her in silence. The church was now almost empty. Rose's eyes were closed as she sat, hands crossed on her lap. She opened her eyes, turning her head to look at him.

"Who are you?"

Peter removed his anorak hood. The rain had turned his blonde hair into dark curls. He rubbed a hand through the fringe shaking free a few heavy drops.

"Peter."

"Why are you here, Peter?"

Peter's breathing quickened. He looked into Rose's eyes. She had a fearless, open way of looking. It wasn't easy to look either at her or to look away and Peter dropped his gaze.

"I need to talk to you."

"You're soaking wet."

"Yes." Peter rubbed his dark wet jeans. "I'm sorry. I'm making a mess." He moved slightly away from Rose, wiping the wet bench with the sleeve of his anorak. He pushed his rucksack under the bench in front.

Rose leaned towards him. She reached out and laid a hand on his arm. "What is it? Tell me."

Peter looked behind to see if anyone was listening. There was only a woman in a beige duffle coat and woolly orange hat at the back of the Church lighting a candle at the statue to 'The Little Flower'. He looked again into Rose's eyes. She looked at him in a relaxed almost amused way. With her hair so short, her eyes seemed even larger, with long black eye lashes and china doll whiteness to her face.

"Your life is in danger."

"Tell me something I didn't know."

"No. I don't mean potential danger, I mean certain danger."

"What do you think the new hairstyle is all about?" Rose removed her hat and rubbed the top of her head.

"What happened?"

"It's a long story. Better you tell me what danger you are talking about?"

"There is a plan to murder you."

Rose took a deep breath, moved closer to Peter and looked him straight in the eyes.

"Who plans to murder me?"

Peter rubbed his eyes with his knuckles.

"This isn't easy to explain. My brother and father are

murderers." Peter looked up at the arched ceiling rather than face Rose's gaze. He heard her question in the softest of voices.

"Murderers?"

"Yes."

"Who have they murdered?"

"Paddy. You knew Paddy?"

"Yes." Rose felt her knees tremble. Her heart banged hard in her chest.

"Who else?"

"Michael."

"Michael McGuckin?"

"Yes."

Rose felt her head scrambling. It was hard to think, to speak. In the pit of her stomach she felt a churning and nausea. She took a deep breath and turned in the bench to look at Peter.

"Would you say that in Court?"

"Yes, I will when the time is right."

"Why not now? There's no time like the present. Let's ring the police."

"Don't be naïve." Peter felt his heart thumping. This wasn't going the way he had planned. He shifted awkwardly on the bench.

"What do you mean?" Rose's voice flowed over him like toffee over a Halloween apple.

"If it was that easy, I would have gone to the police myself rather than come here. You don't know them. They saw you walking home from school on last Tuesday and you're on their list."

"Their list?"

"They randomly pick targets who go on a list."

"Why me?"

"There's no reason. They saw you."

"I don't understand."

"You caught their eye."

"How do you know?"

"I was there."

"What were you doing?"

"They tricked me into being with them when they murdered Paddy O'Connor. Then they threatened to kill me if I didn't help."

"You helped to murder Paddy. I don't understand."

"I was with them. I didn't murder Paddy. Cedric did."

"Who is Cedric?"

"My brother. William is my father."

"Why are you here now?"

"I don't want them to kill you. I don't want to be a part of any more murders. I want the killing to end."

"When do they plan to kill me?"

"I'm not sure. I tried to talk them out of it, but it didn't work. I'm telling the truth when I say that they threatened to kill me. I have a friend who can help – Mr McCabe, a teacher. He's found a safe house for you in Portstewart. You can go right away if it helps. I have the contact details." He pushed a folded piece of paper into her hand.

Rose opened it. "I need to talk to my uncle and aunt. Why should I believe in you? This could be a trap."

"You're right. You've no reason to believe me. Maybe I could bring Mr McCabe. He could explain it better than me. You could believe him. He is a good man."

Rose watched Peter's face flicker red and white, his lips go straight, his eyes drop to the red kneeler. She reached for his hand.

"I believe you."

Peter looked up at Rose. She was smiling at him. She didn't look at all afraid.

"Your aunt and uncle can go with you. It's all arranged. Once you are safe, we can tell the police."

Peter reached into his anorak pocket. "I've something else for you."

As Peter reached into his pocket, Rose asked, "Why did you try to talk them out of it? You don't know me."

Peter handed Rose Paddy's diamond ring. "I never wanted them to kill anyone. I was in the car with them when they spotted you. Your hair was long then."

"Yes it was." Rose blushed. "What's this?" Rose held the ring in the palm of her hand.

"Paddy O'Connor had it with him the day Cedric murdered him." Peter looked down again at the kneeler.

"Why are you giving it to me?"

"I am going to tell them that I've given the ring to a friend. If anything happens to you or to me, this friend will bring the ring to the police. The ring will lead the police back to Cedric."

"They're not going to like that are they?"

"No."

"What will they do?"

"I don't know. But that doesn't need to happen if you go immediately to the safe house. If you do that, I will go to the police. You keep the ring until they are arrested."

"Are you not in danger?"

"I don't care. It doesn't matter what happens to me."

"You can't go back home. It's too dangerous. Why don't you go to the safe house tonight? You need it as much as I do."

The church was empty. A sweet sense of incense hung in the air. Rose looked at her watch. It was seven forty-five. Father Anthony would be coming out to take Confession in fifteen minutes.

Peter's voice became stronger. "I have to go home. I have to speak to Mum. I'm going to tell her everything."

"We both need to go home. I'll talk to Lily and Tom. We don't have a car. I don't think we can get to Portstewart tonight."

"Maybe Mr McCabe could give you a lift tomorrow after Mass? He has a car."

"Maybe."

"Are you afraid?" Peter asked as they walked together to the back of the church. Rose dipped her hand into the Holy Water font and blessed Peter on the forehead before blessing herself.

"Not really. I feel numb. It hasn't sunk in."

Peter kissed Rose on the cheek. Her skin was like silk just as he had imagined – cool, smooth and then warm and flowing. He didn't expect kissing her to trigger an image of Jenny leaning forward across the table with an empty coffee cup to her left. He stood up and placed his hand on Rose's head.

"I'll meet you tomorrow at Mass. I'll try to find out more information if I can but see if you can persuade your aunt and uncle to go with you to Portstewart."

"I'll talk to them." As they left the church, a gang of rioters gathered at the corner of Butler Street. "I'll wait with you until the bus comes." Rose whispered.

Five minutes later Peter boarded the double decker bus for the city centre.

Rose waved at him as he took a seat by the window. He twisted in the seat to watch her as the bus pulled away into the darkness. He watched her open the garden gate and turn the key in the lock.

"Lily, Tom, where are you?"

Tom listened carefully as Rose told her story. Neither Lily nor Rose noticed that he was staring with the whites of his eyes showing above and below his iris rather than only to the sides.

He was breathing quickly and shallowly. Lily sat beside him on the sofa. Rose walked up and down the sitting room in front of the TV, trying to remember every detail of her conversation with Peter. When she finished, Tom stood up.

"The safe house is a good idea but we can't get to Portstewart tonight. Tomorrow we go with Mr McCabe. Let's hope he agrees to that. What time is it?"

Lily looked at her watch. "Eight o'clock."

Tom patted Rose on the head. "I'm going to talk to Father Anthony and see what we can do. We need help. We need a gun."

Tom bent down to kiss Lily on the cheek. Lily pulled herself to her feet and put her arms around Tom's shoulders. "A gun Tom? For God's sake. You need to take a tablet. Calm down. We can deal with this without guns. We always have."

Tom turned without saying a word, hands by his side and opened the sitting room door. "They're not going to kill you Rose. I promise you that."

He opened the door into the hallway. Rose caught Lily briefly by the hand, then dropped it and ran after him.

"Don't, Tom. Please, don't."

The front door closed. Seconds later Rose heard the gate squeak open. A dark silhouette approached the door. She waited. The letterbox opened and a small white envelope fell on the floor.

Rose's heart beat rapidly. It had to be Matt.

She ripped opened the envelope:

Dear Rose

I have been worried sick about you. What a nightmare. I am OK although struggling to come to terms with what happened to Eddie and Max. Can't get that last hour out of my head. They wanted me to stay in hospital for another few days but I

*wanted to be able to see you on your birthday tomorrow. I am
on Crumlin Road duties from six o'clock in the evening. Hope
to see you somehow.*

All my love
Matt

•••

Peter breathed heavily and his stomach did cartwheels as he
turned the key in the lock of the front door.

"You're back", Eileen shouted from the kitchen, clinking
dinner plates in the basin. "Come on in. I've kept dinner warm.'"

"Where are Father and Cedric?"

"You've missed them. They've headed off for a drink at the
Black Beetle. How did rugby practice go?"

"Mum, I didn't go to rugby training."

"Where were you then?" Eileen asked, brushing back a wisp
of hair that had fallen over her eyes.

"Holy Cross Church, Ardoyne."

"Why on earth did you go there? Ardoyne is dangerous."
Eileen slipped off her court shoes and stood on the tiled floor in
stockinged feet.

Peter didn't reply. Instead he asked, "Do you ever wonder
what Father and Cedric are doing when they come home at
three and four in the morning?"

"I do. Then I stop thinking about it because it can drive you
insane imagining all sorts of things which may or may not be
true. They're probably talking and drinking. There's not a lot
more to do."

"What if your worst thoughts were true?"

"What do you mean? Are you saying that you know what
they are doing? Are they not drinking in the Black Beetle?"

"Not all the time. What if they were planning to murder

Catholics? What if they were murdering Catholics?"

Peter pulled the rugby kit from his rucksack and threw it on the floor beside the washing machine.

"What do you mean they are killing Catholics? You shouldn't say things like that, unless you know it's true." Eileen's voice dropped to a whisper. "I thought that you said that you hadn't been to rugby practice?"

"I brought the kit in case Father and Cedric were here when I got back. I haven't used it."

"What do you mean your Father and Cedric are murdering Catholics?"

"It is true."

"How do you know?"

"I've been with them. I was in the taxi with them when they kidnapped Paddy O'Connor and Michael McGuckin. They murdered Paddy O'Connor and Michael McGuckin. I know that for sure."

Eileen shuddered, remembering the ring in the attic tagged with the name Michael, January 1972. The other rings now made sense if what Peter was saying was true.

"What have you done, Peter?" Eileen asked her voice dropping even lower.

"I dragged Paddy O'Connor from the taxi to the garage. I waited with him as Father and Cedric went to have drinks in the Black Beetle. Cedric returned alone to kill him." Peter sat at the kitchen table, holding his head in his hands. "I feel sick. Mum, what can I do to get out of this?"

"Why did you do it Peter?"

"They lied to me. But they're not going to get away with it."

Eileen removed the hot plate with its cod and cheese sauce from the pot of boiling water, where it had been kept warm. She slipped the plate towards Peter.

"Let's stay calm." Eileen whispered. "You need to explain. We will then do what we can and we will trust in God to do the rest. Please eat your dinner." Eileen sat facing Peter. "Tell me why you went to Holy Cross this evening?"

"To warn Rose Martin that Father and Cedric are planning to kill her."

"How do you know Rose Martin? What do you mean that they are planning to kill her? Why?" Eileen jumped to her feet and walked towards Peter. She held his face with both hands and stared into his eyes. "Tell me, Peter. Everything you know."

Why did Peter trust Eileen? How was she so different to William? There are some things which Peter knew without being explained. There was something seeded within Eileen that radiated from every pore of her body. The way she looked at him now was the flower of that seed. Peter's words tumbled from his mouth uncensored.

"Rose lives on the Crumlin Road, opposite Holy Cross Church. I was in the car with Father and Cedric when they spotted her as their next target."

"Rose Martin." Eileen sat down again at the table, "I've met Rose. She has an aunt, Lily. I met Lily at the inauguration of the Art Exhibition. Rose arrived with her uncle Tom and a few friends."

"Yes, she has an uncle Tom. They live facing Holy Cross Church."

Eileen slid her hands across the table towards Peter, who, pushing the plate to his left squeezed Eileen's hands and dropped his head onto her knuckles.

"I'm afraid of Cedric Mum. I saw him with Paddy O'Connor. When Cedric came back from the Black Beetle, Paddy was sitting in a chair with his rosary in his hands. Cedric's face and neck were red as he grabbed him from behind. He brought his arms across his chest and squeezed it hard. He whispered something into his ear. I couldn't hear because I was standing against the door. Paddy started crying, almost growling, and struggling to free himself from Cedric's grip. Cedric pulled his arm even tighter across his chest. Paddy couldn't move. I felt sick in my stomach. I wanted to do something but all I did was open the door. I took one last look at Paddy. He looked at me. He stopped making noises and struggling. I'll never forget the look in his eyes, Mum. He said, "Jesus, Son of God, have mercy on me, a sinner." He kissed his rosary beads. I saw Cedric rip the rosary from his hands, break it in two and throw it on the floor. I left and closed the door behind me. Peter whimpered, "Mum, even now his eyes stare at me; plead with me to do something. All I did was walk away."

"I know, Peter." Eileen got slowly from her seat, walked towards Peter and gently placed her arms around Peter's shoulders as he sat on the chair. She rested her cheek against his soft nest of curly hair.

"It was the same with Michael McGuckin. Father helped Cedric murder him. I walked away."

The kitchen was in silence apart from the ticking of the large white faced clock on the wall, showing nine-thirty pm. The second hand moved rhythmically clicking tick, tick, tick. The net curtain rippled from the draught in the faulty window frame. The rain which was almost turning into hailstones pinged against the window. Eileen watched the sleet-like rain dissolve and melt as the drops caught the light from the kitchen before trickling onto the windowsill and disappearing into the darkness. Peter told her everything he knew.

"Don't blame yourself," Eileen whispered in a low voice, "Maybe it's my fault this is happening."

"What do you mean, Mum? What have you done? You've

never been anything other than kind. What are you talking about? This is crazy enough without you starting to make it even crazier. My head and stomach are spinning. Please talk sense to me, don't make it worse." Peter stood up and paced up and down the kitchen.

"I can't tell you now. I will tell you soon. I have to speak to Cedric first. There is something he needs to know which will change everything."

"What, Mum? Don't talk in riddles. Tell me." Eileen stared into space, ignoring Peter.

"Let's keep calm and think about what is the best thing to do." She paused. "I could talk to Lily." She jumped to her feet to find her handbag perched on the windowsill. She quickly opened it, breathing shallowly. A bead of sweat rolled down her forehead. She didn't bother wiping it away. "I have Lily's telephone number."

She had no sooner said the words when the telephone rang. It was Lily.

"Eileen?"

"Hello Lily."

"Is it safe to talk?"

"Not now." Eileen heard a key turning in the front door, followed by the heavy tread of feet along the hallway. "Lily, I have to go. Peter has told me what's happening. They're back. Tomorrow. Let's talk tomorrow. I'll come to Saville's after you finish work at five. There's something I need to tell you."

Eileen quickly hung up the telephone as the kitchen door squeaked open.

"Mum, this is stupid. Tell me before you tell Cedric and Lily," Peter whispered as William stumbled into the kitchen with a bundle of fish and chips wrapped in newspaper.

"Anyone for a chip?"

Cedric followed behind, walking over to the television and switching it on. "Let's catch the ten o'clock news."

William didn't bother using the plate Eileen placed beside him. He uncurled the newspaper and pulled the battered cod into four pieces dropping the white fleshy meat into his mouth. Cedric lounged back in the chair watching the television. He grabbed a couple of chips from William's newspaper and without taking his eyes off the television screen mumbled with a full mouth, "Peter, we're going to need some help from you tomorrow for that little job. You'll have to say no to any extracurricular school activities. We need you here at six o'clock."

He swung around in the chair, grabbing a second handful of chips. William picked at his front teeth trying to dislodge a trapped fishbone. Eileen and Peter quickly exchanged glances.

"Where's the vinegar?" Cedric asked, slapping William on the hand. "You've had enough. Leave some for me."

"What do you want Peter to do?" Eileen asked in a lighter tone of voice, and a forced smile as she placed the bottle of malt vinegar in front of Cedric. "You know he has homework to do. He can't be out every night. Tonight he had rugby practice. Tomorrow he needs to do school work. He has exams to think about."

"He can do his homework the rest of the week. One night without homework never killed anyone." Cedric wiped his fingers on his jeans. "We need Peter's help. I've learnt that it's better not to procrastinate. There is work to be done tomorrow – not the day after."

Peter and Eileen looked at each other again. Peter's breathing now turning rapid and shallow. His head thumped with every heartbeat. He felt a strange dull pain in his lower back which spread into his stomach and up around his heard. He could hardly make out the words of newscaster reading the News at Ten:

"There has been another sectarian murder in North Belfast. The victim Anthony Magee was a young man of twenty two from the Ardoyne District. His family disclosed that he had recently moved to Dublin to work but returned to Belfast because he was homesick. Last week he was offered his old job back as barman in the National Bar in the City Centre of Belfast. He had left the National Bar this evening following his first night at work and hailed a black taxi in the City Centre. One man already in the taxi allegedly asked if he could share the ride with him saying that he was going to Ligoniel. As they drove up the Crumlin Road, the passenger pretended to be sick. The taxi stopped close to the Mater Hospital on the Crumlin Road. The driver and passenger got out of the taxi, pulled Anthony from the back seat and fired three rounds into Anthony's chest.

In spite of the severe nature of his injuries, Anthony was able to explain what had happened to police before dying a short time later in intensive care in the Mater. Police have confirmed that they have a description of his attackers and are now investigating the connection between this murder and other murders which have taken place over the last two weeks close to the Crumlin Road. Anthony's parents have appealed for anyone who saw the black taxi or who witnessed Anthony being taken from the car to contact the Police. They have asked for no reprisal killings to take place in honour of their son who they say was a kind and home loving young man."

"What a fool. Wouldn't you think you would be a bit more careful who you'd take a lift from these days? I don't imagine his description of his attackers will be up to much. Probably scare tactics by the police." William laughed.

Cedric chuckled. "If you're going to be gullible, that's what happens to you."

"What about Jenny?" Eileen interrupted, clearing the table.

"Jenny who?" Cedric ate the last chip and licked his fingers.

"Oh dear." Eileen wiped the table. "I'm sorry it didn't work out. She was good for you."

Peter pushed his chair to one side. "Mum, you don't mind if I leave the kit for you to clean? I'm off to bed. I'll see you in the morning."

"Of course. Sleep well, Peter."

"I'll have an early night myself." William crunched the fish and chip newspaper into a ball and threw it at the bin, where it bounced off the wall and landed on the floor. He slid his chair back across the tiled floor, making a screeching squeal, hoisted his trousers up at the waist and limped towards the kitchen door after Peter.

Cedric pulled his chair closer to the table. "Any chance of a cup of tea Mum?" William and Peter's footsteps were heard tramping across the floor of the bedrooms upstairs.

"Were you involved in the murder of Anthony Magee tonight Cedric?" Eileen asked, checking that the kitchen door was closed. She pushed it again as the kettle whistled.

"What are you talking about Mum?" Cedric's breathing shortened. He pushed a long oily fringe back from his forehead and leant forward to stare into his mother's blue eyes across the table. "Have you got holes in your head? What would I be doing on the Crumlin Road near the Mater? It's a bloody hellhole. I wouldn't touch it with a barge pole. There's enough work to do in the safety of the Shankill."

"What are you doing, Cedric?" Eileen began to cry gently. "Tell me what you're doing. I don't believe a word you say any more."

"Then what's the point in telling you what I'm doing, if you don't believe me? Has Peter been talking to you?" Cedric's eyes narrowed. Eileen's face was streaked with black mascara.

"It's not about Peter. It's about you and it's about me. We need to talk. I should have done this a long time ago." Eileen's shoulders heaved. She smeared mascara in dark fingers across both cheek bones. "Can you turn the light out?"

Cedric obediently pushed his chair back, ambled towards the kitchen door and switched off the light. Eileen lit a small candle on the kitchen table.

"There's something important that I need to tell you. You don't need to listen to or to obey anything that William tells you to do. He's not your Father. He has no authority over you. Listen to me."

•••

Peter never thought that he would be able to sleep, but after an hour of tossing and turning he fell into a deep slumber. He dreamt that he was in a bedroom which seemed to be a cross between an expensive hotel, a monastery and a prison. He was in a white washed room with a large bed, a small hand basin in the right hand corner and a large oak writing desk and chair on his left. He sat on the bed and looked straight ahead at tall French windows covered with white chiffon which led onto a small balcony. It was daylight. Peter threw back the smooth white linen sheets, placed his feet into the golden slippers beside the bed and walked towards the window. He pulled the chiffon curtains to one side and opened the French doors to the balcony. Below was a Plaza filled with Nazi-like soldiers wearing helmets, heads down, arms raised in salute. From the balcony they seemed like a sea of bobbing lentils. Who were they saluting? It was someone who was standing on the balcony in the room to the right of him. Who was it? Peter looked to his right and could only see an arm waving back into the Plaza. He couldn't see the face or the body attached to the arm. Peter turned around, looking back into the room. Jenny appeared from nowhere, standing beside his bed, smiling at him. He walked towards her, caught her by the hand and together they walked towards the door. Would it open? Easily. They walked hand in hand along a hallway; an older woman approached them,

"Do you want to see the games room?"

They followed her, squeezing one another's hands. She opened a door into a spacious room with a large television screen, a jogging machine, a snooker table, darts board, and a table tennis table. The woman smiled proudly. "There's everything you need here."

A younger woman wearing a pinstriped suit and white blouse approached, smiling. Peter realised that he and Jenny were prisoners. They were to be entertained but not allowed to escape. Peter knew that at some unknown point in time they would be executed but were being allowed to enjoy the time before the killing. In fact they were encouraged to be distract themselves until the planned hour of their deaths. Peter was determined to help Jenny escape even if it seemed that the forces lined up against them were insuperable.

He wakened from the dream with a sense of relief. Jenny was safe in the nurse's home. What did the dream mean? What did the future hold for them? Last night Cedric had implied that everything was over between him and Jenny. Maybe it would be possible to see Jenny, but first he had to take care of Rose. Peter threw off the sheet and woollen blankets and his feet touched the bedroom floor which was cold. As he pulled back the curtains, ice crystals were starting to melt like snowflakes on the inside of the windows. He whispered to himself. "What time is it? Where was Mum? What had she said to Cedric?"

chapter 13

Thursday 13th January 1972

Eileen woke at four in the morning. William snored in bed with his back to her. She watched his back heave, heard him splutter, then return to steady snoring as she quietly pushed the sheets back and found her slippers. She pulled on a warm pink brushed cotton dressing gown, and made her way downstairs. The candle had burnt out, the white overspill of wax solid like a glacier going nowhere on the pine table top. She filled the kettle. There was something comforting in the increasing volume of the gentle hum of water heating to boiling point. She removed it from the gas just as it started to whistle and carefully placed four teaspoons of leaf Assam tea into the silver teapot, poured the boiling water and waited three minutes before opening the front door. Mug of tea in hand, Eileen walked into the garden and stood beneath the cherry tree.

The icy January morning air immediately settled on her eyelashes, face and hands. The short grass was crisply frozen and drops of melting ice seeped through her slippers. Eileen held the cup of tea with both hands and looked up into the clear starry sky. Standing beneath the cherry tree, the branches created a lacy canopy above her. A waning crescent moon cut through the velvet darkness. Eileen watched the stars dancing with their edges flickering, changing positions, winking. Beneath the light of the moon she felt herself bathed in a purity of light. Everything in the sky was perfect, held in symmetry, balanced with mathematical positioning. The moon and stars movement was planned, certain, regular, tracking with precision across the sky, the stars glittering with utter dependability. Eileen touched the rough, cold bark of the cherry tree, its empty branches holding within them life for spring.

As a child she had wondered what it would be like to be a tree, a star, or to be the moon. She imagined that it would be lonely and boring to be a tree, not to be able to move apart from pushing its roots slowly into the bowels of the earth, or swinging its branches from side to side in a breeze. What would it be like to be a star, dancing, burning, flickering in an immense universe, until all its energy was gone? Self-destructing as a supernova, scattering, falling, unknown fragments sinking through the layers of the mud and stone, waiting for millions of years to erupt as a volcano of diamonds or, not finding earth, exploding into infinity, unremembered, jettisoning eternally into a world of mystery, nothingness and blackness.

What would it be like to be imprisoned as the moon, following a designated elliptical route in an inky black universe, unable to quicken or slow its pace? What would it feel like dizzily spinning around the Earth, catching light from the sun and occasionally feeling the pale reflected Earthshine? This morning, Eileen would happily surrender all her sense of aliveness in a world of coming and going – all of her freedom – to be able to settle in the stillness of the stars, to be rooted and unmoved like the cherry tree and to tranquilly observe like a crescent moon,

What dread can the cherry tree feel? What remorse churns

the moon? Do stars itch to escape the discomfort of being? These feelings which she had regarded as being so important in being human, she would now swap for the calmness of the detached observing moon, untouched, accepting, steady, totally trustworthy and reliable. She sipped the warm sweet tea and prayed to the silent moon, asking it to touch and transform her mind with its coolness. She wanted to learn from the moon, from its reflection of what was real.

"Mum?" Peter stood at the door in his pyjamas and dressing gown. He walked into the garden, towards the cherry tree, standing below it and looking into Eileen's eyes. "Were you able to change Cedric's mind about Rose?"

"Sssssshhh. Keep your voice low," Eileen whispered. "We don't want them to waken for a while. Let's enjoy the peace for a moment. It may be all we have today." Eileen took Peter's hand. His eyes were puffy, his sandy blonde curly hair tight with ringlets. He pulled the dressing gown up to his chin, shivering. "I spoke with Cedric for quite some time last night. I'm not sure if I have been able to help him see things differently. He has lived his life for more than thirty year's feeling, thinking and acting in a certain way. Will three hours make a difference? I don't know. I know that one second can make a difference, if he wants it to."

"What did you say to him?"

"I explained why he shouldn't listen to William. I gave him a good reason not to follow William's orders."

"What did you say?"

"I told him the truth."

"What truth?"

"What we have talked about together – about William and I – and more."

"Tell me 'the more'. I need to know."

"It's complicated. I will tell you, I promise; but not now.

It's not going to help now. It could distract you. We need to get through today and then I'll tell you. Do you trust me Peter?"

"Yes I do, more than anyone in the world."

"Then listen to me. I want you to go to school as normal. Don't come back at six. Stay with Mr McCabe. He will take care of you. I will meet Lily this afternoon at five as planned at Saville's."

"Rose thought that it might be a good idea to go to the Police. So did Mr McCabe. Are we making a mistake not doing that?" Peter asked.

"I don't think so. You're right. We need to persuade them not to kill Rose. We've started. It now depends on how Cedric reacts and what he will say to William. Go back to bed now and try to get a little more sleep. I know that sounds impossible but try. We need to make everything seem as normal as possible. It has to be easy for them to change. We mustn't make them afraid of being different. By getting out of the way, we can at least create some space for something better to happen."

"What are you going to do before you meet Lily?"

"I'll make breakfast as normal for William and Cedric. I will then bake wheaten bread and visit some new friends in Glenbryn. Then I will see Lily at five." Eileen sounded decisive.

"What new friends?" Peter shook his head in disbelief. Eileen normally didn't have any friends apart from those in her art class. She spent her life painting, cleaning the house, and taking care of the small garden. The windows sparkled, the furniture was scented with pine polish, the floors with disinfectant. Everything gleamed and squeaked. Small cacti plants were lovingly tended on the kitchen window sill. She made miracles happen with the cacti – like when she helped one cacti give birth to a little button flower, a small star shaped flower hidden under a spiky green leaf. The star shaped flower had a circle in the centre filled with small triangles of yellow and green. Star leaves unfolded from the circle scattering more yellow and green triangles into the air. Eileen would look at it the way a mother looks at a new baby – with amazement, a sense of pride and mostly awe.

"Sammy and Anne. They're ex-neighbours of Tom Martin and Lily. I met them at the art exhibition. They are salt of the earth people. Today is a good day to spend an hour or so with them."

Eileen moved towards Peter, holding him in her arms in the freezing temperatures, hearing the thump of his heart as she pressed her head against his chest, feeling the warmth of his breath in her ear. He stood above her, his arms awkwardly pulling her close.

"Mum, one more thing – I gave Rose the diamond ring that belonged to Paddy O'Connor. Cedric took it from him before he killed him."

"Paddy?"

"You remember I told you last night about Paddy O'Connor?"

"My God." Eileen shivered.

"It was meant to be Molly's ring." Peter sighed deeply.

"Molly?" Eileen looked up into Peter's eyes.

"Paddy's fiancée who was killed in a car bomb in Cornmarket. Do you remember Susan in your art class got caught up in that bomb and lost her legs? Well, Molly died."

"I saw it in Paddy's hand before Cedric took it from him." Peter looked up at the moon and gulped at the air.

Eileen shivered again. "Why did you not tell me before?"

"I didn't know what to say – where to begin."

"Why did you give it to Rose?"

"I thought that I could blackmail Cedric and William into not killing Rose."

"I don't think threats will work with either William or Cedric. But we are where we are now. Let's get you back to bed. Tell Mr McCabe to ring me this evening and let me know that you are safe. Don't come home until I tell you."

Eileen linked arms with Peter and they walked slowly into the kitchen. Eileen closed the front door taking a last look at the cherry tree and the moon.

"Why are you smiling, Mum?"

"In a way I am glad that the truth is emerging. The truth is always good and yet I for one am so afraid of it. I knew that something wasn't right but I didn't want to really know what it was. I was terrified to know. I stopped looking and stopped asking questions. I realise that by not looking and not asking questions and not trying to find out what was going on, I contributed to these murders."

"Is that what you meant last night, Mum, when you said that maybe you were to blame?"

"No. There's more, much more."

"What? Please tell me?"

"I will tell you tomorrow."

There was the sound of someone stirring upstairs. Footsteps padded across the bedroom floor and then shuffled along the hallway to the bathroom.

"Tell me quick, before they get up."

"I need to tell you properly. Not like this. I'll tell you everything when today is over. I promise. There will be no more secrets ever – I promise." She touched Peter on the nose with her finger. "Promise."

The toilet flushed upstairs. Footsteps retraced the path along the landing, towards Eileen's bedroom.

"He's back in bed. He won't move for another few hours. Get some rest."

"I'll try." Peter squeezed her hand and moved towards the kitchen door.

Eileen pulled her hair into a ponytail tying it with an elastic band. "Be strong."

• • •

Cedric lay in bed listening to William walking along the landing. The room was dark, apart from a chink of grey where the curtain hadn't been properly closed. A blackbird hopped onto the window sill, its shadow highlighted as it lifted its head into the air, singing three clear notes before opening its wings and flying into the early morning sky. He rolled over on his side, fumbling for a packet of cigarettes on the table beside the bed. He switched on the radio. Elvis sang,

"There goes my reason for living. There goes the one of my dreams. There goes my only possession. There goes my everything."

He lit a cigarette and inhaled deeply. The tip burned orange, blue smoke curled towards the ceiling. Cedric scratched his sideburns and early morning stubble. His head was heavy against the pillow. Images appeared in his head of Eileen cleaning the kitchen floor with a mop, shining the windows with newspaper, cooking Sunday lunch, making his birthday cake with thirty candles, ironing his shirts and socks, folding his underwear. A voice in his head repeated, "Eileen is not my mother. William is not my father. Peter is not my brother. Who is my mother? Who is my father? Who am I?"

The words ate away at him, like mice chewing through a plaster wall. They gnawed away, probing for answers to questions which he had never asked before, "Who am I? Who was my mother? Who was my father?" Tears streamed down Cedric's cheeks. He wiped them away with his hand, looking at the glistening teardrops beading on the hairs of his hand. He licked them. They were salty. He had never tasted the saltiness of a tear before.

Eileen had told him how much she loved him and that it didn't affect her love for him that he wasn't her natural child. She said that she knew about the murders and even though they were appalling and he needed to give himself up and receive society's punishment she still loved him. What would make her happiest would be if he could feel some remorse for what he had done – could see how wrong it all was and vow never to kill again. That was what she asked of him. That he could feel the suffering of his victims and their families and the terrible tragedy which he had inflicted on so many innocent lives. Then she repeated that she knew that he could only see what he could see and that what he needed was help to be able to see differently. She would give him that help. She would be there for him. There was no way that he could undo what he had done, but he could stop the murders now, he could start to see the terrible error of it all.

Even if it made no difference to Eileen, it did mean something to him that Eileen was not his real mother. He couldn't think about the murders now. The only thing which he could think about was his real mother? Why had she been murdered? How would William react to the fact that Cedric was not his son? What would Peter say? What would Sammy P say? How could he walk into the Black Beetle hearing the sniggers of everyone around him and stay?

Perhaps he should kill Eileen? Who had she told so far? As far as he could see William didn't know. She had said that last night. Peter didn't know. If he killed her everything could be the same. He could make it look like an IRA murder. That would be easy to do.

He took another puff on his cigarette and felt a sense of comfort in the fact that a solution to the problem was beginning to emerge. He would need to act fast. Eileen would have to be dispatched today if he was going to do it at all. He looked at his watch. She could be dealt with before five o'clock this afternoon. Even as he had this thought, he knew it was insane. He knew that he was denying his love for Eileen by attempting to put the images of her out of his mind.

There was one image which kept returning. It was of Eileen last night as the candle flame spluttered, gasping its last. She pushed her chair back and in the darkness walked around the table and finding his hand flat on the kitchen table, lifted it to her lips, saying, "There hasn't been one day, one minute that I haven't loved you as my own son. There is nothing that you have done or will do which will ever change my love for you. I am here for you now and always. I love you. I only ask you to stop killing. Give it up Cedric. Admit what you have done. Take your punishment. Life will be still worth living. You can be a different person. You can be the person you were born to be. This person that you have been isn't real. It's false. The real you is inside and can be set free. There's time. Remember that there is more joy in Heaven over one sinner who repents. Jesus didn't come on earth to hang out with those who were good but to be with those who needed to see differently. You need to see differently. So does William."

Eileen didn't want to sound like a preacher but she didn't know what else to say. She was clutching at words, trying to find the right things to say that would get through to Cedric and yet the echo of her voice sounded so wrong – so clichéd – superficial, patronising, like a Pharisee. What would be better to say? Should she stay quiet for a while?

"When are you going to tell Father ... I mean William?" Cedric stared ahead of him as he asked the question. He ignored Eileen.

"I could tell him. Maybe I should. I have lived a lie all of my life with him. I should be honest and tell him. Am I a coward if I ask you to tell him?"

"I've never thought of you as a coward."

"Could it be the first step back to what's real for both of you? He needs to hear it from you."

"What are you going to do after I tell him?"

"That depends upon what you both decide to do next. It's in your hands. However, I know that I won't accept any further killings. I will do whatever it takes to stop you both killing." For the first time Eileen looked and sounded extremely fierce.

Cedric turned his head to look at her. She was on her feet, hands by her side, fists clenched. Her eyes glowed like dark coals in the golden light of the dying candle. Her hair had fallen out from her French plait onto her shoulders which he wasn't used to seeing. It made her look more childlike. Nevertheless she looked solid, determined and unmoving and what he felt from her was a strange quality of love. "Remember, whatever it takes to stop the killings." Eileen repeated firmly.

He felt that love transmitted by Eileen within him now, like a delicate flame setting tinder alight. A flame is like that – it moves and burns quickly. It was stronger now than what he had felt last night. How strange that the memory of love can burn even stronger than the real thing. Or maybe it was that first touch of love last night that he hardly recognised. It was so removed from anything he had known before, including anything he had felt with Jenny. This morning it was as though a gentle breeze within him fanned the flame. He lay in bed, not really thinking, staring at the ceiling and allowing himself to feel warmed by this fragile flicker within. He sensed Eileen's presence now in the room beside him as though she was breathing into him. The flames leapt higher, became stronger, until he felt them roaring within him. He was burning, being consumed by a certain knowledge that was unknown. He was burning, burning, blazing with an unknown love. He did not want to extinguish that fire. He didn't want to dampen the flames, even though they hurt. He rolled onto his side and allowed himself to cry. The bed felt on fire like a funeral pyre. There was no coolness anywhere – not in the sheets, not on the pillow, not when he threw the sheets from him and faced the frosty temperatures of the room. The only coolness that existed was in the sense of Eileen breathing into him.

He would not kill Eileen. He knew that the painful burning he was feeling for the first time was indeed remorse. The faces of those whom he had murdered flashed before him – expressionless, floating faces, non-judgemental – appearing and disappearing, as real as if alive. The depth of their pain now twisted within him. He had become each of them. They were embedded in his DNA. He felt the knife wounds he had inflicted on them sink into his own flesh. His body shook with terror. He was gripped by an excruciating desire to get out of his body but he had to stay and face it all. This was his prison, this moment of eternal Hell his own self-judgement. As the flame burned within him he knew for sure that he would never murder again. He was afraid as he shuddered now beneath the blankets pulled around him of what would become of him. Who would he become? He squeezed his eyes tighter as though wishing to blind himself and curled his legs up to his chin. He held them with his arms, rolling onto his back and then rocking backwards and forwards in the bed, oblivious now of time, of where he was and what he could do next.

•••

Sammy and Anne listened carefully to Eileen's every word at mid-day, as they chewed on the sultana barn-brack bread.

"That's a lot to take in." Sammy shook his head from side to side. "What time did they say they were meeting up?"

"Six o'clock."

"You think that they're heading for Holy Cross Church?"

"I think so."

"Leave it with me." Sammy got to his feet and shook Eileen's hand warmly. "Tom and I have already made plans for this evening. But maybe we need reinforcements."

"It takes courage to do what you've done." Anne whispered.

•••

Peter caught the train to Lurgan and found his way easily to the nurses' residence. He knocked on her bedroom door. She slowly opened it. She waved him to sit on the one wooden chair as she perched on the edge of the bed. The room had the feel of a nun's cell. There were no paintings or pictures on the white walls. A gold lightshade with a cream fringe dangled above his head. The single bed had a primrose yellow candlewick bedspread. The white sheets turned down over the top looked starched. The room's simplicity conveyed peace.

It was strange for Peter to see Jenny in her nurse's uniform. Her hair was pulled into a bun which sat inside a white hat which looked like it had come from a posh Christmas cracker. He didn't tell her that. She had a dusty blue dress which ended below her knee which was covered with a white cotton apron. She had white plimsolls and wore no earrings or jewellery.

Her eyes were watery as she listened to Peter explain about the reasons for his visit to Rose the day before.

"How is Eileen?"

"I would say focused."

"I'm worried about this evening."

"I promise I will come here tomorrow and tell you what happened." Peter sat with his two hands on his knees. Jenny reached forward and took one hand.

"Can you not ring tonight? They'll call me from my room. I won't sleep otherwise."

"Can I tell you a dream that I had about us?" Peter looked embarrassed asking permission.

"Tell me."

Peter explained the dream about being imprisoned and not able to escape while being 'entertained to death'.

Jenny laughed for the first time that afternoon. "It looks like you're the one who is meant to save me from that woman who looks as though she's wearing a nurse's uniform." Jenny looked over her shoulder and giggled. "Maybe it's Sister Maureen. Although, I don't know where the games room is."

...

At exactly five o'clock in the afternoon, Eileen peered into Saville's jewellery shop. She could faintly see Lily polishing the counter. She tapped on the window and immediately Lily looked up and waved at her and ran to the front door.

She hugged Eileen. "Am I glad to see you. Come in. It's freezing outside." She turned over the red 'Closed' sign to face outwards. "Eileen, what on earth are we to do?"

"Let's talk. Let's put the facts on the table and decide." Eileen perched on a stool behind the counter and waved at Lily to join her on the stool to her left.

Lily first rummaged in her hand bag, zipped open her leather purse and removed the diamond ring.

"Let me start. First of all there's this. You know that Peter gave it to Rose."

Lily placed the diamond ring on Eileen's open palm.

Eileen nodded. "I know that it belonged to Paddy O'Connor. Well, it was destined for Molly."

"Yes." Lily shook her head and sighed. "She never got a chance to wear it."

"Peter told me that Cedric took it off Paddy before he died." Eileen pressed the ring back into Lily's hand. "What would Paddy want to happen to it?"

"I think he would want us to give it to his landlady, Anne. She adored him. Tom can decide. Now you tell me what you wanted to tell me."

They drank sweet tea, huddled over a small electric fire, while the trays of diamonds, sapphires, rubies and emeralds sparkled around them. Eileen explained what Peter had told her.

Lily asked, "How much time do we have?"

"Less than an hour before they leave the Shankill." For the first time Eileen looked agitated.

"My God Eileen, we shouldn't be sitting here drinking tea. We need to do something. Let's go." Lily jumped down from the stool and pulled her woollen gloves on.

"There's one more thing you need to know. I told Cedric the truth last night." Eileen said the words in a calm, measured voice.

"The truth?" Lily straightened her beret.

"This is so difficult. I haven't told either William or Peter."

"What? Eileen, quick, spit it out for God's sake!"

Eileen gently got to her feet and stood as though in Court in the witness box with her two hands clasped together in front of her, her head down.

"I told Cedric that he is not my child. He's not William's son."

Lily looked at her watch and with the first sign of impatience asked, "Whose child is he?"

"Do you remember the Blitz?"

"Yes. I do. Tom and I were living on the farm on the Horseshoe Bend. The night of the Blitz was the night that Catherine was murdered. How could I forget it?"

Eileen raised her head. "Remind me who Catherine was?"

"Tom's sister."

"Yes. She was the one you said was murdered?"

"Yes. We never found out who murdered her or why. Is this relevant to Rose?"

Eileen nodded. "Yes – more than I thought. I remember that night so well. I was in the Royal Hospital."

"The Royal?" Lily interrupted. She continued, "Catherine was in the Royal."

Eileen wasn't listening. Instead she told her story. "The bombs fell over a six hour period. In the first hour I gave birth to a son. I called him Cedric. The ward I was in took a direct hit. Mr Magee arrived to help. He lifted Cedric from his cot and was carrying him to safety. He was six steps in front of me when a bomb hit the ward and the ceiling collapsed. Cedric was thrown from Mr Magee's arms against the wall. Mr Magee picked him up. He turned to me. He said, "I'm sorry. He's dead."

I started screaming and yelling and he put Cedric on the ground, looked for a sheet to wrap him in and then he held me for a moment in his arms. He whispered to me, "Eileen, we have to move. We have to get out of here. I'm so sorry but you can't stay here. Cedric is dead. Leave him to God. Go."

Mr Magee pointed to a corridor leading to an exit sign which I could just make out. He waved at me and turned left along a wider corridor where people were crying. He was needed to help the living. I didn't know what I was doing. I wandered in the direction that I thought he had pointed to. I heard a baby cry. At first, I thought that I had imagined it, but there was a cry coming from behind a door leading into a small theatre. I opened the door. I couldn't see anything at first. It was really dark. The baby's cry was close and stronger. I felt as though I could touch it. I took a few more steps in the darkness listening to the sound of crying. It stopped for a moment. I stood still. My eyes had become more used to the dark. Then I saw them. There were two babies, held in the mother's arms. She was dead. She had been murdered – her throat had been cut. I could see that."

"That was Catherine," Lily whispered.

"Catherine." Eileen hesitated. "Yes. Tom's sister."

"You took Jonas?"

"I took a baby. There were two."

"Maria was his sister."

"Cedric is Jonas." Eileen stared at Lily. There was silence.

"Who killed her?"

"I don't know."

"Did you not go to the police and tell them everything?"

"No," Eileen shook her head, "I didn't. I wanted to keep the baby. It was the only way that I knew how to keep the baby."

"What happened then?" Lily asked in a calm voice.

"I thought that no-one would know. I wanted to take both babies, but I knew that would have been impossible to explain to William. It would have complicated everything. With only the boy I wouldn't have to tell anyone, not even William."

"Mr Magee would have known."

"I know. But Mr Magee had had enough of Belfast. He

decided to move with his family to America two months later. He knew that the real Cedric died. He knew that Catherine's baby had been stolen. He didn't see either the baby or me before he left for America."

"Oh my God, I think that we need something stronger than tea to survive this!" Lily picked up her black handbag and removed a small quarter bottle of gin and poured a generous helping into Eileen's tea and then into her own and gulped it back.

"I don't drink but ... I think I'm going to start." Eileen sipped at her gin tea.

"You do realise what this means?" Lily asked.

"That Cedric is Jonas." Eileen bowed her head again.

"Cedric is also Rose's uncle and Tom's nephew," Lily whispered.

"And ... He's a Catholic. Mr Magee told us that Catherine had baptised him that night of the Blitz."

"How important is that?" Eileen asked.

Lily threw her hands into the air. "Who knows? How will he react?"

"I don't know." Eileen shook her head.

"What will William do if he knows all of this?" asked Lily.

"I really don't know."

"What time is it?"

Eileen glanced at her watch. "Quarter to six."

Lily said, "Mass is at seven. They're going to attempt to kill Rose after Mass."

Eileen nodded. "They asked Peter to meet them at six."

Eileen took a tissue from her handbag and wiped her nose.

"Maybe I should have told William the truth about Cedric this morning. I asked Cedric to tell him. I hoped that he would have more influence over him."

Lily took the last gulp of gin tea. "Let's go. If we can convince

Cedric that he is a baptised Catholic and that he is Rose's uncle that might be enough to stop the killings."

Lily set the alarm, turned off the lights, turned the key in the front door, and they ran to catch the 57 Bus for the Crumlin Road.

•••

"Where's Peter?" William asked, draining his pint in the Black Beetle.

"I don't know," Cedric whispered, looking over William's shoulder to where Jenny used to stand behind the bar. Cedric saw Sammy P walk through the front door with his usual swagger. Cedric leaned forward holding his chin in his hands and sighed, "There's Sammy P, dependably punctual. Let's go without Peter. This is our last job. Peter can get on with his life and I can get on with mine and you can get on with yours."

William straightened himself up. "What do you mean last job? There's more work to be done. We have to do our quota. There's work outstanding."

Cedric smoothed his hair back of his face. "I don't think so. I'm thinking of getting out of here, doing something different, starting afresh – maybe in Australia."

"Australia? Get a grip. Do you want another beer?" William asked, smoothing a long string of black hair across his bald head.

"No thanks." Cedric puffed on a cigarette.

"What's got into you? You're not turning good living on me are you?"

"What about you Sammy P? Never known to refuse?"

"I'll keep you company then." Sammy P slid onto the bench beside Cedric. He took his deck of cards from his pocket and started to shuffle.

"Have you got the car sorted, Sammy P?" Cedric asked.

"I bloody well have the car sorted out. Don't fuck with me when I'm playing cards."

• • •

At six o'clock in the evening Father Anthony closed his eyes and keeping them closed walked into the rose garden in the Grove holding his rosary in his hands, rubbing the beads, concentrating on the Third Sorrowful Mystery, 'The Crowning with Thorns'. It was dark as he sat on a bench facing the rose bushes he had planted fifteen years earlier. He opened his eyes. Even in the depths of winter one or two black spotted leaves still hung on the branches with a single yellow bud, curled leaves bravely facing the winter frost.

The evening star sparkled above him. There was no sign of the moon yet. His hands were sweaty rolling the beads, as were his feet. They felt wet against his sandals even though it was nearly freezing. Crows called harshly to one another, flapping their wings noisily above his head.

Darkness surrounded Father Anthony. He heard a rustling in the freezing grass. He opened his eyes again as a white hedgehog scurried from the tangled undergrowth. It looked at him with small pink eyes and made a snuffling sound. Only when it disappeared under the wet brown fallen oak leaves did he place the rosary into his right pocket. He groped under the concrete bench for the cold nuzzle of Father Martin's gun. Again he counted six bullet cartridges in his left pocket.

"God protect you."

• • •

Rose kissed Matt for the first time at the back of the monastery, near the Woodvale Road where Matt's Saracen was parked.

They were sheltered from view by the evergreen shrubbery and the thick trunks of oak trees. She asked him to show her his back and he heard her take a deep breath when she saw the blue and crimson bruising which covered the area from his shoulders to the base of his spine.

"It's not as bad as it looks." Matt tucked his shirt into his trousers. "It doesn't hurt if I sleep on my front."

Rose kissed him again softly on the lips. "I must go back. Tom and Lily will be wondering where I am. Mass is in one hour. This is the best birthday present ever." She pulled his beret to one side. "You look funny like that."

Matt pulled her pom-pom hat off her head. "You look beautiful like that."

Rose touched his cheek. "Would you do something for me?"

"Anything."

Rose reached into her pocket and handed him Catherine's ring. "Tom and Lily gave it to me this morning for my birthday. It's my grandmother's. Would you put it on me?"

Rose removed her woollen gloves and Matt his leather gloves. He took the small diamond ring and looked into her eyes.

"Which finger?"

"You choose." Rose blushed.

Matt slipped the ring onto the fourth finger of her left hand. "Will you wait for me? It will be a year before I can leave the army."

• • •

Sammy P manoeuvred the stolen red Mini Cooper around the remains of a wooden barricade made from an old bed on the lower Crumlin Road. Cedric and William followed closely behind in the black taxi. It was six thirty and two degrees below zero. The only shop open on the Crumlin Road at that point was an off licence with thick iron bars over the windows and doors. The light from the shop fell across the road and lit up William's face. Grey stubble prickled around his chin. He rubbed it roughly with his hand.

"We'll warm things up here." William glanced at Cedric who hadn't said a word since leaving the Black Beetle. Cedric looked at his hands turned face up resting on his jeans. A cigarette glowed faintly between his lips. His fingers gently curled, as though waiting to receive something.

"What's up? You're acting strange."

"I'm wondering what you feel when you kill someone?" Cedric asked without removing the cigarette from his lips or moving his hands.

"What do you mean, 'feel'? You get on with the job. You do it. You don't 'feel' anything. Are you going soft on me? I tell you how that makes me 'feel' – fucking angry. There's a job to be done tonight and I don't need you to be turning all philosophical on me."

"How did you feel when you killed Paddy O'Connor and Michael McGuckin?"

"You killed Paddy on your own, so don't ask me about that one."

"You had a part to play. You knew that he was going to be dead within hours when you left him. How did that make you feel?"

"I was thinking that you would finish him off and do a good job of disposing of the body so we wouldn't be caught."

"I didn't ask you what you thought. I asked you how you felt?"

"Nothing. I didn't feel anything."

"No. I didn't think you felt anything. I thought that I didn't feel anything either but I was wrong. I felt angry. I felt that this person was responsible for the pain I felt inside. I was angry that he made me feel that he way. I wanted to kill him to make the anger go away. He disgusted me. The way he took it all. He hardly fought at all. I thought he was pathetic." Cedric continued to look at his hands.

"Did the bloody anger go away then? Was it worth it?" William squinted into the distance trying to keep track of Sammy P's mini.

"No. I felt pleased for a minute or two afterwards but five or ten minutes later I was angry again and it was worse than before."

"What happened last night? What was in the bloody fish and chips? You've been poisoned or you've cracked."

"I had a heart-to-heart with Eileen after you went to bed."

In the dark of the taxi Cedric pulled the sun visor down and looked into the mirror. He moved closer. His eyes fascinated him. For the first time he noticed his long black lashes framing turquoise blue eyes. He kept staring into them. The black pupils dilated until there was almost no blue left. He stared into the blackness.

"Why are you calling her Eileen? You never call her Eileen." William took a quick look to the left.

"She's Eileen."

"You call her Mum or Mother. It's disrespectful. What did you talk about? For God's sake give me a fucking cigarette and stop looking at yourself."

William lifted the packet of Benson and Hedges from the dash board, tapped one free, and then snatched the cigarette dangling from Cedric's lips to light it. He gasped for air and then took a puff and exhaled deeply. He coughed and felt his stomach shake. "I'll have to give these up. They're killing me. Anyway what did your Mother say to you to get you into this state? What was your little heart-to-heart all about?"

"Eileen has kept a few things secret from you. She filled me in on the details last night." Cedric laughed gently.

William took the cigarette out of his mouth, kept his right hand on the steering wheel and pressed the glowing cigarette butt into Cedric's palm. "Don't you ever talk about your Mother in that tone of voice! It's disrespectful, I've told you!"

Cedric didn't flinch or move his hands from his jeans. His fingers remained slightly curled upwards like a lotus flower floating on a pond.

"Nice one 'Daddy'." Cedric dusted the ash from his palm. "But you need to know that she's not my mother."

"What's got into you?" William put both hands back on the wheel and pressed his foot on the accelerator. "What are your talking about? Eileen is your Mother. I'm your Father. Get your head sorted."

"You're not my Father."

William tapped a cigarette onto the dashboard, pushed it between his lips and after lighting it with a shaking hand, dropped the lighter on the floor of the car. "You're crazy."

"I'll tell you one more time as you seem to be going a trifle deaf. Eileen is not my mother."

"You're bonkers. Shut up or I'll shut you up." William put his foot to the floor. The car pushed to fifty miles an hour.

Cedric wound down the window and threw his cigarette out. "William, I'd advise you to keep to the speed limit if you don't want to attract the attention of the police."

"Why are you calling me William? He slowed down. What do you mean I'm not your Father? What's going on here, son?" His voice fell abruptly into a curiously gentle tone.

"I'm not your son. Ask Eileen. So when you work that one out, maybe we'll be getting somewhere."

William crunched into first gear instead of third. He turned to look at Cedric.

"What are you talking about?" The black taxi slowed down as Sammy P in the Mini Cooper disappeared into the darkness ahead. "For fuck's sake slow down, Sammy P. You're going to set that bomb off if you go over the ramps at that speed." William cursed under his breath. "Give it to me in one sentence what you're getting at. I don't know what you mean. How is Eileen not your Mother? How am I not your Father? Make it simple for me to understand."

"It will need more than one sentence. There was a 'real' Cedric. He was your son, not me. He was killed in the Blitz only hours after he was born. After he was killed, Eileen tried to find her way out of the hospital. She heard a baby crying. She followed the sound and found a theatre where a woman lay with her throat slit, holding two babies. The babies were both still alive. Eileen took one of the babies – the boy. That was me. She called me Cedric. She introduced me to you as her real son."

William started to cough violently. His tongue stuck out as he gasped for air, his body shuddering with each convulsion. The cigarette burnt into the filter held in his fingers. He stubbed it out in the overflowing ashtray, throwing the butt onto the floor of the car at Cedric's feet. He couldn't stop the words tumbling out. It was as though a magnet had taken his mind back with force to the theatre when he opened the door and walked towards Catherine. In his mind he only saw Catherine's ghostly white face, close to his. He smelt the sweet soap on her forehead.

"I killed that bloody Fenian woman. I sliced her throat!"

"You did what?" Cedric sat up in the seat, licking the cigarette burn on his right palm.

"You heard me. I was on the night shift at the hospital that night. Your Mother was in labour. I had to leave her before the bombs started to fall. There was work to do. Earlier in the day I had to tidy up the room after that woman was wheeled to theatre. It's her ring that you're wearing on your left hand."

Cedric had been twisting the ring on his left small finger. He stopped. "This is my mother's wedding ring?" He sat forward in his seat.

"I didn't know it was your mother's until tonight did I? You had no problem with the other rings. How was I to know it was your mother's ring? You chose it – remember?" The cigarette between William's lips fell onto his knees. He let it burn through his trousers. "I knew from her notes that she was a Fenian. It was easy with the Blitz. I knew that the place would be in chaos."

Cedric leaned forward on top of the dashboard. An image of his mother holding him in her arms with Maria flashed into his head as though he had killed her like the others he had killed with William.

"Did you not go back to check on Eileen and the baby?"

"I was going to do that after I killed her."

There was silence. William strained forward to see Sammy P.

Cedric undid his seat belt and slid back in the seat, staring at the ceiling of the taxi.

"So, you … you … murdered my Mother?"

"How many times are you going to say that to me? Would you shut up? I didn't know she was your fucking mother, did I?"

"I've been lying tossing and turning all night wondering about what happened to my Mother and all the time little did I know that the man lying in the bedroom next door, the man who calls himself my father, was her murderer. What kind of person was she?"

"How do I know?"

"What did she look like?"

"Scared."

"You bastard."

"I didn't know. I could have killed you and the girl. I didn't."

"What do you want? A thank you for not killing me? Maybe it would have been better for everyone if you had killed me."

"Could I have known what had happened to the real baby Cedric? I met Eileen outside the hospital. She had a baby in her arms. She said, "William look, isn't he beautiful?" We walked home with the bombs still falling all around us. We spent an hour in an air raid shelter at the bottom of the Ormeau Road. Eileen breastfed you in a corner, covering your ears with a blanket, and she made me say prayers of thanks to God for saving your life. When we got home, she lit a candle, asked me to kneel on the ground and give thanks to God. Why didn't she tell me the truth?"

"What would you have done if she had?"

"I don't know." William lent forward on the steering wheel and began to whimper. "You're not my son."

"No. I'm not."

William slowed down to ten miles an hour and smashed his head against the steering wheel three times. Blood trickled onto the leather wheel. Sammy P in the Mini Cooper in front indicated left. William didn't indicate; he swung the wheel violently left, forcing the taxi off the Crumlin Road. The wheels slipped, skidded and revved on black ice. His breathing was rapid. His hands gripped the steering wheel tightly; his foot pressed at first the accelerator and then immediately the brakes, swerving to park behind Sammy P. The tyres squeaked and squealed as they rubbed against the edge of the kerb.

"What are you going to do?" William asked Cedric, his eyes soft and doe-like. "You're not going to leave me are you?"

Cedric stared straight ahead in silence. He pulled on his leather gloves. "What does it matter?"

"It matters."

The spires of Holy Cross Church reached into a cloudless starry sky. The front doors of the church were open, pouring a mellow liquid orange light onto the steps.

"What fucking time is it?" William sat straight up in the seat, grunted, wound the window down and spat onto the road.

"Two minutes to seven," Cedric replied in a lower voice, without looking at his watch.

...

"That's them." Eileen gripped Lily's hand as the bus pulled to a stop. She pointed at the black taxi stationery on the side street off the Crumlin Road.

"How do you know?"

"The number plate and the dent in the back door."

"We can do it." Lily threw her arm around Eileen's shoulder. "Quick. Let's go."

...

Rose climbed the steps of the Church, pulling the orange and yellow tea cosy of a hat which Lily had knited for Christmas down over her ears. Her platform shoes slipped on the frosty glaze of the first step. She caught hold of Tom's arm. He pressed her hand. They walked towards the front of the Church where an altar boy lit two candles.

Father Martin walked to the altar to check the readings, his black habit covering the sins of a large paunch. He placed his glasses on the tip of his nose and looked over the top of them at the first reading from the Second Book of Samuel. It told the story of David who had spotted the beautiful Bathsheba bathing.

He asked for her to be brought to his Palace. He slept with her. When she became pregnant, David invited her husband back from battle to dine and then encouraged him to go and sleep with his wife. Uriah refused. He then invited him again and tried to make him drunk but he still refused to sleep with his wife, the stunning Bathsheba. In exasperation, David asked for Uriah to be sent into the thick of battle and there he arranged for him to be murdered.

Father Martin heaved a sigh of relief that it wasn't Sunday and that he didn't have to give a sermon to explain the story. That would have required him to think about how David who had fought Goliath could be so weakened by the sight of a beautiful woman. How could he try to entrap Uriah after Bathsheba became pregnant? Why did Bathsheba betray her husband? What did she think when her husband was murdered? Why did Uriah not want to sleep with his beautiful wife? How could a talented gifted man like David be so flawed? He was confused. Today, he didn't need to worry as it was a weekday and there was no obligation to give a sermon. The congregation would have to work it out for themselves.

He walked back to the Sacristy to change for Mass. Father Martin's boots clicked across the marble floor sending hollow echoes around an almost empty church.

"Is it not meant to be Father Anthony saying Mass tonight?" whispered Rose to Tom. "Where is he?"

"I would have thought so but maybe he had to visit someone ill." Tom scratched at his leg through his trousers.

•••

Eileen hammered on the window of the black taxi. William wound the window down. "What's going on, Eileen? What are you doing here?" William spluttered, wiping his lips with the back of his hand.

Cedric looked past Eileen at Lily, who opened her handbag, lifting out an almost empty half bottle of gin. "We need to talk." Lily's eyes were wide open, thick black mascara eye lashes blinked at Cedric. She took a sip from the bottle and passed it to Eileen as she reached a hand through the window to Cedric.

"You don't drink," Cedric whispered.

"I don't normally, but no-one would call this a normal situation." Eileen closed her eyes and tilted her head back gulping at the gin. "Revolting." Eileen coughed as she handed the bottle back to Lily.

"I find it a tonic." Lily eyed what was left. "We don't know each other but I'm your aunt Lily. You can call me Lily."

Cedric found himself shaking Lily's hand.

William sighed. "Get in the back."

In the back seat of the taxi Eileen held Lily's hand, while Cedric twisted around in the front passenger seat to look at Eileen.

"Well Eileen, I don't know what you're planning, but let me give you a quick news update. It was William who murdered my mother."

"What?" Eileen squeezed Lily's hand tight.

"You said that you heard a baby crying. You found a mother with two babies, her throat slit. It was William who cut my mother's throat."

Eileen leant forward in the seat, dropping Lily's hand. "You didn't murder her, did you William? How could you? How ..." She struggled to find the right words. "You coward!" She thumped at his shoulder three times with a curled fist. "Tell me you didn't do it. Tell me!"

William held his head in his hands and in a muffled voice

whispered, "I did it. She was the one that I regretted most."
William lifted his head from his hands and stared straight ahead.

"How many more have you murdered?"

"Maybe ten."

"Maybe? You don't even know?" She lay back resting
against Lily in disgust.

"Ten."

"I don't believe you. Didn't it start with James in 1941? I've
seen your attic ring collection. It's more than ten. I don't know
how many rings you've handed out as presents."

Lily sat forward and brought her lips close to Cedric's ear.
"You didn't know your mother, Cedric. I did. She would ask
you now to stop the killings. Rose, who you are planning to kill
tonight, is your niece. You are her uncle," Lily continued.

William shuffled in his seat to turn and look at Lily without
making eye contact with Eileen.

"Is there any of that gin left?"

"A drop." Lily handed over the bottle to William in the front
seat.

From the silence in the back of the car, it was Eileen's turn
to lean forward. "I made a mistake, William, not telling you the
truth. Tell them the rest, Lily."

Lily coughed and nodded. "OK. You need to know that
Catherine baptised him a Catholic on the night of the blitz.
You're a Catholic, Cedric."

"What does that mean?" Cedric rubbed his leather gloves
together.

"What you want it to mean." Lily placed a hand on his
shoulder. "Can I ask you a favour?"

"What?" Cedric questioned uneasily.

"Can you show me something? We need to get out of the car
for a minute."

Cedric opened the door of the car and stood outside waiting for Lily to join him. William and Eileen strained forward from inside the car.

"May I?" Lily indicated to his shirt with a gloved hand.

He nodded.

She pulled his black shirt from his trousers. "Look." She pointed at the three hearts above his navel.

Eileen nodded from the back seat.

"Jonas."

Eileen reached forward to William in the driver's seat. She touched him on the sleeve. "Forgive me for not telling you."

"Where's Sammy P?" Cedric broke the silence, tucking in his shirt, climbing back into the taxi and looking at his watch.

"He will have set the timer by now." William whispered. "He is due back here in five minutes."

"OK. If he gets back here before I see him, tell him to go back and defuse the bloody bomb." Cedric pointed at William. "You sort that out if he comes back. I'll see if I can find him. He's maybe still at the car."

Cedric opened the front passenger door, heaved himself out of the car.

"You're not going to kill Rose, are you?" Lily shouted from the back seat.

Cedric bent over and pushed his head through the open window to within a couple of inches from William's face. "No. I'm not going to kill Rose. The killings are over. Aren't they, William?"

He withdrew his head and William nodded. "Yes, the killings are over."

"Are they really over William?" Eileen tugged at his tweed jacket.

"Yes, really over."

Cedric slapped the roof of the taxi twice and then ran towards the Grove, opening the small metal gate at the edge of the road, splashing through puddles thinly topped with ice.

"Cedric, wait for me." Eileen shouted from the car, tumbling onto the frozen pavement to follow Cedric. "Lily, stay with William."

"I will." Lily waved after Eileen. "Follow him Eileen. Don't let him out of your sight."

"William. William. What a mess." Lily leant forward again.

"Is there anything left in the gin bottle?" William looked over his shoulder at Lily.

"Not a single drop."

"Better that way. What will happen now? Will Eileen ever forgive me?"

"Eileen has forgiven you. I know it's hard to believe but you also know Eileen. With Eileen you don't wait for forgiveness to happen. You either forgive or you don't. Time doesn't come into it. She is extraordinary. She sees beyond time. She doesn't need time," Lily whispered.

"The families of the people I've killed won't forgive me. They'll want me dead."

"They've suffered. You will have to live with the consequences. I can't speak for them."

William's left leg twitched and his head shook from side to side. "Do you not hate me?"

"No."

"Why not?"

"I don't know. Maybe you get sick of hating people who hate people."

"I did it because I wanted to do it. I enjoyed killing."

"You are not enjoying it now are you?" Lily said gently.

"No." William rested his head on the head rest.

"Are you OK?"

"I'm OK."

Lily watched two tears roll down William's face, glistening like smoothed diamonds in the moonlight. He sneezed. They shook from his chin like drops of water from a closing umbrella.

"I've been a bad boy." William brushed the tears away with the back of his hand, straightened up in the seat, took the handbrake off and strapped his seat belt on. "Let's drive to Holy Cross Church and see what is happening. There's no sign of Sammy P. He's missed his time check. Something must have happened. He's never late."

"Let's go."

William drove slowly along the edge of the Grove looking for space to do a three point turn. He reversed the taxi, drove to the end of the side street, indicated left and turned onto the Crumlin Road.

•••

Mr McCabe parked his white soft topped MG beside the red Mini Cooper outside the side door of Holy Cross Church. He tried to open it. "It's the main door we're using this evening," a tall man with red hair called over to them.

"Thanks." Mr McCabe rubbed his leather gloves together as he climbed the main steps into Holy Cross Church with Peter. Mr McCabe stamped his feet to warm them before opening the oak door which led into the main aisle.

"Mr McCabe, before we go inside, I want to thank you for accompanying me this evening. You didn't need to do this. I really do appreciate it. You may find yourself in trouble with Mother mind you." Peter bowed low and shook hands with Mr McCabe.

"Your Mother is the kind of woman who will understand."

Mr McCabe rubbed his hands together.

"Let's see if we can find Rose." Peter jumped onto the second step.

"You seem remarkably calm, Peter." Mr McCabe mopped his own brow with a handkerchief.

Peter smiled at him. "You've succeeded in putting me at my ease."

Then Peter spotted Rose. She was sitting in the third bench from the altar on the left hand side. He pushed the coat's hood back from his head.

"Remember to genuflect, my dear boy, and to bless yourself. It is very important to follow the customary rites and rituals. Do as I do." Mr McCabe dabbed Holy Water onto Peter's forehead from the Holy Water font at the front door. He walked towards the front of the church, genuflecting at the end of Rose's bench, blessing himself before putting out his hand to shake hands with Tom and Rose.

"It's a pleasure to meet you both. You must be Tom and of course you will be Rose." Mr McCabe smiled broadly as he shook Rose's hand. Peter shook Tom's hand and blushing took Rose's hand.

"Let the prayers begin."

Mr McCabe knelt.

Tom reached across and patted Mr McCabe's hand. "You must be Peter's teacher. Thank you for coming and for the offer of the house in Portstewart."

Mr McCabe looked at Tom over the rim of his glasses. "It is a pleasure."

Tom smiled. "Thank you again."

Father Martin's reputation for saying Mass quickly was legendary. He didn't disappoint. At seven twenty-five he raised his hands for the final blessing as Cedric burst through the back door of the church. He stood dressed totally in black, legs apart, black leather gloved hands waving above his head.

"No one must move to the back of the Church. Stay where you are or go further forward. There's a car bomb outside."

The first scream came from a woman sitting alone on the last bench. She scrambled to her feet and ran squealing up the side aisle towards Father Martin at the main altar. That started a tsunami as each of the rows on either side of the main altar at the back of the church emptied and rolled forward towards the front. Eileen staggered in through the back door and clicked in her solid brogues towards Cedric. Father Martin stood frozen on the main altar one hand still in the air with a suspended blessing.

Father Anthony virtually fell through the back door of the church clutching a stubby red-faced man by the arm and pointing Father Martin's rifle awkwardly at the man's chest. Father Martin watched Sammy P struggle to pull away from Father Anthony's strong grip.

"This man has put a car bomb outside. Call the police." Father Anthony shouted to Father Martin, who now had almost the entire congregation bobbing beside him on the main altar.

"Wait," Cedric interrupted, "Sammy P can defuse the bomb. Sammy P, you've got time. Defuse it."

"Ten minutes. For these fuckers you must be joking." Sammy P shook his head violently. "I could be killed." He spat the next words at Cedric, "What's got into you? Have you had a brain bypass?" Sammy P shook his head and continued attempting to wrestle free from Father Anthony's grip.

"Give me the keys." Cedric walked toward Sammy P, holding out his hand. "Give me the keys." Sammy P fumbled in his pocket with his free hand. "Now!" Shouted Cedric.

Sammy P threw them onto the marble floor. Eileen picked them up and passed them to Cedric.

"Father Martin, get everyone into the monastery and stay there until you are told that it is safe to leave," Father Anthony shouted from the back of the church. "Move quickly. Get them out of here. We have less than ten minutes."

While the congregation were being jostled off the altar towards the monastery by Father Martin, on the third bench sat Mr McCabe, Peter, Rose and Tom. Mr McCabe whispered into Peter's ear, "I've a rather soft spot for that MG, I hope it survives. We need to move."

"Where are we going?"

"To the back of the church where the action is, it's the only place to be."

"Cedric is there."

"I see that. We have to go into the dragon's den. Didn't anyone tell you, that my dear boy? He appears to have had a change of heart. More of a kitten don't you think than a dragon?"

"I can't be sure. What's Mum doing?" Peter pointed at Eileen who was talking in a low voice to Cedric.

"What should we do?" Tom tapped on Mr McCabe's shoulder.

"Help Father Anthony." Rose pulled off her hat and threw it on the bench. "I'm boiling." Her cheeks were fiery red.

"You might have a temperature." Tom put his hand on her forehead. "You're not well."

Mr McCabe leaned forward. "Tom, I think that you should go into the monastery with Rose and wait for the all clear. That is the safest option." Mr McCabe touched Rose on the cheek. "Do you not agree?"

"Mr McCabe, I don't think so. You don't know what's going to happen. If that is Cedric, he doesn't look as though he is going to murder me or anyone. Why would he warn us about the car bomb? It's Father Anthony who needs help."

Peter got to his feet. "Rose, Mr McCabe is right. I don't know what has got into Cedric but it doesn't mean that you are not at risk. Where's William? How do you know what he will do? " Peter took Rose's hands in his. "Once the car bomb is sorted you can go to the safe house as planned tonight."

"No. I'm staying with Father Anthony."

"Why?" Tom asked. "Why? It doesn't make sense."

"It does to me."

"Explain."

"Father Anthony is my father."

Tom's mouth dropped open. His glasses steamed up in a mysterious way which meant that Rose couldn't see his eyes at all. She could only watch his lips turning slightly purple and continuing to open and close. She grabbed her hat from the bench, pulled it onto her head and down almost over her eyes. In the ensuing silence Rose explained.

"Father Anthony told me that he was my father when I made my First Confession."

"But that was eight or nine years ago. Why didn't you tell your aunt Lily?"

"If Father Anthony had wanted you to know he would have told you. He must have had good reasons for not telling you."

"What were they?"

"I don't know. Maybe he thought that he would not have been allowed to have contact with me?"

"How do you know that it is true? How do you know that he is your father?"

"I know. He explained it all bit by bit. He didn't tell me everything at the start – only what he thought I needed to know. Then year by year he added small pieces like a jigsaw puzzle. In the end I understood it all and saw the whole picture."

"Does anyone else know?"

"No. He blessed this ring a second time, today." Rose held out her left hand showing Catherine's ring.

"I wish you had told Lily and me."

"What difference would it have made?"

"I don't know." Tom rubbed his hands on his trousers and looked at the floor.

"I don't want to leave Father Anthony."

Mr McCabe coughed. "Well, Peter and I had no intention of ever leaving him either. So let's see what we can do to help."

He placed his brown felt hat on his head, nudging Peter who jumped to his feet. They genuflected at the end of the bench, blessed themselves and headed towards the back of the church. Rose and Tom followed.

As they walked in single file Father Martin extinguished the lights on the main altar and the light now came from two small lights on either side of the front door and the small votive candles burning in memory of everyone who had died, or who was sick. There were more than fifty candles twinkling at the back of the church at the feet of the statute to the Little Flower. The sweet spicy smell of frankincense hung in the air, forming a cloud above Cedric's head.

Cedric watched Peter and Mr McCabe walk towards him down the aisle. As Peter approached he rubbed a leather glove through his hair.

"There's no time to explain Peter. I will later."

Peter shouted after him. "What about Rose?"

Without saying a word, Cedric turned on his heels and headed towards the back door. Father Anthony, watching Cedric disappear, thrust Sammy P into Tom's hands.

"Hold onto him Tom until the police arrive."

Tom looked closely at Father Anthony as he took hold of Sammy P. He saw for the first time the dark rings under his eyes, speckled grey hairs around his temple. Father Anthony looked worn out, like a man who had no choice other than to keep going. Tom nodded and caught Sammy P's two hands behind his back. Sammy P wriggled trying to free himself.

"Peter, can you use my tie to secure his hands?"

Peter undid Tom's blue silk tie, twisted it tightly around Sammy P's wrists and tied a double knot. "I'm not sure if that will hold him."

Father Anthony looked at Mr McCabe. "Will you take care of this?" he asked, passing him the rifle.

"My dear Father, I wouldn't have a clue what to do with it."

"It's not complicated. Don't point this bit with the hole in it in your own direction or in the direction of anyone you think not worthy of it."

Mr McCabe took the rifle in his arms, holding it like a bouquet of flowers.

"Tom, don't let him get away. He's strong."

With his black habit flapping behind him, Father Anthony followed Cedric through the front door of the church.

Cedric jumped down the steps three at a time, zipping up his back leather jacket and rubbing his leather gloves together. A crescent moon rose in the east. With the sky completely clear of clouds, Cedric's breath left a cloud of white behind him as his boots crunched on the gravel. He sprinted past the red Mini Cooper and Mr McCabe's white MG, turning right and heading for the Crumlin Road and the army sentry post. He heard the cursing of the rioters on the Crumlin Road and only briefly hesitated before turning onto the road where the smell of burning petrol hit the back of his throat. He coughed heavily. A handful of rioters broke up pavement slabs with heavy picks and hammers while others threw a series of well-aimed petrol bombs at the sentry post.

"Go home, you fucking British bastards."

Cedric stopped outside the church gates and looked left. A Saracen tank turned onto the Crumlin Road from the Woodvale. It spun around, the window flaps opened and the short barrels of rubber bullet guns were pushed through the windows. The roof of the sentry post blazed with a direct hit from a petrol bomb. Another petrol bomb arced into the air before crashing onto the bonnet of the Saracen. Four rounds of rubber bullets rocketed into the rioters.

How could he get a message to the soldiers? If he ran towards the Saracen they would think he was one of the rioters. A crowd of around thirty rioters retreated into Kerrera Street, a side street off the Crumlin Road. Silence followed another four thick bangs from the rubber bullet guns. The black bullets bounced into Kerrera Street, springing into the air after hitting the tarmac road before punching two rioters in the back.

"More! More!" The rioters taunted. Within seconds, undaunted, they swarmed back onto the road with new ammunition, including chunks of heavy paving stones which flew through the air. The rioters now tied handkerchiefs soaked in water around their faces anticipating the arrival of CS Gas. Cedric looked at his watch. Seven minutes to go. Father Anthony's muffled sandaled feet stopped behind him.

"How do I let them know about the bomb?" asked Cedric, pointing at the Saracen tank. His were eyes wide open, his breathing fast and shallow. "We've less than seven minutes."

"Leave it to me. I'll talk to them. Give me the keys." Father Anthony took the car keys from Cedric's outstretched hand.

He moved towards the Saracen tank as it pulled into the middle of the Crumlin Road forming a blockade. Two more Saracens arrived, mounting the pavements on either side. The road was completely sealed off. The soldiers bundled onto the road, visors down, wooden batons hanging from their waists, rifles now pointing into the crowd.

Father Anthony stood in front of them, in the middle of the Crumlin Road, waving a white handkerchief. The soldiers were lined up in front of him.

"Everyone keep back. There's a car bomb. Get way back off the road." He turned to wave the white handkerchief at the rioters who had momentarily fallen silent. He shouted again. "Get back. There's a car bomb."

The rioters withdrew into Kerrera Street, milling around an entry lane which was an artery leading into the heart of Ardoyne. They began to run down the entry away from the Crumlin Road. Father Anthony dropped his handkerchief to his side and walked to the middle Saracen tank which was flanked by the first row of soldiers. He handed the car keys to Matt.

"It's a red mini-cooper and you've less than seven minutes."

Matt signalled to the bomb disposal expert at his side. "Let's go."

Cedric and Father Anthony watched them run through the church gates.

"They'll never do it will they?" Cedric asked Father Anthony.

"God knows. What do we do now?"

"They've six minutes."

•••

William turned left onto the Crumlin Road and saw the nationalist rioters at Butler Street and further up near the top of Brompton Park. "Lily, we're driving into a riot but there's no going back."

He didn't see an armed Ciaran McCann pressed against the red brick wall beside Blackwoods on the corner of Butler Street. Ciaran spotted the black taxi. He recognised Lily inside.

"The black taxi – stop it. It's not one of ours. He's got Lily Martin. Stop him!"

William pressed his foot onto the accelerator but not quickly enough to prevent three rioters throwing themselves onto the car bonnet, while two others caught hold of the side door handles, running along beside the taxi. Three faces squashed against the glass in front of William, lips open, kissing the windscreen.

Unable to see anything, William instinctively began to accelerate and swung to the right and then immediately left in an attempt to dislodge them. He succeeded in losing two rioters hanging onto the handles of the car doors but the three on top of the bonnet held onto the windscreen wipers and stared at William with faces pressing even more heavily against the glass.

"Get off the car," Ciaran shouted, giving a signal that he was going to use his gun. The rioters clinging onto the window wipers let go, rolling head over heels on the ground, and then scrambling onto their feet to melt into the wave of rioters in Butler Street. Ciaran lifted the rifle into the air, aimed it at the tyres of the taxi. Three high velocity shots rang out. The bullets pummelled into the tarmac road, sending dust and debris into the air. He missed the tyres. He caught sight of William and Lily's faces in the light of one of two streetlights still working on the Crumlin Road.

"Get out Lily! They think I'm kidnapping you. Get out!" William braked a second time. The taxi shrieked and shuddered to a stop. Lily opened the front door and fell onto the road. William immediately accelerated. Ciaran gave a signal to the rioters to return to the road.

"Don't let him get away," Ciaran McCann shouted as he helped Lily to her feet.

"He wasn't kidnapping me. You've made a big mistake," Lily shouted as Ciaran McCann took her by the arm and led her to the side of the road. "There's a car bomb. He's trying to stop it going off."

"How do you know?" Ciaran looked at Lily. He aimed once more at the taxi. This time he scored a direct hit as the back windscreen shattered. He passed the rifle to Sean.

"Get rid of it."

Ciaran shouted at the rioters. "After him. Don't let him escape."

He watched four rioters run after the black taxi and turned to Lily. He bent down to dust the gravel from Lily's camel coat.

"What were you doing in the taxi, Lily?" He caught Lily by the wrist.

"Let me go." Lily pulled free from Ciaran's grip.

"Lily, I was worried about you."

"How can I believe that you are worrying about me after what you did to Margaret Mulvenna?"

"Lily, I told Tom I'm giving myself up tonight. I promised Tom. I am handing myself over to the police. I'm only here on the Crumlin Road to be arrested. Tom has set it up that way with your friend Sammy. Now do you believe me? I had to make it look as though I was on an operation, to make it look real." Ciaran dropped his two hands by his side. He stared at the tarmac road as he took a step back.

"What can I say, Ciaran?" Lily patted Ciaran on the shoulder.

"I thought he was one of Paddy and Michael's killers. He fits the description given by the police today for one of Anthony Magee's murderers. Everyone knows they're Paddy and Michael's killers, too."

"I have to go, Ciaran. Keep your word with Tom." She looked into Ciaran's eyes and leant forward and kissed him on the cheek before twisting her way through rioters up the Crumlin Road.

Sean watched and shouted in exasperation. "Have you lost your balls Ciaran? Wise up. Don't take any shit from anyone and that includes Lily Martin." Sean swung round to see three police jeeps race up the Crumlin Road. "Bigger shit on the way Ciaran – here come the police."

Sammy jumped from the first jeep and headed straight for Ciaran, spread-eagling him against the red brick wall, while Sean whistled to Danny. They took a right turn and then a left out of sight, heading towards the action further up the Crumlin.

•••

William pressed his foot again on the accelerator. He watched the rioters near Kerrera Street scamper off the Crumlin Road. Three Saracen tanks blocked the way forward but that didn't matter. He was planning to turn left into the church grounds. That's where Sammy P had left the mini.

Lily watched as William's taxi approached the church gates. She breathlessly continued uphill, pushing her way through another group of rioters bunching together at Butler Street. Sean ran past her, catching up on a gang of four who had nearly reached William's taxi.

Lily's chest tightened. She felt a strange pain in the middle of her back which she had never felt before. Deep within her body she felt something moving, pushing and sinking, sending shudders of nausea up and down her spine rather than into her stomach. Her body was doing something that she couldn't stop for reasons that she didn't know. She attempted to take a few deep breaths but the movement of pulling and pushing in her chest area continued and expanded all the way down to the base of her spine.

She reached the long set of steps which led from the Crumlin Road to the main church doors. The doors were open and the gentle mellow light from inside trickled down the steps into the Grove. She took three steps and had to stop as beads of sweat broke onto her forehead. She tried to take another step but fainted and sank to the ground on the fourth step. Her beige beret slipped from her head, her handbag rolled to one side, and one of her black patent high heel shoes slipped from her foot and tumbled onto the Crumlin Road.

•••

"Let's go into the monastery," Tom suggested, holding Sammy P's arm.

"You go. I can't," Eileen whispered. "I need to find William and Cedric. Peter, please go into the monastery. I promise that I'll see you there later. I'll be back." Eileen pulled a silk scarf onto her head, buttoned up her coat, kissed Peter on the cheek.

"Tom, can I have a word?" While Tom held onto Sammy P, Eileen indicated that they move to the statue of the Little Flower, where she began to talk in a low voice. At one point Tom seemed to let go of Sammy P and then held him even more closely. When Eileen had finished with a few shakes of her head, she rested her hand on Tom's face. She walked then towards Peter. Peter hugged Eileen. She felt small and fragile in his arms, dissolving into them like melted ice-cream. She whispered into his ear, "You don't need to worry about Rose. Cedric and William have promised there will be no more killings."

"Mum, are you one hundred per cent sure?"

"I'm sure."

"Let me come with you? You can't go alone."

"I want you to stay here. You're still needed here. It isn't over yet." Eileen gently squeezed his hand.

"But you said that there will be no more killings."

"I said not from Cedric and William. Keep an eye on him. He

looks dangerous." Eileen pulled back from Peter's embrace and looked in the direction of Sammy P.

Sammy P shouted at Eileen, "Be careful who you're talking about and who you talk to. Remember loose talk costs lives. You're not the only one who has a tongue and tongues can talk. William and Cedric might just find out just how loud tongues can talk after I speak to my lawyer."

Eileen looked at Peter. She smoothed a few curls from his forehead. "It will be over soon. I promise."

As Eileen left the Church and ran down the steps, Sammy P took advantage of the momentary distraction to pull free from Tom. He had already slipped his hands free from the tie which lay unseen at his feet. He caught his two hands together as though he was about to take a putt at golf and then with an almighty swing smashed his fists into Tom's lower stomach. Tom exhaled with a hissing sound, bent over, his glasses crashing onto the ground where the lenses fell out, spinning like coins before settling unbroken onto the marble slabs.

Sammy P grabbed the rifle nestling in Mr McCabe's arms. Peter lunged towards him in a rugby tackle. Sammy P stepped to one side. Peter crashed onto the floor, arms and hands spread out. Sammy P took two steps towards the stretched out body, standing over him, pointed the rifle at Peter's head.

"Any more of where that came from and you're a goner. I don't care if you're Cedric's fucking brother. He's cuckoo anyway."

"Don't hurt him!" Rose shouted, running towards Peter and kneeling on the floor beside Tom.

"You'll be joining him too where the grass don't grow if you make one more move. Or maybe I should quickly finish off the job I came here to do. Why waste more time? You're getting on my nerves."

He pointed the rifle at Rose.

•••

Eileen stood at the bottom of the Church steps unsure of which way to go. What was in Cedric's mind? Where would William be now? Would he still be with Lily waiting in the taxi? She had followed Cedric through the Grove on her right but would she find her way back? The easiest way back to William and Lily would be down the steps in front of her to the Crumlin Road, turn right and then right again. It would only be a short sprint to the taxi but it would be a dash through the rioters bobbing up and down below her like corks in oily water. The noise was unbelievable – the cursing, chanting. Even with the fear of descending into the madness below, it seemed the best option. Once she reached the Crumlin Road, she would have to move into the middle of the riot in order not to make it obvious that she would be heading for the Loyalist side of the Peace Line. She walked quickly down the first flight of steps. As she reached the second set of steps, she saw Lily's beret before she saw Lily herself spread on the steps.

She didn't remember running down the last few steps at all. She didn't see the rioters withdraw like a wave dragging itself out to sea. She didn't see Ciaran McCann spread-eagled by Sammy.

She knelt beside Lily. "Lily, speak to me. Please be alright. What's happened?" She loosened the top buttons of Lily's coat, holding her head in her arms. Lily's eyes were closed. She didn't appear to be breathing. Eileen took her pulse. There was a gentle throb.

"Get an ambulance!" She shouted at one of the rioters. She picked Lily's beret from the step above and placed it back on her head. One of the rioters lifted her shoe from the road and handed it to Eileen. She slipped it onto Lily's foot. She sat on the step beside Lily, holding her head in her lap, waiting. Lily's eyes fluttered open. Eileen smiled at her.

"What on earth happened to you, Lily?"

Lily gave a half smile back. "I took a funny turn but it has passed. Give me a few minutes." She closed her eyes.

"Where's William?" Eileen asked.

"In the taxi. They're after him."

• • •

Tom was on his knees groping for his glasses. Mr McCabe stood still, gasping, one of those gasps which seemed to go on and on like an inhalation where you wonder when and if you will ever exhale. He seemed to be sucking in the world without stopping. Sammy P moved slowly training the gun on each of them fixing it first on Mr McCabe, then on Tom, then Rose and finally on Peter as he slowly reversed towards the back door. He reached the main door. He jerked the rifle in the direction of Rose. Three shots rang out. The gun smoked, he dropped it on the floor, turned and hurtled through the heavy wooden door, tearing down the steps, stumbling into the Grove.

Tom and Peter knelt on either side of Rose who lay unmoving face down on the marble floor of the church with her hands over her head. Mr McCabe stood with his hands over his mouth.

Tom touched Rose's shoulders, rubbing them gently. "Rose. Rose. Please. No." There was no sign of blood. Rose moved her hands and lifted her head to look at Tom.

"Have I been shot?"

"Don't move. Let's see."

Tom scanned Rose's body from head to toe. "No. How did he miss?"

Rose rolled onto her side and sat up. "I don't know." Tom

shook his head in relief.

"I do." Father Martin walked swiftly down the side aisle with the Rector by his side. "They weren't real bullets. They were blanks. That was the Rector's idea. We replaced the bullets I gave you." He turned and smiled at the Rector who held both hands in the air. "It was always a risk, but then the alternative was totally unacceptable."

Tom squeezed Rose and smiled. Then rubbing Rose's shoulders with his hands, he said, "I'm grateful to you both for recognising my insanity and taking the appropriate measures but the madness is not over yet." Tom pushed his glasses back into place. "We need to find Lily."

Tom didn't know where he was going when he left the Church. He stood at the top of the steps and took two deep breaths. He felt strangely calm. A cold westerly breeze made him shiver. He tightened the woollen scarf around his neck. His body buzzed with an unrecognised energy. Something was going to happen. He was sure of it.

"Tom! Tom! Lily is fine."

He looked in the direction of the voice. He saw Eileen holding Lily on the steps below him. He descended, taking one step at a time.

•••

Cedric watched the black taxi plough through the rioters like a battleship in stormy seas. A single shot rang out. It shattered the rear passenger window on the right hand side, piercing the empty passenger seat before exiting through the floor. William's head and shoulders were barely visible above the steering wheel. A petrol bomb sailed through the air from Kerrera Street and burst into flames on the boot of the taxi, flames licking in through the back broken window pane. Bodies pressed together, squeezing from Kerrera Street onto the Crumlin Road. William watched Cedric hand something to Father Anthony. He flashed the headlights twice.

Cedric sprinted along the pavement at the edge of the Grove. He opened the back door and jumped in.

"Lock it." Cedric shouted. "Go, go, go."

"I'm not going to be able to get through them." William turned his head to look at Cedric.

Cedric pulled off his gloves and sat, head in hands. His stomach heaved. He gasped for air. "They know who we are, William."

William wiped the sweat from his upper lip. "Leave the car in the church grounds and hike it to the back of the monastery. We hit the Woodvale!" William shouted and then continued in a softer voice, "Don't lose it son. Hold it together."

Cedric raised his head and looked at the back of William's head. The long strand of black hair to cover the bald patch had become dislodged. It hung loose touching his right shoulder. Cedric bent forward and with his head touching William's damp white nylon shirt, his lips pressed against it, breathing in the saturated musty cigarette smoke, he pulled the long black strand of hair into the correct position over William's bald head.

"Let's go." William pressed his foot to the accelerator. He mounted the pavement, veered sharply left, skidded, bumped off the railing on the right. Sparks scattered into the air like fireworks as he pulled the car left again, trying to regain control.

"No, William, no, not left. Remember the car bomb!" Cedric shouted, lunging forward from the back seat to grab the steering wheel, trying to pull the car right towards the monastery. William instinctively pulled left, bouncing the left hand side of the car off the wrought iron railings.

"Didn't Sammy P defuse it?" William took his foot off the

accelerator, stabbing heavily on the brakes. He tried to reverse. Cedric let go of the steering wheel and fell back into the seat.

"No. Stop, William. Get out and run."

The car was reversing as Cedric, wrestling with the back door, caught sight of the Mini-Cooper and two shadowy soldiers kneeling on the ground beside it.

William abruptly stopped the taxi. Cedric opened the back door and threw himself onto the ground. William wrestled with the front door. It had jammed. He tugged violently at it, screaming. "Cedric. I'm stuck. Help me, Cedric. Don't leave me." William opened the glove compartment, feverishly retrieving a hammer and battering at the door handle. It didn't move.

"Get out of the back of the car, William. Move yourself."

William squeezed himself through the gap between the passenger's seat and the driver's seat and collapsed into the back. Cedric reached in through the door.

"Give me your hands."

William reached both hands to Cedric who hauled him from the car onto the ground.

"Run now. To the Woodvale. I'll delay them."

"What about you?"

"Quit talking. Get out of here."

William limped as quickly as he could towards the monastery and the safety of the Woodvale Road. He glanced over his shoulder and saw the moon slip between the two copper spires of Holy Cross Church.

"Bomb defused," the bomb disposal expert shouted at Matt.

The rioters heard the call and surged towards Cedric.

"Don't touch him!" Tom ran towards Cedric. "Don't touch him! You don't know the truth – the whole story."

Just then a petrol tank exploded on a hijacked bus twenty feet away on the Crumlin Road. A wave of burning gasoline fell onto an oak tree beside Tom. The wood blazed, setting on fire the neighbouring trees. Tom felt his face sting with the heat. He wiped tears away, dropped his arms to his side and looked into the blurred shapes in front of him.

"What are you talking about, Tom?" Sean, leading the rioters, raised a hand to silence them.

Tom steadied his voice, "You're looking at Jonas – Catherine's boy. He is my sister's boy. This is my nephew."

Apart from the hissing flames of the oak tree continuing to crackle and spit, there was silence and stillness from the rioters.

The silence grew. Tom was aware of it, it was real, tangible, holding him, taking away his fear, making itself a blanket for him. In this moment, he knew the silence for what it was – for what it really was. Silence was the emptiness of the womb without a child. Yet it was not barren. It was full of potential. Silence was the child of the empty womb. He knew that it had always been there waiting for him to know it.

The burning oak tree no longer disturbed the silence. Flames instead burnt into the earth and up into the heavens with a purifying fire, allowing silence to breathe, to expand and to grow. Even Sean's question could no longer interrupt the peace which ebbed between Tom and the objects of the world.

Sean either shouted or whispered at him, "What are you saying? Are you saying that we should let him go because he is your nephew?"

The silence was not changed by the question, in the same way that water is not changed by its rippling. Tom shook his head, "No. I'm asking you to let justice be done." Tom reached a hand towards Cedric. "Come home."

The oak tree continued to blaze beside Tom, spitting and hissing and then abruptly bursting into deeper orange and blue flames. Sparks flew into the black sky like fallen stars returning to the Universe. Under the oak tree the smoke swirled a hazy grey tinged with orange. Cedric threw his gun onto the gravel. Dropping onto his haunches, he took Tom's hand and fell onto his knees onto the path beside him.

Tom dropped to the ground and threw his arms around Cedric and held him to his chest. He breathed out, resting his head on Cedric's shoulder. Cedric's leather jacket was wet and cold against Tom's cheek. Cedric shuddered, quivered, trembled and sighed deeply. Tom heard Cedric's breathing slow down. He felt Cedric's head press into his heart. He lowered his head further and breathed into Cedric's ear, "Welcome home, Jonas. It's never too late to come home."

Sean moved behind the burning oak tree. Out of the corner of his eye Tom saw the glint of the barrel of a gun through the leaping flames.

"Don't!"

Tom gripped Cedric tighter. He swung him to his left as a bullet was fired, falling heavily on top of Cedric.

Matt ran towards Tom, pulling him onto the gravel path. Cedric lay unmoving on the ground beside them. Matt searched for Tom's pulse. There was a faint throb in Tom's neck. He rolled him on his side and searched for the bullet entry wound in his back. The green tweed jacket had been shredded by the bullet towards his lower back. There was no exit wound. He removed Tom's jacket and shirt and then his own. Using his shirt, he pushed it against the small penny-sized hole. Sean, Danny and the others watched in silence, as Matt's bruised torso curved over Tom and he breathed into his mouth and then pressed his chest with a strong rhythmical pressure. A sigh of relief rose from the crowd as Tom spluttered and coughed. An ambulance siren wailed close by. Matt waved to the crowd to move aside to allow the ambulance to approach. Wordlessly, they obeyed.

Matt rose to his feet, naked from the waist upwards as Tom was lifted onto the stretcher. Matt turned around as the front door of the monastery opened, light falling onto the path to his right. Rose ran towards him, arms reaching out. To his left Lily and Eileen opened a pathway through the crowd.

Matt softly repeated, "He's alive. He's going to be OK."

Cedric trembled on the gravel as Eileen fell to her knees beside him. Perhaps a hundred or more people crushed together to watch Eileen embrace Cedric and to see his arms move and gently stroke her back. Cedric didn't raise his head, kept his eyes closed, straining to hear a sound – any sound. A hundred voices were silent. He felt the silence around him – every bit as real as the warmth of Eileen in his arms. The oak tree continued to burn, showering golden and orange sparks, some of which fell on Cedric's hands. He winced, pulling Eileen closer to him. There was a soft gasp from the crowd as the tree gave a final burst of flames, illuminating Cedric and Eileen in tongues of fire. Eileen raised her head.

"You see, it's done. It's over. The truth has been told. Don't be afraid of the fire. The fire is love."

DEIRDRE QUIERY

Based in Mallorca where she runs Seven Rocks Consulting, a leadership development consultancy she founded with her husband, Deirdre brings her vast experience of emotional intelligence and mindfulness to bear in her creative endeavours. Taking inspiration from experience, Deirdre has not only painted with Argentinian artist Carlos Gonzalez in Palma and Natalia Spitale in Sóller, she is also a winner of the Alexander Imich Prize in the US for writing about exceptional human experiences, and the Birmingham Trophy Prize in the UK.

Eden Burning is Deirdre's first novel and is shaped by her experiences growing up in Belfast during the Troubles. She is already working on her second novel, **Gurtha**.